Web Site and Release Information:

Read A Chapter
View The Book Cover
Sign Up For Advance Release Notice
TJ's Blog
News
Details
Available at:

WWW.ItsFiction.com

Friends for life, young Ryan and Austin left summer camp for an end-of-the-summer Caribbean sailing trip with promises of high sea adventure. However, a monstrous storm changes their lives forever, leaving them alone on an island to grow from boys to men, and discover a new life of survival in their own way. Years later, a last minute rescue from the hands of angry Cuban soldiers destroyed their joyous tropical life together, while forcing the boys to live according America's current values and expectations, but they couldn't do it. They couldn't forget the love they had on the island, and together, they fought everything the world put in their path, to find a new paradise faraway from home. They couldn't change the events that changed their lives, but they could change where they lived, and how they lived on a new island. They would make it their mission to help others find the peace, joy, and love they found.

Stranded is an innocent love story, packed with adventure and thrills, passion without limits, and enough emotion to pull a tear from a statue. The laughs and tears feel all too real, while the reader discovers the inevitable conclusion of saying, why not a love like this? The story is fiction, but you'll catch yourself looking for their island, as well as a love like theirs!

Books by TJ Johnson

The War Apart - Part I
(A Josh & Zeke Story)

The War Ahead - Part II Revised 2010
(A Josh & Zeke Story)

The Will
(A Brett & Chase Story)

Stranded Revised 2010
(An Austin & Ryan Story)

The Raceboys
(A Jack & Thad Story)

A Writer's Fantasy
(About His Favorite College Basketball Star)
(A Shane & TJ Story)

Gay Grifters
(An Eric & Tyler Story)

The Blackfeet Boys Part I
(A Kiyo & Windtalker Story)

Coming soon:

Crosshairs
(An Eric & Tyler Story)

The War Beyond - Part III
(A Josh & Zeke Story)

The Blackfeet Boys Part II
(A Kiyo & Windtalker Story)

Rock Solid Part III
(An Eric & Tyler Story)

Stranded

By
TJ Johnson

Dedication

A friend for fifteen years, Greg still makes me laugh when he calls, and his hugs still make my spirit soar.

True love doesn't have a happy ending;

True love has no ending.

ED MCKENZIE

ONE

In the early morning hours, he glanced up at the well-used wall calendar just above his bed, wiped the sleep from his eyes with his knuckles and slowly smiled. For almost a year, he had carefully written a large red X over each day as it passed. Today was the last one to mark. The anticipated glorious day was finally here. This was the day he would finally leave his mother's well-decorated home in Portland, Maine, and head south for the mountains of Western North Carolina. He knew he was far more than just lucky, due to the wealth of his family, but also because his family taught him to be conservative, never acting as if they were rich or pompous. Deep down he knew he had the security and peace of mind with plenty of money in their bank, but he never had more than twenty dollars in his wallet. It had been the same for his father and his grandfather. Everything he needed, from clothes to school supplies, almost magically appeared in his room by either his mother or a member of her staff. Christmas was not a big toy-receiving time at his house because by most standards every day was a Christmas-like happy feeling.

In his journey south, he would leave behind a butler, plus four servants that were all four or five his age, a heated swimming pool, and a tennis court. He gleefully made fun of his tutor who picked his nose when he thought no one was looking, and remained as dull as the day he arrived. Nevertheless, Ryan woefully knew he would miss their excellent chef, a man he often insulted when he asked for simple peanut butter and jelly sandwiches. He was polite to his nanny, but would by no means miss her, as he thought he was much too old to have one. If in trade he had a choice of giving up such luxuries for a more simple life on his own, it would easily be worth it, because he would at last be able to leave behind the one person he most detested in the entire world, his despicable and deplorable older teenage sister.

By all accounts, Ryan, known by all he met as a happy-go-lucky ten-year old, loved everyone and everybody except for his older sister Jessie. She was a big exception, a young woman intent on relentlessly spouting a venomous attitude towards Ryan, while daily inventing even more wicked ways to spoil his life on this earth. If he did anything wrong, even accidentally, she ran to mom to tattle on him. Her report of the infraction was as dramatic as the cheap gossip magazines. Jessie could fake a tear, produce a sobbing shoulder or a shaking anguish fit, all of which achieved instant sympathy from her parents. Convicted and punished by his parents before he could even mount a not guilty plea, Ryan accepted his naive parents and his doomed life with his sister as best he could.

If she lied that he had hit her, he found his freedom grounded for a week or more. Ryan lost every round of the battles with his sister, and she marked the successes down in her diary like a gunslinger carving scores on a pistol. She took great delight in her power over his happiness. She was but three years older and clearly bent on destroying him. In front of her parents, she was their beautiful, talented daughter who dreamed of dancing with the

New York City Ballet, but once out of their sight, she did everything she could to obliterate any joy that might befall young Ryan. He felt he knew more than most how Cinderella must have felt. His only escape came in the summertime as he headed south without her.

This was his third year to go off to summer camp, and he loved every minute of it. Going to summer camp was a family tradition. The family expected him to go. This trip was one of the few lessons in his life they insisted on that he wanted to do. Camp was part of his well-rounded education, and a privilege few boys had the opportunity to enjoy. He had been afraid to go his first year, but his parents had flown down with him to reassure that he would enjoy the summer. He had his doubts, but after eight weeks of camp, he learned to love not only his freedom from his sister, but his freedom from his parents as well. They were good parents, confident that he ate, dressed, slept, and studied well. They were also a bit of a stuffed shirt and starchy, steadfastly stoic, and they made no attempt to give affection to him. He spent all of their time planning Ryan's future, and little time worrying about whether he was happy or not.

At camp, Ryan was completely happy, even on a rainy day. He loved everything about the outdoors. His counselors taught him how to fish, something his dad never found time to do. The staff also taught him how to hike, build a tent, and make a fire. Ryan took a class on how to survive on his own by eating the right plants and berries. Last year, he learned to sail a small boat and water-ski. He loved everything to do with the outdoors, on land or water. He even liked the silly campfire songs and skits.

Every summer, after the first one, his parents put him on a plane in Maine dressed in a fancy wool Sunday suit and tie. The suit looked much like the one his executive father wore each day as he flew into New York City for a business or stockholders meeting. He stood at the boarding ramp ready to give his mother the expected peck on the cheek, and though only ten, Ryan knew everyone expected him to shake his dad's large, baseball glove-sized hand firmly but vigorously. After executing his formal going away duties, he turned and eagerly ran down the ramp to his awaiting jet. In his mind he was a winter prisoner given a summer sabbatical of adventure and fun. He did not want to miss a second of it.

Once in the air, Ryan dashed to the restroom and changed clothes like Superman in a phone booth. He returned to his seat wearing khaki camping shorts with at least six zippers and loops, tennis shoes, white socks, and the official camp tee shirt. He also wore a huge smile that everyone on the plane could not help but notice. He returned their smile when he caught them looking at him. He was a walking, talking, and grinning camp poster child.

During Ryan's first year, his bunkmate was a fat jerk of a kid, who farted all night, even while masturbating. Ryan searched around for someone

2

else to hang out with and soon made friends with Austin, and since then, they had been bunkmates and best friends. Austin became the only person in the world he would take time to write a letter for posting. Austin knew more about who Ryan was, what Ryan thought deep inside, and what he wanted to do or be than anyone else on the planet. Ryan's parents had no clue. Austin knew everything, and similarly, Ryan listened earnestly as Austin shared his life with him. They were best friends, buddies, and pals, and thus they began growing up together, one summer at a time.

Unfortunately for Ryan, Austin and his family were in Washington most of the school year. His dad was an asshole of a Senator; a quote Austin heard a reporter say about his father. He did not argue with the reporter's perception, as he knew the man described his dad quite accurately. Austin had loved his childhood mountain home in the state of North Carolina, but at the age of just five years old, his dad won his first congressional election. Less than a month later, the entire family found themselves yanked from their roots in their home state, and sent off to Washington to serve the American people. To him, such a move would never have been his choice, but in his family he rarely had the opportunity or pleasure of choices.

Suddenly, Austin found himself forced to attend private Catholic schools with other young political pricks. Although his family raised him as a non-practicing Southern Baptist, Austin still did not get a reprieve from the traditional stern nuns. He also had an older sister that Austin called Miss W. His sister never figured out the meaning of her nickname or why. Only his best friend Ryan knew this simple secret because Ryan knew every secret Austin had ever invented. Miss W stood for Miss Witch, or sometimes Miss Wicked Witch. Austin often secretly left one of the housekeeper's sweep brooms in his sister's room in case she wanted to take a long ride somewhere. He would have been glad to hold the door or open a window for just such an occasion.

Austin was a healthy ten-year old who read a lot more than most kids his age. He mainly did so to keep from being lonely. It was also because he loved adventure stories. Their house was in the Mount Vernon area near Washington, and there were no kids his age in the neighborhood. One of his father's supporters owned the camp, and thus, they sent him there every summer for the past three years. Fortunately, beginning at an early age, Austin's grandfather had taught him how to fish and hunt. Often they would sit on some isolated dirt road for hours on end, while waiting for his grandfather's hunting dogs to track a Southern fox. Once he had seen a red fox bounce over the hood of his grandfather's old pickup truck before quickly scampering off into the woods in a desperate maneuver to scramble the dogs from his trail. The astonished grandfather and grandson just slowly turned and

3

looked at their thunderstruck faces. Moments later, they busted out laughing as the tail wagging confused dogs ran in circles all around them.

Austin loved wild animals, and as much as he loved the family's hunting dogs, he often prayed the little fox would escape away unharmed. He became deeply saddened when his beloved grandfather died just three days before his seventh birthday. He missed him. He could not remember a hug by anyone that genuinely loved him since that dark day. Just two months later, Austin met Ryan at summer camp, and before long, he became convinced his grandfather had arranged their meeting from way up in heaven. The pain of the loss of his grandfather almost magically decreased after Ryan and Austin became friends.

His plane was also heading a bit south and west, as was Ryan's flight. The seatbelt light went on signaling the time of arrival was near. In one of Austin's khaki short pockets was Ryan's last letter to him. He had read the two-page letter, handwritten on typical standard three-hole punched school notebook paper, no fewer than forty times. He usually read it right before he went to bed so his dreams would be of him and Ryan exploring the vast hills and waterfalls surrounding Camp Pisgah. He checked his watch once more, and became thrilled to note that he had only a few more minutes until he would see Ryan. He had convinced his parents to book him on a flight that would put him in the Asheville airport about the same time as Ryan's flight.

After reading the letter one last time, he closed his eyes, and instantly could see his best friend's face in his mind. Austin was about the same height, weighed perhaps seventy pounds, and had sandy brown hair that turned lighter in the summer sun, with a shade of light red in it, and dark chocolate brown eyes. When Austin laughed, Ryan would delight in seeing two distinctive dimples appear in his friend's smooth face. He talked to Austin's face in his silent walks in the woods, or laughed with him in his dreams. He loved Austin as if he was his own brother. He loved him far more than he loved any of his other friends or family members. After all, victims often share a pain so great the bond between them becomes inseparable, and their major common suffering was their two older sisters. They could not imagine why God would have done such a great job of creating this beautiful earth, only to destroy all their peace and happiness by adding their older, obnoxious sisters.

Austin checked his watch again. He had debarked from his seat on the plane twenty minutes ago and bounced excitedly down the ramp steps. Though a well-trained counselor tried to push him aboard a camp bus like a shepherd herding wayward sheep, he refused to leave just yet, and rushed back to the fence near the runway to watch for Ryan's plane. He opened his wallet to Ryan's picture, not needing to refresh his memory, but rather wanting to assure himself that his best friend Ryan would soon be landing. He carefully folded a picture his counselor had taken of the two just last summer, and placed that picture in the front of his wallet. He looked at it so often he could have even told you how many blades of grass were around the soles of their shoes. Ryan was about his height, with dark brown hair that contrasted substantially with his rich, sea blue, piercing eyes. Ryan detested the dimple in his chin, and once spent every minute of their daily rest hour with his tongue pressed behind his chin trying to retrain the skin to pooch out instead of the natural depression. He had long given up and accepted the ominous fact that God hated him, and that is why he had a dimpled chin, and why God gave him his stupid sister.

Austin spotted the plane long before anyone else along the railing on the runway. The time on the wall clock crawled along like a metronome during an unwanted piano lesson, but finally, the plane landed. A few more minutes passed before the big stainless steel steps rolled up to the plane. Soon the door swung open. The first passenger to disembark was none other than Ryan, Austin's best friend, the only person he felt love for, and knew that equal love came in return. They were true best friends.

Austin leaped over the railing, and with an airport cop chasing after him he darted across the tarmac. Ryan bounded down the steps, two at a time, and began running towards Austin. They met nearly halfway to the plane, hugged tightly, and swung themselves around and around, laughing cheerfully and yelling. The arriving passengers stopped their walk on the hot concrete runway while gaping at the spectacle, but as they finally moved towards the terminal, you could see a smile creeping across their travel worn faces. The scene of reunited best friends, though only ten years old, had touched even the hardest of hearts. Even the cop slowed his pace before finally ushering the two boys to the exasperated counselor and the waiting camp bus.

"I missed you so much!" exclaimed Ryan, ignoring the cop and the counselor.

"And I missed you. This is going to be a fun year!" laughed Austin.

"It's always fun. We have fifty-six days together. It won't be enough, but it'll have to do."

"I promise to make every one of those fifty-six days the most fun we've ever had."

"My golly, in just one winter's passing, you have managed to get even uglier than last year!" teased Ryan with a sly grin.

"Maybe true, maybe not," shot back Austin, "but I could never catch up with your ugly record. You are the champion of all the uglies in the world, except for my sister. She takes the world championship every day of her miserable life."

TWO

The summer began with the best friends teasing, jostling, and poking fun as Ryan and Austin loved to do before they began to catch up on their wretched winter, school, and sisters. Soon they turned to plotting what they wanted to do for fun this year. At the top of the list was rock climbing. The camp rules required a camper to be at least ten years old to sign up for the adventuresome class. The instructor was a senior at Boston College, who smoked pot when off duty, listened passionately to the Grateful Dead all day long, and drove a beat-up green Honda Civic with 220,000 miles on it. He had devoted his entire life to rock climbing and teaching his safe climbing techniques to kids everywhere. He was braver than any other counselor that had any sober brains, and genuinely cared for all his campers like a big brother. Jack had red hair, fair skin, loved to talk about the women he dated and conquered, and unlike most of the staff, he genuinely loved his summer kids. He knew when to yell at them to try harder, and when to pat them on the back for their accomplishments. He especially knew when to give a kid a hug. Austin and Ryan had tried to get Jack as their counselor last year, but could not make it happen. This year, Austin bravely asked his dad to pull a few strings though he hated asking for a favor. He knew if any of his camp friends found out they would tease him, but he figured the risk was worth it.

Jack greeted them at his cabin door with a big howdy guys and his welcome aboard speech. Neither boy heard a word, for they knew when they reached the top of the stairs, Jack was going to give them an official camp noogie. Anticipating the playful fun had silenced their ears.

The noogie always preceded a male form of bear hugging. It hurt a little bit, but only in a playful way. Jack grabbed Ryan in a headlock, then took the knuckles of his free hand and began rubbing across the top of the camper's head. Somehow he had managed to let the headlock slip so he could tickle Ryan's ribs, and soon both boys were doubling over in laughter and giggles. Austin tried to escape, but Jack was too fast as he grabbed Austin by the waist of his khaki shorts. He quickly gave him his official noogie and then tossed the two giggling boys onto a bunk. To any passing parent they would have thought the camp had hired a demonstrative pervert. To Austin and Ryan, the camp employed what their comic books called the ultimate summer hero. Jack showed no favoritism nor tried to take advantage of the fact the boys were from wealthy families. He was only slightly impressed that one was the son of a United States Senator. He liked Austin and Ryan simply because of their abundant enthusiasm and positive attitude.

They just knew the summer was going to be fun. It had to be, they thought. There had to be some reprieve from the families they lived with and the sisters whose shadows made their skin crawl. They desperately needed a period in which boys could be boys and friends could be friends. It was as if each adventure made their friendship stronger and tighter. Ryan and Austin would gladly risk their life for the other. Though they never thought out or discussed their bond, it made both boys more certain and confidant. Ryan and Austin were true best friends. There was never a doubt about their loyalty. They completely trusted their friend. Lifelong brothers or even twins could not have been closer than these two.

After the official welcome by Jack, they quickly changed clothes and ran to the lake for the camp's requisite swim test. After leaping off the dock and into the cool lake, they knew their summer had officially begun. To the boys, the splash into the lake washed their accumulated family problems from their skin like trail dust off the back of a horse. They gleefully shouted triumphantly and then, of course, began splashing each other as they swam around in circles.

Eight Weeks Later

However, this year the summer had flown by excessively fast, and only a few days remained before the camp session was over. It had been a busy summer. The boys perfected their camping skills, polished their horse riding competence, and finally learned how to rock climb. They survived a rainy five-day hike on the Pisgah section of the Appalachian Trail that was high above the waterfall city of Brevard, North Carolina. Moreover, they earned the respect of the entire camp by being the only campers to get a fire going, despite a typical late afternoon downpour. Jack taught them everything he knew about rock climbing and surviving in the great outdoors. He insisted they do pushups every morning and every afternoon to make the climbing easier. Their arms and shoulders were as strong as their legs. They earned two rock-climbing awards, one for achievement and one for bravery, the latter a new medal class invented by Jack just for the two boys. After his final presentation, he said that he had never known two ten-year-olds to be so daring, confident, and fearless as Ryan and Austin.

They learned to sail with more efficiency than even boys that were three years older. They also could paddle a canoe skillfully down a medium class river. Jack made sure they knew how to make a temporary patch in case they ripped the aluminum skin on a jagged rock. Their cabin won stunt night and the best cabin inspection score. The reward for the latter resulted in an awesome watermelon fight. To the boys, no fancy dinner with their own excellent chef could touch the fun of this summer. All the staff liked the two boys, and everyone knew they were remarkable best friends.

Ryan and Austin displayed extraordinary outdoor skills, but despite their adventuresome attitude, their gentleman-like training from their formative years showed through. They were excessively polite to all, apologized for any unintended inconvenience, and quickly offered to make amends for any sorrow or problem they may have accidentally triggered. Even though they were only ten-year-olds, the camp director called Ryan and Austin a beacon of hope for tomorrow's youth, and not a single member of the staff challenged their dual nomination for Camper-of-the-Year-Award. This was the first time the honor went to two campers instead of just one.

It was at lunch when Ryan received a telegram from his mother. He quickly opened it fearing something happened to his family. To his delight, he learned he would not be going directly home to Maine, but would be flying south to the Caribbean on a two-week sailing vacation with his parents. His dad had chartered a big boat, and the idea of a big voyage just overwhelmed Ryan. He leaped with excitement. The best news of all was that his sister would NOT be attending. He was jubilant as he jumped from bunk to bunk, and Austin was happy for him, while silently already feeling the forthcoming loss of his best friend to yet another long lonely winter.

"Can you believe it?" Ryan exclaimed as they left for the dining hall.

"Nope, you're lucky. I get to go back to hot, dreary Washington..." began Austin before catching his attitude. He realized although he was trying to be a little funny, he was sounding selfish. He stopped himself and quickly changed his temperament. He could not let his misfortune of returning to the Senator's house tarnish his best friend's jubilation. So Austin forced a smile to his face quickly as he added, "This will give you a chance to show your dad how much you've learned about sailing this summer. One day, when we're old enough, you and I will sail off on a great adventure together," added Austin as gleefully as he could muster.

Ryan did not respond as usual, but rather stopped so suddenly in his tracks that Austin had to turn around to see what happened to him. Ryan's smile slid down and off his face like the lowering of a theater curtain.

"What's wrong with you? You got gas?" teased Austin.

"You're not going to Washington," pronounced Ryan, as a sly grin slowly began spreading across his face once again.

"Of course, I am. I think it is written in the Bible somewhere. At the end of the summer, young master Austin must return to his slavery cabin in the great capital, and serve his country by being the perfect son of the great senator from North Carolina. What are you talking about?"

"Not this year. I'm going to call mom, and ask her if you can come with us. It says right here," he held up the letter and pointed. "My sister is NOT going. That means there is room for you! I'm sure she'll agree."

"She might, but I don't know about my mother."

"I'll convince her!" replied Ryan undaunted.

"You're crazy," laughed Austin.

"What have we to lose? We can try to have two more weeks together, or we can say goodbye next week. You decide."

Austin stood there silently stewing over the opportunity, but as the moments ticked by, Ryan could soon see the slow creation of his best friend's trademark tender dimples. A warm grin slowly swelled on his face. "Do you really think we can pull it off?" asked Austin.

"Yes, I do! Come on, let's make the call."

"But we're not supposed to use the phone until Sunday."

"That'll be too late. Come on!" demanded Ryan, as he pushed Austin towards the trail leading to the camp office.

They reached the office and silently peeked in the window to find Miss Galloway typing away on a letter. She was the camp's secretary, nurse, and official Mother Hubbard all rolled in to one. She hugged and nursed the homesick little ones, and still managed to stick over a thousand band aids on everyone whether they needed one or not. She felt loved and teased, and she loved and teased them right back. The camp would never be the same without her. No one allowed her to retire. No one even considered the possibility.

Ryan motioned for Austin to follow him. "You run inside and tell her that a swarm of bees has stung some campers by the lake."

Austin protested. "You want me to lie?"

"You want to go sailing?"

"Yes, but then what?"

"Once she leaves, I'll get on the phone to my mom. Once I get her affirmative approval, then you can call your mom. Get moving." Ryan pushed Austin into the hallway where Miss Galloway instantly saw him. He could not back out now, but he wanted to.

"Now what are you up to these days, Mister Austin?"

She was so sweet and kind to him, he hated to fib to her. She was like a grandmother to him. He gulped. "Miss Galloway, you've got to come quick! There are some bees swarming around the dock at the lake, and I'm afraid they've stung half of the campers!" He made it a small lie. It became a simple stretch of the truth. Surely, there was at least a bee or two buzzing around somewhere near the lake, he hoped.

"Oh my goodness! Let me get my first aid kit."

"I'll run and tell them you're coming!" Austin ran out the door, doubled behind the trash barrel, and crept down beside Ryan as they watched poor Miss Galloway hustle out the door and down the beaten path to the lake.

"Let's go!" exclaimed a grinning Ryan as he playfully elbowed Austin.

Their luck held as they made the call and like a real miracle, Ryan easily obtained parental permission. Ryan gave her Austin's phone number and address. His mom promised to call Austin's mom, and make the coordinating travel arrangements. The news thrilled her. Ryan now had some company, allowing him and Austin to fend for themselves, leaving her more time for reading and tanning. She had no idea of how to entertain or plan a day for ten-year-olds, but made no plans to read up on the subject.

9

Austin prayed before dialing. "Please God, I'll do anything, but please let me go. Please. Amen." Ryan almost laughed aloud, but he knew Austin was deadly serious.

To their surprise, Austin's mother reminded him that it was an election summer, and that his father would be heavily stumping for the fall election. He felt she was going to say no. Nevertheless, she thought about all the barbecues and banquets to attend, so perhaps his going on vacation with Ryan might be a great idea after all. Suddenly, she said yes. Austin nearly fainted. She promised to discuss it with his father that evening.

The next day, Austin's mother called and left Miss Galloway a message that Austin's end of summer travel plans had changed. She gave permission for Austin to go on vacation with Ryan at the end of camp, and said she would send the necessary paperwork to the camp by courier. When Miss Galloway told Austin, they nearly knocked her over when both boys ran and hugged her tight around her waist. She became as delighted as well, making her quickly forget about the lie Austin told her the day before, and understanding why it all had been necessary. She laughed as she watched the eager boys run and jump into the air, clicking their heels together, and bear hugging the other in jubilant celebration. She could not help but be happy for them. The excited boys were a jubilant sight for all to see.

Therefore, the day they had once dreaded arrived, but instead of despondency and tears, they were now leaving a summer of adventure, and heading off to the Caribbean for a two-week sailing vacation. Jack arranged to drive them to the airport where they made their final goodbyes. Jack gave each a huge bear hug, a quick 'noogie' for luck, and then presented beaded bracelets he made for them. They wore the bracelets proudly as they boarded the plane for Miami. They were still filled with excitement. If they had but one wish between them, it would be that they never had to say goodbye again, and all their days would be filled with one adventure after another.

THREE

It was the summer of 1978. The Kennedy Cuban crisis had been over fifteen years before their arrival in Miami. Nevertheless, Ryan's dad insisted on telling the family all he knew on the subject, while the family remained captive to his boring narration in the back of the white limousine that delivered the group from the Miami airport to the pier. The Cuban expatriate driver did his best to ignore the man's ignorance on the subject, hoping for a large tip as a reward for both his silence and seething patience. Robert was the birth name for Ryan's father, but everyone called him Bob. His father explained Cuba was a communist country, forcing thousands of refugees to flee the island for the land of democracy. Ryan rolled his eyes at his dad's lackluster speech. Austin nearly busted out laughing at the faces Ryan made while mocking his dad. Mary, Ryan's mother, tried to distract her husband from his lifeless speech by asking him about the voyage they were about to embark on.

"Hint taken," grinned Bob after catching Ryan making a face. "The boat is a forty-six footer owned by my boss, who insisted I take this vacation so I will feel guilty and deliver a new design for turbine engines later this year. What he doesn't know is that I've already completed the drawings, and just want to think about them for a while." He chuckled. "Anyhow, the boat has a forward and aft cabin, and quarters for our captain and cook. Our job will be to have a relaxing sail, do some fishing, and if you boys like, we might go scuba diving. Does that sound like fun?"

"Yes, Dad, it sounds great," replied Ryan expectantly.

"My dear," he said turning to his wife, "the chef, known for her exquisite delicacies, maintains an excellent stock of wine aboard the ship. I think you'll be sufficiently entertained."

"I pray so," she replied without a smile. Austin noted a hint of trouble between Ryan's parents. Ryan on the other hand had known this for a while. He had seen his father with another woman in town one day but kept silent. He did not understand why his mom and dad could not like each other, but he did his best to keep such thoughts from his mind. Austin thought it odd that she brought aboard an entire suitcase of books to read. He could not fathom how there would possibly be a single moment of spare time for anyone to read on a sailing adventure on the ocean. Prior to this cruise, their biggest adventure while sailing was going just around the bend on the camp's lake. Perhaps, he thought, they must observe rest hour like at a camp, and then she could read.

Finally the car parked, and the boys immediately leaped out so they could see the chartered sailing vessel. The boat was spectacular, well polished and preserved. At the end of the dock stood the captain whose shape and demeanor instantly reminded both boys of the television character Captain

Kangaroo. He was almost as wide as tall, sported a large bushy handlebar mustache, and long gray hair that somehow he managed to squeeze into a tight ponytail before pulling on a sailor's hat. The captain had an anchor tattooed on his Popeye shaped arms, on his feet were well-worn leather deck shoes, and sitting beside him was a small brown dog, a two year old miniature pinscher named Bell. The boat's delightful cook was in fact the captain's wife; a jolly old gal whose eyes twinkled much like one might imagine Santa Claus doing on Christmas Eve. She winked at them. Her name was Molly, and she greeted everyone with a genuine smile and beaming blue eyes. She also possessed magical talents because she welcomed the boys with a warm hello, and pan of fresh baked, chocolate chip cookies. Her magic worked, so she and the boys became instant friends.

Ryan's parents took the aft cabin because it was larger, with a view out the stern, and their very own private head, or in the language of the land lovers, a bathroom. The boys took the forward cabin because it was the only one left. The captain and Molly stayed in a central cabin just across from the galley. Ryan and Austin could not picture the captain even fitting through the door, or even how he got in the small bunk bed, but they were smart enough not to be in his way when he tried.

The boat set sail immediately after a bit of orientation. The boys quickly learned the captain was also a big teaser, and yet generous enough to answer their hundred and one questions. He told them everything including what compass bearing they were heading and where it would lead them. They told him about their sailing adventures around the camp lake, to which the captain laughed and teased them about their tiny bathtub boats they supposedly sailed. However, they amazed him when they began speaking the names of all the parts of his boat, and soon he had them raising the mainsail and cranking up the jib.

While the boys napped in the sun, Bob set down with the captain and went over the nautical charts. The captain suggested they take a southerly route around Cuba, and then make a good run to the Cayman Islands. From there, they could head to the Virgin Islands or more secluded islands if they wished. Bob agreed to the plan, mainly because he did not care where they went, as long as he found some time to rest. His tedious work on the new engine designs had been draining him for a long while. He suspected he was getting an ulcer, and he knew his marriage was coming apart as well. He hoped the trip would rekindle his love for his wife, but she seemed moody and arrogant to him, while a saint to others. He didn't know that she knew about the fling he had with his secretary, and he also didn't know that she had a tryst of her own.

The lonely little dog took a liking to the boys. They promptly petted and fed Bell scraps of food whenever they could. Once out of the crowded Miami ports, the captain expertly picked up speed, trimming his sails, and carefully plotting his course. Each passing mile became a bit quieter with no car horns or engine noises. It was then they noted the wind whipping across the sails, and the splashing swish of the bow as it plowed across another wave. The captain knew the ocean swells like a trucker might know the hills on an often-traveled highway. It seemed that when the large captain breathed the sails collapsed, and when he exhaled, they filled once more, and the great ship moved forward yet again. Ryan and Austin began to realize that if they ever ran out of wind, the captain would simply blow them to port all by himself.

Two days out to sea, and the swells began to live up to their name, as the waves became nine to twelve feet tall instead of the usual two to three. Mornings came early in the Caribbean as the sun quickly heated up the interior cabins. Just as Austin produced a big, wide-mouth yawn, the bow lifted on the crest of a wave pitching him from the top bunk to the floor. The next wave sent Ryan tumbling out of his bunk as well, and of course, he fell on top of poor Austin, who was now on the bottom of the pile. Still in their underwear, they made their way through the galley and on to the deck. Camp had a way of driving away thoughts and fears of privacy and modesty. To their surprise, the skies were no longer the bright blue they had become accustomed to, but were now dark, dreary, tumbling clouds that approached from the east, blocking their morning sun. They flinched when flashes of lightning streaked across the sky.

"We'll have to eat on the run today," said Molly as she handed the boys hot biscuits stuffed with country ham. "Better eat quickly, dress, and get your slickers on. You're going to get wet. We're going to enjoy much rain today, but don't you worry, the old sun will come out tomorrow. You just wait and see. A rainy day just makes the good days even better!"

The boys felt better after Molly's rousing, confidence building speech, but the boys also noted the worry lines that wrinkled her forehead. Bob and Mary were already in their rain gear, and quickly went about tying all their gear down. They checked and double-checked everything. As the boys ate their breakfast, they noted the captain returned to the helm and took it off autopilot. He was also working much harder at keeping the boat on course than he did the previous two days of fair-weather sailing. Despite the cooler breeze, sweat drops fell from his head to his well-worn tee shirt.

With each passing minute, the swells grew stronger and substantially larger. In an hour, the boat was going up one wave and crashing down into the next, much like a roller coaster at an amusement park. At first, the giant swells were fun for the boys, as they felt their weight shift downward and then upward once again. However, as the day went by and the waves continued to grow, they were soon hanging on as tightly as possible to the stainless steel railing around the cockpit. Their knuckles were white despite their bronze, summer tanned skin as they hung on for the ride. Mary had already thrown up

13

three times, and Bob just lost his breakfast over the stern. Molly spent the past hour securing everything below. She locked every cabinet and door as tight as possible.

Everyone on deck had grown quiet, but as the thunder grew louder, the rain came even faster, and the skies became as dark as night. Austin and Ryan had never seen rain blown sideways into their faces. It did not matter which way they turned their heads, they gulped another mouthful of rainwater, and sometimes seawater as the swells splashed over the deck. Bell was a smart little dog that knew bad weather was here, and thus, she climbed into the lower bunk of Molly's cabin and hid under the pillow. When the colossal waves grew to twenty feet, Mary became frightened, and made her way back down below. However, the rocking made her seasickness worst. In the moments of silence between waves, they could hear her retching from below. Bob went to console and try to help her calm down, but there was little he could do. The fun was over. Though Austin and Ryan failed to say a single word, the captain recognized the fear he saw in their eyes.

"Don't worry, lads. I've seen worst, and fared the better of it," he yelled. "I'll get us through this one, and that's a promise you can take to the bank. Although, come to think of it," he teased as he winked, "it'd be a long swim to reach one!" He laughed heartily at his own jokes. The boys rolled their eyes and poked the other in the ribs. The captain's jokes were getting stale. Just as Ryan was about to make a smart remark, an enormous wave came over the bow and drenched the boys.

"Better tie in if you're going to stay on deck, or get below and sweat it out. The choice is yours," warned the captain.

"We'll tie off, "replied Austin. " I'd rather see what we're about to crash into."

"Yeah, we're staying," added Ryan apprehensively.

The boys had already put on their bright orange life jackets. They grabbed some line and tied themselves to the railing, using a bowline knot they learned at camp two summers ago. Jack taught the class this unique knot that never slips nor jams. Feeling somewhat secure, they began to rock and roll with the boat, doing their best to make the storm fun.

FOUR

Four hours went by and the storm had yet to pass on by. In fact, the wind had more than doubled its speed, causing even the captain's brow to wrinkle with worry. He was struggling mightily with the helm, and the boys began to wonder if they should offer to help. The boat rocked and swayed recklessly. Several times the rope they used to tie themselves to the rail saved them from being swept overboard. The captain fired up the engine to provide steady propulsion power due to the erratic wind. He explained they he wanted to cut through the waves at a slight angle. He didn't explain he was trying to keep the waves from broadsiding the boat and flipping it over.

Mary had thrown up so much that she passed out, most likely from dehydration, but there was no way to get any freshwater in her until the storm passed. Ryan caught a glimpse of Molly in the galley, and he saw her cross her chest like a good Catholic as her lips said silent prayers. He nudged Austin so he could see her. Instantly, the boys' faces turned white as their fears doubled.

Suddenly, a loud crack rang out above them. At first, Ryan and Austin assumed it was just another of the dozen bolts of lightning ripping across the blacken sky. In this storm, the sonic boom followed the strike a split second later, which meant they were in the thick of it instead of miles away.

"Look out!" yelled the captain. The sail suddenly tore from top to bottom as if it was made of paper.

Ryan turned and his eyes flickered as he saw the main sail descending on top of them. The mast followed like a large telephone pole broken by a runaway car. Ryan grabbed Austin. The pole was coming straight for them. They rapidly began attempting to untie the knots that had swollen in the rain. Their eyes grew wide as huge heavy mounds of sailcloth began falling over and around them. The weight of the wet sail brought the huge mast towards them but stopping briefly as it caught another line, then the line would break and it would drop a few more feet. There was nowhere to run. The captain reluctantly gave up the helm to try to reach the boys, but in doing so, he lost control of the boat. They crossed a large wave, the boat spun wildly, and just as they descended the next crest, the following huge wave slammed into the side of the boat. The mast continued downward and fell just behind the boys but onto the captain, who tripped in the rigging and fell. The mast instantly crushed his neck. He never had a chance to stop it, and in seconds, the captain died. The splintered mast and the ropes dragged his body overboard, tipping the boat wildly out of control. Another huge wall of water crashed over them and then suddenly the stern went under.

Down below, Bob and Mary found themselves tossed from one side of the boat to the other before crashing roughly to the floor. The stern

15

windows were smashed. Water flowed in freely. Molly struggled on her feet, but slowly made her way up the galley steps just in time to see her husband swept overboard. She screamed after him, while knowing she could not save him, and that he was gone forever. The boys found themselves tangled beneath the remaining mounds of wet sail. It felt like a wall had fallen on them. They could not see each other and still could not untie the knots that originally saved them from being thrown overboard, but now threatened to take them to the bottom of the ocean.

"I can't budge the knot!" screamed Ryan.

"Neither can I!" yelled Austin.

Ryan asked, "Where's your knife?"

"Back pocket!" replied Austin as he began to twist and squirm in his seat. The water was crashing over the deck and quickly filling the cockpit. The boys suddenly had a new terror, and in a brief moment, the realization they were sinking took hold. They could drown right where they sat.

Molly crawled onto the deck to try to find them, but before she could reach the boys, massive waves slammed over the deck, one after the other and right into Molly. The crest of the waves lifted her like a small toy boat, and tossed her violently into the dark water, never to see the light of day again.

Austin managed to get the knife from his pocket, and although he had never opened the pocketknife in the dark before, he knew every individual blade like the back of his hand. It was a Swiss army knife given to him one Christmas by his grandfather. Ryan had been the only friend ever allowed to touch the highly valued tool. He opened the largest blade, about four inches long, and fortunately, it was as sharp as a razor. He could not see Ryan, so he began by sawing at the knot just above his own waist.

Ryan could hear his mother's screams as the water continued flooding the boat. Bob struggled to his feet. The boat was turning on its side as wave after wave began devouring the boat like a savage monster chewing its prey. Bob's body was abruptly tossed about the galley like a rag dog in a puppy's mouth.

"Come on, Mary. We have to get the lifeboat in the water. We must hurry! Ryan! Ryan!" he yelled above the loud claps of thunder.

Mary had rolled herself up into a ball on the bed. Fear overwhelmed her as panic and shock set in. She could not move. She would not hear, and she would not listen. Water crashed through the portholes and onto the bed. Bob fought his way through the debris and waist-deep water. As he quickly lifted her up in his arms, she suddenly came alive. She scratched and clawed his face like a terror-stricken drowning person, begging him to leave her alone. In spite of her desperate pleas, he refused to let her go. He struggled to make his way back out of their cabin and through the rising water. Just as he started up the steps to the deck, a huge wave crashed over the boat that sent him sprawling backwards into the wall. He dropped Mary as his head hit a beam, knocking him unconscious. Mary crawled to his limp body while sobbing uncontrollably, and just barely got her arms around him when the water rose over her head. She never let go of her drowning husband. The bubbles flew from their lungs like an air pump in an aquarium. She finally gasped and sucked in water. She instinctively tried to get another breath but took in more water. Then her eyes suddenly stopped moving as she and her husband descended into the dark cold water.

Austin cut through his rope rapidly. Ryan was still struggling to get free of the ropes that held them fast to the rail. He twisted and turned until he could see Austin.

"Hold still!" yelled Austin as he grabbed his friend's rope and began sawing. The knife cut easily through the rope. "You're free!" he exclaimed.

"I can't see!" exclaimed Ryan.

"I'll cut a hole in the sail. I hope the captain..." However, before Austin could finish his revelation, the bow suddenly lifted out of the water, and then slammed under the next wave. In a flash of seconds, the boat and the boys were a few feet underwater and sinking. The saltwater stung their eyes. There had been no chance for a good breath. They struggled to kick free of the debris around their legs. Still clasping his knife, Austin cut a hole in the swirling sailcloth, and though the water was black as night, he could see bolts of lightning. They never knew you could see underwater in the ocean without a diving mask, but even though their vision was blurry, they could see the yellow streaks flashing overhead. It gave them their bearings and a direction to swim towards.

He put his knife deep in his pocket, pulled free of the sheets of sail, tangled ropes and rigging, and then reached for Ryan's hand.

Ryan grabbed his friend's hand, but as he pulled through the sail, his feet became entangled in the loose line. He suddenly found himself being pulled down with the boat. Fear seized him. He kicked harder, which only made it worst. Austin let go of Ryan's hand, swam down and tried to free Ryan's feet. He retrieved his knife and sawed once again. They were fifteen feet down. Their ears popped from the water pressure, but they didn't feel it. Their lungs ached to draw in fresh air. Their hearts were pounding in their chests. Austin cut one foot free and quickly sawed away to free the other foot. Ryan began to shiver uncontrollably. The water felt cold to their skin. Their rain slickers were heavy. He pulled the top over his head. Austin freed Ryan's remaining foot. He quickly folded his knife and stuck it once more in his pocket. Ryan pulled Austin's rain suit off, and then together, they kicked hard and rapidly towards the surface.

Beneath them, they could see flickering lights on the boat as it was sinking. Millions of bubbles were swirling up from the boat and flying by them. The bubbles led them to the surface. They realized the engine had died.

The boat was silent though their ears heard loud creaking noises as bottles aboard the boat exploded. Food and paint cans imploded. Everything floatable on the boat flew up through the water like small missiles. In just under five minutes, the boat sunk to the bottom of the ocean, taking Ryan's parents to their graves.

Austin reached the surface first and stretched his arm downward to pull Ryan the remaining distance to fresh air. Together, they gasped repeatedly, but it seemed for each breath they sucked in, another wave would fill their mouths with saltwater. Ryan coughed hard. Austin threw up, but their arms and legs automatically began kicking as they had learned in their first year at camp. They were treading water. They held hands as the sky went from bright yellow streaks of light to black. They rode the waves. They yelled for Bob and Mary. They yelled for the captain. They yelled for Molly, but they were all gone forever. It was several minutes before they realized their life jackets were keeping them afloat. Only then did they stop their legs and arms from stroking.

"Find something to hang on to," yelled Ryan.

"I see something over there," pointed Austin.

The boys swam to a chunk of the wooden mast that had broken off and floated free in the water. Grasping a tight hold on it gave them a moment of reprieve as another wave crashed into them. They hung on to the mast almost as tightly as they hung on to each other. Ryan screamed out for his lost parents. He bravely did not cry. He was afraid to cry. He didn't want to accept they were gone.

As the hours ticked by, the storm finally passed and sometime during the night, the seas began to recede. The storm had arrived at breakfast and departed in the night with little to no warning at all.

They spent most of the following day fighting to stay on the temporary floating chunk of mast. By late afternoon, the sun finally broke through the trailing black clouds, and as it did so, the boys got a strong realization of their sunken ordeal. They took turns sitting up on top of the broken pole and scanning the horizon. They spotted hundreds of floating wine bottles, a torn jacket, pieces of sailcloth, but little else. The rest of the boat and their supplies had gone down to the bottom. Their survival gear and rations amounted to one knife, and some soggy chewing gum and breath mints.

"Do you see anything?" asked Ryan as Austin took his turn on the floating log as they crested a wave.

"Yes, I do. Something swimming in the water over there," he pointed. "Something small."

Following tradition, the Caribbean sun was falling quickly into the sea. Sunsets were beautiful, but always lasted only minutes. Darkness would soon cover them once more. A day of mostly darkness, followed by an even darker night, brought on a new stage of panic from the stranded boys.

Ryan asked, "What is it?"

Austin hesitated, straining to see over the wave. "It's Bell, the captain's dog! She survived!"

The dog spotted the boys and hurriedly swam in their direction.

"She looks exhausted," said Ryan.

"I'll get her!" Austin swung off the log and swam over to the poor dog. Exhausted, she could barely move her small legs and arms. She scratched Austin's face as she tried to get up on his shoulder to rest. Austin grabbed her like a mother dog grabs a pup, lifting her up and in that instant, poor Bell's exhausted legs fell limp. Her head drooped, but she still managed to lick Austin's grinning face as he swam back to the log.

"One dog rescued!" he yelled with a grin.

"I wish everyone had made it to the surface. I fear they are all lost," stated Ryan. He realized that his family and new friends were most likely dead.

Austin patted his friend's shoulder gently. "Hang in there, Ryan. We made it. Maybe they did, too. Right now, we have to make the best of it. Let's secure ourselves to the mast."

"No more knots!" replied Ryan.

"No knots, just something to allow us to hold on. Maybe I can make a loop to slip our wrist through to make it easier to hold on. I don't know how we're going to sleep, but I know we'll have to. I'll take the first watch. I will hold on to you and Bell. You lay your head on the pole and try to rest. Just float. I'll take care of you." Austin had done his best to sound brave and confident. He knew Ryan needed that and he did, too.

Ryan was too tired to argue, but every time he closed his eyes, his mind replayed the capsizing of the sailboat. Hours later, he finally dozed off. Around midnight, Austin forced himself to wake Ryan, as he could not keep his own eyes open any longer. Therefore, Ryan took his turn on watch duty. Morning could not come soon enough to suit him. He was thankful the storm was gone. The dark clouds were moving away, and one by one, the stars slowly returned to the black sky overhead. He practiced naming the stars as he had learned at camp. He petted and stroked little Bell, and he held on to his best friend as tightly as he could.

FIVE

Throughout the night the boys rode with the waves and unknowingly drifted out of International waters. The southerly winds pushed their little flotilla right pass the imaginary dotted boundary line surrounding Cuba. This route illegally put the waterlogged boys into the territorial waters of the communist country. Political tempers had cooled down a bit since the Kennedy Cuban crisis of the sixties. However, the United States Navy monitored that line with satellites and radar rather than circling the island with their threatening destroyers. With no boats to run into, the boys unfortunately didn't show up in the satellite photos because no one was looking for them.

The boys had no idea where they were or where the currents would take them. In fact, it was difficult to tell they were even drifting, as the ten-foot square of water around them stayed much the same from sunrise to sunset. The next morning they took turns swimming towards the floating bottles. They made a bag out of some sailcloth and loose rope to put the bottles in. Often the bottles were only half-full, which is why they were floating instead of sinking to the bottom. The boys had never tasted wine before, but with no freshwater to drink for the last twenty-four hours or more, every hour or so they forced themselves to take a single swig. The taste of the wine reminded them of cherry cough syrup. The sun was beating down hard, and though the wine tasted strong and nasty to their palate, they still managed to swallow it. Their growing thirst was greater than the rebellion of the wine on their taste buds.

Ryan asked, "What are we going to do?"

Austin shrugged. "I don't know, I guess we wait for a search party. Surely, someone has discovered we're missing."

"I don't think the captain or Molly got a chance to yell Mayday on the radio. How would they know we're missing?"

"I hope he told somebody of his plans. I think he's supposed to do that. Can you see any land?"

Ryan pulled up a bit higher on the floating chunk of mast log and stretched his neck as tall as he could. He scanned the horizon in all directions, but as far as he could see there was nothing but water. The lack of black clouds was the good news of the day. The sky was clear, but the sun was hot.

"Nothing but more water," he replied as he dismally fell back into the water dropping below the surface to wet his head and back up again.

Austin stroked Bell, who somehow managed to stay perched on top of the log like a seagull. They let her lick drops of the wine from their fingers.

Ryan asked, "What are we going to eat?"

"We've got nothing to eat, and we don't have any fishing line to catch anything with," replied Austin.

"That's good, because I don't think I could stomach raw fish."

Austin grinned. "If we get hungry enough, I bet we could eat raw dog."

Bell's ears suddenly stood up.

"He's just kidding, girl. We wouldn't eat you," laughed Ryan as he petted her once more to reassure her.

"We just have to conserve our strength, keep our wits about us, make the wine last as long as possible, and hope to goodness a boat or plane passes by soon. This is the Caribbean. There's bound to be a lot of fishing or tourist boats somewhere around here. We'll spot someone."

Ryan said, "Let's make a flag to wave in case we see someone. Do you see any more loose sailcloth dragging on the rigging?"

"There's a steel cable dragging beneath us. I'll swim down and take a look. Hold on to Bell for me."

Austin took a breath and then dove under while going hand over hand down the cable. He opened his eyes in the saltwater to look around, but his vision was blurry without a swim mask. He had gone about ten feet when sure enough he found an entangled section of sail. He took out his knife and began cutting a section of it. He had just about finished when suddenly the sail slightly unfurled revealing the captain's hand, and some of his big hairy forearm floated upwards towards Austin. The dismembered hand terrified the youngster beyond any event his short life.

Austin shrieked at the sight and then rapidly clawed his way to the surface. "Aw!" he yelled as broke through the water.

'What is it?" asked a bewildered Ryan.

"There's a human hand floating down there. I think it was the captain's!" he gasped.

"Oh lord! Are you all right?"

"Yeah, I guess. My heart just about leaped out of my chest!" exclaimed Austin. "Here's the piece of sale to make the flag." He pulled it from the water and handed it to Ryan, and then slumped over the log to rest.

"I think we'd better put the flag over our heads for now, or we're going to fry in this sun. Kind of weird isn't it. We've got millions and millions of gallons of water around us that we can't drink, and though it is slightly cool, it can't keep the sun from burning our skin."

"You think of weird stuff when you're floating in the ocean for hours, don't you?" teased Austin as he pulled the white sailcloth over their heads. Bell quickly moved under the shade cover as well.

"I tell you what's weird. I got to go to the bathroom," replied Ryan.

Austin said, "Number one is easy, just pee in your pants. Are you saying you've got to do number two?"

Ryan slowly nodded.

"Oh, jeez, I guess you'll have to do just like we did on the campouts. Drop your shorts and drop your load!" laughed Austin.

"Funny, what am I going to wipe with?" asked Ryan.

21

Austin chuckled. "Those millions and millions of gallons of water you were talking about!

Ryan splashed him. Austin splashed him back. Bell barked at them when some of the splashed water hit her, as if warning the boys she didn't want to ever get wet again.

Five days passed. They tried to ration their supplies, but they had already emptied three bottles of wine, one swallow at a time and sharing a little with Bell. The boys wisely re-corked the empty bottles so they would float in their bag to help keep it alongside them.

The following day began with Bell barking her head off. They turned in the direction she was barking and spotted an odd-looking object barely floating on the surface. It was dark green and tan with a snakelike head. It drifted just over twenty feet from them. The boys were just about to panic when they realized the head was the snout of a giant sea turtle. The playful turtle submerged under them and surfaced on the other side, but reluctantly decided they were too big to eat. Austin became brave enough to swim down, and ride the turtle's back for a few feet before the turtle took a hard turn and dumped him off.

"Wow! That was cool. Go try it, Ryan!" yelled a grinning Austin.

Ryan dove and immediately noted the turtle was not alone. There was a group of about twenty turtles of all sizes swimming around them. He rapidly swam to the nearest one as it turned and began rapidly paddling away. Quickly, he grabbed on to her shell, but he rode a bit too far. He surfaced about twenty feet from Austin.

"You're too far, Ryan! Come closer. Don't take a chance on us becoming separated!" yelled Austin.

Ryan didn't need a reminder as he quickly ducked his head and swam rapidly back to the log.

"You're right about fun. I just wish they could take us to land. Surely they know where it is," added Ryan.

"Sure they do. Do you speak turtle talk?" chided Austin.

Ryan laughed. "Nope, but I often speak to a smart aleck fool!"

They splashed each other while enjoying some fun before settling down to floating the rest of the day.

A few more days passed. Their strength was failing their young bodies. If the water had been cold they would have already been dead, but the Gulf Stream waters were warm, even after sunset. While there are drunks all over the world who could live entire months and perhaps years on bottles of wine, the boys possessed no plentiful body fat to provide the nourishment they desperately needed. Bell was rarely barking or moving, and slowly she was dehydrating. From time to time, she licked the sweat off the boys' faces. The

22

sailcloth protected their bare heads from the sun, but unless they found land, food, and water soon, they would surely die.

The nights were a mixed blessing, as they continued their ritual of taking turns sleeping and standing watch. During the few hours they could sleep, the boys had a chance to dream. By dreaming, they were able to relax, and feel a little better and less fearful. However, when the drifting boys awoke, the depressing reality of drifting in an endless sea, with no food or water, often sent them back into deep despair. Secretly, while standing watch alone, the boys would cry for a while. Bell licked their tears.

SIX

At dawn, the boys took another swig from the last bottle of wine. They had no idea what they were going to do when the wine was gone. Austin gave a small amount to poor Bell. Just as he was stowing the bottle, Ryan called to him.

"Look! Oh jeez, Austin! Look!" he exclaimed.

Austin tied the bag off and turned to see where Ryan pointed. Off the horizon was a large dark cloud. Bolts of lightning were already streaking through the sky. They could even see the sheets of rain as it fell to the ocean. It was all coming their way. Neither boy had anything to say. There was no way they could out swim the storm. The waves were already picking up some height, and a breeze began blowing their sail shade cover.

"Better stow the sailcloth in the bag and tie it off good," stated a somber Ryan.

"You're right and I know you don't want to think about this, but I think we'd better tie Bell and us to the log. The waves will get huge and I..."

Ryan gulped. "I know. Do it, but keep your knife handy in case we have to cut ourselves loose in a hurry."

The seas were already cresting at fifteen feet when the rain engulfed them. Just as they crossed the top of the wave, Ryan yelled out.

"Yow!!" he exclaimed. "Something bumped me underwater!"

"What was it? Did it bite you?" asked an alarmed Austin.

"No, but..." he stopped in mid sentence. " Austin look! It's a shark!"

Austin turned to where Ryan was staring. They began shaking and trembling as they stared at the menacingly looking predator. Fear was overwhelming them as the shark swam back and forth just fifty feet away. They were afraid to speak and too afraid to move.

The rain suddenly began coming down in buckets that soon made it difficult to see the shark. The boys prayed silently. The waves continued to rise, cresting at twenty-five feet. The sky grew black, making the lightning bolts bigger and brighter than ever before. Even with the ropes tied around their wrists, they were fighting to hang on and keep their heads above the water. Repeatedly, Bell would lose her footing and slip into the water, but the boys had tied her collar to the log. Gently, they would push her feet back up and try to steady her feeble body. She'd bark a little, but her strength was failing her, too. She just did her best to hang on by digging her little claws into the wood. When he could, Austin caught the poor dog mouthfuls of rain, and then gently encouraged Bell to lick the water from his mouth. The little dog also quickly lapped up the water hitting the log and waited for more. Ryan soon took his turn feeding the dog with mouthfuls, while Austin swallowed as much rainwater as he could.

The storm and the huge waves seem to force the shark to go deeper and fortunately away from the boys. They didn't know that for sure, but they saw no other signs of the beast, and hoped they wouldn't. The storm and the shark were almost more than they could bear, but the freshwater from the sky lifted their spirits a bit.

The storm lasted for hours, moving them almost four times faster than the drifting speed of the past few days. Just as the center of the storm passed over the boys, the rain suddenly turned to sleet, and then to marble-size hail, thumping the boys on the head.

"Jeez, that hurts!" exclaimed Ryan.

"It's ice!" laughed Austin.

"Why are you laughing..." began Ryan before he caught himself. "It's edible!"

"It's something to eat!" they both yelled.

Quickly, they began catching the ice and pushing it in their mouths. Austin and Ryan also took turns putting small pieces in Bell's mouth. She quickly crunched them down and barked for another one. The ice was like manna from heaven and for almost twenty minutes, they ate all they could.

"Put some in the bottles," yelled Ryan.

"Good idea, but how?" asked Austin.

"Melt it quickly in your mouth and then spit it in."

"That's gross!"

"Can't think of any other way, can you?" asked Ryan.

Austin pretended to be thinking hard before grinning and replying, "Let's do it!"

They caught the ice for as long as it fell, managing to almost fill two bottles with water. Suddenly, the wind picked up, and the rain began falling once more. They hung on as they tossed and rolled over wave after wave.

"I can't hang on much longer," complained Ryan.

"You have to. You can do it," encouraged Austin.

"How much more of this can we take?"

"We'll get through. Hang on. I need you."

"I need you, too!"

Suddenly, a huge wave ran them over, leaving them gasping for air. Then another wave spilled over their heads, and soon yet another. The rolling waves seemed endless. The sky was black. The air filled with rain. Both boys felt sure the end of their lives had arrived.

"What's that noise?" asked Ryan suddenly as he lifted his head to hear.

Austin pulled himself up a bit on the log to free his ears from the water. They topped the crest of a wave and he heard it again.

"It sounds like a roar of some kind. Could it be a boat?" asked Austin.

25

"I don't see any lights. There it is again! Do you hear it?" asked Ryan.

"Yes, but I don't know what it is."

For the next twenty minutes, the noise continued, becoming louder and louder. The sun had fallen, and the storm was passing. The sky was black. The lightning moved on past them and finally the rain stopped. The roar sounded like a huge waterfall. It got so loud they began to fear it.

"Yowl!" yelled Ryan. "My leg scrapped something. It's the shark! It's back!"

Austin's eyes went wide, but suddenly his feet scrapped sand. "Wait, I'm walking!"

"Walking?" replied Ryan. Gingerly he allowed his feet to drift down into the black water. "I can touch, too!"

The undertow pulled them a bit. The realization suddenly hit them.

"LAND!" They yelled simultaneously.

"Hurry, Ryan. Let's untie ourselves, and try for shore before we drift by. This could be a small island or something. Hurry!"

Ryan and Austin dropped their feet to steady themselves, quickly untied their hands, and began pulling through the water with their arms, while fighting the tide and the undertow. A wave crested overhead and then crashed just forty feet ahead of them. The roar had been the sound of breaking waves on the shore. It was so dark they could barely see the white frothy water of the breaking waves. They could barely see each other but they kept moving closer.

Soon they were standing with their necks and chests free from the water. They stubbornly kept moving towards shore. When close enough, they made a run for shore, with Austin pulling Bell from the mast, and Ryan dragging the remaining bottles ashore. The undertow tried to drag the determined boys back to the sea, but they would have none of it. They doggedly pushed their way to shore.

Once they were finally out of the water, they fell on the sand, gently dropped Bell and the bag, and shouted for joy. The log soon came crashing ashore behind them. They grabbed it and pulled it up to dry land; half-afraid they might have to leave the island the same way they arrived.

It was nearly nine o'clock at night, so it would be at least eight or nine more hours before they could see where they had come ashore. They moved a bit farther up the beach feeling exhausted and tired. They drank two swigs a piece from the water bottles, and gave Bell a double hand scoop of water. The threesome stretched out on the sand, sleeping all night without a watchful eye and without a care. Though their energy was spent and their bodies exhausted, they had remarkably made it to land. Their last thought before drifting into a deep sleep was simple. They were safe.

Maybe it had been a nightmare, or a long ugly dream, but slowly Austin forced his sleep worn eyes open. He found himself puzzled, as all he could see was something gray. He struggled to keep his still exhausted eyes open. Then he opened and closed the lids a few times as if testing to see if they still worked. Though he was starving, he managed to make his eyes focus. The gray he saw was powdery sand, lots of sand, and it was damp sand. He was lying face down in it. He pushed himself up to his knees and turned around. He shaded his eyes from the bright sun that blared at him from across the waves and the ocean. The realization took hold. It hadn't been a dream, but it was a nightmare, for as far as he could see, he could see nothing but the blue ocean. It had been so appealing in pictures, so much fun riding the waves on the sailboat, but it had become a killer, and now he hated it.

Turning from the reality of his situation, he turned to see about Ryan and immediately inhaled a deep breath. Ryan was gone! So was Bell. He turned left and right as he looked up and down the beach, but he found no sign of them. Suddenly alarmed, he stood there alone. He feared that perhaps the raging current dragged Ryan down into the endless water. Austin began to shout for him.

"Ryan! Ryan! Ryan!" he yelled over and over. He ran to a sand dune and climbed on top of it so he could see farther. He cupped his hands around his mouth like a megaphone and yelled again. "Ryan! Ryan! Ryan!"

"Over here!" he heard from behind him. He turned towards the jungle and instantly found the opposite of the entire ocean blue he had floated on. The jungle was green, birds were flying, tree branches swayed left and right, and the gentle breeze felt good to his skin. It was a beautiful place. He spotted Ryan. "Come here," Ryan beckoned with a big exaggerated wave of his hand.

Austin ran for a few yards, but his weakened state caught up with him. He stumbled into the sand. He pulled himself back on his feet with sheer determination and guts. It took five minutes to make the seventy-five yards to Ryan, but he made it.

"You'll like this stuff!" grinned Ryan, his face white from the milk of a busted coconut. "Drink! It tastes wonderful."

Austin exploded into the biggest grin Ryan had ever seen on his best friend's face. Austin took the open coconut and ate a bite of the soft white mushy substance. The juice dripped down his chin, but he caught every falling drop and pushed it back in his mouth. Ryan reached into Austin's pocket, removed his knife, and began drilling a hole in another big brown nut. Once he broke through, the boys drank even more of the milk, and took turns feeding Bell at the same time. Their body and spirits slowly became nourished. The loss of energy was somewhat replenished and their hopes cautiously restored.

"Let's go exploring. Perhaps we can find some bananas or oranges, or something. I'm still hungry," protested Ryan.

"I think I'll be hungry for a year. Where are we?" asked Austin.

"No idea, but I haven't spotted any sign of life just yet. Let's see," he paused as scanned the horizon left and right. "The sun is straight out from where we came. It is morning, so that must be east. Let's go north up the beach and explore. I think this is an island, but how big, I do not know. Maybe this is the back side of Cayman or it could be Cuba."

"Cuba?" replied Austin suddenly alarmed. "What about the communists?"

"I don't think they'd hurt a bunch of hungry ten-year-olds, but we won't know where we are until we go find out. Are you up to walking?"

"Anything but swimming and drifting," replied Austin.

Ryan grinned, and then leaned in, putting his arms around his friend, and gave him a playful noogie as they began walking up the beach. They found driftwood and shells, and one smelly, rotting dead turtle. They held their noses as they passed the decaying dead animal. Bell barked at the poor turtle and then made her way around it. They spotted a few empty bottles, a broken barrel, and a rusty belt buckle. They found no other signs of human life, and except for the birds, no sign of animal life. Bell grew tired after an hour of walking, and just plopped down on her belly with her legs spread wide to rest in the sand, but they wanted to keep moving, so Austin cradled her in his arms. She liked it when he picked her up. She thanked his generosity with a wet lick of her tongue.

After a few miles of walking, they sat down and drank some of the water from their wine bottles that Ryan carried over his shoulder.

"I think we're turning west." He once again turned towards the water, and then looked left and right while noting the sun's position. "This is looking more and more like an island for certain," stated Ryan.

"Look, there's a banana tree!" yelled Austin as he stood, set down Bell, and began running towards the tree with Bell scampering after him.

"How we going to get them down?" asked Ryan, trotting after him.

"We find a smaller tree and climb it," replied Austin rather wisely. The thought even astonished him as he ran a few feet up to the trunk of a banana tree. A few overripe bananas had fallen, but they were too nasty to eat. They walked farther into the jungle, and instantly, they felt the temperature drop about ten degrees, as the foliage of the trees shaded the sun from their bare shoulders. The grass was cool beneath their feet. After just ten minutes of searching, they found the perfect banana tree. Obviously, a storm had blown the tree over when it was young, because it grew at an angle that was lower to the ground. Tons of fruit filled the branches of the tree. Most of the bananas were green. They searched for ripe ones and began pulling them off, peeling,

28

and gulping them down. Bell had never eaten a banana, but on this day, she ate a whole one.

They cut off about half a stalk, placed it in their bottle bag, and hiked back to the shore. Once there, they continued their journey of following the beach, which now took them westerly. By nightfall, they had made it halfway around the island. They were too tired to make a fire and create even a makeshift shelter. They settled down amid the sand dunes with Bell between them and soon drifted off to sleep.

SEVEN

The next day was similar to yesterday, but the long hike came to an end when the boys discovered they were right back where they originally landed. They sighed heavily, accepting the realization of their confinement on a large island. Their footprints were still in the sand that led to that first coconut tree. They ate a night meal of bananas and coconut milk before drifting off to sleep. Their bodies were slowly gaining some strength. However, their morale suffered, creating a dark melancholy stage of silent depression. Their mood turned somber at the realization that there was no immediate rescue in sight. They were just young boys, but found themselves forced to accept the fact they had found no one that could help them and nowhere to walk to. This desert island held them captive. Yet they were thankful they were alive and out of the ocean, and very thankful for some food.

When morning came, Austin woke first and walked down to the beach to rinse the sand off his skin. He was thinking hard, very hard. He hadn't lived long on this earth, but in his mind he rewound and replayed everything he had ever heard, everything that he had been taught, and everything he had read over and over in his head. He was forming a plan, a plan of survival that even he didn't realize, but something inside him told him he couldn't give up, he couldn't just die, he had to fight, he had to live, he had to survive.

Ryan joined him with a yawn. "What's up?"

"I've been thinking."

Ryan grinned. "I thought I smelled smoke!"

"I'm serious. We have to build us a place to live because we both know it'll rain again and probably soon. We have to find more food and maybe a source for freshwater. If not, we'd better collect enough coconuts and use the shells to collect rainwater because without water, well, we're done for."

"You sound like you read Swiss Family Robinson," replied Ryan without much thought.

The sudden realization of the thought hit them both. "You're right," smiled Austin as he shook his fist in the air. "That's exactly what we have to do. We will build a place to live, and we need to make a signal fire, too. Who knows when a boat may pass?"

"Or even a plane overhead," added Ryan.

"Right, let's go inland and do more exploring. Let's look for a place to build a hut, and find more food and hopefully some freshwater."

For the next several days, they hiked and foraged inland in different directions before returning to the beach minutes before nightfall. On their fourth day out, they were following a natural trail through the jungle when Ryan tripped over a fallen limb and fell flat on his face.

"What's the matter? You forget how to walk?" teased Austin.

"Thanks, smart ..." Ryan stopped in mid sentence and stared at the dirt just inches from his face. "Jeez look at the tracks. They're animal tracks, but what kind of animal?"

Austin knelt down and allowed a finger to trail one of the tracks. I don't know for sure, but it looks like a pig or hog or..."

Suddenly the limbs of a bush moved nearby. Both boys stood up quickly. Then they heard a loud grunt.

Ryan whispered, "What is it?"

"I don't know. Let's slowly move on down the trail."

They turned to walk away when they heard a growling sound.

"What if it's a tiger?" whispered Ryan as they took a few more steps away.

"Then run for the nearest tree," replied Austin, as he silently retrieved his knife from his back pocket and opened the largest blade.

The growl grew louder. The bushes started moving one after the other. They heard a swish-swish sound as something made its way through the low growing palms, and then the sound of sticks and twigs breaking. Whatever it was, it was coming straight for them, and it was coming rapidly.

"Run!" exclaimed Austin as he pushed Ryan along.

Together, they were running down the trail with Austin sneaking a look behind him to see if he could see what it was. The grunts grew louder. The limbs of the bushes were breaking and moving. Then he spotted an animal about three feet tall, with a dark hairy back, two short tusks, and it was heading right for them.

"Faster!" yelled Austin.

"I can't find a tree we can climb. Just tall palm trees," replied Ryan.

"Keep running. We'll find something."

They rounded a curve, went down a slight slope, and ran head on into a large pool of water. They stopped at the edge and saw all kinds of animal tracks. Then their heads turned quickly as the animal rounded the curve, stopped suddenly, and growled loudly at them. Ryan and Austin began to shake with fear. The only climbable tree was across the pool of water to the far side. The animal slammed its front hoofs in the ground much like a bull at a bullfight. It snarled at them. The boys had obviously traveled into its turf. Without further notice it charged them.

"Austin!" screamed Ryan.

Austin turned to face the animal with his knife, but immediately thought better of trying to kill the big beast with just his knife. "Come on, jump in and swim to the other side. Perhaps this beast hates the water."

Ryan didn't stop to argue as they both ran into the water, and dove towards the middle, throwing little Bell into the water ahead of them. They

31

surfaced about fifteen feet out, and turned to see if the animal came after them. It hadn't. It stood in the mud onshore and snarled at them once more.

"What an ugly mother!" grinned Ryan now relieved they were safe.

"Do you think it is a boar?" asked Austin as he treaded water with Bell trying to stand on his wet slippery shoulders.

"Yeah, I guess, like a wild pig," replied Ryan.

Austin asked, "Do you think it is edible?"

"Pigs are, but how in the hell are we going to kill and roast it?"

"I guess we hadn't realized that we had better arm ourselves. We'll make some spears and perhaps a tomahawk. Maybe even some sharps stakes to carry with us as long knives."

"We also need to build a fire. I guess we'll have to do it like we did on the campout," stated Ryan.

"Taste the water," said Austin.

Hesitantly, but confident Austin wouldn't ask him to do anything that would hurt him, he stuck his tongue out like an overgrown puppy and gave the water a lick. "It's fresh! Freshwater!"

"Right, now all this makes some sense. That trail is what the animals use to come here to drink. This must be the only freshwater on the island. If so, we're going to have to find a way to get some animals to leave, or share it, or get along or something."

"Where'd Bobby go?" asked Ryan pointing to where the wild boar had stood on shore.

"Bobby? Bobby who?

"Don't you remember? The counselor that talked in a monotone voice last year that everyone made fun of. They nicknamed him Bobby Bore, didn't they?"

"Ryan, you think of the weirdest stuff at the weirdest time. I believe that certifiably makes YOU weird!" stated Austin.

"There he is!" exclaimed Ryan as he pointed to the far side of the pool."

"Jeez, he is working his way around the pool. He knows we can't swim in the middle of the pool forever."

Ryan asked, "What do we do?"

"Swim faster. We have to get to that tree before he does."

Austin and Ryan swam towards a huge cypress looking tree with many huge flowing branches, some of which touched down into the water. There were a few other similar trees nearby, but this tree was by far the biggest. All the rest of the trees they had seen had been palms and bananas trees, or just bushes. This was a real tree.

Austin got to a branch that ran right down into the water and crawled up on it. He put the knife in his pocket, and reached down to lift the sail bag from Ryan's shoulder. The bag still contained their only possessions: mostly empty bottles and it now contained little Bell because when tired, Austin

32

would place her in the bag so she could ride. Ryan climbed out of the water, and together, they began walking up the branch into a high section of the tree.

"Where is he?" asked Ryan.

"There he is. We'd better get a little higher, but I think we're safe. If that old boar can climb a tree I'll die of laughter anyhow," grinned Austin.

Ryan chuckled. They climbed higher as the limbs grew wider and thicker. The boar reached the bottom of the tree and snarled. He kicked at the ground and even once or twice, he kicked the trunk of the tree, but the tree was far too big for him to push down. The boys sat down on a big limb to rest. Ryan pulled Bell from the bag so she could see what was going on.

"Bell, meet Bobby. Bobby, meet Bell," laughed Ryan as he gestured from one to the other with his hand.

Austin was rolling his eyes at Ryan, but he stopped when he looked up. The boys had been so busy looking at the ground for the boar; they hadn't noticed that nearby was the top of a huge tree.

"Ryan. Be quiet!" ordered Austin quickly.

Alarmed, Ryan brought Bell in close to his chest to protect her and to keep her from falling. "What is it?"

Austin nodded upwards. Fifty feet over their heads was an old, large, tree house. The weathered construction had some floorboards missing, but nonetheless it was there. Built in connecting sections and levels, based on the shape of the tree, the tree house had an odd, but effective design. A narrow deck or porch circled the tree house on each level. The thatched roof, built from dried palm leaves, needed some updating and patching. Bamboo and dried vines created the walls, which featured modern-like windows and doors, all made from bamboo and branches. Gray saltwater moss grew along the edge of the roof, and down the sides, effectively camouflaging the tree house from the ground below. The tree grew right out the top of the house another thirty feet or more, and its big branches and leaves hid the tree from the sky overhead. The tree house, covered in leaves and dust, had to be very old.

Neither boy said anything for a few minutes as they steadied their gaze on the structure, carefully watching for signs of life. Even Bell sensed possible trouble, so she perked up her ears to listen. No one noticed the boar had given up on a possible free lunch and made his way back in to the jungle.

"Do you think anyone is around?" asked Ryan quietly.

Austin whispered in reply, "I don't know. The house has obviously been here a while."

"What if they are pirates living there?"

Austin chuckled. "Pirates don't live in trees. They have giant ships…" Then he caught himself. "Ryan, pirates were in the seventeenth and eighteenth centuries. I think we are safe from pirates. Come on, let's take a chance and see if someone is there."

"Are you sure?"

Austin opened his knife. "Yep, come on."

33

Ryan put Bell back in the bag and looped it over his shoulder. Austin led the way as they leaped from branch to branch up the tree. The limbs were so huge, they could walk on them like big steel pipes, while holding on to smaller branches to steady their balance. They walked almost forty feet out on one big limb before they were under the tree house. They climbed upwards for another twenty-five feet. When they were within about fifteen feet of the surrounding deck, he motioned for Ryan to stay put and keep Bell quiet. He then turned and made his way to the surrounding porch deck, half expecting some jungle wild man to come running out of the house and cut him to shreds with a sword. He listened attentively, but he heard nothing, so with his heartbeat pounding in his ears, he made his way onto the deck and looked in the first window. It was semi-dark inside as he scanned the room.

Suddenly, a big bird flew straight at him and out of the window. Austin yelped and ducked down. The bird flew right over his head.

Ryan whispered, "Are you all right?"

Austin gulped but nodded affirmatively to Ryan. His nerves were on edge. He made his way around to another window. The place was empty. He waved to Ryan to come on up. Together, they pushed open the framed bamboo doors and stepped inside. The floor felt funny to their feet, due to weaving of the vines with the curves of the large bamboo pipes. They saw a table and chair made of real wood. There was even a bed frame against the outer wall. Austin found a burned down candle stuck in a carved wooden holder, but no matches.

"Looks like nobody had been home for quite a while," stated Austin.

Ryan set down the bag so he could look around more freely. Bell immediately climbed out of the bag and started sniffing the floor around the room. "Austin, look at this bookshelf. There are dozens of books, but what language"

Austin joined Ryan as he picked up a book and blew the dust off the cover. 'It's in Spanish." He picked up several of the books and determined they were all in Spanish. The only one he recognized was the Bible. They continued exploring the room finding wooden bowls, utensils, and a black piece of a steel drum that had a small metal grill placed on top so someone could cook in the tree house.

"I wonder what these ropes do. There must be seven or eight of them," asked Ryan, tugging one.

"Pull it and see. Whoever lived here must be long gone. There is dust everywhere. I think we should claim this as our new home."

"But shouldn't we stay closer to the shore...oh jeez!" The rope pulled easier than he thought because it had a counterweight that went through the bottom of the tree house floor and looped over a sailboat pulley. Instantly, the house flooded with light as one section of the roof, or about five feet square, lifted at an angle letting the light and the air in.

"Cool," replied Ryan.

34

Austin suggested, "Let's open the rest and air out this musty smell."

Quickly, they dashed from rope to rope, and in seconds, the entire tree house was bright and clear again.

"Here's a broom, we can sweep out the place," said Austin.

"But shouldn't we live near the ocean, in case a ship comes by?"

"Yeah, you're probably right, but there are no trees on the beach to get us off the ground, and I'm not so sure I want to be a sleep on the ground when old Bobby Boar comes snorting around."

Ryan gulped. Austin grinned at his friend. Bell barked showing her compliance.

"See, even Bell agrees."

EIGHT

Ryan began sweeping the dust out while Austin returned to the deck, and began making his way around the outer shell of the tree house. He had never been in a tree this large. He stopped when he came back to the door. After shading his eyes from the sun that just barely made its way through the thick leaves, he looked up. He spotted a rope ladder much like the kind the trapeze artists in the circus use to climb to their takeoff perch. Filled with curiosity, he began climbing after carefully testing the strength of the rope. After just a few minutes of climbing, he realized he had almost reached the top of the tree. The ladder ended at the edge of a small platform just three feet square, and in the center was a solid brass pole. Austin took hold of the pole, and pulled himself up on to the platform. Flabbergasted, he stood up to find that he was standing just a bit higher than the top of the tree. The trimmed limbs gave the occupant a full 360-degree view of the island and the ocean.

From this view, he knew the island was not as large as it seemed when they were hiking around on the beach. He found himself surprised at the big hills in the center of the island. They looked like small mountains. He even spotted a freshwater stream bubbling out of the side of one of the hills. He made a mental note where he was it.

He then took note of the brass pole, and marveled at the spyglass attached to the top. The beautiful brass and teakwood tube displayed fancy intricate ornamentation on it. He quickly dusted it off, pulled away a few spider webs, and then closed one eye while putting the other eye up to the lens. Through it, he could see quite far from the island, so he turned around in a slow circle scanning the horizon, but found no signs of any boats. He then moved the view downward a bit to the island and began scouting the entire landscape. He spotted a herd of wild goats on the hills, but no signs of human life. It disappointed him just a bit, but the exciting discovery kept him from feeling sorry for their predicament.

"Ryan!" he yelled. "Come up here!"

"Where are you?" asked Ryan as he came out on the deck.

"Up here. Just climb the ladder!"

Ryan made his way up and onto the perch. He, too, marveled at the view, especially through the small telescope. "The builder of this tree house and especially this perch knew what they were doing. You can see the whole island from here. It's like being at the top of the mast on a sailboat. You know, a crow's-nest. Do you reckon they were watching for boats, too?"

Austin replied, "Yes I do. This is better than the beach, because we can see all around us. What do you think that big black pot tied to the railing is for?"

Ryan studied the cooking utensil with a puzzled look on his face. He knew it had to be the type of pot folks used to cook over a fire with, but why were they cooking way up in the top of the tree. Then he grinned. "I know what it is for. I bet they had dried wood in the pot to prepare to signal with smoke should a boat come close enough to see."

"Yeah, that's it," laughed Austin. "I tell you what. We are incredibly lucky. Any other island might not have had any shelter on the beach, leaving us soaked on rainy days. By stroke of luck or fortune, this place becomes our home, at least until we're rescued. I say we take possession."

"After all that sweeping I've done, we've already taken it," replied Ryan wiping the sweat from his brow. "Now that we've got a roof over our heads and we're high enough to avoid being eaten by wild animals, what are we going to do for freshwater, food, and clothing?"

"Think about the Swiss Family Robinson story again. We will find some gourds or hollow bamboo chambers to hold water. We can also fill the wine bottles. I think we should make some weapons, too. We can use my knife to make some sharp sticks, you know, like spears. I wonder if the people who stayed here had any weapons?"

"I found an old trunk in that upper bedroom, or least I guess that was a bedroom. There's a hammock hanging in there with bird crap all over it," said Ryan. "I can probably wash it in the ocean."

"A trunk? Come on! Let's see what's in it! Maybe it is full of gold," laughed Austin as he made his way quickly down the ladder.

"A lot of good that would do us," complained Ryan as he followed. "Where are we going to spend it? There are no hamburger places out here."

"Come on, finder's keepers!" chuckled Austin as he made his way onto the deck. Down below, Bell barked cheerfully at the boys, and gleefully ran in small circles as they once again descended the rope ladder to the tree house floor.

The trunk was a big sea chest, and it probably took more than one person just to get it up there. In the bedroom, they found more examples that the house furnishings had come from a ship, or most likely from a shipwreck. There were pulleys and tie cleats stored against the wall, a pile of rope, and even part of a helm wheel. The trunk had an old rusted lock on it. The boys took turns shaking and pulling on it, but they couldn't get it to budge.

"Find something to hammer it with," urged Austin as they began rummaging around. Ryan found a short but thick stick. They began pounding the lock. It took the better part of an hour, but they had nothing pressing, and they were too excited to quit. One last hit and the lock suddenly sprung open.

They each took a deep breath and slowly opened it. Instantly, the musty smell of the sea went deep into their nostrils. They both coughed while rubbing the dust from their eyes. They lifted out several smaller wooden boxes, and then found several dresses like those used to go to church, but the clothes were way out of style. They found what appeared to be a pistol like the cowboys used and some bullets. They removed a box of rock salt, pads of stationery, various cooking utensils, and a steel iron, the kind you heat in a fire to get the wrinkles out of your clothes. Ryan lifted out a large bundle of old newspapers and mail, tied up with a faded red ribbon. Austin found a white sailor hat, so he promptly put it on his head and saluted Ryan. They both laughed and feigned marching as if they were in the military. Austin leaned down and lifted out a sealed box containing a long white wedding dress. It had been beautifully hand-stitched with many patterns of lace. When they reached the bottom of the trunk, they realized there was not a single clue as to owned all this stuff.

Time had flown by with the sun was already setting. "I'm hungry," protested Ryan.

"I'm way past hungry," agreed Austin. "Let's climb down, find some fruit, fill our bottles with freshwater, and then get back up here to spend the night."

"Maybe we should leave Bell."

Austin nodded. "I hope she'll stay and not fall off."

"She's a smart dog," replied Ryan as he knelt down to pet her. "Stay girl. We'll be right back. Be a good girl. Stay." Understanding, little Miss Bell turned in a few tight circles until satisfied she had found the right spot, and then plopped down and rested her chin on her front paws. The boys petted her once more and then began making their way down to the ground.

After a feast of more coconuts and bananas, and some cool freshwater, the tired boys returned to the tree house. Ryan took Austin's knife and made a mark on tree branch that worked its way through the main room of the tree house. "I think this is Saturday, August 15th, 1978. I don't know how long we're going to be here, but I'd like to know what day it is. I'll make a mark each morning, and I hope I can remember how many days in the month of August."

"Let's hope we're found soon. I think tomorrow we should get some dry wood stuff in the lookout tower in case we spot a ship or plane."

"How are we going to start the fire?" asked Ryan as he yawned.

"Well, we can make a cooking fire in here. Do you see those flat rocks and that piece of a steel barrel? I think they put it on the rocks to keeps from burning the floor, built a fire inside, and put the grill over it to cook. We can try to keep some ashes going all the time, but I think we'd better hunt for some flint rocks or something to keep in the tower. We have a lot more exploring to do on this island. I saw some goats earlier. That means meat if we kill one or milk it."

"Goat's milk?" replied Ryan with a smirk as he turned up his nose as if disgusted at the thought.

"Are you going to eat coconuts the rest of your life?"

"I think we'd better store up all the food we can. Who knows what the weather is going to be like. Is this hurricane season? Does it rain a lot? Does it get cold?"

"I doubt if it gets cold. We're in the Caribbean," said Ryan.

"You're right, but we need to be prepared. It may take a while to find us. Fire and food should be our main priorities."

"I miss mom and dad," stated Ryan, as the sun dipped out of sight beyond the horizon.

"I know old friend. I'm so sorry. We haven't had time to talk about it," replied Austin.

Silent tears slide down Ryan cheeks. "It happened so fast. It is like a dream. I keep hoping I'll wake up. I can't believe they're dead." The grief he had held back for so long finally overcame him. He began to sob.

Austin slid down beside him and put his arm around him. He didn't know what to say. He tried to remember what people said when his grandfather died, but no words from his memory would come. He sensed perhaps that it was best to let Ryan just cry it out. The weary and still shocked ten-year-old boys curled up together on the floor, and then allowed Bell to crawl up between them. Soon they all drifted off to sleep as a slight ocean breeze caused the big tree to sway just a little, but gently enough to rock them into a deep, relaxing sleep.

The next ten nights ended just as this one did. The night's shadows brought back the memories of Ryan's parents, and soon tears slid down Ryan's face once more. Austin would cradle him in his arms until they were both fast asleep. Daytime was much better for both. They were too busy to think about the past. They worked hard from dawn to dusk. Each day they ventured further into the jungle. They found perhaps the same spring the previous guests used in a deep hole not far from the base of the tree. The waterline was at least three feet down from the rocky bank so the animals drank from the larger shallow pool of water where Bobby Bore chased them, and one in which the animals could easily wade into. This clear cool deepwater spring was theirs alone. Every day they used the same system. One boy filled the jugs, while the other stood guard armed with two spears, and Austin's knife. A few days ago Ryan made a tomahawk just like he had seen his counselor do at camp for their Indian pageant. They found the head of an old ax and hoped to carve down a stick they found to make a handle for it. This morning they discovered some flint-like rocks to make some sparks. They prepared dry wood in the kettle in the perch. Once an hour or so, one of them would make the climb to the top and scout for boats.

They fared well and even managed to spear a couple of fish swimming in shallow ocean pools. They roasted the fresh seafood over the fire they eventually made using the magnifying glass from Austin's Swiss army knife to start the flames. They would have to practice starting fires with the flints. They quit wearing their shirts and with no shoes, the pads on their feet were getting tougher, but generally, they looked and felt healthy.

They spent two days tracking the goats but failed to spot the herd. Today, they were preparing to hunt after they stowed more water in the tree house. Ryan began making arrows so they could arm themselves with bows and arrows like Indians. Most of the field games they played at camp became ideas they used to survive.

They hiked a couple of miles up a long, winding, natural animal path tracking the goats. Tired and weary from the climb, they sat down on a big rock, and began to take sips of water from a wine bottle, while eating a couple of bananas they had carried with them.

"I'm beginning to wonder if these darn goats exist," protested Ryan.

"I saw them. I promise..."

The sudden whizzing roar of a military jet interrupted Austin, as it streaked across the sky just a hundred feet over their heads. The plane skirted across the top of the waves and was already miles away before they could even take their next breath.

"What in the world..." exclaimed Ryan as he held his ears from the sound of the screaming engine?

"It was a jet. A jet!" yelled Austin.

"Do you think he saw us?"

"I doubt it. He was flying way too fast, and we are sitting on the downside of the hill."

"Maybe he'll fly back. Maybe this is a flight pattern."

"I hope so. What time is it?" asked Austin.

"Why?" replied Ryan as he looked at his watch? "One o'clock."

"If he passes again tomorrow at the same time, we'll be ready for him," stated Austin without expression. His mind was racing for solutions on how they could attract the attention of a jet going five hundred miles an hour. "Come on, let's go."

They topped the hill, and there below the tree line in a valley was a fifty-foot waterfall. Drinking water in the pool at the bottom of the fall was a small herd of twenty or so white goats. Austin quickly grabbed Ryan's hand and pulled him into the grass.

"Shh, you'll spook them."

"How are we going to catch one?"

Austin grinned. "The goats are the foxes, and we're the hounds."

"What?"

"You remember the camp game Foxes and Hounds. You'll circle in from the left near the edge of the water. I'll hide behind a tree just down the trail from the pool of water. You'll deliberately make a ton of noise. They'll immediately run down the trail right at me. I'll throw my spear at the nearest one and soon we'll have roasted goat for dinner."

Ryan looked at him somberly. "You're weird. I think you should scare the goats because you're uglier than I am."

"I am not. You should see how dirty your face is."

"I rinsed it off in the pool yesterday."

"Yeah, me, too, but I think after twelve days on this island, we're going to have to find a way to get a bath. We need some soap."

"But what about the goats?"

"Oh yeah, well, you got a better idea?"

"Nope, I guess we'll try yours," replied Ryan as he began making his way down the hill as quietly as he could.

Austin went down the other way and once in place; Ryan came running upstream, yelling like a wild Indian. The goats didn't flinch at first because they had never seen a wild Indian, but soon they took off running away from the pool and right at Austin. With his throwing arm cocked back, Austin jumped from behind the tree. Just as he was about to throw the spear the big goat leaped right into him, knocking the wind from his lungs and rolling him into a heap under a bush. Ryan busted out laughing. Austin was not happy the goat got the best of him, so he jumped up, grabbed his spear, and took off running after the goats. He made a throw or two, but soon had to give up as the goats had long outrun him.

"Some fierce hunter you are!" laughed Ryan as he came through the brush.

"Next time, you throw the spear, and I'll chase them," replied a grinning Austin.

"Shh," whispered Ryan as he pointed behind Austin.

"What?"

"A rabbit," replied Ryan softly. "Give me the spear."

Ryan tiptoed gently down the trail. The rabbit had never seen a human and thus, did not run. Ryan paused for a second, not wanting to hurt any animal, but the hunger pains he felt in his stomach were real. He took a breath and let it out slowly, just as he and Austin learned to do in their archery class. He threw the spear swiftly. It caught the rabbit just behind his left eye nailing him.

"Yee-hah!" exclaimed Ryan.

"You did it."

"It's not dead," said Ryan as he ran up to it.

"Here, club him with the tomahawk."

"Jeez," protested Ryan.

"Put him out of his misery. You have to. I know it is hard. I wouldn't want to hurt him either, but we have to eat to survive. Do it!" said Austin more firmly.

Ryan took the tomahawk, shut his eyes, and slammed it down hard so he would not have to do it twice. They put the rabbit over the spear and began making their way back to the tree house. They would eat well tonight. Rabbit and something that looked like potatoes Austin had found while digging. After eating every possible morsel of the roasted rabbit, the boys once again curled up together and soon fell asleep. Sleeping on a full stomach

41

made the pain of their loss subside. Bell slept between them, but this time she rested her head on an already well-chewed rabbit bone, protecting it while she slept.

NINE

Ryan counted the rows of chiseled marks again. If he had counted right, and if it was not a leap year, then they had survived a full year on the island. They celebrated the day with a feast of roasted boar. Ryan already selected the new bamboo pole that would be the start of the possible three hundred and sixty-five marks of their second year on the island. He set it alongside their first pole, which would be a year old tomorrow, and then tied it in place. He slid his fingers gently over the marks he had carved, reflecting on how fast the days turned into weeks, months, and now a year. Since the sinking sailboat marooned the boys on the island, they had grown a bit taller, while their hair, bleached white from the sun and saltwater, now hung in loose curls to their shoulders. The soles of their feet had become as tough as the shoes they once wore back in the States. Their bronze smooth skin was taut and lean, and though they took care of them as best they could their teeth were a bit yellow. They had yet to figure out how to make a toothbrush so scrubbing with their fingers and piece of cloth was the best they could do. With only their knives as shears, they took to barbering the other about once a month, but kept their hair long enough to protect their ears from the sun. Overall, they were a happy pair, perhaps even adapting better than adults might have on a desert island. Grown-ups would have experienced more in life than the boys and perhaps miss their old world even more. They played the games they could recall and invented new ones when they grew tired of the old ones. Sometimes, complete days would pass by without even a mention of something from the past.

They were not yet strong enough to take on the big boar that had chased them through the woods in their first week on the island. However, they did manage to set a trap for a smaller boar, and sure enough, on the fifth try, they caught a forty pound boar, clubbed it to death, and slowly roasted it all-day on a skewer over the fire. Killing for food grew easier. They knew a good diet was essential to their survival. Day by day, they made the tree house a real home, with all comforts they could manage. They had taken one of the pulleys hanging on the wall with a couple of long ropes, and created an elevator out of a two-foot square section of bamboo flooring they made. They also added a short railing, and on the other end of the rope, they had made yet another platform that held counterweights of rocks. With just a little effort of their strong muscles, the crude elevator would raise the both of them from the ground to the deck in just seconds. They built it for convenience to help bring up their food and water, and other items to either cook with or offer some protection. It made getting up and down from the high tree house much easier. Their little dog Bell enjoyed the ride as well and barked gleefully all the way to the top. The clever project, the result of a memory from the Swiss Family book, had taken several days to complete. They were proud of their work, and it helped to keep their minds occupied. It was another challenge they accepted with full vigor. It made the boys determined to overcome and win every obstacle they faced.

During the year, almost every project required the use of their growing muscles. Their arms and legs were bulging with power. Every day they went hunting, fishing, or exploring. Their chores involved cleaning, hauling, or cooking. They climbed a lot when they were in the trees and could hold their entire weight with just one hand. They ran after all types of game, and constantly tried to outrun the other. Every day they swam in the ocean. They dove deeply while holding their breath for about three minutes. They pulled up a lobster from the bottom corral beds and hauled it ashore to prepare a feast. Their dark tanned chests were strong, and their abs well defined. Daily work had been good for their minds as well as their bodies. Their childhood baby fat had long left their lean frames.

Most of the time, they left Bell in charge of protecting the house because they were afraid a wild animal might gobble her up after meeting Bobby Boar. Bell had her spot out on the deck where she peed and potted. She was a clean house dog, and a good protector who barked fiercely when a bird perched too close to the tree house. The boar crossed their paths on several occasions, but each time they managed to outrun or outsmart him. Austin once shook his fist and swore to the boar that one day soon he would roast him over a hot fire, and then they would deliciously devour him.

They collected salt from the tops of rocks along the shore, rubbing it on leftover meat before drying it in the sun to preserve for a future meal. This was important to them, because if they caught larger game, they could not eat it in all in one day. Storing the dried extra meat successfully helped with the occasional all-day rainstorms or bad days of hunting.

They toasted each other with a drink they invented by combining coconut juice and berry juice. They knew nothing of how to ferment wine, but they knew how to play games, and how to act as they did in their camp skits. They acted out a party scene and pretended drunkenness. Their wild imaginative games became their best entertainment.

Austin left the grass mat he was sitting on and went to turn the handle on the skewer. "It smells delicious." He poured a little more mixture of water and pineapple juice over the meat to let it steam.

Ryan protested. "How much longer?"

"The sun isn't all the way down and besides, the boar needs to cook a little longer. What's your hurry? You going somewhere?"

"Yep, I thought I take the yacht out for a cruise to Miami and back," shot back Ryan.

Austin laughed. "The wine is getting to your head. You've turned in to a two-legged coconut!"

They had long ago started teasing each other about marooned on the island. It was a childlike way of making the best of an unusual and difficult predicament. After all, they did not have to go to school or church so that was

44

a huge plus. There were no clothes to wash, fold, or put away as their old clothes would not fit their new bodies. There were no taxes to pay, no political speeches to endure, no long walks to school in the freezing cold, and no one telling them to go clean their room. Ironically, now that they were on their own, they cleaned the tree house daily. Responsibility became a point of pride between the two. To them, the best part about being on island was they no longer had to put up with their older sisters. They had no idea where they were, but they did know they were far away from the habitual aggravation their sisters once inflicted on them.

The jet plane returned about a dozen times over the past year, but not similar times or even regular days. They found no schedule to the flights they could count on, although they logged each one carefully on some paper they found in the trunk. Not once had they seen a boat and this greatly surprised them. They thought that surely a lost or exploring sailboat would pass, or perhaps a cruise ship, or even a freighter. They did not understand why not, and had no clue what they could do to attract the attention of something that did not exist. They kept dried kindling in the kettle in the top of the perch after adding a flat rock as lid cover to keep the rain out. They remained prepared to signal if the opportunity presented itself. Several times a day they would take turns climbing the rope ladder to the top, and scanning the horizon in all directions in hopes of spotting something on the vast ocean that surrounded their island paradise. Not once did they spot anything but seagulls, whales, dolphins, or sharks.

The meal had been delicious. There would be few leftovers tonight. Austin ate until he thought he was going to explode. Ryan managed to eat even more. He was a few inches taller than Austin and often bragged about it. Bell ate well, too, and delighted in the new pile of bones she amassed. One by one, she dragged the bones over to her corner of the house, and hid them under a torn piece of sailcloth by pushing them with her nose. They guessed it was her way of burying a bone minus the dirt.

Tired from the day's adventure, Austin walked out to the deck. He began following his nightly ritual, by first peeing over the rail. They called this POR like at camp. Several months ago, they found a natural sponge on the beach, so he dipped it into a bucket of water, and splashed it all over his body to wash off the juice and grease from their dinner. He then took their well-worn towel, which they had found in the trunk, dried off, and knelt down to sleep.

The fire was simmering down and there was little light left. Bell crawled into Austin's arms as he was drifting off to sleep on his side. Ryan was shivering just a bit as the slight ocean breeze blew across his damp skin after his turn at washing. He knelt down beside Austin, slightly shook to shake off the chill, and curled up close to Austin. He noted the chill bumps on Austin's bare butt, so he reached down to pull the sailcloth they used for a sheet over them. He moved in tighter behind Austin, slid one arm around Austin's stomach, and snuggled in to get warm and sleep.

This was their customary way of sleeping night after night. In many ways, they became the echo of the other, while still keeping a slight variance in personalities. Often speaking the same sentence at the same time, they seemed to know the thoughts of the other. They took care of their best friend, and quickly became the other's mirror image by wiping dirt off their face or finger combing misaligned hair.

About three o'clock in the morning, the skies became black because of some rain clouds moving in from the south, and Austin abruptly awoke as the damp breeze suddenly flared around the middle of his back. He turned without opening his eyes, expecting to find Ryan, and wanting to cuddle tighter so he would be warm. As his arms reached for Ryan, he discovered his friend was not there. The realization took another moment to stir his sleepy brain. Suddenly alarmed, he sat up quickly.

"Ryan?" he whispered, not sure why he did so, as no one could hear them for hundreds of miles, but he spoke gently nonetheless. Ryan did not reply. "Ryan?" he called a little louder. Still no answer came. Austin sat up. Bell stirred, but still fat and full, she curled up into a tight ball, and went back to sleep in a furl of the sailcloth. "Some watchdog you are, girl," grinned Austin as he gave her a little pat, then stood up and walked towards the deck. Just as he got to the entrance, he saw Ryan's bare feet stretched across the deck. He turned the corner and found Ryan lying face down on the deck, his head hanging over the side.

"Ryan!" Are you all right?" Austin feared he might be dead.

To his relief, Ryan stirred. "I'm sick. I've been throwing up repeatedly."

"Let me get you some water. Do you think it was the boar?" asked Austin as he went to get a gourd of water. Before Ryan could reply, he retched once more, but nothing came up. Austin thought it was a horrible sound, and it almost made him sick to hear it. He could see the deep convulsions in Ryan's back as he desperately tried to throw up whatever it was that was making him sick. Austin rinsed Ryan's mouth out just as his mother used to do for him when he ate too much birthday cake and ice cream.

"I don't know what it could be. I've been thinking about it for hours. You ate the meat and you're not sick," replied Ryan before retching once more, and this time so hard, that it made Austin's skin crawl. Ryan began to cry. His insides ached painfully. Austin felt Ryan's forehead and instantly realized Ryan was burning up with fever. Austin got just a sip of water into Ryan's stomach before Ryan threw it back up. This time, he retched even harder and then passed out.

Austin turned him over and dragged him back inside. He stoked the embers in the fire, and threw on a few more wood sticks to warm them up and provide some light. He could see drops of sweat across Ryan's brow. He dipped a cloth in the bucket of water, wrung it out, and placed it across the forehead of his best friend. He tried to recall how his mom had taken care of him when he had a fever. The boys did not have any aspirin, nor a thermometer, and worst of all, no telephone to call a doctor for help.

He changed the wet rag repeatedly until dawn. It had begun to rain, and it looked like the rain would last all day. Austin was thankful they had learned to store up plenty of food for the unpredictable Caribbean storms. He held Ryan in his arms for hours. Ryan suddenly stirred, sat up, and spoke gibberish to Austin, then collapsed in Austin's arms. Fearing he would die, Austin pulled him in tighter, as if clinging to Ryan would save him.

For the next few days, Austin managed to get just a few drops of water at a time into Ryan's stomach. Then diarrhea took over Ryan's body. He would still dry heave from time to time, and the squirts came because of his body's rebellion of some unknown virus or food poisoning. This forced Austin to do something he had never done in his life. He had once seen his aunt taking care of his little baby cousin, changing his diaper, wiping his butt, and he also remembered how the stench sent him running from the room. He never understood how his aunt could handle the smell and the crap all day long for months and months until the baby grew.

However, to his surprise, the smell of Ryan's weak bowels did not intimidate him. He would quickly clean Ryan up with another rag, just as his aunt had done to her baby. He rinsed the rag out in the rain as it ran off their roof. After hanging it on the porch rail for the rain to continue to rinse the overused rag, he went back to trying to get some water down Ryan's reddish throat.

By the fifth day, Ryan's tanned skin had turned pale, his lips parched and cracked, and his fingers were an odd, light blue. Woefully and fearfully frightened, Austin knew his beloved friend could die. He began to pray, cry, and then pray some more. As he hugged his friend tightly, his tears would bounce off Ryan's chest to the floor. Bell sensed something was wrong. Every few minutes she would lick Ryan's cheeks to try to stir him, but her sweet doggie kissed failed to heal him.

Austin slept no more than a few minutes at a time for almost a week. He never left Ryan, but he knew he would soon have to as their supplies were dwindling. Dawn arrived more than an hour ago. An exhausted Austin bounced his eyelids a few times before drifting off. He was on his back with Ryan's head buried in his chest, his limp arm draped across Austin's nude body, and together, they were fast asleep.

Austin's dream was not a good fantasy, but this time it was more of a nightmare. He could see himself pushing the dirt over Ryan's cold corpse in the bottom of the grave that had taken him all day to dig. His face was dirty, and the tears that rolled down his cheeks were creating streams of clean skin bordered by dark fertile soil stains. He fell to his knees and sobbed when the last of the dirt completed the mound over his friend. It was a fitful, disturbing vision. Austin wanted to wake himself, but he could not, and every time he finished covering the body the dream would start all over once again.

"Austin?"

Austin's brain heard the voice, but he had been dreaming so deeply the sound did not make sense to his exhausted ears.

"Austin, wake up. Are you all right?"

Austin's eyes suddenly popped wide open. The sun had broken through the trailing rain clouds, lighting up the house for the first time in a week. Ryan was looking up from Austin's chest into his friend's eyes. Austin stared down at him. The realization took hold. Ryan was awake. He was not dead, as he had seen in his dream. He was alive.

Austin exclaimed, "I'm all right! You're the one that's been sick for seven days." Then softer he asked, "How are you? Is the temperature still there?" Austin felt his forehead and grinned when he found none remained.

"I'm weak and thirsty," replied Ryan hoarsely.

"I'll get you something," said Austin as he started to move out from under Ryan.

"No, I can wait a bit. Don't move. I have been so cold that resting here with you, well, it makes me feel so wonderful and warm."

Austin smiled and put his arms around his best friend, pulling him closer. He gently bent down and kissed Ryan's forehead. "I thought I had lost you forever. You scared me to death. I couldn't bear that. I love you."

"I love you, too." Then after a few moments, "I ain't going to leave you on this island alone. You know I'm the brains of this outfit," teased Ryan in a whisper.

"Brains? I'd be willing to bet that if you had any brains, which is dubious, they're fried now. You were burning up with fever. And besides, you probably threw up your little brain marbles, too," shot back Austin, and then gave Ryan another hug. "I'm glad you're back. I thought I lost you." He started to cry. "I couldn't stay here without you. I've missed talking to you." His shoulders sobbed as the tears flowed from his face.

"Same here, old friend, the same here." After a few more moments, "Would you stop crying? You're drowning me!" added Ryan. They both began laughing and giggling. They held each other as tight as they possibly could. They survived yet another crisis on the island. Ryan had been so sick, and yet without medicine, his body fought his battle for him. Austin, wrought with the fear of losing his friend, fought a mental war that depressed him more than any other time in his life. However, they once again overcame a major obstacle, and the joy they felt was greater than any present or event in their life before the shipwreck.

TEN

Two months after their thirteenth birthdays, or three years and two months on the island, give or take a missed counting of a day or two, they experienced their biggest adventure so far. Their only wristwatch had stopped working last year, so they kept time by the sun, as if time needed keeping when you live on a deserted island lost somewhere in the blue waters of the Caribbean Ocean. They long ago gave up longing for items they used to have back home in the United States. Their past life just seemed too long ago and some of their childhood memories were fading. They talked of the old days like two hunters on a campout. They talked about the first goat they killed, and how big old Bobby Boar chased them for two years, until they trapped him in a big camouflaged pit they had dug and killed him. His death taught them how to smoke the piles of meat and cure it so it would last longer. They had all sorts of dried wild game hanging from the rafters of their tree house. They also learned how to make candles from the animal fat but rarely used them.

The boys rose at dawn and went to sleep not too long after dust. They filled their days with adventuresome work. They ran fast, played hard, and swam strong. They could now surface dive to twenty-five feet or more and hold their breath underwater for five minutes at a time; at least that's how long they thought they could. They once spent an entire day playing with a dolphin, and soon the dolphin pulled them playfully through the water. Austin discovered when he stretched out face down in the water with his feet together and toes pointed down, the dolphin would come up behind him, and put his long snout into the balls of Austin's bare feet. Stroking rapidly with his big tail, he would push Austin gleefully across the top of the water like a racing boat. They took turns skimming the water, and loved playing and stroking their new friend. They laughed heartily when it seemed the dolphin was laughing at them.

The next morning they rushed to the ocean to play once more with the dolphin, but they were sadly disappointed to find their ocean friend must have moved on. For several more days, they checked the ocean hoping to spot him, but he never returned.

They filled their shelves with colorful conch shells, boar tusks, peculiar black stones, carved coconut shells, and other odd things, giving the tree house a home-like feeling. They were healthy and strong. Their bodies had grown some, their voices were changing, and hair grew where it had never grown before. Every strand of hair on their tanned bodies was completely blond, the result of so much sun and salt. The white of their eyes contrasted significantly with their deep dark tans. They wore no clothes because they didn't have any garments that fit and kept no secrets. They told no lies other than the tall tales they told when they were pulling each other's legs with a joke. Teasing became an art form, and they constantly challenged their language skills trying to think of something clever to pick on the other with. They made up their own jokes while telling the same puns and stories quite often. They celebrated their birthdays by making something special for their only friend.

Last year, they discovered a cave while chasing a goat up a big hill. They returned home to make torches while making plans to enter the cave the following day. They feared what animal they might find, but their curiosity overwhelmed them. With spears in hand, they entered the cavern with torches held in front of them like burning shields while attempting to clear a path through the thick maze of spider webs.

They had gone but twenty feet inside cave when suddenly the narrow passageway opened into a big room that was almost forty feet by forty feet. A cold spring dripped down the side of the passage and flowed deeper into the grotto. Ryan knelt down to taste the cool water, and found it clean and refreshing. Just as Austin knelt down to drink, Ryan turned slightly to keep his torch from catching Austin's hair on fire, and spotted a print in the dirt, a human footprint.

"Austin! Look!" exclaimed an excited Ryan.

"What?" Austin turned, saw the print, and traced it with his finger removing years of dust on his finger.

"Someone was here."

Austin replied, "Of course, they were. Remember they built the tree house, but I wonder if the person that built the house was the same man as this track, or does this suggest someone else was on the island?"

"I wish we had found a print of the man who built our home."

Austin nodded while agreeing. "I wish we had found the man that built the house alive. Then he could tell us where in the hell we are. Whoops, sorry, I know I promised not to curse."

Ryan giggled. "You'll have to say prayers tonight and wash the dishes."

"Yes, mother dear," mocked Austin. "Come on. If someone has been here before maybe they left a treasure chest."

"Yeah right," sighed Ryan. "We'll be lucky if we find something we can use."

Deeper into the cave they went. Chill bumps soon covered their bare bodies as the air in the cave became cooler with each step. Austin led the way as they followed a narrow pathway on the far side of the big room. Stalactites hung down from the ceiling.

"Watch your head," warned Austin as he ducked under a big one, but just as he turned to warn Ryan, the soft soil beneath him gave way. He fell to his butt, and started sliding downward as the earth was wet and claylike. He hung on to his torch, searching for the bottom that was somewhere ahead of him. "Help!" he yelled, but it was too late. Ryan also stepped forward as he ducked under the stalactite and almost instantly, he began sliding right behind Austin as well.

Bouncing repeatedly between the narrow walls, the echoes of their screams intensified. Austin suddenly hit the bottom of the hill with a strong thud. Seconds later Ryan crashed into him, and nearly set him on fire with his torch.

"Yow!" exclaimed Austin as he pushed Ryan's torch to the side. "Where are we?"

Ryan stood and then pulled Austin up. They raised the torches and found their backsides covered in mud. There were in a room that was about ten feet square. They quickly discovered human skeletons filled the floor of the room. The boys shuddered at the sight, and it wouldn't have taken much for them to start yelping and trying to climb out of there. Slowly, they made their way among the skeletons searching for clues.

"Well, no gold," stated Austin, a bit disappointed, while feeling a bit braver.

"Wrong. That man there has a gold tooth. Should I pop it out with my knife?"

"No, where would we spend it? Let the dead rest in peace. Do you think these men were pirates or something?"

Ryan bent down and picked up a skull. He noted a big hole on one side. He set the skull down and picked up another with a similar puncture. He set it down and slowly waved his torch over the skeletons to get a better took. "Austin, all these men have been shot in the head. See the hole in their right temple. Every one of them has the same hole in the same place. Nevertheless, what happened to their clothes, belts, and shoes? There must be some clue."

"They were shot in the nude. But why?"

Ryan said, "Let's get out of here. This room gives me the creeps."

Austin held up his torch to figure out how they were going to climb out of what they now thought of as the grave room. "Come on. There's a path over there."

"Where we going this time?" asked Ryan. The last time I followed you I ended down here in this giant pit.

'Who knows, smart-ass, just out of here, okay?"

They walked for about forty feet when they began hearing a faint roar. They feared it was an animal, but it wasn't a sudden roar and then quiet, but rather a continuous growing one. Curiosity once again got the best of them, and so they continued moving forward with the noise gradually becoming louder. They rounded a bend, crept through a small shaft that suddenly opened into another huge room. Across the room, they spotted a small waterfall that fed into a quick moving stream. Their discovery amazed them.

"Time to wash the mud off," said Austin as he stuck the butt of his torch in the ground near the edge of the stream so they could see into the water.

"I bet that water is freezing," replied Ryan as he stuck his torch in the dirt as well.

Austin abruptly leaped off a rock into the water, doing his best cannonball. Ryan waited for Austin to surface to see the reaction on his face, so he would know just how cold the water was, but Austin did not immediately come bursting to the surface as Ryan expected. Ryan waited. A minute passed. Ryan nervously chewed his lip. Another minute passed. Even without a watch, Ryan knew how long Austin long could hold his breath, because it was exactly as long as he could. When he felt the five-minute mark had passed, and Austin still didn't surface, Ryan leaped off the rock, fearing something happened to Austin on the bottom.

He crashed into the crystal clear water and immediately realized he had been right as the water was cold, very cold. Rapidly, he turned left and right, but didn't see Austin anywhere. He swam to the bottom and immediately discovered another human skull. Shots of fear ran up his spine. He swam left and right, but found no sign of Austin. His lungs were screaming for air, but he forced himself to stay down a minute more to search for Austin. He suddenly caught sight of something shiny on the bottom to his right. He swam towards it. He realized it was a gold and silver sword, as shiny as perhaps the day it was made. He swam within five feet of it, when suddenly the water seemed to surge, pushing him away from the sword. He quickly realized a current had snatched him, and before he knew it, the swirling waters pushed him over the sword and then downward. He bounced through the churning water and then under another waterfall. Then he swam to the surface where he grabbed some air, and quickly saw he was in another room in the cave. He screamed out for Austin, but he was not there.

The current continued carrying him to the far wall of the room. He grabbed a breath and quickly ducked under to avoid smashing into the rock ledge above his head. Again, it pushed him downward. He did not fight the flow by relying on the swimming skills he learned at camp, and the rule of never swimming against the current. He planned to ride it out until it weakened, and then swim to safety. He bounced up and grabbed another breath of air. He briefly spotted a bright light ahead of him, but the water pulled him down once again. He turned back to look beneath the water for Austin. Suddenly, the stream flung him into the air as the river he had been traveling in fell downward and crashed on the rocks about fifty feet below. Ryan had abruptly become airborne. Frightened, he began flapping his arms as if he were a bird. He also tried to figure out where he was on the island. Then just as quickly, he crashed into a pool of water that nearly knocked the breath out of him. He fought his way to the surface and came up quickly gasping for air.

"Fun, huh!" laughed Austin who began swimming over to him.

"Fun? Are you crazy? I was nearly killed, drowned, or whatever! Are you all right?" asked Ryan after finally catching his breath.

Austin was treading water as he circled the pool looking for signs of any dangerous animals. "I can't imagine how in all our hikes and exploring we missed this pool of water."

"Or that last waterfall."

"Right," laughed Austin. "Come on, let's swim for shore."

They tried exiting the area by hiking up several different animal paths, but each one appeared to be a dead end. After about an hour, they found a way to crawl upwards from rock to rock and suddenly, they were on a hill that was just opposite the tree house and a few hundred yards. The constant roar of the ocean masked the sound of the waterfall.

"Well, I'll be. No wonder we didn't see it. The darn thing is almost impossible to get to."

Ryan chuckled. "Well, if pirates ever come after us, we'll lose them in the cave. Then will swim out and crash in the pool once more, climb up this hill, and watch them leave disappointed they couldn't kill us like those men in the cave."

Austin asked, "Did you see that sword?"

"Yeah, that's how the stream snatched me."

"You, too? I think somebody put it there to trap us."

"Well, it worked."

"Let's go home. I'm hungry," complained Austin as he shook the water from his hair.

Ryan stretched and yawned. "Me, too. I'm worn out, too. I'm been in enough water today to last me a longtime."

"At least you smell better," teased Austin.

"I wish I could say the same for you," shot back Ryan as he popped Austin's head with his index and middle fingers, and then took off running down the hill with Austin racing after him.

They feasted on ham, baked pineapple, root cakes, and a mixture of pineapple and coconut juice mixed with water. It was Austin's recipe. The meal talk was all about the cave adventure. They took turns trying to invent various stories about the skeletons. Moreover, the sword created a completely new series of their imaginary tales. The stories became wilder and more inventive, and they were finally laughing so hard that Bell began barking at them. Austin grabbed and playfully tickled her belly, which caused her hind legs to jerk uncontrollably, about like when you tickle a human repeatedly. She loved every minute of it, but always tried to get away. She scampered to her favorite corner, then came running right back to them, and they started tickling her all over again.

53

"I'm going to bed. I'm whipped," stated Austin as he stood to take a long overdue pee off the rail.

Ryan stood beside him and tried to piss farther than Austin. Everything between them was a contest, and because of the competition, they became stronger and better. When they swam, they raced. When they dove, they went deeper and stayed longer. When they went for a walk on the beach, they would soon be pushing and shoving each other, which would always result in a longer chase. They played tag and even hide-and-seek. In the water, they played Marco Polo, though one or the other usually cheated by peeping. They threw hand carved knives, spears, and tomahawks. They shot arrows with their bows, and then the winner bragged excessively at becoming the champion. Rock throwing had become an accurate skill, and they were as good as some baseball pitchers. They made a target on a tree trunk in the shape of circle painted in boar blood. They started at twenty feet. Then moved back to thirty feet and soon they could still hit the target consistently at forty feet.

ELEVEN

They carried their heavier supplies or weapons to the tree house by using their homemade elevator. However, they often preferred a faster route by skillfully climbing hand over hand on a single strand of rope to the top. For a long while they had to use their legs to assist their arms, but soon they could climb using only their upper body strength. They left various ropes at strategic points around the railing so they could grab one and swing to the ground. Sometimes they would yell as they swung like the Tarzan they had seen on television, making Bell bark repeatedly at them. While pretending that pirates were chasing them, they practiced escaping from the tree house in all directions. Though most everything was a game, it was also making their brawny bodies tougher. This gave the teenagers a new measure of confidence in their new skills and abilities. With endless time to practice without disruptions, their performance level remained very high. At just thirteen years old, they made decisions as if they were adults.

However, learning how to consistently make a fire was by far the most important skill they had accomplished since arriving on the island. This meant they knew how to sustain their lives by preparing and cooking. Other than the campout cooking they did as kids at camp, they had no idea how to cook like their chefs at their fancy homes. They learned by trial and error, sometimes resulting in one or both throwing up after eating one of their new island recipes. This usually occurred because they misjudged by either overdoing the meal with the spices they invented, or not cooking something long enough. They saved everything they found because they always used even the smallest root or rib bone to make something new. They used saltwater to cook their roots, and a pinch of the dried salt made the fresh meat taste better, too.

Though they never discussed it, they also learned to love. They loved each other immeasurably, and though they teased and played like carefree Huckleberry Finns, they were intensely serious when providing adult-like care for one another. A few months after Ryan became very sick and nearly died, Austin unintentionally followed suit, but also recovered. Several times a year, one of the boys would become ill. They feared these tense times of sickness the most. They had neither medicines to stop a sickness, nor the knowledge of making remedies or treatments. The lack of medicines or treatments brought an element of fear to their young lives. It made the boys mindful of everything they killed, dug up, cleaned, and cooked. They invented a few remedies that would help, but mostly the patient had to endure the agony of the illness, while the other boy nervously waited and prayed. So many times, the boys thought the other was about to die and therefore, the bond between them grew stronger. While they often taunted and teased each other, they sometimes playfully fought and wrestled the other to the ground. Occasionally, the boys made empty threats to kill the other if they did not shut up. However, if anything or anybody had dared hurt one of the boys, the other friend would have been all over them. Throughout their stay on the island, each partner saved the life of the other on dozens of occasions that soon became too numerous to keep a count.

Puberty set in without them knowing it, too. There was no announcement, no telegram, no books to read, and no mortified fathers explaining the details or proper hygiene. There were no girlie magazines, no locker room descriptions, no bar mitzvahs, and no ceremonies. They knew nothing more than their natural environment offered. They formed no opinions or inhibitions. They barely knew any four-letter words and hadn't a clue what they meant. They had never seen any crude drawings on a bathroom wall. No prejudice ideas were forced-fed to their brain, and no angry preachers spouted Scriptures to their ears. On this island, they received no environment training or educational brochures as to how they were to act or behave. Their thoughts were natural, or it didn't exist in their heads or their hearts.

The idea of 'best friend' exceeded even the extreme life-and-death foxhole friend during wartime, perhaps even the friendship and loyalty of a prison roommate. It felt as if during their entire life they had been the best of best friends. They trusted each other with every morsel of food, while counting on the other to deliver nutrition not poison. They had lived countless months in isolation, while fending for their survival. They made their own jokes and stories, and their own rules, but the one rule they did not have to create was that they loved and counted on each other like a couple, and they always would. One, without the other, was nothing. Society never had a chance to form them into a proper mold.

They would lie down to sleep as they always had, side by side, one curled into the other. They would sometimes wake finding their partner's head resting softly on their shoulder, or their lips nuzzled against a neck. They thought nothing of such acts of tenderness and love. They needed affection just as they needed comforting in times of sickness. Can one imagine living an entire life without feeling touched, hugged, or loved? Can a person survive without receiving the joy or pleasure of a kiss? They reached out to the other for all their needs and received all they required. No one had told them it was odd or different for two boys to be affectionate or intimate. No one told them anything. They did as they wanted and desired because something deep inside their hearts genuinely wanted love.

They knew each others body as well as they knew their own. They took care of each other in every possible way. They washed each other's hair, pulled splinters from one's feet and backsides, and nursed the other to good health when needed. They made fun of each other by often howling with laughter at something their partner did. However, they quickly came to the

56

rescue when a leech in the pond stuck to private parts that resulted in more teasing and laughter.

Ryan was behind Austin with his arm under his partner's head. As the cool night breeze filled the tree house, Austin reached and pulled Ryan's free arm over his chest. Ryan slid in closer, an act they did nightly as the crickets chirped below in the dune grass. During a deep sleep, Ryan obtained an erection that pushed gently against Austin's butt. Austin felt nothing as he was sleeping soundly. Ryan abruptly awoke from a dream he couldn't remember. He felt odd. His skin was sweating, but then he felt a sudden chill. His penis felt warm. He touched it, but felt a sticky substance, and immediately pulled his hand away. It had never done that before. He didn't know what to make of it. He was afraid he was sick. He got up, went to the rail, and felt himself once more. He had to urinate and so he did. He gradually felt better. He washed himself off with a dip of a gourd from the water bucket. He dried off, returned to bed, and was soon asleep once more.

The following morning Austin asked, "What the hell is that?" He had just awoken and felt the now cold, gooey substance on his bare butt.

Ryan chuckled. "You'll have to pray again. You said hell."

"No. Get serious. What is this on my butt? Did you sneeze snot on my butt?"

Ryan laughed. "No," shot back Ryan. Then he softened his voice and turned pale. "It came out of my dick. I don't know what it is. I'm sorry. I didn't know I got any of it on you." Ryan ran and grabbed the wet cloth on the rail and quickly cleaned Austin up. They both did things like this for the other. Their butt was an area they just couldn't see for themselves. They were each other's mother when hurt or sick, they were each other's father when the other needed scolding, and when they woke up in a bad mood, they were each other's older sister. Life was simple, but the unknown often confused them. Apparently Ryan's new illness passed, as Ryan no longer appeared to be sick at all, but felt rather pleasant and happy that day. Probably it would never happen again, thought Ryan.

However, it did happen again, and a few months later, it began happening to Austin. They talked about it as they talked about everything. They were never ashamed to admit that they had gas, diarrhea, or even afraid to try something that might taste gross. There were no secrets between them, but rather full honesty and trust. It was all part of their bond and loyalty to each other. It was also part of the love they shared.

Austin awoke one night with his back to Ryan, but he felt the pressure of Ryan's arm over his waist and the warmth of his hand over his genitals. It meant nothing to him, but the sensation of the warm skin that wasn't his own made him feel good. His member began to enlarge. He put his hand over Ryan's and played with himself, and astonishingly the mysterious juice returned.

The next morning he was discussing it with Ryan when all of sudden Austin started burst out laughing.

Ryan asked, "What's so funny?"

"I just had a long ago memory pop up. Do you remember our third year at camp, and we were on an overnight camping trip with our cabin and cabin number …"

Ryan broke in, "Cabin seven?"

"Yeah, that's right. Do you remember the counselor's name of cabin seven?"

"Let me think. Jeez, I'm getting old. I believe it was Steve."

"You're right! Way to go, coconut head," laughed Austin. "Think now. It was late at night, and I woke up and had to pee something fierce, so I woke you up."

"Yeah, we crept out of the tent. The campfire was still burning. We walked towards the river. As we got closer the noise of the cascading waterfalls became louder, but suddenly, we heard …"

"Voices. You're doing well. Whose voices?" asked Austin, testing Ryan's memory once more?

"It was the counselors, Bob and Steve!"

"You're right, banana breath," laughed Austin. "We both peed off the trail, and then crept over a big rock and spied on them. We thought they were probably drinking."

"We were right. They had several cartons of beer with them."

"We were half right. Remember, they had no clothes on and they were lying on a blanket."

Ryan suddenly blushed. "They were playing with each other's …"

"Penis." He paused, and then said, "Yep, they sure were, sort of like we were doing last night."

"I wasn't doing anything. I was asleep."

"You had your hand on my weenie before I woke up."

"So?"

"So it felt good, but stop interrupting my story. Remember what happened next?" asked Austin.

"They were moaning, but then one of them turned upside down," stated Ryan.

Austin chuckled. "Upside down?"

"I mean, Bob swung around and put his head down where his feet used to be. They came in close to each other and started …" He didn't finish his narration, but the boys nodded at each other, as if confirming the accuracy of the story.

"There were many rumors about those two counselors, and the next summer they didn't get asked back, because they were sucking each other."

58

Ryan chuckled again. "I can't believe we're talking about this now. That was over four or five years ago."

"Do you remember a few months ago when we tracked the herd of goats up to the high country? As we crept up on them, one of the goats, a male, had his front hoofs on the back of another goat, and his butt was moving forward and back real fast, and we both pointed and laughed at them?"

"It was like those turtles we saw doing it in the water," laughed Ryan.

"That's right, or those two birds we saw doing it in the air."

"That's sex?" asked Ryan boldly?

"I guess so."

"That's how babies are made?"

Austin nodded. "I think so. That's probably why they appear to be so happy when they're doing it."

"But Bob and Steve looked happy and giddy when they were doing it. I don't think men can have babies.

Austin busted out laughing. "Maybe they can. Maybe we can. Maybe we can have children!"

Ryan laughed hard. "You'll have to be the mother because I'm bigger than you."

"No you're not!"

"Yes, I am. I am one inch taller than you."

"My dick's bigger."

"My brain's bigger."

They began an argument they repeated at least once a week, month after month. They forgot the discussion for now. They ended the argument by quickly swinging down the ropes to the ground and beginning the day's hunt for fresh meat.

TWELVE

At the beginning of another month on the deserted island, the roar of a jet plane awakened the boys as it rushed overhead. Like fireman in a firehouse, they quickly scrambled up the rope ladder to the perch. It was almost the beginning of their fourth year on the island. Over time, they continued improving their signaling ability. They recovered pieces of a broken mirror and assembled the fragments inside a gourd sawed in half. One of the benefits of the sperm they now produced was its ability to glue and adhere to substances. From time to time, they made stronger glue from the melted hoofs of goats and boars, but they had to heat it for use. They felt lucky to have an endless supply of sperm glue just waiting inside their bodies for use. It didn't take long to learn that after playing with their penis, they could produce more sperm than needed. It was also portable and readily at hand. Inspired, they soon found many reasons to glue stuff around the tree house. They even decorated their bamboo poles with tiny shells.

Ryan reached the perch landing and immediately started striking the flint rock to get the fire going. He also broke off some green leaves from the tree and placed them in the fire to produce more smoke. Austin put his eye to the spyglass and began scouting the horizon until he saw the jet. Almost always, the plane would race across the island, and then out of sight over the horizon, but this time, the jet made a turn to the left, then another turn, and was now heading towards them.

"He's coming back! Maybe he saw us!! More smoke!!" yelled Austin as he took the gourd with mirrors, turned it until it caught the sun and began jiggling slightly left and right, while also rotating the gourd just slightly to give the appearance of a flashing signal.

"I see him!" yelled Ryan. "Get ready!"

The jet, still several miles off, made a heading straight for the island. However, when it was within about two or three miles, the pilot unexpectedly pulled back on the stick, and began racing straight up, while doing a slight roll as he climbed. It was as if he was practicing combat maneuvers, as the plane suddenly pulled out of the climb by turning west, while rapidly racing out of sight.

"Do you think he saw us?" asked Ryan, knowing the pilot couldn't have possibly seen them.

"No. We might as well put the fire out and prepare for the next chance," stated Austin. "Time for breakfast."

Twice more that year a jet would race overhead, but not once did they get a fair chance to make contact with a signal, but they always kept trying. Several times a day, one of the boys would climb to the perch to continue scouting for planes or boats. They also did it for their safety and protection.

It took a couple of months, but each night before they went to bed, they began trying to recall another chapter from their favorite book Swiss Family Robinson. They began from the beginning, each boy adding something the other forgot. When they reached the end of the story, they would start again. With each review of the story, they recalled something they previously forgot.

One of their recollections was about a gruesome gang of pirates that attacked the Robinson family. They didn't believe that pirates existed in 1982, but they knew there were plenty of bad people in the world, not to mention the communists they heard so much about in school. Ryan even remembered his dad's telling them about the communists and Castro taking over Cuba, as he had explained in the limousine when they were heading from the airport to the docks in Miami.

Somewhat out of boredom, and a serious attempt to provide protection, they decided to take precautions. They first devised a plan of escape from the tree house by securing ropes from a series of sequential limbs that led them away from the tree house. They left the ropes dangling downwards. To the casual observer the ropes would have looked like vines hanging from the tree. Should an enemy attack their tree house, the plan they devised was simple and fast. They would retreat out the back of the tree house onto the porch, grab the first prepared rope, and swing out and away from the house to the next rope. They would grab it in mid air, let go of the first rope, swing to the next, and so forth just like Tarzan did in the movies they saw when they were little. They practiced swinging in complete silence. Over and over they drilled their escape plan until they performed it flawlessly. Their arms and shoulders had grown so much over the years of climbing and swimming, that holding their full weight on the rope was as easy as lifting a gallon jug of water. There was not an ounce of visible fat on their lean, muscular bodies. They could run fast, swim hard and deep, hold their breaths well beyond five minutes, and leap five feet or more in the air. For castaways, they were in superb shape.

The last rope let them drop halfway up a hill. Once on the ground, they would swiftly scamper over the ridge and out of sight. They would assume someone might have seen the direction they were heading. Therefore, once out of view, they created a diversion by taking a hard left on the path that led to a pool of water. The rope swings had taken them to the north side of the hill. The new tact turned due west. They would quickly run up a fallen tree trunk and dive into the water. They would swim to the far side, climb out, and then take a path through the hills to the cave. In the cave, they prepared gourds of water, food, and weapons, and hid the emergency cache should they need them.

Ryan and Austin made a backpack out of the leather skin of boar. In an emergency, they would quickly put Bell in the pack, place it on Austin's back, and begin their escape. They practiced several times with Bell, and miraculously the little dog just nestled down into the soft leather. Often she licked the sides of the skin during the journey. The only part she didn't like was the leap into the water. Austin would recover her from the pack and leap into the water, letting her go as he hit the surface so she could swim on her own to shore. She made good speed despite her short legs. When they reached the cave, she received an award of a nice new boar, goat, or rabbit bone. To her, it was worth the journey, and almost worth getting wet, just to get that new juicy bone to chew on.

They created a series of hidden rock markers in the cave to make it easy for them to find their way to the waterfall. They practiced moving through the cave in the dark by counting the eight marked stones aloud until they reached the big cavern. They never practiced going through the waterfall with Bell, but if they were discovered in the cave, riding out the underground stream was their only avenue of escape. They would take Bell anyhow. After a bit of practice they learned the backpack was almost waterproof, so the plan changed. Bell could stay in the backpack, but they would reverse it so the open end was the bottom. The trapped air allowed her to breathe while they swam through the stream.

Their voices completed Mother Nature's cycle of change when they were fifteen and in their fifth year. Blond strands of hair continued growing down their legs, which helped to cover the little scars they incurred while hunting and playing, and accidental scrapes they experienced in growing up on the island. Ryan was nearly six feet tall. In one year, he had grown three full inches. Austin was growing but not as fast. He was only about five feet eight inches tall. Their bodies remained lean and rippled like a bodybuilder. They were thin, wiry, but strong. Muscles bulged from their arms and shoulders as well as their calves and thighs. They now cut each other's sun-bleached air about every other month, having determined that shorter hair was easier to keep clean and dry quickly. Their eyes glistened with confidence. They even managed to keep their teeth reasonably clean and white after making a crude toothbrush they shared.

They were strong and healthy, and while they weren't sick very often, each time nearly always scared them. They feared one would die, and the other would be alone forever. Left on the island without their only friend far surpassed the fear of an attack by pirates. They became the other's better half. Each boy produced the only love the other received. To lose that love and that friend would be harsh enough, but to continue living afterwards, might be impossible, they thought.

They discovered a few plants roots that had some medicinal purpose, but they did not know which one to use, or how much to take. They fought all maladies the same way, sip as much water as possible, sweat out the fever, and pray they were never sick at the same time. In their early months on the island, they wisely took turns trying to eat something new they had found or discovered. Only one boy would taste the potential new food, and then they waited to see if the explorer became sick or not. If he didn't, then both would eat it.

They were lucky in that there were no sick strangers around, and no kids with colds or the flu, so they had little chance of catching any of the viruses they often caught when they were in the States and going to school.

They were sure it was late September, but the date was off a few. While they could remember the words leap year, they had no idea when it occurred. It had been a good hunting day as Ryan shot his bow and arrow, and hit a good-sized bird, a rare treat for them. They were not sure what species of bird it was, but once roasted over the fire, and basted with pineapple juice, it chewed up just fine, almost like chicken. They devoured it.

The bird was one they hadn't seen before and soon assumed it must have flown from another island. This left them feeling they can't be too far away from civilization. While it gave them a measure of hope, it left the boys bewildered as to why no one came by their island.

Several nights a week, with their hormones raging, they would play with each other, and then fall asleep contented but exhausted. Unlike the AIDS crisis in the States, they had no fear nor did they possess any knowledge that sexual activity could lead to diseases. In their isolated situation monogamy was forced on them. They were one in body and spirit, eating the same food, drinking the same water, exercising with the same intensity, and even thinking alike. They continually finished each other's sentences and easily gave affection to the other. They soon relished receiving a hug, a kiss to the head, or slap to the bare butt. The human touch did not exist in the plants they dug, the items they ate, or the animals they hunted. They knew it felt good to have sore muscles rubbed, backs washed, and comfort freely and lovingly given.

About four in the morning, the nightly sea breeze picked up speed. The temperature began to drop a few degrees and it began to rain. The wind increased, blowing lightweight gourds off the shelves. Bell's repeated barking awakened the boys.

As he stroked her head Ryan asked, "What is it, girl?"

Bell just looked off towards the ocean and continued barking.

"Looks like a big storm," warned Austin.

"We'd better secure everything. I hope it doesn't last long." Forgetting about the sleep they wanted, they rushed around placing everything fragile or of some worth in the trunk. They pulled down the sky hatches and secured them tightly.

"I'm going to run up to the perch and check on the storm," yelled Austin.

"Be careful! Don't get blown off the tree," warned Ryan as he huddled with Bell in the center of the tree house. He placed his back to the trunk of the tree as it came right up through the center of their domain.

Austin ran to the porch deck, grabbed the rope ladder, and began to climb. Halfway up the wind began blowing him back and forth, making the later part of the climb almost impossible. Nevertheless, he was tough, surefooted, and refused to quit. He was strong enough to climb the rope without using his feet anyhow. He made it to the perch, which was swinging wildly back and forth, much like the perch atop a sailing schooner in rough seas. He scanned the horizon to the west and could see nothing but rain and blackness. The rain drenched his naked body. He turned back to the south and immediately became alarmed. He saw a funnel cloud whenever the streaks of lighting lit up the blackened sky far off to his right. He had never seen a hurricane, but had heard about them in school. He had seen pictures of them in Life Magazine when he was about eight or nine. It appeared to be heading straight for them. Suddenly, he was plummeted by falling hailstones, forcing Austin to retreat from his perch to the tree house. The wind blew the rope ladder into the trunk of the tree nearly knocking him from his tight hold on the rope. He dropped the final ten feet to the deck with a wet thud.

"I'm not sure we should stay in the tree," he yelled over the howling wind.

"Why? It's just another storm. It'll pass," replied Ryan loudly.

"I think it is a hurricane!" he exclaimed. "I saw a huge funnel, and I think it is making a beeline to us!"

Ryan asked, "Jeez, what do we do?"

"Let's head for the cave but we'd better hurry. It is moving rapidly."

They grabbed the backpack and loaded Bell. Then they quickly packed some food and belongings in a second backpack, ran to the makeshift elevator, and dropped quickly to the ground. Limbs and leaves were flying quickly through the air as they began to run towards the hills. Even the though it was almost pitch-black, they knew the way by heart. A flying coconut grazed Austin in the back of the neck, knocking him to the ground. It stung a bit, but he quickly stood and they moved on. The wind was already up to sixty miles an hour making it almost impossible to walk, but they trudged on nonetheless. Leaves and sand blew into their faces and eyes, but they refused to give up.

They could hear the whine of the hurricane. It was like the sound of a massive freight train racing towards them. As they climbed higher up into the hills, they began to see it firsthand. The hailstones were falling rapidly all around them, bouncing off their bare heads. The ground began to turn white like a snowstorm in Maine.

"Hurry!" yelled Austin from behind Ryan.

"I'm trying! I can't see my hand in front of my face, and the wind keeps blowing me off the trail!"

Suddenly a huge burst of wind knocked them off their feet to the dirt. Shards of flying tree limbs pricked their bare skin, but they were tough and determined. Survival was priority one. They had already survived so much that they wouldn't dare give in to anything, not even a hurricane. The last twenty feet to the entrance of the cave became extremely difficult. The funnel cloud was less than a few miles from shore. The seas were slamming into the beach and rolling far into the jungle. Palm trees twisted in spirals, and then snapped into big chunks. The high-speed winds tossed the dense logs end over end into the forest like matchsticks. Austin held Ryan down as a huge, flying palm tree trunk hurled over them much like a batter slinging his bat after hitting a home run.

The explosive wind snatched a giant sea turtle from the shore water and threw it up on the beach. One moment fish were swimming in the saltwater, and the next the wind rolled whole schools of fish to the top of sand dunes. Having experienced hurricanes before, the wild animals on the island knew exactly what they had to do. The boars rushed into the freshwater pool. The goats huddled down inside a ravine. The birds flew into the backside of the mountains and found holes in the rocks to hide. The fish and sea creatures went to the bottom of the ocean surrounding the island while moving to deeper waters.

No longer able to stand, Ryan grunted and crawled towards the cave. Austin was struggling behind him. Bell was barking inside the backpack. The wind was now over a hundred miles per hour. Jungle debris pelted them. They could no longer hear their screams. The funnel was close, too close. Austin handed Ryan his backpack with Bell inside. Ryan crawled onward until finally he made it inside the cave. Quickly, he set down the backpack. Bell scampered out and instinctively ran farther into the cave. Ryan turned to pull Austin in and unexpectedly realized that he was gone.

"Austin!!" he yelled, but the roar of the hurricane was far louder, but he yelled repeatedly. He moved back out of the cave to search for Austin. He was as scared as he could remember, and more terrified of losing Austin than of being killed by the hurricane. He trudged on.

The wind slammed Ryan into the hill, temporarily knocking the air from his lungs. He struggled to his knees. The hurricane hit the southern side of the island. They had only minutes until it reached them. Entire clumps of uprooted trees flung end over end into the air, some rising a hundred feet before crashing into the ocean. Ryan had to shade his eyes from all the sticks, rocks, and sand that were flying at high speeds through the air as he searched for Austin.

A bolt of lightning shot through the air and during the brief flash he spotted Austin hanging to the side of the cliff by just the root of a tree. Ryan knew that below Austin was a drop of about fifty feet, however, at the bottom was not a pool of water, but rather a huge pile of rocks. Ryan quickly climbed down a few feet. The wind tried to blow him right off the hill, but he clung onto whatever root or twig he could find.

Suddenly, the speed of the wind dropped way down. In that moment, Ryan realized the storm no longer raced towards them, but rather they were in the middle of it, the real eye of the monster. It was as if the big hurricane had stopped moving and stood right on the edge of the shore. One side the hurricane sucked debris into a horrifying funnel. The other side spit it out like water from a giant fire hose. Another bolt of lightning streaked across the sky. Austin was six feet below him.

Ryan continued to climb downward. Austin's feet were bouncing wildly off the cliff. He couldn't find a footing. He was more than strong enough to support his body with just one arm, but for how long and would the root hold out under the strain of Austin's hundred and thirty pound frame, he wondered?

"Hold on!" yelled Ryan.

"Don't you'll fall!" yelled Austin, fearing for Ryan's life.

"Shut up and hold on!" replied Ryan.

Ryan found another root to grasp tightly. The hail pelted them but neither boy noticed because they were in the midst of a life-and-death struggle. It was like the bottom of the fifteenth round and the boxing match tied. It was a do or die moment. Austin didn't know how much longer he could hold on. Ryan didn't know if he could reach him in time, but neither boy ever thought of giving up and quitting. He leaned way down with his free hand. His foot slipped. He struggled briefly before finding another toe hole, and dug the tips of his feet in as far as he could. The roar of the spiraling hurricane was deafening.

"Grab my hand!" he yelled as loud as could.

In less than a second, Austin looked up, saw the hand, swung his free hand up, and snatched Ryan's hand as expertly as a trapeze circus performer. Austin began to pull his body upward as Ryan tried to retract his arm. Austin nearly slipped but clung on. He bravely let go of the root that had saved his life, swung his hand up, and grabbed Ryan's elbow. Ryan held his position, allowing Austin to climb up his body to his level on the side of the cliff.

Once secured, Ryan took a breath. "What the hell you doing out here? There's a hurricane on the beach you fool!" he grinned as the rain poured down their faces.

Austin grinned, while letting out a big sigh of relief.

To Ryan, Austin's grin was the most beautiful sight in the whole world. Austin laughed. "Whoops! You cursed. You got to say prayers tonight!"

"I'll say the darn prayers if we live through this!" yelled Ryan as he pushed Austin farther up the hill.

Once at the top, Austin glimpsed back at the funnel cloud as it began moving once more. "Better get our butts in that cave right now!"

Together, they pulled each other back across the trail where they crawled their way into the cave. Austin rolled over on his back to catch his breath. The roar grew louder. It felt as if the air was sucking them right out of the cave. Austin began to slide across the ground on his back towards the entrance. The hurricane seemed angry for not killing him on the cliff. The wind created a vacuum in the cavern. Rocks and debris began flying pass Austin and out the entrance. Ryan grabbed his hand and pulled him farther in.

"Run!" he yelled as he pulled at Austin.

Austin scrambled to his feet, and together they ran about forty feet farther into the cave, and quickly huddled down behind a rock, safely out of suction created by the path of the hurricane. Bell, hidden deeper in the cave, trotted swiftly to Austin's waiting arms.

For the next forty minutes, the fierce storm wrecked total havoc on their island paradise. The storm attacked everything, making it scarred, torn, or twisted. A squadron of bombers could not have managed as much damage as this single hurricane. There was nothing they could do but wait it out.

THIRTEEN

By dawn, the rain subsided and the clouds cleared. As if by magic, the sky became a beautiful crystal blue and the sun a bright orange. When the boys stepped out of the cave the sunlight revealed the total devastation of the island. They climbed to the top of the hill with Bell trailing after them, and off to the west they could see the horrific hurricane roaring away in the distance. When they turned around to the east, they saw bright beautiful skies. However, when they looked down, they saw only the harrowing destruction and obliteration of their island.

To their surprise, the house was still in the tree, but most of the roof, some walls, and even some flooring were missing. The house was in the biggest and perhaps the oldest tree on the island. It clearly had weathered similar storms, but still refused to give in and let go. Its roots were deep into the ground and thus, it defiantly remained steadfast.

The rolling saltwater waves flooded the nearby freshwater pool. The winds blew away all their hanging dried food. Entangled in the flying limbs were the ropes for their escape routes. For more than an hour, they just sat beneath the tree house, and looked up at the havoc that surrounded them. However, as they had done so many times after smaller storms, they would rebuild, and they would make it stronger, better, and more durable, and by doing so, they would forget how long they had been on the island, and how sorry they might have felt for themselves. Nevertheless, they were not sorry, they were thankful. They were thankful they had survived. They were alive, unhurt, and to them, that was all that mattered.

Once again, the possibility one of the pair might be critically hurt, made them all the more fearful of such storms. They possessed no knowledge on how to prevent a storm, only the desire to prevent these events from hurting them. They sat side by side on the ground deep in thought. Their minds replayed the events of the nighttime attack of the hurricane. It had nearly wiped them out, but somehow they had survived. Ryan reached over and took Austin's hand to comfort him. Austin squeezed it trying to give solace in return. They spoke no words. They did not know the words that would console someone after such a horrendous, narrow escape with death. They leaned into each other, while wrapping arms around their shoulders, and sobbed with relief and the joy only a survivor can feel.

Minutes later, they suddenly heard a mechanical noise in the sky. They stood up and turned around for it was not the high pitch whine of the jet plane's engine, but a lower pitched prop plane motor. The engine grew louder and was coming in from the south. Austin and Ryan quickly made their way through the broken limbs surrounding the base of their tree, climbed ropes to the perch as the elevator ropes and pulleys were tangled, and quickly pulled away the numerous limbs blocking their path to the perch. Once they made it up the rope ladder, they quickly discovered the plane was less than a half-mile away. It was a big boxy plane. They didn't know it, but it was a hurricane chase plane. Austin searched for the mirrored gourd in the debris on the perch, but the storm had taken it away, too. Thankfully, the handle for the pot had been tied to a limb, but for there no chance for a signal fire as the pot was full of water and the prepared kindling gone.

Seconds later, the plane turned westerly, and then flew over the island as the boys stood helplessly in the perch above their ramshackle house. They stood there with nothing in their hands to signal with to catch the eye of the pilot. They didn't even have a shirt to wave in the air. They knew help would surely come if they could signal, but the pilots never saw them. As the plane passed, they silently stood arm in arm, wondering what the rest of the world was doing, and where that plane was going. They watched until too far to see anything but the disappearing storm. They shed no tears for there was too much to do. In just a few hours, the powerful storm had destroyed their island paradise. Now it was time to rebuild.

For over fifty days, they worked solely on restoring their house, restocking their food, and hauling freshwater after their spring was refreshed. They lived off the food previously stored in the cave in case pirates or anyone attacked them. Their back up plan saved the boys from starving. The hurricane taught the castaways to work and store up more food and supplies in the cave, as well as weapons and torches. If they ever spotted a storm again, they would instantly drop everything they were doing and run to the cave. Nothing was more important than their survival together. Determined that if weather or humanity's worst should befall them again, they would endure, they would triumph, and they would survive.

After several weeks, they completed the rebuilding project. They decided it was time to take a full day off and go fishing. That night they were preparing a celebration feast that began just after dark. Bell learned to like fresh fish, so they carefully deboned a chunk of meat and filled her bowl to the brim as well. They had made the house stronger than before. Nature had storm pruned the jungle, but already they could see new fruit beginning to grow. Thankfully, the freshwater spring and pool recycled, providing quality and easy to obtain drinkable water again. However, just in case, they hauled numerous survival items to the cave until confident there was nothing more they could do. They restored their tree house and supplies in fifty days. They were smaller in height than the giant swirling beast, but they knew that in their hearts they could survive any storm, especially this hurricane that they now called the bastard.

They were proud of their work and jubilant in their celebration. When it came time to settle down, they cuddled into each other and started to play around until sexually satisfied before drifting off to sleep. A few hours later, Ryan slightly awoke from his deep sleep feeling his enlarged penis rubbing against Austin's bare backside. The soft flesh in the crack of Austin's butt made his member grow even more. With his eyes still closed, he nuzzled his lips to the back of Austin's warm neck. He pushed his penis closer down Austin's butt. He was not sure what to do, but with his eyes shut, he recalled their spying on the two counselors who were having sex. He wondered a bit about the how and the why, but not too much pondering. He was not thinking at all. Everything he did felt natural and good. He was in a euphoric mood.

He found Austin's butt to be dry. Sometimes when their bare butts itched or scratched, they would rub some leftover cooking grease on it. They did the same for masturbating. Without hesitation, he reached in the bowl lying near their cooking area, retrieved a finger of grease, and silently rubbed it on his throbbing penis.

Austin stirred slightly, but he did not push away from Ryan. He felt a sudden chill. He moved himself backwards just slightly into Ryan's chest, and without apparently awaking. He pulled Ryan's arm over his own chest and wrapped his hands in his. Ryan returned his arm around Austin's chest, and then pushed his now lubricated penis into Austin's anus and pushed in just a bit. The feeling overwhelmed him. He pushed a bit more. He felt Austin's heartbeat from inside. After a few seconds, the hole relaxed, and so Ryan pushed farther inside.

Ryan recalled the goats they had spotted having sex. Soon he, too, began slowly and gently moving in and out, much like the animals they laughed at. Austin woke up slightly as the sensation began to warm him all over. Confused at first to what was happening, he did not move or say anything. The feeling was nothing like he had ever felt before. It felt good to him, and he was in no pain. His member grew larger than he had ever seen it do before. He slid his hand down and began playing with himself. A moment later, he realized Ryan was inside him. It confused him. He had thought about such a thing when they saw the goats doing it, and was sure it must hurt, but it didn't. The feeling was incredible. It was not like getting his back massaged with the feeling being on the outside, but rather it felt good on the inside. He soon became even more aroused. Slowly, not wanting to stop Ryan's magical rhythm, he pushed Ryan's hand from his chest to his own penis. Ryan gripped him tightly while slowly pulling on it. Austin pushed back towards Ryan, allowing him to go deeper. Austin gasped at the exciting feeling.

Austin turned his head around so his lips could find Ryan's wet lingering lips. They kissed passionately and deeply, while their bodies instinctively kept up the rhythm. Minutes later, they both exploded in simultaneous orgasms.

"Do it again. That felt great," whispered Austin as he broke off the kiss.

"Did I hurt you?" asked Ryan, always protective of the other.

"No. Is that what the counselors were doing?"

"I guess so or the goats."

"I ain't no goat," replied Austin with a chuckle.

"You smell like one," shot back Ryan.

They did it again, and then they traded places and Austin did it to Ryan twice as well. Exhausted, they faced each other, and for a long moment, they stared intently into each other's eyes. With no words spoken, Ryan leaned in just slightly and kissed Austin's forehead. Austin responded by kissing Ryan's cheek. Their kisses soon found their partner's lips, and tongues took turns exploring and exciting the other. After a while, they were making love once more.

FOURTEEN

It was January 22, 1985 and the boys had been on the island for seven and half years, and were now about eighteen years old or so. After shaken awake just an hour before dawn by a jet plane roaring across the sky, the boys quickly sat up from where they slept on the floor. The entire tree house and everything in it shook viciously from the loud, thunderous jet engine as it screeched by just fifty yards over their heads. A night plane was a rare event, but they felt that it provided a greater chance of discovery. Due to the lack of sunlight, they set aside the primitive signal mirror that had been rebuilt in a new gourd after the hurricane. They knew a bright fire would travel a lot farther in the blackness of the night, and afforded the greatest hope of detection. Quickly, they climbed the ladder to the perch and made the fire, but just as they struck the flint and lit the prepared kindling, they realized it was already too late. The jet streaked across the dark night sky and just kept right on going as it had always done. It soon disappeared into infinity.

They both sighed heavily and even felt a bit angry. The boys, yanked from their warm beds by an airplane, stared in disbelief as the jet left without the slightest chance of spotting them. Just as they were reluctantly putting out the fire, Austin spotted a bright star that was moving across the sky. "That's a big shooting star. Do you see it?"

Ryan stirred the kindling, separating it so the flames would go out. He stopped briefly and stared up to where Austin was pointing and immediately saw the star as well. "I don't think it is a shooting star, as they only last a second or two and then go out. What do you think it is?"

"Maybe it's a satellite or something like that."

"Cool. Yeah, that's probably it."

After watching for a few minutes, they climbed down the rope ladder to the deck of the tree house, and somberly went back to bed. They began their day a little later than usual since their trek to the perch so early in the morning. Ryan felt horny and so did Austin. They had discovered sex in the mornings was even more exciting than right before bedtime. Their lovemaking made the earlier disappointment of the plane easier to bear.

They kissed during their morning swim, feeling happier than ever during their seven years on the island. The boys could no longer remember how many years the Swiss Family Robinson clan had stayed on their island, but they knew they had survived longer than anyone they had ever heard of.

They decided to make it a lazy day by doing only their necessary chores, replenishing food and water supplies, picking some fresh fruit, and taking Bell for a walk so she could potty on the ground for a change. Once her paws hit solid ground, she always scampered around quickly sniffing and circling until she found just the right spot to squat. Soon they returned to the house to work on a net they were weaving to make it easier to catch fish. Near noon, with the sun high overhead, Austin decided to take a break from his weaving and began stretching his legs by climbing to the perch.

When he got there, his eyes scanned the horizon as they always did, and suddenly his heart leaped as if he was about to have a heart attack. Just five miles to the west were eight gray Navy ships. He spotted at least a dozen helicopters in the sky, and even higher, airplanes circled a large area of the ocean.

He gulped a deep breath and patted his chest. "Ryan! Come quick!" yelled Austin.

Ryan laid down his section of the net and went out on the deck to look up at Austin. "What's up?"

"Hurry!" yelled Austin.

"I'm coming. I am coming. Keep your shirt on," he replied out of habit, and then laughed at what he had said. The boys had long ago quit wearing clothing. Nothing they had fit. They used almost every piece of cloth, leaving nothing for clothes. Once they tried tying palm leaves around their waist, but the leaves scratched their private parts. They were naked and did not care. "I guess you don't have a shirt to keep on. Heck, you don't even have pants to keep on," he chuckled as he climbed the ladder, and at the top, he reached and playfully pinched Austin's bare butt.

Ryan climbed up onto the perch and stood up. Austin was busy looking through the telescope.

"Look!" grinned Austin as he pointed to the northeast as he shook his index finger repeatedly towards his fantastic find.

Ryan stared out into the ocean and immediately spotted all the commotion. To him it seemed as if ships were everywhere. "What the hell is that? Is there a war on?"

"Whoops! You got to say prayers tonight," teased Austin at having caught Ryan saying a four-letter word. "It looks like our Navy. I spotted a United States Flag on the biggest ship. Do you see it?"

He moved the scope back and forth until he found the flag. "Our Navy," he almost whispered reverently. "Well I'll be! I will build the fire. You start signaling with mirror."

Quickly they began their signaling, hoping at least one person out of that large task force of ships, planes, and helicopters could see them. All the years before they had never seen more than one plane at a time, and now there was a whole fleet of people just five or six miles offshore. Perhaps this could finally be their day of discovery. This could be the day they fancied about in their dreams. The day they wondered about and possibly the day they feared.

They signaled frantically at the boats for the better part of an hour, when suddenly they saw a shooting star like the one spotted before dawn, soaring right through the bright blue sky. The star suddenly slowed down as three huge parachutes opened, and the helicopters started closing in on the rapidly dropping thing or whatever it was, wondered the boys. Ryan and

Austin desperately kept signaling, but everyone involved in the military operation appeared to be looking at the descending star.

"I think that must be a space capsule," said Ryan slowly and somberly.

"I bet you're right. It has to be. It is landing in the ocean. It is landing right in front of us. Surely they'll see us!" exclaimed Austin excitedly and more determined than ever to keep up the signaling.

"I'll get more dry wood," stated Ryan as he hurriedly climbed down the ladder to the deck. Bell was barking as she could hear the helicopters, and instinctively knew something special had happen.

The spacecraft crashed into the ocean, then divers jumped out of the encircling helicopters, but Austin kept flashing the sky with his new gourd mirror. They pulled the astronauts from the spacecraft, placed the men in a large basket, and hauled them up and into a large helicopter. Afterwards, they rushed off to the biggest ship of the fleet, which must have been an aircraft carrier. Most of the helicopters returned to the other ships as they turned to steer to the west. However, one of the helicopters, with a network camera crew aboard, turned into the wind for a better angle. The camera operators kept busy filming shots of the craft as it floated in the water. One of the reporters, feeling a bit nauseous because of the bobbing and weaving of the helicopter in the wind, glanced up from watching the recovery in the water, and instantly saw the flashing mirror.

"What's that?" he asked the pilot through his headset as he pointed at the island.

The pilot turned from watching the divers surround the space capsule, "I don't know." He began checking his map on the clipboard attached to his thigh. "That's the deserted island of," he paused while he searched the map for the correct name, "Shark Island."

"That's probably a human signaling. Maybe they need help. Can we fly over?" yelled the reporter over the whine of the big turbine engine.

The pilot shrugged his shoulders, "I guess so. I will radio in that we are going to make a circle approach. That island belongs to Cuba. We are just barely out of their waters. Do you see that flotilla of boats to the north? That is Castro's navy just waiting with trigger fingers to shoot at us if we get too close to Cuba. Nevertheless, I doubt if they will bother us for accidentally flying over an empty island of theirs."

Ryan climbed aboard the perch, removed the backpack filled with dry twigs and immediately placed them on the fire.

"Ryan!" exclaimed Austin suddenly. "That one is coming towards us. The helicopter is coming towards us!"

"Break out the flag!" yelled Ryan.

Austin knelt down and unfolded the white flag they had made years ago for just this occasion. They had removed the bottom of the wedding dress discovered in the trunk, ripped it up into large pieces, and sewn the pieces together to make a heavily seamed white flag. He quickly tied it to the stick, then stood, and began waving it rapidly back and forth.

The helicopter pilot spotted the flag and the smoke, and steered towards them. In just another minute, he realized two boys were waving the flag. He yelled over his microphone to the crew that he was going to land. He hovered for a minute or two just offshore waiting for approval from the ship's flight deck. The news reporter elbowed his camera operator, urging him to take pictures of the boys. The camera operator focused his lens on the boys, and then began zooming in with his lens for a closer look. The helicopter was just seventy-five yards away. The wash from the blades caused the big limbs to sway just a bit. Though well tanned, their naked bodies and blond hair led the pilot to believe the boys were Anglo-Saxons, and not Cubans or other islanders. He wondered where they came from. He saw no ships or boats around the island.

"The boys must be shipwrecked or abandoned for some reason," he said to the news reporter.

"Let's go get them," yelled the reporter to the pilot.

"I have to wait for permission of my captain before I can do that," he replied. He began radioing once more to the big ship.

While the helicopter waited for instructions, the boys began jumping up and down with excitement. Rescue had finally arrived. They were jubilant. Bell barked from the deck below. Safe salvation for the marooned boys was just yards away.

Suddenly a jet whirled pass the helicopter not more than 30 feet off the water. The boys did not know it, but the jet belonged to Castro. The helicopter pilot nearly wet his pants. Occupied with discovering the boys he had not seen the jet coming. He received no warning, as his command office was busy with the space capsule recovery. Abruptly, his radio barked at him. His captain yelled at him and immediately ordered him to withdraw. A professional Navy pilot did not like having to back down from a communist threat, but he was illegally inside their territorial waters. Not much, just a mile or two, but he knew he would be in the wrong. He was also no match for an enemy jet fighter. Grudgingly, he turned his chopper away from the island.

Immediately, the hearts of the islanders sank, as did the flag that Austin reluctantly quit waving. The jet plane turned and roared past their island once more. This time he was so low, the dejected boys could easily see the flag painted on the tail of the plane. Although they did not know it was

Cuban, they knew it did not belong to the United States. They could see the pilot's helmet turn towards them as he cruised pass their tree house. He saw them.

"The reporter kept screaming into the headset for the helicopter pilot to return to the island, but the pilot couldn't break the direct orders of his captain. Once aboard the vessel all the reporters began filing their stories about the success of the Apollo landing, but Bill Sherr suspected he had an angle on another story that no one else had. His camera operator set up a color monitor away from the competing news staff. Together, they reviewed the tapes. This time they caught sight of the perch structure in the top of the tree to facilitate scouting the shore. This meant the boys built the perch, and probably been there long enough to do so. They saw their spyglass. They saw the big black cooking pot and the smoke that was bellowing out of it. They noticed the naked boys were without tan lines. They saw the cord that went round the boys' waist to hold their knife sheaves. Who were those boys? He wondered. How long had they been there? How did they survive?

He decided to put out the story, hoping someone would recognize the boys and call him. The video editor enlarged a single clear shot of their faces. The public would be his researchers. It took several hours to piece the story together. He filed the story with his NBC news bureau in Miami. That night on the evening news, the viewers saw the unbelievable close-up shots of the Apollo craft descending to the ocean, then after a break, the anchor came back with the story on the boys.

FIFTEEN

Senator Robert London was busy in his study in his Arlington, Virginia home working on a speech on free trade that he was scheduled to deliver the following morning on the floor of the Senate. Last year he won election once again, making him a three-term Senator. His wife, Bonnie, sitting in the den of their Washington home, stitched some needlepoint for a pillowcase to keep her often idle hands busy. Their daughter Kathleen called earlier from college to tell her that she had some big news, and she would be home this weekend to explain. She also mentioned that her boyfriend Tim was coming home with her. Soon Kathleen would complete her Masters Degree in Education, which made her parents very proud. Bonnie quickly surmised the big news must be the announcement of her daughter's engagement to Tim. She was already looking forward to planning the wedding.

Bonnie had been watching the local and network news for just about an hour but grew bored. She had just reached for the television remote control to change the channel when the story about the Apollo landing ended and the story on the boys appeared. Everyone assumed the boys had drowned with everyone else over seven years ago. There were never any bodies found, and the search teams determined the ship was most likely lost at sea. A few items from the ship had floated towards the Cayman Islands, and picked up by cruise boats, but nothing else. She hardly heard the words the reporter was speaking because she was staring first at the two boys, and then intently into Austin's eyes. Her son was ten years when she last saw him. There was no way she could imagine what he would be like now. However, it was those eyes she had kissed so many times when he was a baby that she would never allow herself to forget. She did not have to imagine them. She knew them as well as her own. She gasped as tears streamed down her face.

"Robert! Come quick!" she exclaimed as she dropped her needlepoint work to the floor and brought her right hand to her chest in disbelief.

"What is it?" he called while looking over his bifocals in the other room.

"Get your ass in here now!" she demanded in such an unusual and harsh tone that he immediately jumped to his feet, fearing she had somehow hurt herself. She almost never swore and he could not remember when she last did so.

He ran into the room. "What is it, dear?"

"Look at the boy on the right. Look at him!"

The senator knelt down beside her on one knee, removed his reading glasses, and stared at the blowup that just appeared on the screen. He first noted the two wild boys were nude, but as the camera zoomed in closer and closer, he, too, saw the resemblance. "Oh my God!" he suddenly blurted. He glanced quickly at his wife and smiled as his eyes watered. He reached out and gently squeezed her hand

"It's him. That must be Austin and Ryan. They survived!"

"Where are they?" asked the senator.

"The reporter said Shark Island, in Cuban waters."

"I'll find them."

Robert rushed from the room, called the local NBC Network office, ordered an immediate copy of the tape, and told them to deliver it to his house as soon as possible. He then called the Navy command center in Washington, and using his power as a senator he soon talked to the captain of the helicopter aboard the ship. He learned the pilot had gotten close and was preparing to land, but suddenly deferred by a menacing Cuban jet. The senator then talked to other officers, and finally to the admiral of the aircraft carrier. Out of habit he jotted down the names of everyone he talked with. It made their names stick in his memory. He called the reporter who filed the story. He was in a hotel room in Miami.

"Hello," said Bill Sherr as he picked up the phone.

"Mr. Sherr this is Senator Robert London. Do you know me, sir?"

Taken back a bit at the surprise call Bill managed to reply quickly, "Of course, I do Senator. It is a pleasure to hear from you. What can I do for you?"

"My wife and I saw your piece on the two boys in the tree on Shark Island. I have just talked to your pilot. We believe the boy on the right to be our son. He was sailing with his friend's parents when their boat when down." He swallowed hard, ducked his chin down, and took a much-needed eager breath before continuing. "That was seven and almost eight years ago. We thought they were dead. I have ordered a copy of your tape. Do you have anything else you can add that would help us identify him?"

"No sir. The boys were nude without tanning lines. They appeared healthy but much like wild boys or natives. Their hair was blond. They are definitely Anglo-Saxon. I am sure of it. Their smiles were huge. They were tall and they desperately waved a white flag at us. I am so sorry we couldn't land. I'll never forget their waving of that big white flag. I begged the pilot to land. I felt so helpless after we were forced to return to the carrier."

"Yeah, I heard the commie bastards ran you off. You've been a big help. I'm sorry, but I have to run. Thanks for your help. You may have just saved my son's life. Thank you, Mister Sherr. Thank you."

The senator hung up before Bill could reply. He hoped to get a follow up on his story from the senator, but sighed deeply, realizing if one of the boys was the senator's lost son, then like any parent, the father would now be running at full speed to bring him home. He began writing new notes in his pad and then swung around to his computer to begin doing research on the sailboat that had gone down.

Hours later, the senator, and his wife watched the delivered videotape repeatedly, and soon they were convinced beyond any doubt the boy on the right to be their son, Austin. The senator went to his desk and began calling in favors from all over Washington.

In Havana, a team of government news watchers had been studying the United States nightly news reports. When the story about Shark Island appeared, they quickly sat up and began rapidly taking notes. Hastily they made many phone calls. Castro, informed of the situation, decided the Cuban government must rescue the boys so that his country would be a hero in the world's eyes and not villains as the Americans conceived them to be. The boys, possible pawns in a trade for food for his country, created a key opportunity. Castro ordered a helicopter team to be on Shark Island at dawn to pick up the boys and deliver the lads directly to his headquarters. Twelve soldiers suited up and flew out an hour before dawn. Their training required checking their weapons, although rarely needed them on a rescue mission, they were told to prepare in case the Americans also sent out a team to get the boys.

Austin and Ryan ate their evening meal in silence, something quite out of character and almost impossible for the boys. Always one or the other had something to say, ask, or entertain by inventing a wild adventurous tale. Silence was something they already had enough of. Many times, they had watched the jet engine flames disappear over the horizon, never giving it much hope. However, to be fewer than a hundred yards from a helicopter that they knew saw them, and then leave without landing, put the teenagers into a dark, dreary mood. They always felt someone would liberate them from the deserted island, but they never imagined the rescuers would turn away after finding them. When it came time to go to bed neither boy could sleep. They took turns rubbing each other's back and later they cuddled together. Sleep wouldn't come because they remained wide-awake and wondering. Their brains replayed the day's events from start to finish in their heads as they tossed and turned while trying to block it out of their minds so they could sleep.

They did not know the camera operator had captured their faces on videotape. They had never heard of videotape.

SIXTEEN

The roar of a helicopter suddenly swung directly over their tree house just minutes after the sun came up. The tree swayed rapidly back and forth, but Austin still managed to climb up the ladder to the perch. Just as he reached the top, the helicopter swung around to his right. There was no American flag on the tail.

Austin ducked down out of sight and yelled down to Ryan. "It's the communists! What should we do?"

"Don't let them see you."

"Too late, they probably saw me already. They're landing on the beach." Austin scampered quickly down the ladder.

Ryan asked, "Do you think they'll harm us?"

"I don't think we should find out. It's time to evacuate! Let's go!"

Austin and Ryan scurried about quickly, grabbing things they needed and placing them in the backpacks, including Bell. They ran to the far deck where Austin leaped in the air to the first swing rope without hesitation and swung to the next tree. He swung the rope back to Ryan, while he swung on to the next tree. When Ryan arrived, they moved around to the back of a big tree trunk about thirty feet aboveground, hid amongst the leaves, and waited to see what would happen.

The squad of twelve soldiers included a captain eager to achieve a higher rank. He thought this simple, well-publicized mission might just be the key to his success. He ordered the men to search the jungle for the path that led to the tree house. Within minutes, about ten of the armed men began spreading out, while searching for the boys.

"They don't look so friendly," whispered Ryan. "They've got machine guns!"

"Shh, they might be here to kill us," replied Austin.

Finding the tree house, a corporal ran to tell the captain. The captain hurriedly made his way to the tree. Then he called out in English laden with a heavy Spanish accent. "Come down, boys. We mean you no harm. We're here to rescue you."

He waited, but the boys did not reply as they watched the squad from their hiding spot in the jungle. The captain said, "Stir them up a bit. We have no time to lose. The Americans might be here soon. Fire a few shots into the house to flush them out," he ordered.

The overzealous soldiers immediately fired a burst of hundreds of shots into the tree house. Ryan was pissed at the damage the soldiers were causing. He almost leaped out from around the tree trunk to smack them around, but Austin held him back. Austin gave him a signal for them to move on. Ryan nodded and immediately swung silently across to the next tree. Austin followed him. Even Bell was quiet in her backpack. They were heading for the safety of the cave. It took a series of five ropes to get them to the hill. The captain called for a cease-fire then sent two men up to look for the boys. When one of the men came out onto the deck and surveyed the surrounding jungle, he spotted Ryan swinging to the last tree.

"There they go!" he exclaimed as he pointed several trees away.

The captain turned around and realized the boys were escaping behind him. He could not let that happen. He could be court-martialed or worst if he lost the boys. His superiors would not take failure easily. He ordered the men to go after them.

Austin waited for Ryan to reach the last tree limb. He caught him as he swung across. They jumped to the ground and quickly ran up the path over a hill and out of sight.

"They're after us!" exclaimed Ryan.

"Yeah, but they can't keep up with us. You take Bell and go on ahead of me. Stay low in case they have someone from another helicopter watching for us. I'll see if they found the path."

"Austin, be careful. They have bullets, and we have mere bows and arrows."

"I will. Go on now. I'll be there shortly." Austin gave Ryan a quick slap to the butt and winked at him. He then turned to his left, stepped off the trail, and then up and over a big boulder. He could see the soldiers scouting the bottom of the trail and was not surprised when they started climbing up the side of the hill. Austin was angry they had shot up their home they had worked so hard and long to rebuild after the hurricane. He sat down his quiver of arrows. Each one had taken a full day to make. The blades of the arrowheads were polished sharp, and the shafts as straight as any store-bought ones. The feathers came from the tropical birds on the island and displayed a rainbow of colors. He drew an arrow and laid it across his bow. Ryan was the better archer, but Austin was obviously a close second. He did not want to kill anyone, but thought he might try to discourage the men a bit and get even for the damage the soldiers did. His well-practiced hunter instincts took over his thought process, but killing a bird or a wild pig was not the same. He aimed at the thigh and not the heart of the first soldier working his way up the hill.

Taught many summers ago at camp to exhale just before releasing, Austin quietly and gently let go of the taut string. Zip! The arrow was fast and true, hitting the man dead center of his thigh muscle. Austin grinned at his marksmanship as he quickly retrieved another arrow. The man let out a loud yelp, dropped his rifle, and fell to the ground holding his now bleeding leg while staring in disbelief at the arrow stuck there.

The captain came up the trail quickly. After taking a quick look at the wounded man, he ordered two soldiers to take the soldier back to the chopper. Austin had just cut the squad from twelve to nine with just one arrow. His confidence was bolstered. One of the soldiers spotted a likely hiding spot and immediately fired several rounds into the rock. Zap! Zap! Zap! The bullets creased the rocks spewing dirt and pebbles into the air, but did not harm Austin as he wisely moved to another big rock after firing his first arrow.

The captain yelled at his men to rush up the big hill, but they were cautious and afraid they were chasing wild natives that might shoot them with arrows as well. When the soldiers made it to the big rock, Austin was long gone. The soldiers looked in all directions, finding themselves perplexed to where he went so rapidly.

It had taken Austin and Ryan a long time to haul the sections of logs from ten different trees and pile them up against long stakes. A long rope, tied to the top of a single stake and attached to a strong tree farther up the hill, held the logs in place. Once cut, the logs would roll and tumble down the hill just like the ones the boys imagined in Swiss Family Robinson. The hurricane had created an abundance of logs. The boys felt they might be able to put them to good use.

Austin secretly watched as the soldiers made their way up the path. He was fearless. To him it was just like games at camp. He, the fox, and they, the hounds, but this fox was smart, cunning, and fast, and enjoying the game. He liked making the men look stupid and afraid of him. Austin waited patiently at the top of the hill.

Ryan reached the cave and went inside to put Bell down. He set his backpack down gently, and then ran back to the entrance to get his bow and stand guard. He could see Austin waiting from behind a big bush. From the cave entrance, Ryan stood on a rock so he could see the remaining nine men advancing. He jumped down, quickly took his knife, and cut some fresh brush, attempting to camouflage the entrance to the cave. He then dragged the head of a bush across the path, wiping away their footprints. He then ran back to his view on the rock.

The captain sent two men ahead of the squad who made their way up the steep bank. Austin turned around and found Ryan watching him. He put a single finger to his lips while smiling. Ryan nodded silently indicating he understood to remain quiet. When the two men stood in a spot he and Austin had agreed on weeks before, Ryan used his index finger and pretended to slice his own throat. Austin grinned, laid down his bow for a second, retrieved his well-sharpened knife from its sheath tied to his waist, and cut the rope tied to the tree.

82

Immediately the stakes snapped under the strain and the pile of logs began rolling rapidly down the path, toppling one after the other. The alarmed solders on the narrow path soon discovered there was nowhere they could run. Two soldiers reacted by shooting the logs, but that did not slow the bouncing logs. It was like an avalanche of sixteen feet long utility poles. A log crashed into and snapped the first man's right leg, the second soldier caught a bouncing log in the chest, and soon the logs mowed over most of the squad. The captain screamed for his men to take cover before he darted behind a rock, but his orders came too late. Three more of his men went down. When the logs finally stopped rolling, six more soldiers had been rendered useless and limping back to the chopper.

Though tempted, Austin wisely did not shout out at his success, but rather quickly made his way up the remaining section of the hill and into the cave, where he leaned into Ryan and gave him a triumphant hug. Ryan wiped away the remaining footprints in the sand in front of the cave, and together they went deeper into the cave pulling the brush behind them to hide the entrance.

The captain, now extremely angry and knowing he must not fail his superiors, urged his remaining men up the hill. He desperately advanced onward. For the next few hours, they searched around every rock on that hill for the boys, but could not find them. While the soldiers searched around the hill in the hot sun, inside the cool cave Ryan, Austin, and Miss Bell were safely resting while chewing on some beef jerky. They could stay in the cave for a week or two if necessary. The one flaw in their hiding place was they had no means of observation as to the commotion going on outside. They would not know if the enemy was still there, but felt waiting the men out was the safest thing to do.

Austin enjoyed the battle of wits and his curiosity was killing him. Silently, he crept back to cave's entrance. He often heard the soldiers talking within six or seven feet of the cave. Not once did they see the entryway. The sun had risen to high noon. The sun and island humidity made the men dreadfully hot from all the climbing and searching. The captain eventually allowed them to stop and rest, and so they sat down in a shaded spot just a few feet from the cave. One of them lit a cigarette. Austin could hear them chatting about the search, but they were speaking rapidly in Spanish. He did not catch all they were saying. The only Spanish he knew was from a couple of Spanish campers from Mexico, and he had forgotten most of it long ago. Austin could see the sweat on their bare necks. He stood there cool and calm while the soldiers were burning up outside in their hot sweaty uniforms. He grinned, feeling even more confident they would soon abandon their attempt to capture them.

One of the men soon noticed the cool air gently flowing into the back of his neck. It felt good so he turned to allow the breeze to hit his face. It puzzled him the breeze would be coming from the wall of rocks behind him. He eyes noted something a bit unusual. He saw several bushes seemingly growing at the base of the rock, but there were no roots or trunks, and the limbs were not attached to anything. He pulled at one and it easily moved.

"Captain, look!" he exclaimed as he began pulling the bushes away.

Austin immediately retreated, grabbed his backpack and with Ryan and Bell, they moved farther into the cave by counting silently the marker stones. The men found the cave entrance and promptly broke out flashlights from their field packs and entered the cave. Austin and Ryan assumed they would search until they found the first chamber, and then perhaps stop, as the paths became smaller and steeper from that point. If they made it to the room of skeletons, perhaps that would discourage the men as well. If they made it to the waterfall, Ryan, Austin, and Bell would be long gone in the underground river.

The frustrated soldiers turned on their flashlights and searched the cave trail for footprints, but their feet had grown strong with calluses and the men expected to find boot prints. Ryan dragged a brush limb behind them to cover their tracks, but in their hasty retreat, he missed a few. One of the men spotted a single human print, and then one of Bell's prints, so they began following the path to big room, but by then, the boys headed down the steep hill leading to the skeletons. After many months of exploring, they learned an easier way down the hill than sliding on their butts like the first time. Unfortunate for the captain and his two men, when they hit the cold clay-like wet mud, they fell on their butts and tumbled down the hill swiftly. One of their guns accidentally went off, sending several bullets that ricocheted off the walls, nearly deafening them. The men ended their slide in a pile much like Ryan and Austin had done on their first trip to the cave. As the soldiers gathered their flashlights from the cave floor, the realization that they had fallen into a pile of skeletons sent shivers up their spine.

"Captain, Captain!" rambled a terrified man. "We've got to get out of here."

The captain rebuked the frightened soldier, but then an idea struck him. While saying loudly so the boys could hear that they would leave, he was using his hands to tell his men he was going to stay behind. He cut off his flashlight, took a few silent steps to a corner in the cavern, and watched the remaining two soldiers make their way up the hill and out of the cave. He sat silently, barely breathing and waited. He soon heard their voices. They were speaking English. He knew a few words of English, but could not make out what they were saying.

84

SEVENTEEN

"We did it," whispered Austin.

Ryan replied, "Yes, they're leaving. Maybe the Americans will return now."

"I hope so, but the Cubans might return with a bigger force. We don't have that many tricks left."

Ryan asked, "How long should we wait?"

"A bit longer to be sure," replied Austin.

The captain began crawling in their direction. Silently, he made his way along the path towards the voices.

Austin asked, "Did you hear something?"

"Nope, did you?"

Bell started to growl. The boys became alarmed. Suddenly, the beam of the captain's flashlight blinded their eyes. "Now I got you!" he said in broken English. "How long have you boys been on this island?"

"Seven years or so," replied a stunned Austin.

"That long? Well I am surprised you survived at all. You've hurt many of my men, and for that you're going to pay. My orders were to bring you back to Havana, but I think I'll kill you here, and pretend we didn't find you."

Suddenly, he grabbed Ryan's arm and jerked him forward. He put his pistol to the boy's throat. Little Bell charged and bit at the man's leg. The captain gave Bell a swift kick, sending the little dog sprawling and squealing into the dirt. Austin quickly picked her up and cuddled her into his arms, then set her down and shooed her towards the back of the cave near the path leading to the waterfall. He then came back towards the captain.

"Sir, we meant you no harm. The way you shot up our tree house made us afraid of you. I'm sorry we hurt your men. Honest." Austin stuck his hands up as if giving up. The tips of his hands were above the flashlight beam. He took a step forward, feeling the top of the cave without looking up. He could not find what he was feeling for. He moved another step. His fingers were groping while he was walking. Ryan knew the plan and hoped the captain would not shoot him.

Austin asked, "Do you have sons, sir?"

"Yes, I do."

"My mother only has one son and it is me. I haven't seen her in seven years. She probably thinks I am dead. Please, sir. Don't kill us."

"You can plead all you want you little savage, but you're going to..."

He cocked the pistol. Austin finally found the hidden rope stretched tightly across the ceiling of the cave.

Austin suddenly said, "Rabbit in the nest!"

85

It was the code phrase the boys agreed upon. The captain's brow wrinkled as he tried to translate the phrase in his brain. Austin yanked the rope. The rocks that had taken days for them to gather and place on a ledge abruptly tumbled down on the captain. The moment he looked up to see what was coming, he moved the gun and the flashlight, and in that instant, Ryan and Austin vanished. The rocks knocked the captain down, but did not seriously hurt him, but it made him angry. He cursed the boys and the words echoed throughout the passageways. The falling rocks bumped the switch on the flashlight to off. He felt around until he found it, snatched it up, turned it back on, and began searching the room for an opening. He found the path that led to the waterfall.

Austin and Ryan grabbed the backpack and Bell, and darted down the path in the darkness. They reached the waterfall room.

"Set the trip line," reminded Austin as he placed Bell in the backpack and tied it tightly together. Ryan quickly found the line and hooked it to a stick they had pounded into the ground many weeks ago. He then quickly came running to the edge of the stream.

They heard the captain curse when he bumped his head smartly into a jagged rock. Blood trickled down his face when he reached the waterfall room.

"Jump Ryan! I've got Bell. Go!"

The captain spotted the boys and fired his pistol at them. Ryan hit the water and swam to the bottom to prevent a bullet from reaching him. The beam of flashlight flashed across the water. Ryan spotted the glistening sword for just a brief moment, and then swam directly into the current to begin the journey to the pool. Austin lingered long enough to see the soldier hit the trip line and fall face first into the dirt where they had prepared a field of sharp sticks. One stick caught the captain in his arm causing the pistol to fall free. Another stuck him in the leg. The captain screamed out at the pain, and began cursing as he tried to free himself from the sharp sticks. He was furious and more determined than ever to get the boys and kill them.

Austin jumped towards the stream while reversing the opening of the backpack in the air so the top was now at the bottom. He felt Bell begin shifting so he juggled her inside the bag so her butt was downward, and her snout at the top of the bag. He crashed into the water and swam downward as fast he could. Trapped air filled the cavity of the backpack. Bell could breathe for a while if he could hurry along. He spotted the sword and for a short moment, the current lagged. Austin heard a splash. The bleeding captain had jumped in the water after him. Austin instantly grabbed the handle of the gold sword as the current caught him and Bell, and sent the two rapidly downward through the shaft of water.

The captain was not a great swimmer. The current enveloped his body and unfortunately for him, he panicked and tried to swim out of it, exhausting himself and his oxygen. It was a big mistake. His anger caused a dangerous lapse in judgment. He should never have jumped into the pool of water. He did not know about the current of the underground river.

Ryan soon passed from room to room, grabbing air where he could, while constantly looking back for Austin. Austin no longer feared the captain, but feared the journey would not be fast enough for Miss Bell. He held on to the bag as tightly as he dared and clung to the sword. A full minute later, he passed into the third room, grabbed a breath of air, but just as he went under the captain suddenly grabbed him by the hair. The soldier, terrified of drowning, grabbed the boy not just as a captive, but also in a desperate effort to get to the surface of the stream.

Austin knew that if he did not break free from the soldier, they would all drown. Without hesitation, he quickly spun around while bringing the sword back and then stuck the captain just above his stomach. The captain immediately let go of his grasp on the boy and grabbed his chest. His red blood began swirling around him. The remaining air in his lungs escaped in huge bubbles. His life was over.

Austin knew time and oxygen were running out for him and Bell as well. He began rapidly kicking his way down the flowing river channel and seconds later they broke free of the cave and were in the air sailing towards the pool of water.

"Catch!" yelled Austin as he tossed the backpack to Ryan, as he remained treading water while waiting for them. Ryan caught Bell as expertly as a tight end for the Dallas Cowboy football team going for a touchdown. Austin crashed into the pool of water while still hanging on tightly to the sword. When he surfaced, Ryan had the bag open and triumphantly, Ryan, Austin, and a much-relieved Bell swam to shore.

"We should call her super dog!" laughed Austin as he gave her wet kisses. She responded by barking gleefully at him while licking his face.

Ryan asked, "How'd you get the sword?"

"The current let up for just a second and I just grabbed it. I'm glad I did because I had to use it on the soldier."

No sooner had he said the words than suddenly the captain's bloody, lifeless body flew through the air before hitting the pond flat and hard. He was dead. It was drifting to shore where the boars would soon feast on the corpse.

"Let's get out of here. We've made the Cubans angry with us. We'll have to hide."

"Maybe the Americans…" began Ryan but Austin cut him off.

"Don't get your hopes up. We depend on each other and no on else. I love you."

"And I love you." They hugged tightly celebrating their triumphant success, picked up the backpack and put a reluctant wet Bell inside, grabbed the sword, and off they ran through the jungle.

Carefully, they made their way towards the tree house, but feared a trap just as the captain had tried in the cave. They could see the sun glistening off the blades of the parked helicopter. They watched the men as they waited for their captain. The two remaining men had gone back inside the cave, but could find nothing but the captain's gun and flashlight. They searched all the way to the underground river, but found nothing but his blood on the sharp sticks. Giving up, they returned to the helicopter, boarded and took off.

Still suspicious, Ryan hung on to Bell while Austin carefully swung from rope to rope, and silently entered the tree house with his knife in front of him. Though shot up and messy, the old tree house had survived a storm of bullets this time, and so Austin whistled for Ryan to come on in.

Bell, thrilled to be home in the tree and out of the hot backpack, quickly drank from her water bowl, took a quick pee on the porch deck, and feeling exhausted she then curled up and began a nap. She had experienced more than enough excitement for one day, and was not planning to move from her favorite spot for hours. Austin and Ryan quickly climbed the ladder to the perch and scanned the horizon. The sun was going down, but there was not a boat on the horizon. They were safe and alone once more, and this time, they were glad they were. Over dinner, they decided a rescue could be as dangerous as staying on the island the rest of their lives. They would have to work creatively on some new defensive plans because they knew most likely the soldiers would be back.

They ate quickly, cleaned up the tree house, restocked some of their supplies, and began to plan their next escape. Tomorrow, they would take action on new plans. Confident the enemy would not return after sunset, they vowed to rise early and stand watch.

Though exhausted from the day, Ryan and Austin had much to celebrate. Their battle plans worked for the most part, and they had not a scratch to show for it. They were also still alive. They hugged each other tightly and then made love passionately. They discovered new ways to love while soaking up the affection and tenderness like a dry sponge to a puddle of water. They could not get enough caressing. They craved the other. They longed for the other. They were a team, a unit, and a success. They were family. They were one and together they had conquered a foe much greater than old Bobby boar.

Austin woke just before dawn. Quickly he climbed the ladder and scanned the horizon.

Ryan yelled up to Austin as he took his morning piss off the deck. "Do you see anything?"

"Trouble!" called Austin.

"I'm coming!" called Ryan as he shook the dew off his lily as the boys called it, and scampered up the ladder like an experienced sailor on a large sailing ship. "Where?" he asked as he climbed onto the perch? Austin pointed with one hand and held the spyglass with the other. Austin then held Ryan's free hand while he waited for Ryan to see the four gray military boats heading directly for them. "They look like destroyers or something."

"Look at the flag!" Austin squeezed Ryan's hand.

"Jeez, they're not American. Is it the Cuban flag?"

"I'm not sure, but it is the same flag painted on the helicopter that landed her yesterday. My guess is that we have pissed them off, and they're going to blow us out off the island with those big guns. Do you see them? They're huge!" exclaimed Austin excitedly.

Ryan pulled his head away from the spyglass and sighed. "I say we just hide with no fighting or fussing. After a while, they'll give up and leave us alone. Surely they have more important things to do than chase a bunch of kids around an island."

Austin loved to fight to win, but he knew boatloads of armed soldiers were not a game at camp. Reluctantly, he smiled. "I agree. Where do we hide where they can't find us? They already know the cave. They'll probably dynamite it thinking we're still in there."

"Let's go to the crater."

"Yeah, the walls are steep there. Maybe we can find a place to hide. Grab food and water. We'll pack quickly and get out of here. Hurry!"

They had just scrambled down the ladder from the perch when suddenly a silver helicopter came out of nowhere and began lowering itself almost on top of the perch. The wind caused the tree to sway. The boys suddenly felt like they were experiencing a hurricane once more. Bravely, Austin climbed the ladder to see if it was the Cubans. The Cuban helicopter had been green. It gave him a small measure of hope, as this one was silver. Ryan clung on to Bell while trying to gather his backpack and his weapons. He placed Bell in the backpack, gave her some beef jerky to chew on, and waited for Austin.

More than once, Austin slipped on the ladder, but cautiously he continued the climb. When he got to the perch, he did not stand up immediately, but carefully rose until his eyes spotted the whirling blades of the helicopter. He allowed his eyes to follow down just a bit until he saw what he had prayed for on those many nights when he had cursed and forced to say the evening prayer. He saw the unmistakable red, white, and blue flag of the United States of America. Austin stood up and waved. Ryan saw him waving.

"Ryan!" yelled down Austin. "It's the Americans!"

Ryan quickly dropped his weapons and set down the backpack, and climbed the ladder. Together, they waved their arms. The helicopter pilot saw them and moved in closer, just a hundred feet away. One of the crew pushed back the big aluminum side door. The boys stood side by side waving their arms repeatedly. They immediately noted a soldier with a flight helmet on helping a passenger move closer to the door. Once the man had sat in the outside seat, he took off his flight helmet. Immediately, Austin recognized him.

"Dad?"

Ryan asked, "That's your dad?"

Austin didn't reply to Ryan, but quickly yelled as loud as he could, "Dad!!!!"

The senator waved and mouthed the name of his son. Austin!

It seemed like forever, but the pilot had gotten a radio message and swung the craft around so he could see the Cuban ships rapidly approaching. However, the helicopter did not leave this time. He quickly began setting the helicopter down on the beach. The boys left their perch, snatched up the backpack with Bell inside, and made their way to the ground. They let Bell out of the backpack. Austin ran ahead of Ryan and Bell. Tickled to be back on the ground and out the stuffy backpack, Bell promptly peed, and then set off after the running boys.

As the chopper wheels touched down into the sand, the senator jumped out. Austin ran from the jungle onto the beach and turned towards the chopper. He saw his dad running towards him. He knew that face. The hair had changed to gray from both the seven years and from the senator's many rough and tough political battles, but Austin would always know that face. The senator was surprised to see how much his son had grown. He was tall, lean, and filled with muscles. He had not even noticed the boys were naked. He was too glad to see him.

They met just ten feet apart, paused for a second to renew their memories of each other's face, to gasp for a brief gulp of air, and then triumphantly they grabbed each other and swung themselves around and around. The soldiers in the helicopter broke into huge smiles.

"Dad, this is my best friend Ryan," stated Austin as he broke the embrace and pointed to Ryan who picked up Bell in his arms.

"I am pleased to make your acquaintance, Sir. I've heard so much about you," stated Ryan steadfastly and politely as ever as he shook the senator's hand firmly. He still possessed his polite manners taught to him by his mother.

"I'm pleased to find you as well."

"Did my parents make it?" Ryan knew the answer, but there was still one glimmer of hope left.

The smile left the senator's face. Sadly, he replied, "No son. Not a sign of them. We didn't know where to look, and unfortunately we couldn't look on this Cuban Island.

"Sir?" interrupted a lieutenant. "We have to leave immediately. The Cubans are closing in."

"Be right with you. Boys, we have to leave now."

"Now? Okay, but let us run get our things," stated Austin.

"Austin, we must leave now."

"Five minutes, Dad. Just five minutes."

Austin and Ryan took off running. The senator and the lieutenant followed. So did the tail wagging Bell. The senator rode up the elevator and soon found himself astonished at the tree house. The boys rapidly packed what they could, including the sword, and in fewer than the five promised minutes, they sent the elevator down with the senator and the lieutenant as they ran for the chopper.

Holding hands, the boys took one last look at the home that had saved their lives. It was hard to go. They embraced and then slid down the ropes triumphantly and grabbed their backpacks and Bell, and ran for the helicopter. They took off before strapping in and for the first time in more than seven years, their feet left the sand of their island home. From the air, they could see what had been their oasis for their duration. The water turned a deep blue around their island. The island rapidly became smaller and smaller. The Cubans arrived too late. They would protest the invasion by the Americans, but the Americans would deny even being there. There was no evidence they were. Castro would not be happy. Someone in Cuba would pay a price.

After two hours of flying they touched down at the Key West Naval Air Station in Florida. The boys were given white sailor shorts to put on, and laughed as they carefully zipped the zipper without the benefit and safety of underwear. The short pants felt strange to the boys. They stepped barefoot off the chopper onto the hot cement, but the heat did not bother their jungle tough feet. Austin's mom ran from the fence where she had been waiting, grabbed her son, and hugged and kissed him repeatedly. Austin introduced Ryan and she gleefully hugged and kissed him as well. Austin and Ryan were nervous. Everything was happening so fast. It was like a dream. They held hands. Everything around them seemed odd and bewildering. They saw cars they had never seen before and people carrying big stereos on their shoulders called boom boxes. The soldiers took the pair to the base hospital for complete and thorough physicals. Some bureaucrat had to be sure they were not bringing any unknown diseases into the United States. They were also given medical shots they didn't want.

After devouring a sandwich, they ushered the boys into a room to meet Bill Sherr, the reporter who had started it all. As agreed with the senator,

Bill briefly interviewed the boys while the camera relayed the signal by satellite to New York. Three hours later, their faces appeared on every television in the country and by morning, their faces covered the front page of newspapers around the world.

Afterwards the kitchen staff brought in trays of food, and the boys ate everything they could get their hands on except for the fresh pineapples and bananas. They ate every morsel of the roasted chicken and even licked the plain butter off their bread plate. They took hot soapy showers. They found new clothes waiting on the table. It took them a while to dress. They had forgotten how to tie new shoes. The shoes did not fit right and hurt their feet when they walked. They took the shoes off and went back to walking barefooted.

By evening, they were alone in a bedroom in a house belonging to a friend of the senator's in Key West. They had not slept in beds for seven years. It felt strange to them. The twin beds were four feet apart. They had not slept apart in seven years. After an hour of restlessly turning over and over because they were unable to sleep, Austin climbed out of bed. He listened to cars driving by as he slipped out of the silly pajamas his mother had bought them. He pulled the covers back on Ryan's bed and gleefully dove in. The boys immediately snuggled in close to each other. Austin grinned when he realized that Ryan had already slipped out of his bedding clothes as well. Since they could not fall asleep, they decided to celebrate this incredible day they had just gone through. Finally, the boys felt rescued. They were safe and happy. One excuse is as good as another is, or so they imagined, and they made love. Afterwards, they kissed for the longest time, nuzzling each other in a tender and caressing way, and then fell asleep in each other's arms feeling warm and at peace with themselves.

EIGHTEEN

The senator's staff cranked up the publicity machine, affording and allowing every opportunity to promote the senator's rescue of his son, and of course, put in a plug for his political aspirations. The senator's staff leaked a rumor to the press of his expected nomination for vice president at the upcoming republican national convention. In four more years or more, he could be running for the president. In one television interview after another, his publicist remained busy expanding on how hard the senator worked to find his son. The senator stated how pleased and proud his son survived all the elements of nature while saving his friend. He laughed as he described how his son fought the cowardly commie Cubans and fought victoriously. He never noted Ryan's share in their success. In fact, he rarely mentioned Ryan at all. With the senator, Ryan didn't even rate best friend status.

After breakfast, the chauffeured limousine drove to a nearby hotel banquet room. They stood with Austin's parents on a small stage in front of over a hundred reporters and photographers who shot thousands of pictures of the pair and the senator. Their story, typed out by the senator's office, read as if professionally edited, enhanced, made politically correct, and then passed around to the press as if it was something the boys wrote themselves. Considering their limited childhood education, all the words over six or seven letters were not words from their vocabulary.

As soon as the questions and pictures were completed, the boys quickly excused themselves and headed for the bathroom. They had eaten too much rich food too soon and their digestive system turned on them. Their intestines grumbled and churned before the dreadful cramps set in so severely it made the boys double over in pain. On the island, Austin and Ryan ate moderately. In the States, their digestive systems rejected the large quantities of food, and especially the various spices. They found side-by-side toilet stalls and quickly jerked down their pants. The room immediately filled with miserable grunts and groans as their bowels loosened. All the squeamish restroom patrons quickly fled the area. It was not a pleasant experience for anyone. They returned to the anxious senator feeling dizzy and sweating with bleak pale faces. The senator never noticed but his wife did.

They loaded up in cars and drove to the airport. They flew not to North Carolina as Austin hoped but directly to New York. There they appeared on two different talk shows and the following day on the morning news programs of all three networks. It was a scheduling nightmare carried out with surgical precision by the senator's aides. In less than full day, they had flown from the peaceful warm breezes of Shark Island to the frenzy, backstabbing world of politics and power. Austin and Ryan, naive in thinking the world genuinely cared, saw no political motives. However, they became suspicious when the senator insisted his involvement in every photo opportunity and interview. The senator often answered the media's questions

93

before the boys could. They wondered how he knew what they did on the island? The truth was he didn't know any more than the few minutes he had allowed them to talk.

The senator's staff arranged everything from limos to lunch. The boys tired quickly. They hated the makeup powder splashed on their faces, and grew tired of answering the same old questions. In the few private moments they had, Ryan spoke his mind to Austin, but in front of everyone else, he was as usual, the perfect gentleman. However, Austin wished Ryan would quit the polite act because he needed an excuse to put a stop to this. On one of the morning news shows a female television anchor asked where they went to the bathroom while on Shark Island. This ridiculous and private question infuriated them. Austin had finally had enough of this hoopla and blew his top. The moment they went to a commercial break, he announced to his dad he planned to leave immediately with Ryan and fly to Maine to pay their respects for the loss of his parents. He knew he also needed to help Ryan secure some of his childhood things for their return to Austin's real home in North Carolina. He pulled off his microphone and began leaving the studio. He told Ryan to do the same.

"You can't!" exclaimed the senator. "We've got another talk show to do tonight."

Austin's face turned red and his voice grew louder. "You do it. I don't need it. I've told my story enough. We did what we had to do, and we're proud of our friendship. I wouldn't have made it without Ryan. He comes first in my life, not you and not politics."

The senator's aides turned pale. They knew what was coming. They had seen it before. "I don't appreciate your tone of voice, young man. Now you will do..." the senator's neck began turning red as well, and his eyes bulged because he rarely allowed anyone to stand up to him.

Austin had heard this speech before and like riding a bicycle, once you have, it all comes back to you. He cut the senator off quickly. "Sir, with all due respect, I'm no longer your little boy. Ryan and I proved our courage out there. We have nothing to prove to you. We're going and that's that." He paused for an unplanned dramatic effect, "And in case anyone else wants to know, we peed in the woods and we took a dump there, too! And no, we didn't have any toilet tissue! If that's enough, I'll drop my pants and let them have a look at my ass!" Austin grabbed Ryan's hand, and together they bolted from the room. The aides quickly smiled at his bravery, but lost their approving grin when the desperate senator looked their way for a solution to his problem. They offered none.

The senator began arguing with his staff about the situation when his wife came up and calmed him down. The quiet tone of her steady voice brought the senator in line immediately. She leaned in as if to whisper something and looked him straight in the eye. No one knew what she said, but the accomplishment was always the same. Then she smiled and kissed him on the cheek as if she had offered some encouraging words of wisdom or a bit of praise, and then she hurried out the door to catch Austin and Ryan.

She had politely told the senator what an ass he was making of himself and if she said it, he knew it was true. She felt great pride in Austin for standing his ground with the senator, and furthermore, she knew her son was right. She had seen her husband take advantage of opportunities before and she felt relieved that this opportunity had ended. The sudden massive exposure the boys had been through was just too much. She was determined that she would not lose her son again.

"Austin! Ryan! Wait!" called his mom as she hastily pushed through the studio doors to the street. The boys had just reached the seemingly endless sidewalks of New York and were standing on the corner trying to figure out what to do. She hurried down the busy sidewalk to catch up. "Honey, I'm so sorry. I should never have let this get this far. I was just so proud of you and Ryan." She gave them both a good hug. "You boys are something special and you stood up to the senator. That was really amazing. My goodness that was a great speech!" She laughed. "I believe you are a man all right. I guess I wanted the whole world to see what a great kid I have. I do not want to lose you again, so how about this. Take my American Express credit card and ..." she swung her purse around and ran her hands quickly through her contents, "and here's three hundred dollars. Catch a cab to the airport and get on the next plane to Maine using the credit card. Call me when you get to a hotel or something so I'll know you arrive safely. I will fly home to Washington tonight and on to North Carolina tomorrow. Go see Ryan's relatives. Wish them my best, and then the both of you catch a plane and come home to the Carolinas. No more Washington politics, I promise. I imagine Shark Island somewhat of a paradise, but North Carolina is a special paradise, too. Please bring Ryan home with you and let's show him the beauty of our great state. Is that fair enough?"

Though a bit dumbfounded by her sudden plan, the boys nodded yes. Austin smiled and hugged his mom once more. She cried a bit, letting the tears slide down her cheeks, then smiled and reached to pull Ryan into the hug as well. "You're my favorite sons. I will not let anyone do this to you again. I promise."

"Thanks Mom."

"You be careful. Flag down a cab. You're men now, but if you can handle the Cubans, maybe you're tough enough to handle a New York cabbie," she said with a laugh.

The boys hailed a cab, but after entering the backseat, they turned and waved goodbye to her with big smiles on their faces and followed the plan just as she said. Holding hands in the back of the cab they rode to the airport. The cabdriver noticed they held hands while waiting at a red light, but he did not say anything until after the ride ended and he had secured his tip.

Then he nearly growled as he yelled out the window. "I'm glad you faggots are leaving our great city. I hope your plane crashes!" He drove off leaving Austin and Ryan dumbstruck. No one had ever called them faggots and the tone of his voice stung their pride.

They tried to shrug it off as best they could. They assumed perhaps the fumes of driving around the streets of New York got to him, and thus, the cabbie must be crazy. They bought plane tickets and received instructions on how to get to their gate waiting area. The plane did not arrive on time from Pittsburgh, and like the rest of the waiting passengers, they quickly became bored and tired. The seats at the gate were getting hard, the junk food tasted bland, and the air-conditioning barely worked at all. Ryan and Austin had not sat in chairs this long in over seven years. It made their backs hurt so much that they got up and moved to an empty wall and sat down on the carpet. As time went by, they leaned in to each other for reassurance and comfort. Austin drifted off to sleep with his head on Ryan's shoulder. Ryan stayed awake a little longer, but soon his head leaned into Austin's and they fell fast asleep.

A half hour later, they were awakened with a start when a preacher in a white clerical collar with a strong Southern country accent came up to them. He immediately started yelling scriptures from the Bible that condemned homosexuals, and then he began yelling how God would destroy them just as he did the sodomites. He threw his large soft drink on them, cup and all. The man then stormed off to one of the nearby restaurants to buy another drink. The horrendous episode left them in shock. Everyone stared at them. They did not know what to do, nor did they understand why he attacked as he did. They were even too stunned to retaliate. If only they had their bows and arrows, they thought. They grabbed their overnight bags and ran towards the bathroom to clean up. Thankfully, when they returned the boys assumed the preacher had moved on down the corridor. Their plane had begun boarding. The flight attendant at the entrance to the plane spoke nicely as they stepped aboard, apologized for the late flight and pointed towards their seats.

Just as the boys were feeling a bit more at ease, another man who had seen and heard the preacher suddenly cursed them as they passed by his seat. They turned around to see which man was cursing, but the owner of the voice did not face them. When they turned to continue walking down the aisle, they saw the preacher sitting just several rows ahead with his prim and proper wife. The preacher just glared at them with a smug, disgusted look. It unnerved them. Their pulse rate began to climb.

The boys suddenly felt claustrophobic and frightened. They both began to tremble, but deep inside their souls, they were ready to fight. Unfortunately, they left most of their weapons back home. All Austin had on him was his Swiss army knife. He missed his sword as it had been shipped back home to North Carolina from Key West. They were facing new enemies than those on the island, and they did not know how to defend themselves. In the States, words were weapons, and they had no words in which to defend them. When the same flight attendant that had welcomed them aboard came towards them to check for locked seat belts, she abruptly turned her nose up at them. The boys sunk down in their seats feeling like everyone aboard hated them. They could not wait to get off the plane in Portland.

They had not thought far enough ahead in their travel plans to call Ryan's sister, so there was no one waiting to meet their flight. They decided to get a motel room, as it was nearly one in the morning, and they were exhausted. They planned to call Ryan's sister or his favorite aunt in the morning. They found a Ramada Inn with a vacancy sign on, paid with the credit card, found their room, stripped out of all their soiled clothes, and together they headed for the shower. They wanted to wash the remaining sticky Coca-Cola off their necks and arms, and wash from their ears all the file and evil words yelled at them. They also wanted to clean their nostrils from the stench of the city and from the smell of the mean-spirited people. One of the first things they noticed on returning home was the smell of other humans. The constant fresh breeze on the island made just about everything smell nice and fresh, but every person they met possessed their own artificial smell. Some perfumes nauseated them. Smoke filled hair and suit jackets made their faces turn sour. They already missed the clean, sweet smelling, flowering fragrances they experienced on their daily walks around Shark Island.

The sleepy hotel clerk placed the boys in a room with a single queen-size bed. They blessed him for the gift. Compared with the twin beds they were supposed to use in Key West, the hotel bed looked enormous. However, it did not matter how large it was because as soon as they quit talking, they made out, rolled in to each other's arms, and drifted off to sleep in the center of the bed.

Jessie, Ryan's sister, had received a call from him while he was in Miami. She had no clue he would be coming home sooner, but delighted nonetheless to get his call the next morning. She and her boyfriend planned to pick them up about noon. As tired as they were, they had survived. Thankfully, they had gone ten hours without feeling accused of being demons. They felt peaceful again, as they sat in the safety of the motel bedroom alone but together. They played around a little, ordered room service for breakfast, and decided to watch a little television. The first channel began with a talk show and the topic was about transvestites. The boys had enough of that channel before the first commercial. They decided to watch a cartoon, something they could understand.

They waited with their bags in the lobby until Jessie arrived. She leaped out of the car and ran to Ryan. Austin began to recall all the mean things she had done to Ryan, and how much Ryan had hated her, and how even he hated her for hurting his best friend. He almost expected her to be wearing a black pointed hat and arrive by riding a broom. However, Jessie was now as tall as Austin, and she possessed long dark hair. Her big blue eyes and her face radiated warmth as she beamed the biggest smile possible at the sight of her only brother. She stopped talking and just stared at Ryan. She fidgeted with her bright blue dress as she tried to straighten out the wrinkles. She was clearly nervous. Austin's opinion changed for Jessie as he watched the joyful tears stream down her face. He laughed when she kissed Ryan's cheeks leaving a little lipstick mark, which made him blush. He noted how pretty and feminine she was, and yet she still managed to pick Ryan up off his feet, and swing him around like a life-sized rag doll. He quickly decided Ryan's sister must have grown from her teenage past and deserved a second chance, and so had the boys. Austin began laughing at Ryan, at least he did until she grabbed him and swung him around, too. Now both boys had bright red lipstick smooches on their soft tanned cheeks courtesy of Ryan's only sister and only other member of his immediate family.

Still clinging to her brother's hand she blurted out, "I'll say this. You look great, little brother. You're lean, tanned, muscled..." she leaned into him and gave a playful elbow to his ribs, "and the girls are going to be dropping dead over the 'twos' of 'yous'. You just wait. I've got all my classmates dying to going out with you." Her thick Maine accent left the boys lost and confused at to what she said, but they laughed anyhow. "Oh, I forgot, this is Marvin," she winked at the big guy standing behind her as she took his hand and introduced him. "Marvin and I plan to marry next June."

Obviously, Marvin played on a college basketball team because he wore a block letter basketball jacket with several gold awards pinned in the block. He was six feet seven inches tall. That is about seven inches taller than Ryan and more for Austin. One of his hands was bigger than their heads. When he shook Ryan's hand, Austin saw the flesh of Ryan's hand disappear as if he had laid his hand in a catcher's mitt. Without a word, the boys decided Marvin was not a dude to reckon with. Austin knew it would take a good size log to knock him down the mountain. His nose, broken somewhere in his past, was big and crooked. Marvin's neck was bigger around than Austin's thigh, but he smiled almost timidly as he shook their hands. The boys decided Marvin might be a possible friend.

They ate lunch at a fast-food place where the cautionary boys slowly and carefully chewed each bite repeatedly before swallowing. They savored the taste while hoping their intestines would like what they were sending down the pipes. They watched the other customers and found themselves floored by the clothes people wore, their wild hairstyles, and even the music on the radio. Seven years had been a longtime adventure and a lot had changed in the world.

98

They ate most of their burgers and some of their fries, being careful not to overdo it as they had before, but they topped off the meal with strawberry milkshakes. To the boys from Shark Island, they had just devoured a royal feast. They felt deliriously happy when they left the restaurant, and on the way to the car, they innocently held hands just as they had done on many long sunset walks down the beach. They had just about reached their parking space when a car full of teenagers roared by screaming the words faggots and queers at them. One of the boys threw a bottle. Austin and Ryan reacted by letting go of their hands and shielding their faces. The bottle missed the intended target, but exploded into the side of the car next to Marvin's. Jessie and Marvin did not see the handholding, and thus they were confused why the teenagers selected them to yell and scream obscenities. Marvin's smile fell from his face. Quick-tempered, he shook his fist in the air and called the teenagers all kinds of names. After they were out of sight, he calmed down a bit and got in the car.

Sadly, Ryan's house sold years ago, so they spent the night in Jessie's apartment on a foldout sofa bed. It was lumpy and hard, and nothing like the bed at the Ramada Inn, but nonetheless, they were together. They decided to be careful, and not be sexually active since they were in the living room, and his sister's bedroom door was only six feet away. They quietly kissed, cuddled, and went to sleep.

NINETEEN

Ryan felt odd in Maine. If they had found the bodies of his parents and placed them in cemetery graves, he could visit their gravesite seeking closure. Part of him still needed to mourn and say goodbye. He spent the next day visiting relatives, aunts and uncles, cousins he knew, and some he did not know. He ran into a former neighborhood friend and chatted for a bit while Austin threw rocks in a pond. Having left when he was ten, Ryan no longer felt any strong connections to Maine. Even the reformed and now sweet Jessie seemed different to him. Before the shipwreck, Ryan had never shared a single intimate thought with his sister. She knew none of his secrets. She had been his enemy and she loved the role. He knew in his heart that he should love her, but it still just felt wrong, but he was thankful for her kindness to them.

They stayed a second night, and Marvin offered to treat everyone to a movie after dinner. Jessie made pizza, which the boys loved, but still they ate slow and sparingly. The movie was a new James Bond action adventure. They noted the crowded theater. The four of them sat about halfway down the aisle and in the middle of a long row. At times, the movie seemed tense, but something else bothered Ryan and Austin.

They had not sat in the middle of a large crowd of people in a long time. After being alone for almost eight years, suddenly they felt trapped and enclosed with hundreds of strangers. It made the boys feel closed in and claustrophobic. In the dark, Ryan slipped his sweaty palm into Austin's open hand. Austin felt nervous, squeezed Ryan's hand, but let go. That response puzzled Ryan, as Austin had never let go so quickly before, so Ryan pouted a bit by pulling his knees up to his chest and wrapped his arms around them. A grim expression appeared on his face. His stomach churned. He felt like he had gas. He tried to keep watching the movie, but his mind kept replaying their recent days since arriving in Key West.

Austin was apprehensive, too, and knowing Ryan as well as he did, he knew something was wrong. He put his arm around Ryan's shoulder and patted him a few times, while leaving his arm around him. That small amount of affection made Ryan feel better. James Bond suddenly leaped out of a plane and skydived his way to a beautiful island surrounded by gorgeous blue seawater. Bond crashed into the water and then made his way to the white sandy beach. Palm trees swayed in the background. The vegetation was green and fresh. Tropical birds were in the trees and bushes. The beautiful spectacular scenery suddenly mesmerized the boys. They felt like they were watching a movie about their own home. Oddly, they felt homesick, not for Maine or North Carolina, but for Shark Island.

The scene only lasted a few minutes as Bond leaped into a waiting jeep driven by a beautiful blond with big teats and clothed in a bikini. She whisked him off to a casino built in the center of the tropical island. The boys immediately lost interest in the story. Marvin had his arm around Jessie while she had her hand on his knee. No one could have cared less about this affection in a movie, but when Bond had reached the sandy beach, the bright scene suddenly lit up the theater. Marvin noticed that Austin had his arm around Ryan. He stared with a scowl at the boys, but they did not see him. Marvin began to remember the incident at the fast-food restaurant. His temper began festering. Jessie asked why the change in his mood and he nodded at her brother. Jessie's face became puzzled as she noted Austin's affection towards Ryan.

When the movie ended the four of them began walking to the car. Jessie whispered to Marvin, trying to get him to forget it while hoping to help him control his temper. Like most of the players on his basketball team, Marvin hated queers. The sight of a queer incensed him. He waited until they all four were in the car and then drove a few blocks towards home. After abruptly stopping at a red light by squealing his tires, Marvin's temper suddenly blew a fuse.

He jerked his head around so he could see the boys. "What the hell were you two lovebirds doing in the movie?" They instinctively knew it wasn't a really question but rather a way of yelling at them.

Startled, Ryan and Austin said nothing.

"Honey, don't. They have been away a long time. They had no one else," pleaded Jessie. She tried to justify it in her own mind, but she did not feel right about the boys holding hands either.

"That doesn't give them the right to be queers!"

Austin and Ryan's faces went pale. They pushed back into their seats, trying to get as far away from Marvin's menacing face as possible. They heard what he said. It bewildered them. It confused them. There was that word again, queers. They were only ten years old when they were last in the States. They did not know what the word queers meant. They also did not understand the word faggots. In addition, the phrase 'gay people' would have been even more of a mystery to them. The only new phrase they knew was when the teacher told them about Afro-Americans. That was not a big change for Ryan as he had hardly ever seen a black person. For Austin, he had heard the word nigger most of his life, but in his family they frowned on its use. The senator used the word black people, but never in the boys' lives had they heard any of their family members or friends use the word queer. The tone of the way people yelled it absolutely frightened them. They did not know what to say in response, so they sat in silence.

"Don't deny it! I saw you with your arm around Ryan like 'yous' guys were lovers or something! Do you kiss each other? Do you have sex?" He yelled as bits of his salvia fell in their lap.

Thankfully, the light turned green. Jessie punched Marvin's arm. She started to cry. She did not know what to think or do. She had seen them in the theater as well. She tried to think like a liberal, but the idea of a queer brother was not something she wanted. She felt somewhat open-minded, but not that tolerant.

They drove the final two blocks to their place in silence. When they got home, Marvin didn't cut the engine off and head for the apartment as usual.

"Aren't you coming in?" asked Jessie to him as she got out? The boys quickly got out as well.

"I ain't staying in a place with queers. I should shoot the dirty faggots. Get the hell out of my car!" He cursed at them and drove off squealing his tires.

Jessie started crying and ran to the apartment. Left standing in the street, Austin and Ryan wondered what all the fuss was about and what they should do.

Austin spoke up first. "I think we should leave, but if you want to stay, I'll understand."

"Do you mean me stay and you leave?"

"No. I'm not sure what is wrong, but I get the feeling that you and I shouldn't hold hands or show any kind of affection. I love you more than anybody in the whole world. I never thought of you and I as husband and wife. I just love you."

Ryan replied, "I know and I feel the same way. I even love the sex we do together, but I guess I felt like that was teenage stuff and we would grow out of it."

Austin thought about that answer for a while before answering. "I guess you're right. I mean I sometimes ache for your gentle touch. Maybe that is how a man aches for a woman. I don't know. Bond did well," he added with a grin.

The grin failed to work on Ryan. "I don't want you to leave. I don't even know what I'm doing here. I don't feel I belong here anymore. Maybe we should go."

"It's your call, it's your sister. I'm sorry all this happen."

Ryan thought for a long minute. "Let's go get our stuff and say thanks for letting us stay a while and make our goodbyes. We can hitch-hike to another town and get a motel room."

"Are we heading north, south, west, or east?"

"We can't go east we'd fall in the ocean," he said matter-of-factly, and then slowly grinned at the thought. "We're supposed to be heading to North Carolina so maybe we should go to Philadelphia or somewhere. At least we would be heading south," stated Ryan.

Jessie cried even more when Ryan said they were leaving. They both apologized, and said they would stay in touch, but the boys felt better once they were out of there. It felt like a heavy backpack of piled pressure fell off their shoulders. Jessie called Marvin the moment they left to get him to come home to her.

Ryan and Austin walked about two miles without saying a word to each other. They did not know what to say. Life seemed so much more complicated now than when they were ten. However, walking was something that was still easy for them as that was their only means of moving around for seven years. Walking felt like freedom to the boys. The only difference was that the darn new shoes still hurt their feet. A trucker picked them up, and by midnight, they were in Philadelphia, in a motel room, and once again enjoying each other's body before drifting off to sleep.

The next morning they decided to spend the day sightseeing around town. Austin had never been in the North before, and Ryan had only flown through Philadelphia, never getting a chance to go sightseeing. They bought a typical tourist map and started with the museums. By eleven o'clock, they were hungry, as they had not eaten any breakfast, so they found a corner market. There were several people just hanging around outside the store, and although they dressed differently, Ryan and Austin did not look at them. They went to the back of the market to the diary section and got a quart of milk. They missed the taste of fresh milk and just could not get enough of it. They also bought a package of cheddar cheese, something they missed from their childhood. They bought a small loaf of fresh bread, figuring the food would hold them over until supper. While Austin waited in line to pay, Ryan noticed Austin's collar partially turned in so he straightened it and gave Austin's neck a squeeze. They smiled and winked at each other. They failed to notice the people outside watching the two strangers.

Austin smiled pleasantly to the clerk, but the guy sneered in return, as if the boys were some lowlifes. He did not care whether they shopped again or not. Austin thought this response was just a typical Yankee attitude. Ryan was still thinking about Jessie while waiting for Austin.

As they left the store, the dozen or so fellows on the street corner stared Ryan and Austin up and down. One of them spoke towards them. "Hey, babes? How about a threesome with me?" He puckered his lips and blew a hateful mocking kiss at them.

They didn't have a clue as to what the man meant, but the tone of his voice and the tone of the laugher from his companions, frightened the boys. Ryan took Austin's elbow and pushed him on down the street because he could already see the veins enlarging on his friend's neck. He knew that if Austin lost his temper there would be a fight, and he did not think that would be smart for them to engage in. They had nothing to defend themselves with except bread, milk, and cheese. "Keep walking," whispered Ryan under his breath. "Just ignore them."

"Come on back, guys. I'll let you suck me right now," yelled a big black guy.

103

Austin turned around defiantly, but Ryan pulled him forward once again. They soon turned a corner, found a park bench a few blocks away, and sat down. Austin did not feel like eating at first, but Ryan kept talking to him while offering some of the food until finally Austin relented and ate.

"I don't think I like Philadelphia much," said Austin.

"I can't say I blame you. I don't think Philadelphia likes us either. You know what? I miss our island."

Austin grinned. "Me, too. I was thinking the same thing. We always do that, don't we? We tend to think the same or say the same thing. Weird, huh? People would laugh at us if we said we wanted to go back there, wouldn't they?"

"They'd probably lock us up," chuckled Ryan.

"I guess we need to figure out about going to school. Most guys our age are in college."

"I wouldn't even know what to study, and we've missed at least seven years of school. How do I know what I want to be when I grow up? Is a beachcomber an occupation?"

Austin replied, "I have no idea what I want to do either. I guess marriage will come soon, but I want my wife and I to live in the same town and near you. I'm not ready for us to separate. You're the only person I trust. You're my best friend," stated Austin solemnly.

"And you're mine. I love you, even when your veins pop up and you look like you're about to lose that temper of yours," teased Ryan.

"What temper?" pretended Austin slyly.

"You know what temper," replied Ryan looking around to where they were and for anyone that might be watching them. "I've lost interest in sightseeing."

Austin replied, "Me, too. Should we go to the airport and fly home to North Carolina?"

"Do you think I'd be welcome there?"

"Of course, you will. My mom thinks you're the greatest."

"But remember how Jessie reacted."

"I think the affection we show each other is fine. They're the ones with the problem, but I guess we should be careful in public. They just don't understand that we're best friends and yes, we do love each other."

"Maybe after we have kids and a wife…" started Ryan but Austin immediately laughed.

Ryan tousled Austin's hair. "What's so funny?"

"I think you mean a wife and then kids not the other way around."

"You're a smart aleck, aren't you?" shot back Ryan as he thumped Austin's head with his forefinger and took off running. Austin quickly chased after him.

TWENTY

They had been in North Carolina in the small town of Pisgah for over three months. The senator had only been home twice during that time and only for brief stops as he was busy on his re-election campaign. He tried to get the boys to let a reporter do a magazine article about them, and how he had saved them, but they both refused. Once he was gone, Bonnie told them she was once again proud they had stood up to him, and he probably would not challenge the issue again. They were also thankful that the reporters had already stopped calling and trying to arrange interviews. They finally became yesterday's news and this pleased them. The last story was with the local paper. Their reporter shot their picture a month ago, did a little story, but that was a onetime event. The next edition displayed opinions on the price of tobacco in the farm fields. The castaways were not a big deal in Pisgah. Everyone treated the boys like locals and they liked it.

Springtime in the mountains could not have been better. Everything was in bloom and the air smelled clean and pure. They began doing some of the outdoor skills they had always liked to do in the mountains at summer camp. They enjoyed hikes on and off the Appalachian Trail, which was not far from Austin's home, and Ryan especially marveled the famous trail led all the way to his home state. They agreed that would one day they would make the journey from the trail's beginning in Georgia all the way to Maine.

In May, Gary Bolt, the camp director at their old summer camp, made an urgent call to them. He had an idea after reading their story in the newspaper. He wondered if they would consider teaching a survival class as well as supervise various hiking groups at camp this summer? This thrilled the boys and Bonnie approved as well. So on the first of June, with great anticipation, they packed up their gear, which included most of the new clothes Austin's mom purchased, and headed off to camp just as they did when they were ten years old.

There they met a spirited and funny staff, and the boys soon felt at home. About three days before the kids arrived for the first session, the director announced they were having supper at their sister camp, and afterwards there would be a dance. Austin and Ryan suddenly became nervous because other than slow dancing together on the island to what little songs they could remember, they did not know how to dance.

"I think we're in trouble," protested Ryan.

"The dance?" guessed Austin.

"Right," he said slowly while nodding. "I don't think slow dancing to Silent Night in a fifty-foot tall tree house qualifies us as expert dancers." Ryan's tone was serious, but Austin busted out laughing anyhow.

105

"You're funny. Don't worry. I bet these big lugs from our staff don't know how to dance either. We'll fake it. At least we don't have to sit through another orientation class tonight."

"That was the best part about the dance announcement."

"Come on, let's hit the showers and get ready," said Austin as he tossed a towel into Ryan's face and took off running out the cabin door.

The showers at camp were similar to bathhouses at most camps, especially a camp for boys. The room was about six feet wide and twelve feet long, and there were eight shower nozzles all around the perimeter of the room with central drains in the center. The shower room always smelled musty and dampish in spite of the gallons of bleach sprayed everywhere throughout the summer. Mothers inspecting the camp facilities on visitor's day always turned their noses up at the room. Dads thought it was a rite of manhood.

Ryan and Austin were standing next to each other when two other staffers came in the shower to get ready, too. One of the boys was a kayaker from Dartmouth College. He was about two inches taller than Ryan, weighed about twenty pounds more, and was built like a college weightlifter. He had obviously been working out a lot. His neck bulged, his tummy was a washboard, and his biceps looked like they were ready to pop. His name was Jim. He talked like the jock that he was.

As Jim stuck his head under the shower spray he asked, "Hey, man, are you ready to party tonight?"

"Yeah, I guess so," replied Austin.

"I hear the babes are hot this year. I got a glimpse of a few at the airport," stated Jim.

"That sounds good," added Ryan feeling stupid.

Jim soaped himself up with ten times more lather than necessary and started playing with himself by shooting soap blobs off his member onto the floor. "Ooh, that feels good. I'm getting my tool ready for hot pussy tonight."

Austin and Ryan tried to avoid looking at Jim once they realized he was playing with his penis. They quickly finished their shower, dried rapidly, and hustled out the door still half-wet. Ryan did not say anything to Austin, but he felt like he was getting a hard-on in the shower. They quickly dressed, loaded up in the van with the rest of the staff, and headed out on the winding camp road to the party.

The staffers made many crude jokes about girls in the van, but Ryan and Austin just sat there very quiet and listening. When they arrived, they were more than glad to get off the van and head into the dining hall. The girls had decorated the place, and for a few awkward minutes, everyone just shyly stood there. The camp director for the girls was about seventy years old and probably seen everything and handled it. She managed this situation, too. She grabbed the hand of the closest girl to her and dragged her towards the first boy she found. It happened to be Ryan. His face turned a bright red blush as he introduced himself to Jennifer Hagan. The poor girl turned pink as well, especially when the entire audience burst in to applause. The director then ordered everyone to the middle of the dance floor and told the staff to dance. They did. The old woman smirked at Ryan's dancing ability, so she slapped him on the butt and said, "Shake that thing, honey! Loosen up and shake it!" The crowd laughed. Ryan turned even a darker shade of red as he rolled his eyes at Austin who was giggling and laughing as hard as any time in his life. He had somehow managed to escape and stand behind an upright piano.

The director, not one to waste any dance steps, grabbed Austin's hand, dragged him across the room, and introduced him formally to Jan Wilson. They, too, felt embarrassed as they were pushed to the dance floor. In just five minutes, the old camp director had every staffer on the floor having a great time. They made jokes about her, but in their hearts, they were grateful. She knew that, too.

Ryan and Jennifer were dancing to a rock and roll record. Ryan had only seen a little of the modern dance styles on a television show called American Bandstand. He did his best to copy Jennifer and keep his body moving, as Austin suggested. Austin was busy trying to follow his own advice because Jan did like to dance as she twisted and turned in every direction. Austin, clueless how to keep up with her, stiffly shifted from left foot to right and then right to left. At least he was moving, he thought.

After the first song, they all continued to dance and thankfully, Jennifer broke the ice by asking Ryan where he was from. It relieved him she knew nothing of the Austin and Ryan's adventure on Shark Island. He explained he was from Maine but now lived in Pisgah, and that he started coming to summer camp when he was just seven years old. He did not mention he had taken a break from camp for almost eight years, but added Austin was his longtime best friend.

Jennifer was from Charleston, South Carolina and hated the high humidity and the hot sweaty days of summer in her beautiful historic town. She went to a private school called Porta Gaude, and to Ryan, she seemed extremely smart. At the very end of describing her life, she all of sudden said that she was not a virgin.

Ryan nearly wet his pants, especially when she asked if he was a virgin. He said, "Of course not." He had no idea what a virgin was but he guessed it was somewhat sexual by the whispering way she said it.

Austin was breaking a sweat from all the dancing he tried to do while Jan seemed as cool as possible. Suddenly, they played a slow song, and she quickly wrapped her arms around his neck and pulled herself in close to him. He felt his penis hardening and it shocked him. She told him she was from Savannah, and that she and Jennifer were longtime friends just as he and Ryan

107

were. He doubted the girls were as close as he and Ryan but said nothing. She, too, wanted to get out of hot Savannah for the summer and escape her strict Catholic parents, so she became a staffer at the same camp she had attended since she was nine. A few times during the dance, she pivoted her hips and pushed her groin right into him. Austin began nervously sweating bullets.

They all danced for about an hour before finally taking a break. The girls led the boys out on to the deck to see the moon rising over the beautiful mountain lake. They loved the gorgeous setting. Frogs and crickets provided the background music, as did an occasional whippoorwill. The air felt cooler and Austin and Ryan were thankful, as they were both hot and worried.

After they engaged in mindless small talk for a while, the girls whispered something to each other, and then Austin watched as Jennifer led Ryan down the steps on a walk towards the lake. Jan then took Austin's hand and led him down the same steps, but she headed out in a different direction. The wise old camp director watched from the balcony.

"Stay in the main yard, girls. You know my policies. I'll break your butt if you do anything stupid," she warned.

"Yes, ma'am," the girls answered in unison.

The girls put their arms around each boy's slender waist and strolled innocently along the yard. Gingerly, the boys put an arm on the girl's waist. Unknown to the boys, the girls constantly kept an eye on the camp director while waiting for the right moment to occur. Sure enough, a few staffers came up to talk to the director, her stern beaming gaze averted for a moment, and in that split second the girls led the boys off into the woods. Ryan and Austin had no idea what the girls were up to. They were as uneducated, unspoiled, and about as innocent as a person could be.

Ryan and Jennifer end their walk at the archery range. He would have gladly showed off his skill with a bow, but she had stowed a blanket in the archery hut, and soon had Ryan pulled down on the blanket where she began feverishly making out with him. He had never kissed a girl, other than his mom, and had never kissed a girl like he had kissed Austin on Shark Island. Her hands roamed all over his body. A few minutes later she began squeezing on his penis. His body reacted accordingly. When he failed to reach and fondle her breasts, she encouraged him by undoing her blouse and putting his hands on her perky teats, while pushing her tongue farther down his throat.

Austin, surprised by Jan's boldness, followed the hot and horny girl quickly. She led him down to the boathouse. On a huge stack of orange life preservers, she managed to get his shirt off and her blouse off in less than a two seconds. She, too, played with his private parts while thrusting her tongue down his throat. She even rubbed her teats in this face and told him to lick them. He did. He felt weird. He had never felt like this.

108

Suddenly, a loud whistle blew.

"Oh no! She knows we're missing. Quickly dress and let's walk," Jan ordered.

Although in different parts of the yard, the girls started walking in the same direction once again in unison. The girls, experienced at sex and equally experienced at avoiding capture, knew exactly how to avoid the director's search. They casually walked towards the party and sneaked in through a side entrance. While the camp director searched all the usual make-out spots, Ryan, Jennifer, Austin, and Jan returned to the dining hall and began dancing on the floor. When the camp director returned, she felt surprised to see the foursome on the floor. She gave them a serious evil-eyed gaze to let them know she was indeed suspicious of their behavior. She felt like the girls might have won this round, but they would not win the next one.

Ryan and Austin heard all the talk in the van and obviously rumors were already spreading quickly that the two innocent boys from Shark Island had indeed been sharks with the girls. The boys denied nothing and let the stories grow, and thus at the beginning of this new camp season, they became known as the only two staffers who had scored on this first opportunity of the summer.

TWENTY-ONE

They had been back in the States only a few months, but Austin and Ryan quickly learned to be more cautious about their affection for each other. When you are a counselor of a cabin and living fifty feet away from the person you love most in the world, and surrounded by a hundred big eyed, big-eared campers, you have every reason to be cautious. Rumors can kill you in the camp business. Ryan and Austin thought a lot about the dance and the sexual activity with the girls, but this confused their minds about the affection they had for each other. Now they both had dreams about a girl's teats. They both could still feel the grope of the female bodies, but intertwined among those dreams were replays of their many special nights in the summer breezes in the tree house. Emotionally, the summer began just as bewildering as their return to the States.

On their first night off, Ryan and Austin decided to head for Brevard for a quiet dinner alone. Afterwards, they drove north up highway 276 to the Blue Ridge Parkway, and then turned south until they reached a popular tourist spot called Pendel Peak. This was the spot of their last rock climbing experience as campers. It was a special place because everyone had said it would be too tough, steep, and scary for the ten-year-olds to succeed. They bravely ignored all those put-downs and made it to the top anyhow. The reward for their determination was a picturesque three hundred and sixty-degree view of the famous Blue Ridge Mountains.

Today they arrived just before the spectacular summer sunset and leisurely took the tourist path to the top of the mountain. They did not need ropes for their journey up the newly paved path, just their strong legs. Soon they were sitting together and alone for the first time since orientation started three weeks ago.

Austin slipped his hand in Ryan's hand. Ryan squeezed it back and held on. It felt good to hold hands again. Soon they kissed once tenderly, and then they kissed again, and yet again, but far more passionately. As the bright yellow color of the sun slowly changed to a dark orange hue, they slipped out of their clothes, piled them on a huge flat rock, and made love. They had not experienced such a perfect amorous moment since leaving Shark Island. They would have stayed all night, but they had a midnight curfew. They missed the intimacy they shared for over seven years, and in a special way, they missed the peaceful world of Shark Island. The next opportunity to enjoy each other's body would not come soon enough.

After their night off to Pendel Peak, they began counting the days and looking forward to their first full day off. They planned to go hiking and camping alone in Shining Rock Wilderness after learning from the wilderness instructor that it was a beautiful and isolated forest. On the day before they were to leave, Ryan got a heavily doused perfume letter from Jennifer sent to him via the camp's mail. Jim spotted the assumed love letter and snatched it out of the mailbox. It was the camp's custom to give out the mail after concluding the lunchtime meal.

Campers and staff alike always looked forward to this special time of the day. They announced the recipient's name for each piece of mail, and everyone clapped and cheered for the guys who received mail. Once the end came to the dispersing the mail, Jim stood up. He said loudly, "I found this letter on the ground outside. I'm sorry it must have fallen out of the mailbag. It's for Ryan and it smells wonderful," he added slyly. "I bet it's from JENNIFER! You lucky dog!"

"Oooooo!" The entire devilish group replied in unison before laughing.

Ryan blushed. So did Austin. Jim made gestures with his pelvis as he delivered the unwanted mail to Ryan. Everyone started begging him to open it, but he quickly and firmly declined, and thankfully, the director saved him from more abuse by excusing everyone from their tables. The group trotted out of the dining hall for rest period. Ryan found a quiet spot and opened the envelope. There were two letters inside. He read his quickly and then walked towards Austin's cabin. Once close enough for Austin to hear, he whistled the birdcall of a whippoorwill. Austin was sitting on his bunk while his kids were taking their naps. He knew instantly who whistled.

He met Austin near the bathhouse. "Here's a letter for you. It was inside with mine. You were lucky they didn't call your name out. Go ahead, read it."

Austin read it quickly and blushed. "Jeez, they want to go hiking with us. How'd they find out we had a trip planned? What are we going to do?"

"I don't know. If we don't let them go people are going to talk about us."

"And they'll talk if we do, wouldn't they?" asked Austin knowing the answer.

"I think so. I don't like the position this has put us in. People will talk no matter what."

"I know, but hey, we are guys and they are girls, we've got to learn about this stuff some time."

Ryan sighed. "I know, but what about love. Aren't we supposed to be in love first?"

"I know what you mean. It seems from all I hear from the staff is that sex is sex and love is something entirely different. I don't think our fellow staffers give any thought to the latter, only the sex."

"It's not that way with us," stated Ryan.

Austin frowned. "I know, but we can't do it forever. We're supposed to marry, get a job, and …"

111

"Yeah, I know. Off the island, life sure is complicated, huh?"

Austin slapped him on the butt as they headed back towards camp. "What an adventure this is going to be," stated Austin sarcastically.

"Yeah, worse than Bobby boar chasing us through the jungle!" They both laughed.

It was the shortest hike Ryan and Austin had ever taken. The girls did not want to leave Austin's car. They managed to go a mile before they wanted to set up camp. They found a beautiful mountain stream where Austin spotted some trout swimming in little pools of water. He quickly forgot about the girls, cut a limb from a branch and started carving a spear. Ryan helped the girls set up the tent. The girls were more trouble than help as they kept deliberately asking Ryan to help them, and when he did, they took every opportunity to push their boobs into him or pinched his butt when he bent over. His face stayed a constant pink. Austin had speared eight trout by the time the trio finished the campsite. No staff member using a modern rod and reel had ever caught that many fish in so short a time, but Austin practiced spear fishing almost every day for seven years. He learned to fish for survival. He brought the fish back to camp to clean.

"Hungry?" he asked because nothing else would come to mind.

"Hey, you did good partner," said Ryan with a grin while giving his friend a thumb up sign. He was thankful that Austin was back. He felt way out of his league with the amorous girls. He wished he had gone fishing as well.

Jan and Jennifer replied in unison, "You killed them? The poor little fishes."

Ryan rolled his eyes and grinned slyly. Austin laughed. "Well, time to clean them. Want to help?"

"Not on your life," stated Jan flatly.

Austin shrugged his shoulders, found a flat rock to work on, knelt down and went to work. Ryan started building a fire. The girls chose to help Ryan, as he did not smell like the fish. In an hour or so, Austin served the grilled fish with some potatoes and corn they brought from the camp kitchen, while Ryan cut a fresh cantaloupe into quarter moon shaped slices. The girls were surprised at how well the dinner tasted, so they placed Austin once again in their good graces even though he now smelled a bit fishy.

After dinner, Jan leaned over to thank Austin for the dinner and kissed him. "Oooo," she said as she held her nose. "You smell like fish!"

Austin blushed. Ryan laughed. Jennifer giggled.

"That was too mild. Austin smells more like a dog that's treed a skunk," teased Ryan. "You need a bath."

"You're right," stated Austin trying not to sound disturbed by their comments. He was determined not to let the teasing get to him. "Last one in is a horse's pa-toot!" Austin quickly slid out of his shoes, stood up and pulled his tee shirt over his head. Not to be outdone, Ryan followed suit. The girls sat there astonished. For days, they had planned and schemed all kinds of conniving ways to try to get the boys out of those clothes, and without even dropping a hint, their clothes were flying in the air everywhere.

With no worry or thought of modesty, Austin dropped his canvas shorts, slipped out of his underwear, and started running for the river. Ryan dropped his pants, too, and off he trotted to the cold water. He looked back over his shoulder at the girls as they sat there with their mouths open. They were staring at the handsome young men and their lean, well-tanned bodies. Ryan grinned and yelled, "You girls too shy to join us!" He then galloped and dove off a rock into the water where Austin was already swimming.

Not to be outdone, the girls giggled and scooted out of their clothes, and ran full speed to the water. The boys did not know it, but skinny-dipping was also a big activity at the girls' camp. The only difference was now there were boys present. They splashed and played like kids for a while, but the water was too cold for the ladies so they soon retreated to the fire.

Austin was still playing when Ryan turned to watch the girls walk carefully over the rocks towards the camp. Without shoes, the pebbles and stones hurt their tender feet. Austin grinned and then dove under the clear cold water, swam behind Ryan, and stuck his head beneath Ryan's balls and blew bubbles before gently caressing them as he surfaced behind Ryan.

"You're crazy. They could have seen you," warned Ryan in a whisper, but without a smile.

"So, I don't care. We're just playing."

"I'm going to drown you," replied Ryan slyly as he leaped on top of Austin and pushed him playfully underwater. For the next twenty minutes, the boys took turns throwing the other in the air and playing in the water just as they had done off Shark Island. What the girls did not see was the grabbing of each other's privates, the underwater kisses, and a little massaging of their private parts.

When they joined the girls at the fire, the girls had toasted marshmallows and fed one to each of the boys. The boys dried off with their towels, and then loosely draped the towels around their waists, but the girls had no plans for those towels to stay there. The boys soon discovered the contriving amorous girls had hid their clothes. Jennifer led Ryan towards the tent, instantly removing his towel, and pulling him to her sleeping bag. Soon they were busy making out. Jan had rolled her bag out by the fire so she took Austin's hand and placed it inside her open blouse. She kissed him deeply while pulling his towel from his waist. His erection rose immediately.

Though inexperienced when it came to girls, the boys had nothing to worry about as the girls took complete charge of the situation. The girls brought condoms and expertly applied them to the boys in just a few seconds. Austin and Ryan had never even seen a condom. They had no use for them on Shark Island, and no use in the States since until now as they had only made

113

love to each other. Without checking on the progress of the other, they soon had the boys on their backs. The girls planted themselves on top of the boys' swollen member, and rode it hard and fast, while moaning loud enough to drive even the early evening cricket chatter away. At least three times over the next few hours, the boys and their tools found action. Austin and Jan soon entered the tent as the mosquitoes and 'no-see-ums' were after them, and by midnight, the girls were asleep.

Austin tried to sleep but remained wide-awake. His mind was replaying the evening with the girls. He guessed he liked Jan, but not like he loved Ryan. That made the sex different from what he did with Ryan. He decided he should give it more time. He recalled that more than once he found himself thinking of Ryan when Jan played with penis. Austin did not feel passion with Jan, but it was fun and it felt good.

Ryan remained on his side with Jennifer cuddled in his arms. His back was to Austin who also held Jan until she fell asleep, but a while later Jennifer rolled away from him. Ryan turned on his back to think for a while.

Austin sensed Ryan was awake, so without a word said, he gently slipped his hand beneath Ryan's open sleeping bag and touched his bare skin. Austin instantly became erect though his penis felt sore from all the action. Ryan gently turned to face Austin. He quietly leaned over and kissed him, whispered good night in his ear, then took Austin's hand in his and soon all four of them were fast asleep.

TWENTY-TWO

The foursome dated all summer, but at the end of the camp session, the girls headed back east while Austin and Ryan went back to Brevard. Being around all the other staffers that went to college helped them decide they should try to go as well. The family delighted in the decision. Registering so late seemed impossible, but the senator pulled some strings and presto, the boys drove the following weekend to Chapel Hill, North Carolina to attend the University of North Carolina. They had heard from friends that the school's basketball team was the best in the country, and they both liked to shoot hoops. The school's population was well over twenty thousand students. The beautiful sprawling campus required they keep a folded map in their rear pocket to keep from getting lost. Because of their circumstances and the senator's influence, they found themselves excused from the usual entrance exams, but instead began remedial classes to try to accelerate the education they missed. They did not have a dream or a plan of what they would do when they graduated, but together they felt happy to be there. They made friends, dated the girls assigned as their tutors, and managed to stay in school.

A week before Thanksgiving, Austin began crossing campus on the way to class when he heard this man yelling from the center of a crowd of students. As he walked closer, he realized the man had begun preaching by standing on a park bench and yelling at the top of lungs. The man's pale face contrasted with the purple blood veins bulging in his neck as he continued to scream out his sermon. By endlessly quoting scriptures, he denounced and condemned all homosexuals. Out of the thousands of verses in the Bible, he chose to use only the ones he felt made his case, and conveniently left out verses like "Love on another" or "Be kind to one another." A smaller group of gay students began arguing with him. Some of the crowd disagreed with the preacher while others started calling the gays queers.

Austin stood there, desperately trying to put the puzzling pieces of information together. Everyone talked at the same time, but not even the crowd of fifty could drown out the loud and experienced street preacher. Austin climbed up on another bench so he could see. He saw several of the gays and lesbians defiantly holding hands with their partners. Two men deeply kissed just to piss off the preacher and it surely did. The preacher said the heathens would go straight to hell. A gay person replied by yelling that would be the only time they would go straight anywhere. The students began pushing one another just as the campus police arrived. Quickly the cops disbursed the crowd while escorting the uninvited and unauthorized preacher off the campus.

Austin had listened to all the comments the crowd made. The event left him feeling astounded. He went straight to the library and looked up the words he had heard: gays, homosexuals, faggots, and queers. He then sat still thinking while digesting the facts. He began running his thoughts repeatedly

115

in his brain like a computer working a giant math problem. He looked up a few books about gays, and quickly scanned through the pages of information. His vocabulary remained at a young adolescent level so some words went right over his head, but he wrote each unknown word down so he could look up the definitions in the dictionary. He studied intensively for several hours before finally leaving, and even then he did not return immediately to his room. He walked around campus still pondering what he had learned. In his head, he recalled what he had read and heard, but in his heart, he knew the day's events and revelations had changed him forever. The man he loved waited for him in their dorm room, but he feared the new knowledge could doom their special friendship.

Austin had told himself that he and Ryan would grow out of the sex they enjoyed between each other, but he knew his love for Ryan would silently continue. Often he dreamed about Ryan, especially during this past summer at camp where they slept apart for the first time since returning from the island. Their sexual activity continued to slow down since the beginning of the summer. Jennifer and Jan kept the boys busy this past summer, and now that everything was out in the open, well, almost everything, they had made a good foursome for going out, bowling, parties, movies, and dinners.

Austin knew the attraction was progressing for Ryan and Jennifer. He thought nothing of it at first, but now he began to feel like he was going to lose Ryan. Just yesterday, Ryan received an invitation from Jennifer to spend Thanksgiving in Charleston with her family. Austin reacted fairly by saying he knew he would have a good time and called him a lucky dog. However, after Ryan left the room for class, Austin fell on his bed, chewed his lip nervously, and nearly started to cry. He became depressed and could not sleep. He did not want to lose the friendship he had with Ryan, and wondered if he was a homosexual and perhaps Ryan was not. Austin knew he would have to let Ryan go. It was a lot to consider and worry over, and he didn't exactly like what he knew might happen if and when he told Ryan his thoughts.

Austin did not think of himself as homosexual. He knew he felt attracted to other guys, but he had never had male sex with anyone but Ryan. He wondered if perhaps because he loved Ryan's gorgeous body that this caused his attraction to other men. Nevertheless, maybe he was not gay. After all, he had sex with Jan on many occasions. Austin's feelings remained mixed up. For the next several nights he often remained awake.

Feeling desperate, he decided to call Jan to wish her a happy Thanksgiving, thinking perhaps she would invite him to Charleston as well, and then he and Ryan could go together. She kept the conversation polite and sweet, but said she met someone else and naturally, she was no longer interested in Austin. She ended the call by telling him she would not be back to summer camp next year. He knew their fling was now officially over. He knew he would miss Ryan when he went to Charleston alone, but the lost of Jan as a girlfriend did not bother him at all.

He spent most of Thanksgiving weekend by himself in Brevard, and then reluctantly returned to school alone. On Ryan's return, Austin politely listened as he bragged about all the things he and Jennifer did in Charleston. He tried to appear too busy to listen to all the details, and soon packed up his stuff and headed off to the library. He tried hard not to show it, but he felt hurt when Ryan returned from the trip and gave him a good hug, but left off the usual kiss Austin had been waiting all weekend for. Despite his age, he could not help but pout a bit.

Three quick weeks passed and then their assignments were finally finished. There were no more papers to write or exams to take, and temporarily their freedom from studying had finally been achieved. They were adapting to the college world and studying better than anyone thought they could. Thanks to the good and friendly tutors, they covered much ground this semester, and hoped by next fall to be able to take college entry-level courses. After their last class, they rapidly packed their car and headed west on Interstate 40 to their home in the Pisgah Mountains. Mom prepared their favorites for the dinner that night. The senator flew down from Washington, and the house became a buzz of commotion, most of it political in nature, as he had spent Wednesday visiting with local political contacts. Bonnie recently completed the ardent task of sending photo Christmas cards to all the people who helped the senator, their friends and co-workers, and their families. They included Ryan in this year's picture indicating he was a special nonofficial member of the family. It made Ryan feel good to be a part of Austin's family. The senator secretly hoped the social adoption of Ryan made him appear more compassionate to the voters.

Austin hoped the time home for the holidays would be a revival time for him and Ryan. They had not been as close this past four months, as intimacy in a dorm remained almost impossible. Their lengthy and difficult studies, plus Ryan's romance with Jennifer, contributed to the lack of sex between the two friends. The next morning Ryan and Austin went on a winter hike on a day that began with temperatures in the thirties. Thankfully, the bright blue sky and the crisp clean air increased their enthusiasm for the hike. As the sun began to climb it provided some heat to their cold hands and faces. The leaves on the trees had long blown away, thus improving the breathtaking distant views of the mountains of Western North Carolina. The valleys, filled with sections of fog that appeared to just cling to the rivers, gave the area a smoke-filled, forest fire appearance. This type of daily view gave the Smoky Mountains their name. They hiked most of the day, but took a break about two o'clock to sit on the edge of a cliff on a huge rock. They dangled their legs over the side while taking in the awe-inspiring view.

117

As they sat there taking in the view, Austin slipped his hand in Ryan's and squeezed it. Ryan did not squeeze it back as he had done on most other occasions until now. Austin noticed it immediately. An unforeseen chill ran up his back. After they talked for a while, Austin put his arm around Ryan, and soon leaned over to kiss him. Ryan kissed him back but only briefly. He broke away and stood up.

"What's the matter?" asked Austin, defensively put off and almost angry at the rebuff.

"I don't think we should make out anymore," stated Ryan swiftly and boldly.

"And why not?" asked Austin, though he knew why in his heart.

"Guys don't do that. I think I am in love with Jennifer. She's coming up to school the week we go back to Chapel Hill as her classes start a week later."

"Oh," replied Austin dejectedly.

"Don't do that!" exclaimed Ryan as he threw a rock off the cliff as far he could.

"Do what?"

"Give me that pout look of yours. You knew we had to grow out of it sometime. I love you Austin. I'll always love you, but I'm not in love with you. Do you understand?" Ryan came back and sat down.

Austin stared out across the tops of the trees below them. He threw a stick off the side of the cliff and watched it roll over and over to the bottom. "I love you, too," he finally said.

"Then you agree," urged Ryan wanting to get this subject behind them.

"You want me to agree not to hold your hand, not to kiss, not to...."

Ryan cut him off in mid-sentence. "Stop it! Don't even say it. I don't want to have sex with you anymore, but I don't want to stop loving you. We can hug occasionally in private, and I might even kiss you on the top of that ugly head of yours, but if I love Jennifer, then I should only make out with her." Ever the diplomat Ryan made a desperate attempt at humor, hoping to lighten the conversation up a bit.

"We've had some good times, haven't we?" asked Austin, but it was more of a statement than question.

"Yes, we have, but now that we're back, we've got to get on with our lives. You'll always be a special part of my life, just not my wife," laughed Ryan.

"I know," replied Austin somberly.

"How's the relationship with you and Jan?"

"I like her, but I don't think the attraction is there like you and Jennifer. I know very well why Jennifer is attracted to you. I know your body inside and out, pardon the pun. I don't think Jan sees me as a handsome dude, or something," he added.

"Wrong. You're handsome. Not as handsome as me, mind you," laughed Ryan, "but second only to me. Start shopping for another woman. You and I have some catching up to do when it comes to girls."

"You know, it's weird. If we were still on the island, we'd still be in love with each other and still doing it."

Ryan got angry. "Drop it, Austin. We're not on the island and we're not queers!"

Austin had never heard him use that word.

Ryan continued, "I know what it means. I looked it up one day in the library. That's when two guys are in love with the other. Austin, you and I are special to each other, but that's it. Come on, let's go!"

Ryan stood up and started walking without looking back to see if Austin was coming. Austin sat a moment longer, threw another stick over the side of the cliff, then reluctantly stood up and followed. The rest of the day they were civil to each other, but had little to say. The ride home became a long quiet trip.

That night Austin replayed the day's events over and over like a video stuck on replay in his mind and slept little. He felt as if the doctor had told him he had cancer and only a few days to live.

In the past three and half years, Austin and Ryan caught up on their education and excelled. The self-discipline, forced on them on the island, now paid off at home. They possessed a stronger capacity to concentrate on a single task, and soaked up studying and learning with a far more determined spirit and maturity than most college kids. They were no longer afraid to ask questions in class, and many a professor survived a round of twenty questions from the boys after class in their office. Ryan graduated with a degree in English and minor in education. He had decided to become a teacher. Austin graduated with a degree in business. He had no idea why he picked the business field, but to him it was better than choosing English or politics as a major. The senator, as usual, lined up a job for him with a friend of his at a North Carolina bank. During college, Austin became interested in computers and luckily, the new job involved collaborating account accuracy involving computer work. Austin started training for his new job just two days after graduation at the bank's Raleigh headquarters.

In two weeks, Ryan planned to marry Jennifer. Naturally, Ryan chose Austin as his best man. Bonnie, excited about the wedding, assisted Jennifer where she could. Jennifer chose the famous First Baptist Church of Charleston for the special event. Ryan attended the church services in this two-century-old church on several occasions with Jennifer and her family. Thanks to Bonnie's help, a nearby Brevard School became his first teaching position. Jennifer and Ryan would be living in a small house Bonnie also arranged for them. Although thrilled they would remain in her part of the state, Bonnie felt like she lost her own son to Raleigh, while keeping her

119

adopted son nearby and gaining a daughter-in-law. She thought how great it would be to have a grandchild to spoil. Above all, she would miss Austin dearly. They had been close when he was little, somewhat close when he returned from Shark Island, but in her heart, she knew he was growing distant, and it worried her immensely. She had no idea why.

Several of their school and camp friends flew into Charleston for the wedding. They rented several rooms on the top floor of the historic Francis Marion Hotel, a recently refurbished four-star hotel overlooking the infamous Charleston Harbor. The view of Fort Sumter, the site of the start of the civil war, was breathtaking from the suite of rooms on the top floor. Ryan politely complimented the senator and Bonnie for the great view, because he knew the senator paid for it and his adopted father always got what he wanted.

Their pals threw a wild bachelor party for Ryan including a local stripper they hired for the occasion. They also drank a lot of booze, a whole lot. When the party was over, they stumbled to the room. Ryan was smashed. Austin somehow remained only slightly drunk. As they undressed, Ryan playfully popped Austin on the fanny with his bare hand. Austin responded by throwing a pillow at him that knocked the intoxicated and weaving Ryan to the floor after bouncing off the bed. They busted out laughing. Ryan crawled around bed, struggled to his feet, and managed to get a headlock on Austin. He pulled Austin around in circles, trying to give Austin a noogie, but Austin deflected Ryan's attention by yanking Ryan's underwear down. When Ryan let go to reach for his shorts, Austin tried to run from Ryan's grasp. Ryan forgot about his fallen shorts, but did get a good grip on Austin's underwear and accidentally ripped them right off as he tried to leap out of reach. They both stood there naked. They gasped at the revelation. It has been a long time since they had seen the other naked.

"I'm sorry, man. I didn't mean to rip 'em," muttered the drunk, but always well manner and apologetic Ryan. He then impolitely burped rather loudly. His face flushed as it turned into a sheepish grin.

"Right, you're just wanting one last piece of my good butt before you go and marry Jennifer," teased Austin.

"It's your mouth that's good, not your butt," shot back a giggling Ryan.

"Oh, is that so. I remember a time when I couldn't get you off me!"

"You loved it and you know it," bragged Ryan.

"That was the good old days before you went and fell in love with a woman."

"You can marry, too, you know," added Ryan before burping again.

Austin sighed as he walked back over to Ryan who stood there naked and already slightly aroused. "You may not have noticed, but I don't even have a girlfriend."

"You'll find the right woman. Just keep looking."

Ryan stopped and through bleary eyes, he stared at Austin's groin. He chose not to say anything, but instead reached over and began playing with Austin's penis as he had done on Shark Island. Austin fell on the bed. They began making out and having sex as they had done so many times before on the island. Austin, more sober than Ryan, threw everything he had into their lovemaking. He pushed back and squeezed with inner butt and leg muscles as Ryan went deeper and deeper into him. Ryan responded with great enthusiasm. When done with Austin's butt, he spun him around and sucked every possible drop out of his penis. Two hours later, they both passed out in each other's arms.

Ryan woke up about ten the next morning when the house cleaner knocked on the door to touchup the room. Surprised to find Austin in his arms, he became alarmed at the discovery of their nudity. He tried to recall the evening but his head hurt. Holding a pillow over his groin, he told the housekeeper to come back later. Austin turned over, woke up, and out of old habit tried to pull Ryan to him.

"Stop it!" said Ryan as he left the bed. "I can't believe this happen."

"It's okay. We haven't done it in years. You're getting married. It was a last fling. I know you love me and you know I love you, and yes, I know you're not in love with me," stated Austin without saying he was in love with Ryan.

"Get in the shower," added Austin when Ryan did not reply. "I'm starving."

Ryan nodded and got in the shower. No words would come to his recovering, alcohol infused brain. His thoughts remained perplexed as he let the hot water pour of his body. He had played around with Austin last night though he knew by the standards he had learned since returning to the States it had been wrong to do so. He would be lying to all, especially himself, if he said he did not enjoy it, but he would never tell Austin that thought. Austin has to grow up, he thought as he washed his hair. Austin has to find someone, too, and once he does, then all will be well, and the four of them will be the best of friends. He hoped it would happen that way because he feared losing Austin altogether.

TWENTY-THREE

After the wedding and for the first time since their return from the island, they were no longer living together. Austin went back to Raleigh to work, and Ryan and Jennifer went on their honeymoon to the Bahamas. Afterwards they returned to the house in Brevard that Bonnie and Jennifer decorated. Except for a few days, Austin and Ryan had been together every day for over a decade. Now it had been a month since they went their separate ways. Austin had trouble sleeping because every time he tried his mind would rewind like a videotape and replay the lovemaking sessions on Shark Island, or the last time he and Ryan had done it in Charleston. He masturbated every night and many a morning with eyes clad shut to help recall his visions of their lovemaking.

Austin ate lunch at the same restaurant every day. Not because the food was exceptional, but simply because of its proximity to the bank office, and he did not have to drive to get there. His over-the-fire cooking skills did not work too well in his apartment, so he rarely made dinner at home. He usually ate out for lunch, making it his big meal of the day. Though they briefly talked twice on the phone, it had been three months since he had seen Ryan. During today's lunch, Austin met someone. Austin studied the waiter approaching his table. He guessed the young man to be about twenty-three years old, tall, with tanned skin, smooth face, brown hair, and beaming blue eyes. Austin noticed the eyes first. The waiter's neon radiant smile came second.

"I'm Gregory, I'll be your waiter," began the waiter as he set a fresh glass of ice water in front of Austin and handed him a menu.

Austin interrupted him with a smile and quick quip, "That's a relief, for a minute there I thought you were my dentist!"

The comment so stunned Gregory he actually giggled and snorted. His tiny nostrils flared in and out just a bit, like a horse's nostrils when he neighs and snorts. Austin laughed when he saw the nostrils of the waiter turn a shade of pink. It became a special moment for them.

"Okay, okay. I see I have a hostile patron, and that means I get to take matters into my own hands," teased Gregory.

"Okay, Gregory. I'll play along. What would I like to eat today?"

Gregory blushed again. Austin suddenly realized Greg was gay so he quickly added, "I mean food, dude! What special creation has the chef done up today?" Austin was not sure why he knew Gregory was gay. He was not excessively feminine, nor did he act gay. He wore no pink triangles nor carried a rainbow pen. His hair and his clothes were spotless. His eyebrows brushed. He wondered how many guys brush and maintain their eyebrows? However, he had long ago learned gays possessed something unique, which

122

remained unseen by the heterosexuals, but it outed gays to other gays. They called it 'gaydar'.

Gregory rolled his eyes. His heart skipped three scheduled beats. He felt himself immediately attracted to Austin. He had never seen such glowing skin and remarkable fluid eyes. He became captivated with him and could not stop stealing glances. He became warm and began fanning himself with the menu. Their conversation fell into slow motion. He felt his smile widening more than usual. He gulped, "Oh, well, let's see, for starters, we have egg drop soup that is to die for. I know this isn't a Chinese restaurant, but you're going to love it. While you're eating that, I'm going to bring you the pasta with chicken, topped with grilled cashews, and I guarantee it will be the best chicken you've ever tasted." Gregory did not have a clue why he had suddenly become so bold. He had been waiting tables for about a year now, and he had never said those words to any of his customers. He felt his decision to change jobs to this restaurant from across town had been a good one. Besides, he had grown tired of the redneck clientele at Sam and Joe's Barbecue House.

"Sounds great. I'll have ..." began Austin.

Greg broke in, "Ice tea, sweet tea to be exact, with a lemon to be even more precise. You always like tea, never a good stiff drink."

"I work for a bank. They expect you to be sober when handling their money."

"What a shame. Okay, I'm off and running. I know you'll miss me, but I'll be right back," giggled Gregory bravely. He felt both amazed and at ease with Austin, very much like waiting on an old friend.

Austin laughed. He was enjoying the moment. This had never happen to him before, a gay waiter flirting with him. Thankfully, the lunch crowd today was a little sparse. Gregory had just another couple to wait on so he spent more time than required with Austin. They quickly became lunch friends, but after a few days, Gregory became a bit bolder.

"Austin, I might be fired for this, but would you like to go dancing tonight?"

The offer came unexpected. Austin looked up into Gregory's beaming blue eyes. He saw a hopeful glow in them. The eyes begged him to say yes, and the eyes relayed he would be safe with his new friend. Austin thought for a long second. Gregory thought the moment lasted a lifetime. He felt like his heart momentarily stopped beating. Austin was in a town where none of his family lived. No one knew him other just a few office people. He thought, why not?

"I'd love to," said Austin.

Gregory's heart immediately started pumping again. "Would eleven be okay?"

"Eleven? Why so late?"

"Are you new to the scene?" asked Gregory cautiously.

"Yes."

"It's a late crowd. Go home after work. Take what we call a bar nap so you won't yawn while we're dancing, and dress nicely because I want to show my new handsome friend off to all my friends. Can you meet me at Ingles on Walker Street at eleven?"

"Yes. I know where it is."

"Good. Ciao. I'll see you soon!" Gregory spun around like an ice-skater and floated his way to the kitchen. Austin paid his bill, laughed at his boldness, and then began having a series of second doubts about what he had done.

Austin had spent a nervous evening trying to figure out whether he should go or not. He took a nap as suggested. Afterwards he showered, headed out the door, and drove to the Ingles grocery store. He found Gregory leaning against his car waiting for him. He had changed clothes from his usual black pants and vest, and white shirt, or standard wait staff issue, and instead wore a handsome sport shirt and jeans. It was the first time Austin had seen him without his uniform. He grinned slyly at the new and improved Gregory.

"I thought you might not show," said Gregory as he leaned over to Austin's car and shook his hand.

Austin asked, "Am I late?"

"No, and by the way, if you call me Gregory tonight, I'll have to kill you!" teased Gregory.

"I thought that was your..."

"Only at work. The owner thinks it makes our place appear classy. I think it makes me feel like a dork. Just call me handsome, call me gorgeous, or if that's a bit too much, just call me Greg!" They both laughed. "Come on, we'll take my car. I'll show you around Raleigh because I can tell you're new here."

Austin agreed and soon they were visiting a few tourist spots along with the key state government buildings, since Raleigh is the capital of the state, and then suddenly, they pulled into a parking lot in a dreary part of town. It would have been a perfect place for one of the senator's television commercials promoting the need for his urban revitalization got-to-have-your-vote programs. However, as soon as Greg cut off engine, Austin could hear the music blaring from the building just ahead of the car. He adjusted his eyes to the poor lighting and found the lot filled with cars. As they began walking towards the music he spotted many more cars all around the place, as well as parked up and down every possible side street and over the curb. It only took him a full sixty seconds but alas, he caught on to the sight of only men walking towards the entrance. Some held hands. Many of the men laughed and teased the other. Austin took in the jaw-dropping scene. The gay men delighted in this late night freedom to express their affection to the love of their choice. The disenthrallment stirred him deeply.

124

"Don't be nervous when we go in because you're going to be the star attraction. Everyone loves a newcomer," stated Greg as he ushered Austin through the door. They stood in line to pay at the counter while chatting nonsense about their busy day. Austin stared at the posters announcing upcoming drag shows, and dropped his jaw at a huge poster of a famous male stripper scheduled to appear in two weeks. Once they paid, the electric lock on the inside door clicked and then opened to reveal a packed dance club. The fire marshal license on the wall stated the club had a capacity of three hundred people. Austin easily guessed over four hundred men were dancing on the dance floor, in the aisles, and even on the bar. The sheer numbers amazed Austin. He thought gays were a minority. Secretly, he increasingly read everything he could about homosexuals. He even read Raleigh's gay newspaper in the library. He knew the club name from an ad he had seen there. This was the place to be, he thought. Although the flashing lights blared into his eyes, he noted various men sizing him up and down as they walked by. It made him feel like a celebrity. His face displayed a huge smile. Greg grabbed his hand and pulled him through the crowd and up a few steps to a well-lit dance floor. Austin, shocked to see hundreds of people dancing, quickly did the math. At least ninety-five percent were men and most likely gay or gay friendly. He spotted a few lesbians and fag hags dancing, but mostly the hot, shirtless guys filled the floor. Greg never gave him a chance to back out of dancing, but squeezed his hand a little tighter and pulled him to the center of the dance floor.

Austin, though nervous at first, soon relaxed in midst of hundreds of men dancing. The crowd was so tight he was sure no one could see his feet anyhow. As the minutes ticked by, he began feeling better. He forgot how lonely he felt in Raleigh. He even forgot about Ryan, at least for a time. The packed dance floor hid his poor dancing skills, but it really didn't matter as no one cared if he could dance or not. They liked his cute face and awesome butt. Greg chatted with him by yelling in his ear, teased him a bit about being so gorgeous, and they just kept on dancing and laughing. The more he chilled the better Austin danced. They took a break after an hour to get a beer. Greg had to pee so he temporarily left Austin at the bar. Ten seconds later a handsome dude with tons of muscles leaned into Austin and asked him his name. Austin pulled away and replied politely.

The man said, "You look good enough to eat."

Austin blushed. "I'm sorry. I've got to pee." He quickly darted away before the man could reply. His face became hot and pink. In the first hour of being inside the club, he received at least twenty compliments, and he soon lost count of how many times someone gently pinched his butt. He liked it all. His confidence soared. Greg knew everybody and soon Austin felt like he had met most of the entire huge crowd. They danced and drank until four in the morning. Lacking the stamina of a great dancer like Greg, Austin became exhausted and thought Greg might have to carry him out. Finally, they said their goodbyes to some of Greg's friends and began walking back to Greg's car.

Greg suggested they go by his place and Austin, feeling euphoric, easily agreed. Greg grinned approvingly and placed a warm hand on Austin's inner thigh. Austin felt he had gone this far in his exploration of the gay world, so psyched with a few beers and his worn out dancing legs, he decided he wanted to know what it felt like to make out with another man. Once inside Greg's apartment, they sat and talked on the couch for a while before Greg started making out with him and Austin let him. It felt different but his body reacted accordingly. He felt guilty for thinking of Ryan a few times. He knew it probably was not fair to Greg, but Austin kept his thoughts of Ryan to himself. He enjoyed the sex. It felt wonderful to be touched again, as it had been so long since another human had caressed him. He enjoyed the flattery. He especially enjoyed the playing around. Greg became a great first date, but for now, he was not in love with Greg because he was still in love with Ryan. He knew he must give up his desire for Ryan before he could be really happy with someone else. Austin felt he would need more time to accomplish that task.

TWENTY-FOUR

Over the next two years, Austin became a regular at the gay clubs. On the dance floor, he could be himself. He accepted the fact that he preferred the company of men, but still could not call himself a homosexual to others. His brain kept replaying all those nasty phrases people said to the gays on campus. He also knew his associate employees hated queers. He felt the whole world hated gays as they often used the popular fag insults as just something they said to their friends in jest. Every weekend he scooped up the latest gay newspapers on the table as he exited the clubs. He read everything he could get his hands on that contained the word gay in it. The guilt began piling up on him. He kept his gay life secret from everyone, including his mom, the senator, the bank, and especially Ryan. He did not particularly enjoy keeping it from Ryan, as he had always been the one that Austin could be open and honest with. With Ryan now married and in Brevard, and Austin single in Raleigh, there just wasn't much for them to talk about. The phone calls became less and less between them. That left him with no one to share his new feelings. Greg had been honorable and kind enough to teach Austin about safe sex. After reading several articles on sexually transmitted diseases, Austin made sure he always used a condom. He and Ryan never had these problems in their paradise on Shark Island. Daily he felt the need to be touched. They made him feel handsome. However, he never believed anyone when they said they loved him. Ryan's love still mattered to Austin. His feelings for Ryan remained strong, so he countered by dating many guys, but always kept his distance, afraid his love for Ryan would dwindle if he began caring for another guy.

As the months went by, he called Ryan and Jennifer even less and only went to see them twice in two years. In fact, he didn't come home to see his mother who always wanted him to stay a while longer. He felt home was too close to Ryan, and he would felt obligated to see him. Home felt like returning to a cage while Raleigh gave him the freedom he wanted.

Jennifer wanted a child but they had not yet conceived. It was not from the lack of trying, bragged Ryan in one of their few conversations. Austin replied that Ryan probably had a low sperm count because of all the wild boar and goat meat he ate as a child. They both laughed at the silly response because the conversation felt awkward. When they were alone taking a walk, or fishing for trout, it was like what he called the good old days, at least it was how Ryan felt. For Austin, it was a difficult time of self-control. Now that he had experienced the joy of gay sex, and met numerous gay couples that spent years together remaining proud to be a real working together couple, he knew he couldn't settle for less. He knew of the trips these male lovers made together, the concerts they attended, and he saw the magnificent houses they built together. From Ryan, Austin knew that he would get the usual, almost obliging hug when he got there and the same hug

127

when he got ready to leave. Emotionally and physically, there would be nothing more. If Ryan's body had hinted of any sexual desire, Austin's wall of self-discipline would have fallen apart. If Austin attempted anything, it would have pushed Ryan farther away.

Ryan and Jennifer came east to see him a time or two over the past two years, but this made Austin nervous, fearing discovery. He ushered the couple to out-of-the-way restaurants, hoping to avoid running into any of his gay friends. He did his best to avoid showing Ryan his apartment while stating he only had one bed, and then made a reservation for the couple at a nearby hotel. He knew it was all too possible a gay friend might stop by his apartment and disclose him. He justified lying to his best friend because he could not stand the thought that Ryan would be ashamed of him. He cared nothing about what Jennifer would say, only Ryan, but if Ryan detested him, then he felt there was just no point of being alive.

Reluctantly, after much pressure from Ryan, including about eight phone calls over the past few months, Austin agreed to go with Ryan on a camping and fishing trip in the Smoky Mountains near Balsam Gap. This trip would be just for the two of them. They planned to hike up to a place called Leap Off at the end of a long narrow ridge between two mountains. Folklore revealed that a frustrated Indian brave had indeed leaped off the cliff to his death because the girl he wanted had married another. When Austin read the story in the guidebook, he thought it was just too surreal, and urged Ryan to change their plans, but he could not say why, so off they went to Balsam Gap.

They left early in the morning, and the moment they left Ryan's house, Ryan began to feel and act like old times had returned between the two. Austin kept asking him about his school, the faculty, and his love for teaching, as well as he asked about his students and his plans for the summer. He deliberately gave Ryan little time to ask Austin about his new life. Austin kept his avoiding tactics working throughout the day.

Ryan naturally told him everything about his life. He felt he wanted to talk and hold nothing back. It had taken some talking, he said, but Jennifer had finally agreed to join Ryan in working at their old camp next summer. She planned to take on the challenge of teaching arts and crafts while Ryan could not wait to teach camping and hiking along with the usual survival classes. The couple visited the camp on many alumni occasions, and eventually she began to warm up to the idea of sleeping in a summer cabin again. She was a city girl, he added, and not happy with the limited shopping opportunities Brevard offered. About every six weeks, she would meet her mother in Atlanta for two days of shopping. Austin noted the comments, but said nothing. Unlike Ryan, Austin did not feel like this hike brought on a feeling of old times because his mind raced to keep Ryan talking about his life instead of asking about Austin's world. While Ryan began to relax, Austin remained tense.

They drove most of the morning to get to a parking lot near the trail. They grabbed their packs and hiked three miles across a ridge with many switchbacks. By lunch, they reached a long stretch of trail that went almost straight up the next big hill. Although they were both in shape, with the gear on their backs this climb winded them.

"Looks like it is easier to teach than work out," teased Austin as he sat down on a big rock. Ryan plopped down beside him. He had indeed put on about ten pounds while he marveled that Austin had not gained even one, but in fact looked a bit skinnier.

"That's funny. I was thinking it was easier to type on that computer than for you to jog," shot back Ryan with a puffing grin.

"I work out three times a week at the spa."

"The spa? I'm impressed. We don't have a spa in Brevard. I have some weights but by the time I set them up, well, it's just not worth it, and Jennifer doesn't like for me to leave them lying around. Our house is small, at least in comparison to the senator's."

"I know what you mean. I live in a two-bedroom apartment, but fortunately, the second bedroom is empty so I keep my fun stuff in there."

"I guess that's the joy of being single. Are you dating anyone special?" asked Ryan bluntly.

"Nobody special. I am not ready to marry. Is married life what it's cracked up to be?" asked Austin shifting the subject away from his life once again.

"Yeah, it's great. We're happy, very happy. I just wish you'd find someone."

"I will, all in due time as they say. You ready to go again?"

"Yeah, sure," lied Ryan as he dreaded starting up the next hill. He felt a little surprised at how out of shape he was.

Two nights later, fifteen miles now under their boots, unshaven, smelly, and a bit dirty, they relaxed by the campfire. Their spoons scooped the last of the rice and chicken Ryan cooked to go with the trout Austin caught, much to Ryan's chagrin, since he caught nothing. They were hungry so they licked their plates, the pot, and even the utensils.

"Is Jennifer a good cook?" asked Austin innocently, and then wished the question hadn't just popped out of his mouth.

"No, she's not," he gave a quick cold reply. "I mean, she tries." Ryan paused and then added honestly, "I do most of the cooking."

Austin laughed. "You do most of the cooking? Remind me to send her a sympathy card and case of stomach medicine."

Ryan pretended to be insulted. "I cook very well thank you. From the look of your plate, it looks like you liked it."

Austin laughed. "It was only rice. Out here I could eat dirt I'm so hungry. We've done well, haven't we? We've completed over fifteen tough miles of mostly uphill climbs. I am glad to be in a gentle flowing valley that is low enough so we could camp and fish. My body and I dread the six-mile climb to the upper ridge tomorrow. Oh, my aching back and legs," he added, rubbing his calves.

Ryan surprised him by asking, "Do you need for me to massage your back and legs?"

Even the question shocked Austin. On Shark Island, they daily took turns giving each other massages. However, since Ryan singularly decided they would quit cold turkey on all affection, he had not once broken his rule.

"Yeah, if you don't mind. They're killing me. I think sitting at that computer screen is straining my back."

Ryan nodded. "I imagine it is the stress that's getting to you, not that little old electronic box. What are you doing to relieve stress after work?"

Austin slipped out of his shirt and laid face down on his sleeping bag. Ryan went down on his knees and straddled Austin's butt, then reached out with his hands and began squeezing and working the tired muscles of Austin's shoulders as he had done for seven years on the island. The touch of Ryan's hands to his bareback made an erection occur immediately for Austin. Thankfully, he was lying face down so the bulge remained hidden. He feared Ryan might stop if he saw Austin getting aroused. He lifted his butt a little while reaching down to aim his penis for more comfort.

"Oh, I work out a few nights a week and hang out with my friends. I joined a bowling league." The moment the last remark fell from his lips he wished he had not added it for the team he joined was outrageously funny and part of a very gay bowling league.

Ryan laughed as he began working down Austin's back, pushing, pulling, smoothing, rubbing, and mashing the muscles. Austin sighed loudly.

Ryan chuckled. "Bowling? You?"

"Yeah, Tuesday nights, it's fun." He remained thankful Ryan would probably never be in town on Tuesday nights to discover his team was gay.

The conversation continued while Ryan kept working and massaging Austin's back. "Slip your trousers down so I can work those pitiful legs of yours," said Ryan. Austin gladly did, knowing massaging his weary legs would be even better than his back. Ryan suddenly blurted, "What the hell?"

Austin turned his head around to look at Ryan, half-afraid that a leech or tick was on his legs.

"When did you start wearing boxer shorts?"

"Several months ago. They're comfortable," laughed Austin as he lay back down. They had always worn the same size briefs. Ryan went to work on Austin's bare legs.

"You look like my father ..." began Ryan before catching himself as a childhood memory of seeing his father in his boxers in the hall waiting for

130

his sister to get out of the bathroom replayed through his mind. He immediately felt saddened, thinking of the loss of his parents, then caught his tongue and added, "That's what the doctor has me wearing."

"The doctor? Why would the doctor tell you to wear boxer shorts?" Austin moaned as Ryan pushed the legs of Austin's boxer shorts up to his butt, wrapped his hands around Austin's big thigh muscles, and began squeezing them hard. After a while, he began working his way down his legs all the way to his toes. Austin was in blissful heaven on two counts, the massage and the long lost touch of Ryan's hands. He realized the human touch of his friend remained high on his list of memories.

"Jennifer is insisting that we have a baby, but we are not able to make one. The juice comes, but nothing happens, if you catch my drift. I'd be happy to adopt a sweet kid but not her. Her mother keeps talking about how she cannot wait to have grandchildren. The doctor ran some tests on me and it seems I have a low sperm count, and no smart remarks from you," added Ryan as he popped Austin's buns as a warning. Austin's erection grew stronger. He shifted his body a bit to once again give his growing penis some more room.

"Oh jeez, I'm sorry. Do you and Jennifer want to borrow some of my big mother load so y'all have a cute baby like me?" Austin laughed so hard that Ryan could feel his convulsing giggles right through his skin.

Ryan pinched his leg. "Don't make me mad or I'll stop massaging your sorry, scrawny body."

"Oh, don't do that. I take it back. I take it back," pleaded Austin by putting his hands together in a prayer-like position and begging him to continue while still laughing.

"Loose balls produce more sperm. Have you ever seen the balls of a big old bull? They hang loose and he gets it on with the whole herd!" They both laughed at the thought and then fell silent again.

Ryan paused and in a quieter voice he stated, "We've been fighting a lot and I think the home stress is the problem. Jennifer is..."

Austin stopped enjoying the massage and turned around. He knew Ryan must be hurting emotionally. Ryan noted Austin's exposed erection that crept out the waistband of his short but said nothing. "I'm sorry, Ryan. I didn't know you were fighting. Are you having just the usual marital squabbles?"

Ryan dropped his head, a bit ashamed to admit the problem, but Austin was his best friend, so he told Austin everything. "Mostly over money," he replied quickly. "You know teachers don't make much money and she works at that realty office. She feels like the money she makes is hers but the money I make is ours." He sarcastically stressed certain words in his response.

Austin thought about his declaration a bit, and then tried to cheer Ryan up by laughing. Ryan grinned a little at his confession. Austin asked, "Is money that tight?"

"Yeah, we need a new car. Mine blew the clutch and not a week after I got it fixed, then the transmission went."

"I have some money. How much do you need?"

"Lie back down. I can't take your money. I'll do your other leg and then it's your turn."

Austin replied, "Oh, now I see why I got the massage treatment. You figure that if you made my muscles feel better, I'll be able to do a good job on you."

"Wrong, I expect you to do a great job on me!" replied Ryan with a grin, while playfully pushing Austin's head onto the sleeping bag.

TWENTY-FIVE

A half hour later, Austin sat on Ryan's butt massaging his best friend's back. He could not believe Ryan allowed him to rub and massage the muscles of the man he loved most in the whole world. He did a great job, and Ryan's moans and groans were applause enough to keep Austin going, even though his hands were aching. His erection pushed through the limp slit in his boxer shorts, but Ryan could not see it as he laid face down.

Ryan suddenly spoke up, "I wish I could get Jennifer to rub my back. I used to ask her but that's a waste of time. The answer is always no. I rub her feet and then she falls asleep."

Austin asked, "Do you still love her?"

"Of course, I do!" shot back Ryan. "Why do you ask?"

"Just the tone of your voice when you talk about her. It sounds likes more of an endurance contest than love."

Ryan grew silent. Austin instantly felt the tension in Ryan's back stiffened a bit. Austin rubbed harder. Soon Ryan's muscles relaxed once again. Austin knew his question had hit a nerve.

"How'd you know?" Ryan asked, showing his honesty at accepting Austin's analysis. No one else in the world knew."

"Know what?"

"That she's seeing someone else."

Austin abruptly stopped rubbing. "I didn't know and I'm sorry. She is?"

Ryan leaned around and looked up at Austin. "Back to work, slave. Yeah, he's a stupid salesman in her office. I didn't catch them yet, but I know it's happening."

"Ryan, I'm so sorry." Austin began massaging once again.

"I feel like the whole town knows. I had a dream the other night that the famous Transylvania Times headline said Local Teacher's Wife Sleeps Around Again. Next!"

Austin almost laughed but caught himself. "Hon'," he nearly bit his lip off, knowing he had chosen the wrong word to use. "Uh, Ryan, what can I do to help?"

"Do the thumbs up the spine thing like you used to?" Ryan was attempting to change the subject.

Austin moved both of his thumbs to the waist of Ryan's underwear, placed a thumb on each side of the spine, and pushed inward deep and hard. Slowly he began sliding his thumbs up to Ryan's neck. Once there he rotated hands squeezing and working the muscles until he came back to the waist once more. Ryan would sigh and Austin repeated the procedure over and over again. Ryan pleasantly moaned the whole time.

Ryan suddenly said, "Pull my shorts down and start at the base of the spine like you used to," ordered Ryan. Austin's hands froze as his heart skipped a bit.

On the island, they never wore clothes, so it was easy to start at the bottom of the spinal cord. Ryan lifted his waist up briefly so Austin slowly pulled Ryan's plaid boxers down below his butt. Austin adjusted his own boxers to cover his penis. His erection now made his boxers look like a pierced pup tent. He did not know it but Ryan had an erection as well. Once again, he began pushing his thumbs in deep while working up and down Ryan's back. Later, he bravely pulled Ryan's underwear off and out-of-the-way, and began doing his legs better than he had ever done.

Exhausted after another hour of massaging, they crawled in their respective sleeping bags to sleep in the nude. Ryan's breathing slowed, suggesting he had fallen asleep. Austin, however, remained awake. He held his eyes tightly shut so he could replay in his brain the new pictures of Ryan's bare back, legs, and butt.

The next day they slowly began hiking up to the top of the ridge. After a few difficult hours, they reached the summit. Puffing, they sat down quickly on some big rocks to catch their breath. While sweating profusely from the hard climb, they took in the view. Their bodies had changed since leaving the island four years ago. Unused muscles had softened. Even their once tough feet had turned soft and tender. They were also eating foods with higher fat contents. After climbing out of their backpacks, the two friends were just sitting on a rock, admiring the view.

Austin stated as he pointed down into the valley below, "Look how far we hiked. I can just barely make out the stream we crossed early this morning."

"I hope going down will be easier than going up," sighed Ryan.

"Not usually as it is the down angle of the foot that stretches the legs, and you end up even more sore than we are now."

"Thanks for bashing all hope of an easier journey," teased Ryan.

"Sorry."

"I wish Jennifer enjoyed camping or at least fishing. I can't get her to do anything outdoors," complained Ryan.

Austin did not know how to respond so he said nothing. Ryan threw a rock over the edge. "I once got her to go with me to a marriage counselor, but she didn't like that either. She acts as if nothing is wrong with her. I believe she's going to leave me for that salesman. He drives a Mercedes. He's got plenty of money."

"I'm sorry," said Austin. "I don't know what to say. I don't have much experience in this area. Heck, I don't even have a girlfriend," he added trying to make Ryan laugh. "Maybe it's your deodorant or the lack of it!"

Ryan grinned. "It's good enough that you try to make me laugh with your silly jokes."

Austin changed the subject by asking, "How's your job?"

"It's okay. I like the kids. No change that. I love the kids but the endless school meetings on things that aren't important, and the stupid forms and paperwork we have to fill out drives me crazy. In addition, the lack of funds, the stupid parents, and of course, my principal is a jerk, well, I don't know if I can take it much longer. If they would just let me teach my kids and go home, I'd be fine. The kids are by far the best part. I had a mother bless me out the other day because her daughter made a B on a test. She accused me of being biased, giving the boys better grades. I told her test grading was the result of numerical scoring, and her daughter's score added up to a ninety. I had no choice but to give her a B. I went home, counted the grades I gave the boys and then the grades I gave the girls, and the girls had better scores than the boys did. She was wrong, but she pissed me off by accusing me. I had to hold my tongue, be polite, and act as professional possible, but I darn near punched her in the mouth! Oooo, she made me mad!" he added angrily, and yet he was glad he could finally get that off his chest. Jennifer would never have listened to him.

"I can tell. You'd punch a woman?"

"She's no woman. She's a full-grown bitch!"

Austin laughed. "I bet you feel better now. Why don't you call her something else? Name this rock after her and then throw it over the cliff."

Ryan looked at Austin as if he had lost his mind, but then the idea took root. He picked up the rock and said, "Miss Jackass, to hell with you and by the way, your breath stinks, too!" He threw the rock as hard as he could over the cliff. They both laughed. Ryan felt better. Austin had become a good amateur psychologist.

They sat for a while in silence, thinking, admiring the view, and just wondering about life a bit. Ryan cleared his throat and said, "You know, I miss the island. I never thought I would say that, but I miss the roar of the waves, the year-around warm breezes, and even the gentle swaying of the tree house."

"I miss it, too. Do you think the house is still intact?"

"Oh, I hope so. I never thought about it. Jeez, you don't reckon a hurricane got it."

"I pray not."

After a pause, Ryan asked, "How's your work coming?"

"My work is all right, but nothing to write home about. I can't imagine I'll be doing this computer work stuff the rest of my life," said Austin.

"The camp is looking for a new guy to do the field promotion work. You know, traveling and showing the camp film, answering their questions, assuring the parents, picking up their applications and checks. You'd be great for that," added Ryan encouragingly.

"But I'd have to move back to Brevard."

"You like Raleigh?" asked Ryan.

"It's big and there's too many cars, and the people act like you don't exist, but I get to go out and have fun. Where can you go out in Brevard?"

Ryan laughed. "You can go to Shoney's Family Restaurant. The breakfast bar is just $2.99!"

"I'm single. I need action. You can't meet …" He caught himself. He didn't want to lie. "Well, you know what I mean."

"You'd be closer to home." Ryan held a stare at Austin that was perhaps a plea.

Austin smirked. "I assumed that is supposed to encourage me. I miss mom, but I don't miss the senator. Everything he does is for one purpose: his upcoming election." He laughed slyly. "We all support his reelection, don't we?"

They both laughed because they might actually vote for the senator's opponent.

Austin continued. "Do you know he never explained the birds and bees to me?"

Ryan chuckled. "You're crazy. We were on the island when puberty came and went. I had to explain it to you."

Austin laughed. "Hah, you didn't know anything either. Only the animals kept us from being confused as hell!"

Ryan laughed even harder. "Those were the good old days weren't they?"

"Yeah, here we are at twenty-five years old and talking about old days as if we were over fifty years old!"

Ryan slapped him on the back. "You're crazy!"

Austin laughed and grinned. He wanted to give Ryan a hug, but was afraid to. He took a step towards the path, but felt Ryan grab his hand. He turned to see what was up and Ryan suddenly gave him a bear hug. He did not let go right away but finally whispered, "You're my best friend in the whole wide world. You're more important to me than anyone. I couldn't make it through this world without you. You're still my best friend, my rock. I may need your help to get through the divorce. She's already told me she wants out of the marriage. My parents taught me to never give up, but if she's not willing to work it out together, well then, it's over."

"I'll be there when you need me. I promise. You just call. I love you," added Austin softly.

"I love you, too."

They squeezed each other a bit tighter before breaking the hug off and walking back to the hiking trail.

TWENTY-SIX

The camp hired someone else for the public relations job. Austin never applied. He deliberately did not tell Ryan, just letting him think the camp hired someone better. Ryan made it through one more year of teaching. His wife did not join him at summer camp that year. Austin had to be away at a banking conference and thus, Ryan celebrated his twenty-sixth birthday by himself. Meanwhile, Jennifer packed everything of hers and all the wedding gifts, plus everything her mother bought them, and moved out while he was away at camp. It had taken a full year for the divorce to become official as North Carolina did its best to demote the idea of ending a marriage. When he came home from camp and saw everything gone, he reacted by simply taking off his wedding ring and vowed never to put it on again. He tossed it in a drawer.

He had some free time so he decided to go see Austin on a lark. He didn't want to stick around in the empty house. He made a call but got Austin's answering machine. He did not leave a message. Failing to catch Austin on the phone did not discourage him. He quickly threw some clothes in a pack and then threw the bag in the back of his car. He headed north on Highway 191 until he reached Interstate 26 and headed northwest briefly before making the turn east on Interstate 40 in Asheville. He stopped once for gas and then drove straight through to Raleigh. He had not been there in over a year, but he remembered exactly how to get to Austin's apartment.

He arrived there around eight o'clock and felt relief to see the lights on in Austin's apartment. At least he was home. They could talk and then get some dinner and maybe a beer and crash. Mentally and physically exhausted, Ryan desperately needed to unwind. He had even thought about begging Austin for a massage. He grabbed his bag from the backseat and walked the steps to the apartment door. He could hear music playing from the inside.

He should have knocked. Later, he wished he had knocked, but now it was too late. He thought surprising Austin would be fun, and he would laugh at his astonished face. He had thought about nothing much on the road. Now he planned to shock Austin by suddenly turning up. Grinning, he turned the knob and pushed in on the door. He expected to find Austin plopped down on the couch watching television with their old dog Bell. Jennifer didn't want Bell in her house so Austin won Miss Bell without a grumble. She was getting old, but was still frisky and temperamental when she wanted. Ryan pushed in on the front door.

"Ah!" screamed the smaller man."

"Ah!" screamed the second man."

Neither one of the men was Austin. The two traumatized men were making out on the couch, oblivious to the music video on the television. Their shirts were open, and both their pants unzipped and pulled partly down. Each man's right hand squeezed the hot flesh bundle beneath the underwear of the other.

"Don't shoot us!" yelled the smaller man as Ryan continued coming through the door and into the room. He regretted his plan of surprise immediately.

Ryan stood there stunned. He had not expected anything like this. He felt bewildered. He did not know what to say. He could not move. His heart pounded in his chest.

The bigger man realized that Ryan did not have a gun, but rather carried a clothes bag. "What do you want?" he asked gruffly.

"I'm sorry," began Ryan. "I must have gotten the wrong apartment. Do you know where Austin's apartment is? Uh, Austin London that is. Did he move?" Sweat drops formed on Ryan's brow as he tried to look away from the lovers.

"No, this is his apartment. We've been house-sitting little Miss Bell."

Bell had heard Ryan's voice and leaped off Austin's bed in the back of the apartment. Ryan looked down at little Bell as she came running from Austin's bedroom and tried to jump into Ryan's arms. He knelt down and to the house sitter's surprise, Bell leaped into Ryan's arms. He caught her and she immediately began licking his face. He had missed her a lot, but obviously, she had missed him more, especially with Austin gone.

"Jeez, I've never seen her do that before. She usually growls at strangers," said the younger man as he zipped up his pants and sat up on the couch.

"I'm not a stranger. Miss Bell and I are old friends."

"Wait a minute," said the bigger man as he zipped and then stood up. "You must be Ryan, Austin's best friend?"

"I am. Where is he?" asked Ryan while rubbing Bell's ears. She practically purred like a cat while he did. He gave her many little kisses as she wagged her little tail almost as fast as the wings of a hummingbird.

"He's in Atlanta, or well, he was in Atlanta. He's due home tonight. He's been there on some training sessions. He just got a promotion, you know."

"No, I didn't know," replied Ryan still standing in the doorway.

"Yes, he's now the regional coordinator. He got a raise, but the downside is he has to travel more, from bank to bank. This is the third time we've house-sit for him in two months."

A car pulled into the parking lots. Briefly, the headlights flashed up the stairway. The shorter guy walked to the window and peeked through the mini-blinds. "Speak of the devil, or little devil in his case, he's here!"

"I guess we better get going," said the taller one as he grabbed his stuff he had stacked on the end of the couch.

"Yes, we'll leave you two alone," replied the other as he helped gather some personal stuff, two overnight bags, and walked to the door.

Ryan stepped aside as the two men cautiously went by and down the steps. They met Austin coming up the steps carrying his suit bag and briefcase. Austin, dressed sharply in a three-piece, pinstriped, navy blue banker's suit, displayed a huge grin. Ryan thought he looked great but did not feel like talking about that.

Austin asked, "Hey, where you going?"

"You have company. Miss Bell is fine. There are messages on the kitchen counter. We have to go. I'll call you later. Bye." They were talking and waving goodbye, but kept hurrying towards the parking lot.

They quickly got in their car and left. Austin, puzzled at their quick responses and rush to leave, came on up the steps. He failed to note Ryan's car in the big parking lot. The door to his apartment remained open so he walked on in and found Ryan sitting on the arm of the couch with Bell still in his hands.

"Oh my gosh! Ryan! I'm so glad to see you. Why didn't you call?" began Austin as he went over to hug Ryan. His eyes quickly scanned the room, hoping his friends had not left anything gay around the house. Bell started gleefully barking.

Ryan did not stand, but politely leaned over to hug Austin a little, but gave no squeeze. Austin noted the difference but said nothing. This was not like the hug he had received on heading back to Raleigh from his last visit in Brevard on their hiking trip.

"I tried but I got the answering machine. I needed to get out-of-town and so I thought I'd surprise you, but I was the one that got the surprise."

Austin, puzzled at the response, returned to the door and closed it. He set his bags down, and turned to catch Miss Bell as she leaped to his arms from Ryan's lap. "I got promoted!" bragged Austin as he ruffled the little dog's ears. She gave him many doggie kisses in return.

"I heard. Congratulations."

"Oh, Pete and Bill told you. Those two fellows can't keep a secret if their life depended on it," began Austin nervously as he stroked Bell and moved to the far end of the couch to sit down.

"Pete and Bill is it? They were making out when I got here."

Austin dropped poor Miss Bell to the carpet. "What?" She barked and jumped right back into his lap.

"I heard music playing, I thought you were home, and the door appeared unlocked, so I barged on in planning to surprise you. I discovered them on the couch half naked and groping each other."

Austin's heartbeat accelerated, as did his brain. "Damn, I'm sorry. Good house sitters are hard to find. They do take great care of Bell and the apartment. They are clean freaks. I once planned a trip just so they would clean the house for me." He had tried to make Ryan laugh. It failed to work.

"They're gay, aren't they?" asked Ryan accusingly.

139

Austin swallowed. He could not directly lie to Ryan. "Yes, they are. I'm sorry they embarrassed you. I'll have words with them later. They do love each other," he added bravely.

Ryan sighed. His manners kicked in. "No, it was my fault. I shouldn't have barged in. Maybe I shouldn't have come."

"Nonsense, I'm glad to see you," began Austin hoping to change the subject. "Why the sudden trip? Is Jennifer doing okay?"

"She's moved out. The divorce is final. I guess she's living with that man now. I don't know for sure and I guess I don't care. I came home to an empty house. She took almost everything and suddenly, I didn't feel like staying there, so I thought I'd come see you."

Austin grinned. "I hope you're hungry because I'm starving. Let me wash my face and we'll go." Austin headed towards the bedroom to drop his suitcase and briefcase. He called back to Ryan. "Would you check Bell's water and food bowl? Make sure she has some of both."

"No problem," replied Ryan, but he was still thinking about the men he had met. Bell had plenty of both so Ryan sat down on a stool at the kitchen counter to wait. He noted the mail stacked neatly on the counter so he assumed Austin must have been gone all week. Someone had sorted it according to personal mail first, bills, junk mail and magazines. The house sitters must have opened two magazines that were delivered in black plastic discreet bags. Ryan's eyes focused on them. He had never heard of the titles before. One of them was 'OUT' and the other was 'Freshmen'. He picked up the first one and let the pages slide through his finger. The 'Out' magazine was not a porno but rather an informative, political gay publication. However, there were beautiful, full color suggestive ads of men and women in gay poses but nothing racy. The other magazine, 'Freshmen', was just the opposite. He found the pages filled with gorgeous, young, nude men. He noted the mailing label on both of the mailing bags. Ryan let it fall back to the counter and made his way to the living room just as Austin appeared wearing a fresh shirt, hair brushed, face re-shaven, and smelling good, all in less than 10 minutes.

Austin smiled. "Let's go. I know an Italian place you're just going to love. Their pasta is the best in Raleigh."

After ordering, they began drinking wine. Ryan rather quickly downed a glass or two. This surprised Austin but he said nothing. He figured it was all because of Jennifer's leaving Ryan. Austin never liked her because he did not like the way she treated the man he loved, but he never said so, not even to Ryan. They ate awesome salads with the house dressing, and then the best linguini Ryan had ever tasted. After dinner, they started their second bottle of wine. Ryan was not eager to go so they sat there and chatted a while.

After a half-hour of mindless talk, Ryan suddenly blurted out, "Austin, are you gay?"

Austin's heart stopped. Prepared for years for his mom to ask, and maybe he'd prepared a long-winded speech in case the senator should ask, but he still did not feel ready to answer. Just last week he handled his boss when he asked the same question on the day of his promotion, but he found himself a bit unprepared to answer Ryan. He felt pleased his boss did not care. In fact, the boss seemed relieved because he knew Austin could commit to the job and not to a wife and kids. Nevertheless, Austin knew he could not lie to Ryan. He had to tell the truth. He took a quick sip of the wine. Then a gulp of the wine, and then finally downed the glass and replied, "Yes, I am."

"You do it with other men?"

"Sometimes, but I'm not in love with anyone, but yes, sometimes I need affection. Everyone does. You've been the lucky one. You had a wife you could..." He stopped then slightly repeated himself. "You could be intimate with. I missed intimacy the most when we came home."

There was a long silence. "How long have you known?"

"Since I moved to Raleigh."

"That long? Why didn't you tell me?" asked Ryan in less of a question and more of an accusation tone.

"I was afraid."

"Afraid of what," Ryan's pitch became sterner.

"That you would hate me. I couldn't take the chance on losing you as a friend. As my best friend," he corrected. Austin's eyes had become wet and full.

Ryan took another swallow of wine, "Last term, a kid I had taught my first year of teaching, came by to see me after school one day. He brazenly told me he was gay. He said his father recently found out and kicked him out of their house. I read up on the subject. I am appalled so many gay teens kill themselves. I refused to let this kid get that low. I found a home for him with some parents in PFLAG. You know what PFLAG is, don't you?"

"Yeah, Parent and Friends of Lesbians and Gays. I've been to fund-raisers for them. I donate time and money to most of the gay charities in Raleigh."

"Well, he's doing well. He didn't commit suicide, which was a relief, as he had told me he had been thinking about it the day he came to me for help."

"That's great, Ryan, but don't stop being supportive. He will still have some tough years are still ahead of him. At some point, we have to accept who we are. I don't know why I'm gay, I just am. God made me that way just as he made you heterosexual."

"I wish you had told me. I realize now why you became so distant. I thought because I stopped being affectionate with you that you were mad at me."

"No, I'm not mad. You did the right thing. I loved you with all my heart. If you had been gay, I would have wanted no other man but you."

Ryan pondered that a moment. "Why haven't you found someone?"

"I guess no one can match up," said Austin gingerly.

"Match up? To what?"

"To whom? I thought you were a teacher. No one can match up to you. When you're loved by the best, nothing else can compare. To paraphrase that stupid song I hear all the time, 'If I can't have you, I don't want nobody else...'" sang Austin as if in a musical.

Ryan grinned. "That's silly. You need a partner, someone to share your life with," replied Ryan.

"Why, so I can end up divorced like you?" teased Austin.

"Time to go. I have to pee. I think you'd better drive. I've got a severe buzz," said Ryan as he stood up and swayed a bit.

"I did drive and you're right. You drank plenty."

They arrived at the apartment hearing the phone ringing as they came up the steps. Austin quickly unlocked the door and dove for the phone by the couch. Bell quickly scampered out-of-the-way and ran to the end of the couch so Ryan could pick her up. Her tail wagged back and forth rapidly. She licked the taste of the meal from his fingers.

"No, I can't go. I have company. I know I promised, but ... I'll just have to make it another time." Austin paused while listening. "I'm sorry. Next time, I know, I know. I can't go. I have to get off the phone. I'll call you later. Bye."

"Sounds like you're in hot water," said Ryan as he sat down while stroking Bell.

"Yeah, sort of, it's Greg's birthday party." Austin laughed. "He's throwing it for himself. Last week I promised I would meet a bunch of friends there, and then we were going dancing."

"Let's go," said Ryan unexpectedly.

"What?"

"Call what's his name back and tell him you're bringing a friend, a good friend."

"It's going to be mostly gay men there and we're going to a gay club to go dancing."

"I figured that out. I can handle it. I don't want any more secrets between you and me, so show me what you do and what you like about being gay, but first, I have to shower and change. I smell like an Italian sausage maker."

Austin laughed. "You're sure?"

"Very sure. You don't smell me?"

"Yes, I do, but I meant sure about going."

"I can handle it. Call him back."

TWENTY-SEVEN

Austin held his breath, crossed himself as if he were a Catholic instead of the rebellious Baptist, and double-crossed his fingers as they entered the house for Greg's birthday party. He was deathly afraid something raunchy and racy would already be happening like he had seen at many a gay party. He sighed with great relief, as all appeared calm, so he and Ryan cautiously entered the house. Greg had been drinking heavily, hoping the alcohol would help him forget he was now another year older, but when he spotted Austin, he forgot his troubles, ran to him, and kissed him quickly on the mouth. Austin blushed. So did Ryan. Austin began introducing Ryan to his friends, while Greg pranced off in a drunken sway as he set about welcoming others to his party. The party was a big one with over fifty men and about eighteen women in attendance. Over half of the crowd was out on the deck behind Greg's house. Ryan watched as men hugged and kissed Austin. Ryan took it all in and said nothing. Austin expected Ryan to bolt from the house at any time, but he was thankful he had the car keys in his pocket, so Ryan would have to walk to leave without him.

Over the next several hours, Ryan met all kind of gay people and felt pleased to discover several other schoolteachers in the group. They soon chatted about educational politics, lengthy paperwork, and told stories about the students and their parents from hell. He talked with others about hiking in the beautiful Blue Ridge Mountains, or fishing for trout in the Smoky Mountain National Park. He even talked about his love for sailing with two guys he had just met who were about to take their first chartered sailboat for a cruise in the Caribbean. They had worked hard to get their Charter Boat Captain License, and found themselves filled with excitement about their upcoming sea adventure together. Ryan was immediately envious of their planned journey and surprised when the couple invited Ryan and Austin to join them when they could. It was an invitation Ryan hoped to take them up on. The couple said if this trip went well they planned to buy a big boat. Ryan learned the men were of different economic backgrounds, but somehow had the money to enjoy life. Austin explained it was because they had no kids to take care of, no wife to keep happy, and no worries about saving for college education for children. Another man added that gay households generally have about three times more spendable income than heterosexuals do. Ryan laughed and agreed by stating he always remained a step above broke, therefore he must be a devout heterosexual. Everyone around him laughed, as did he.

At precisely 11:20, the crowd made their goodbyes and exits, and then the entire group headed to the local dance club. Austin felt pleased Ryan liked his friends. Some of them were a bit silly after a few drinks, but overall, Ryan liked them. Ryan assumed the alcohol was making some of the men appear to have the attitude of acting like what he called a tease or a flirt. He

143

just laughed it off while making sure he didn't get too close, as they seem to grope everyone just a little for fun. It surprised him when many of the guests gave him a hug before leaving. Stiff at first, he soon relaxed and warmly tightened the quick embrace.

Ryan had no idea about what to expect at a gay dance club. He found himself surprised to see hundreds of gay people dancing the night away in such a carefree and happy mood. He and Austin pushed their way through the crowd to the packed dance floor. It felt good to dance. He had drunk quite a bit that night, certainly more than the occasional beer he had back home, and soon found he felt rather gleefully buzzed. Greg brought a couple of beers to them to enjoy while they were dancing. The delirious dancing crowd was pushing in on Ryan's left and right. He got his butt softly pinched by many a handsome man, but he just smiled while shaking his index finger in a no-no at them. Austin felt Ryan was either drunk or at least close to it, so he stayed close to him the whole night so he could protect him if required. He knew that in any bar in the world there was always one person that pushed too hard and went a bit too far. In a few hours, Ryan was dirty dancing with Austin like the other men were doing with their dance partners. They made a tight line of about six of Austin's friends all grinding and swaying to the music. Austin felt Ryan was genuinely having a great time. He was by far the happiest he had seen him since returning from the island.

Later, Ryan needed help to climb the stairs to Austin's condominium. He leaned heavily on Austin's shoulder. Together, they struggled upwards. Once inside, Ryan fell on the couch in a heap and passed out, or so Austin assumed. He went to the hall closet and got a blanket, and then like the perfect gentleman, he gently covered Ryan up and headed to his room. Exhausted from the early tension of the night, and then from the hours of dancing the night away, he stripped out of his clothes and walked naked to the shower in the hall. One of several things Austin detested about the club scene was all the smoke that engulfed his clothes, his body, and deep into his nostrils. He could not wait to wash it out of his hair and off his body. He had just finished his hair when suddenly a hand reached into the shower and grabbed his arm. Austin screamed as he jumped away and bumped the shower wall. Ryan busted out laughing.

"Gotcha!" he yelled.

"Shh! You'll wake the neighbors," warned Austin with a playful finger to his lips while smiling back at Ryan.

"Sorry. I had to piss. Jeez, I smell awful." Ryan started peeing in the toilet.

"It's the smoke. You're not used to it. I'm not used to it. That's why I always head to the shower as soon as I get home."

Austin heard the water flush and assumed Ryan had left the room. Suddenly the curtain parted and Ryan stepped into the shower, naked except for his socks. In his drunken stupor, he had forgotten to take them off. The socks were instantly soaked. So was most of the bathroom floor as Ryan had swung the curtain outward while getting in. He is definitely drunk, thought Austin. Austin grabbed the curtain and pulled it back in. He laughed when he looked down at Ryan's water soaked socks.

"What are you doing?" asked Austin.

"I'm taking a shower. I stink. You smell good." He grinned at Austin through very drunken eyes and planted a playful kiss to Austin's neck.

"You're drunk."

"And they said you weren't a rocket scientist," he replied mockingly. "I'm drunk and I've never felt better," slurred Ryan with a huge mischievous grin on his face. Austin could have sworn Ryan's eyes remained crossed and dazed.

"Are you washing your socks, too?" asked Austin with a smirk while pointing down to Ryan's feet.

Ryan looked down at his feet a long time while thinking hard about what he was looking at. "Whoops, too late now." With that, he bent over, pulled them off, and tossed them over the shower curtain with no particular aim. Bell had entered the room to see what was going on in the bathroom, but she had to duck away as the wet socks flew over her head and landed in the middle of toilet bowl. Water splashed on the wall. She frowned at the mess and decided it was time for her to go back to bed because if she feared if she stayed in the bathroom she could end up as wet as the socks. She didn't like to get wet.

Ryan asked, "Where's the shampoo?"

"Right here," replied Austin as he handed the bottle to Ryan. It slipped from Ryan's hand and bounced off Austin's foot. "Ow!!" Austin reacted by bending forward slightly. Ryan had already started to go for the shampoo bottle. They instantly bumped heads.

"Sorry," grinned Ryan.

Austin decided he had better take charge. "Here. Let me wash your hair. Swap places and get down on your knees so I can get your hair good and wet. I also don't want you to fall out of the shower."

Once they accomplished bypassing each other, Ryan turned around and faced Austin, and then knelt down. Austin immediately realized his penis was hardening. He couldn't help himself. Before him was the man he loved and on his knees. The very man he dreamed about. He was his best friend but he wouldn't take advantage of a drunken Ryan. That was not the way he wanted Ryan. He wanted Ryan's undivided love. He wanted to live as they had in the tree house, but he knew that love was gone forever. Austin poured a puddle of shampoo in his hand, and then reached down and began gently washing Ryan's hair.

Ryan started swaying as the alcohol continued to do its magic. "Whoa, partner. The shower is moving."

Austin said, "You're the one moving. It has been a long time since I've seen you drunk."

Ryan reached out with his hand and placed them on Austin's bare waist to steady his swaying.

"Okay, rinse off."

Ryan stood gingerly, and then turned and rinsed off with Austin's help. He then turned back around. "I think you'd better wash the rest of me, or I'm liable to fall in the floor."

Austin sighed and rolled his eyes. "You do realize you are in the shower with a naked gay man, don't you?"

"That's okay, you're in the shower with a straight, divorced, ex-teacher, and former lover," chuckled Ryan.

"Cute, very cute," laughed Austin. "Hold your arms up so we can wash that B.O. off you!"

Ryan asked as he turned his nose under his arms to smell his armpits, "What B.O.?"

In a mock John Wayne cowboy voice Austin replied, "Body Oder. Hold your hands up, Pilgrim, and hold still or I'll shoot."

Ryan grabbed Austin's waist again, but his right hand slipped a bit and so he squeezed one of Austin's buns. "You have been working out, I see." He gave Austin's butt another playful squeeze and then held on to steady himself.

Austin rubbed the soap over Ryan's chest and then downward to his tummy. His own erection was obvious. Ryan was limp. He ignored Ryan's attempts at conversation.

"Get my legs, mate!" laughed Ryan. "Hey man, it looks like we're playing submarine and your periscope is up!"

Austin knelt down and did Ryan's legs. He then turned Ryan around, did his back, and even lightly washed his buns. Ryan rinsed and then turned back around.

"You forgot my totem pole," said Ryan with a grin.

"You do it."

"Naw, you're gay. You do it! Give me a thrill," laughed Ryan while steadying himself with his hands on Austin's shoulders.

Austin sighed, rubbed some soap between his hands, then gingerly reached down and washed Ryan's penis and genitals.

"Aw, that feels good," said Ryan, as he surprisingly took hold of Austin's enlarged organ. Ryan's penis began to grow.

Austin froze where he stood. He knew he should stop. After all, Ryan was drunk. He kept telling himself that's all it was, but as Ryan stroked him, he felt suddenly light-headed. He stroked Ryan back. Ryan pulled him in closer, slid his free hand to Austin's backside, and began rubbing there as

146

well. Austin was afraid to look up. He was still shorter than Ryan. A few seconds went by. Ryan kissed his neck. Austin moaned. He allowed his head to travel upward. Ryan kissed him on the mouth, deep and hard like they had done on the island. It was a deep physical moment between them that suddenly went cold, or at least the hot water did.

Austin screamed and frantically shut the shower off. Ryan laughed. Austin grabbed some towels, and quickly dried off Ryan and then himself. Ryan followed him out of the bathroom, but when he got to the hall, Ryan grabbed his hand, pulled Austin to him, and kissed him again. Austin's legs went limp like a lady in a cowboy flick. Though drunk, Ryan lifted Austin in his arms, took three staggering steps to the bed, and fell awkwardly with Austin in his arms to the mattress. Bell scampered off the bed onto her own little bed in the corner. She smartly knew the time had come for her to run to yet another safe place.

Ryan continued kissing him the whole way although he nearly knocked a tooth out in the fall to the bed. They kissed deeply with their tongues exploring, and for the moment Austin kept his eyes closed and imagined they were still on Shark Island. Austin didn't know it, but Ryan and Jennifer had quit having sex long ago. Ryan was starving for it. He went down on Austin. Austin wiggled free and spun around so they could both enjoy each other at the same time. Then Ryan spun Austin on his stomach. Austin quickly reached for the lubricating lotion he kept by the bed. He managed to get a little in the right place, and before he knew it, Ryan was inside him.

Later, Austin was on his back, his legs parted, Ryan was slowly moving in and out of him while leaning down to kiss him. After a wonderfully long time Ryan came inside him again. Most drunks couldn't have performed this well, but not Ryan. His intensity grew with each thrust. By dawn, they had drifted off, completely exhausted, but cuddling tenderly in each other's arms. Austin was dreaming deeply. He hadn't slept so soundly since returning to the States. The alcohol wore off. Ryan knew what he had done. The alcohol might have helped him start yet he knew he could have stopped himself, but he didn't.

It was almost noon when Austin finally opened his eyes to discover he was staring at Bell's sleeping butt. He winced when she almost silently farted and rolled over. He stretched out his arm in the opposite direction, gently probing and feeling for Ryan. Suddenly, he sat up when he realized Ryan was no longer in bed with him. He leaped out of bed, but as his feet hit the carpet, he realized his legs and butt were sore and aching. It was a good discomfort, he thought as he grabbed a bathrobe and walked to the bathroom. No sign of Ryan, only his wet socks hanging over the shower rod. The still damp socks made Austin smile and shake his head in wonderment at the shower they had shared together. He walked to the kitchen, and then on to living room expecting to find Ryan eating breakfast, but apparently he had already left. Austin didn't find a note cussing him out and stating he'll never see him again, just nothing.

Austin returned to the shower where it all began and washed the lotion and semen from his loins. He closed his eyes and imagined Ryan was in the shower with him once more. He soon had another portable place to hang his washcloth. He spent the day thinking about nothing else but Ryan. He loved him. He had always loved him. He could never love another. Ryan was truly his first and only love. It was impossible to love another. He was monogamous in his heart and in the love he gave as well.

TWENTY-EIGHT

It was two weeks before Christmas when Austin came home one cold day from work. He knelt down and gave Bell a good scratch behind her ears. Bell never felt she received enough attention to her ears, thought Austin. He sat down on the stool to go through the day's mail. Near the bottom of the pile was a postcard of a beautiful mountain scene in Colorado. Puzzled, Austin quickly turned the card over and looked at the name on the bottom. It was from Ryan. Austin started reading the three-sentence note as rapidly as he could, savoring every word. He had not heard from Ryan since the day he left the condominium in Raleigh.

"I've been busy traveling for the camp and freezing my butt off in the Rocky Mountains. I miss the warm island and you."

Austin had read it aloud even though no one else was in the room. It was as if he was testing himself to make sure the scene was not just another dream. He read it repeatedly before finally he allowed the last two words to sink in...and you.

No sooner had he finished the card for the fourth time when abruptly the phone rang. It jolted him back to reality. He planted a soft kiss to Ryan's signature on the card while still looking at it. Still deep in thought about Ryan and the card, he almost absentmindedly picked up the receiver and somberly said hello.

"Austin?"

Austin eyes went wide. "Ryan?"

"Hey, buddy. How are you?"

"I'm fine."

"Did you get my card?"

"As a matter of fact, I was just reading it. I haven't heard from you in a long time and didn't know where to write or call you."

"That would be pretty hard. I took the camp promotion job after the other guy quit. I'm in a different town almost every day. Next week I'll be home for about a month before heading south for the Florida camp movie stops. Being on the road alone took some getting used to. It gives me a lot of time to think. Listen, I'll come to the point. I felt guilty about what I did the last time I saw you. I took advantage of you. I know you want someone to fall in love with you, but I'm sorry, I'm straight. I didn't call because I didn't know what to say. You're my best friend, and you always will be." Ryan then abruptly changed the subject. "Bonnie wants me to stay at your parents' house for Christmas. I would like to if you were going to be home. Can you get off and come?"

"Yes, I can. It's been a long year, especially with the promotion and all the traveling I had to do. I didn't even take a vacation. I have two weeks off. I'll be home Thursday."

149

"Good, I'll call Bonnie and confirm I'm coming. I'll tell her you're coming, too. She'll be thrilled. She's still your biggest fan, you know."

"Thanks, and thanks for the card, too. It is good to hear from you." Austin was still in shock, but other thoughts and words just wouldn't spring off his lips.

"Same here. We'll talk more when I see you. Bye, buddy."

"Bye."

Austin hung the receiver and wondered aloud, "When did he start calling me buddy?"

Austin had planned his return to Western North Carolina well. He knew he would finally arrive home after a long five-hour drive on Interstate 40 that was hopefully uneventful. He was well groomed with a nice sweater and creased Savane slacks. Known by friends and co-workers for his perfect hair, today he had taken special care to make sure every single strand was in its proper place. Yesterday Greg came by to wish him a safe trip and to trim his eyebrows. Austin wanted everything to be just perfect.

He stopped for gas, paid the cashier, and then returned to his car smiling at the thrill of seeing Ryan again, however, he was extremely nervous about his homecoming. He knew of course that his mom would grill him about whom he was dating, while asking when he was going to find the right girl and settle down. The senator would cross-examine him about how he was doing financially, and if had he joined the local political party. He would directly ask if he had taken the time to register to vote, and firmly state that Austin should exercise his mind as well as his body. Austin, of course, rehearsed the answers to all these questions and more while driving west on Interstate 40 towards home. However, the real and most important reason he felt apprehensive was meeting Ryan again.

Ryan pretty much said what Austin expected on the phone. He missed his friend, but there was nothing more there than fooling around. Oh sure, he still knew that Ryan loved him as his best friend, and Austin still loved him the same way, but also far more. Austin called from his cell phone as he drove through Asheville and turned southeast on Interstate 26. Bonnie took the call. She was thrilled he was only 45 minutes away. Dinner was almost ready. The senator had arrived, as well as Austin's sister Kathleen and her husband Tim, and they brought along Jasmine, Austin's new niece.

He waited impatiently for the house phone to ring. "Mom, would it be okay if I bring a guest for dinner?" asked Austin as he changed lanes.

Bonnie's buoyant eyes lit up at the sound of her son's voice, and that he wanted to bring someone home with him. She felt as if her hopes and prayers must have finally come true. Austin was bringing a girl home to meet the family, she thought. "Why of course, dear," she beamed.

"Thanks Mom," Austin said slightly away from the phone receiver, but where Bonnie could still hear. "She can't wait to see you."

150

Bonnie laid her open palm to breast, as if to catch her breath. "And I can't wait to see her too? Drive safe."

He glanced down at the speedometer and then up to the rear mirror to make sure that one of North Carolina's finest wasn't about to give him a ticket. "I'm cruising at about seventy-four miles an hour and my ETA should be about thirty-one minutes."

Bonnie frowned. He was breaking the speed limit. The senator would not approve if Austin's picture ended up in the paper as the result of a big ticket or car accident.

"Don't worry. I know what you're thinking. I'll slow down and be safe. Bye, Mom. See you soon. I love you."

Bonnie smiled with a twinkle in her eyes. He had read her mind precisely. "I love you, too. Bye."

Ryan entered the kitchen feeling fresh from a shower after unpacking his bag their old room. Since seventeen, they had lived together as brothers, almost like twins. A few people in town thought Ryan's last name was London instead of Wilson.

Ryan came down to the kitchen. Bonnie glanced up from her food preparation, smiled, and gave Ryan a friendly wink. "Oh, hi dear, that was Austin on the phone. He's about thirty minutes away and guess what?" Her eyes were beaming. Ryan grinned at her excitement.

Ryan picked up a sliced celery stalk that Bonnie had been chopping on and popped it in his mouth. "I give up, what?"

"He's bringing a girl with him," her dimples fell in as Ryan's eyebrows went up.

Ryan nearly choked on the small piece of celery. He coughed loudly. He was a bit stunned. "A girl? Who?"

"He didn't say. He just asked if it was okay to bring a guest for dinner. Then in the background he said 'she' was looking forward to seeing me. Isn't this just the perfect Christmas present?" She spun around and took another tray of food to the dining room with a bit a joy in her steps. Kathleen came in holding the baby and immediately Bonnie began telling her the story as well. Ryan listened to her tell it again. He couldn't believe that Austin was bringing a girl home. Had he decided to go straight, he wondered? Was he just trying to fool the family, and if so, he felt bad for the poor girl? Did the girl know, he wondered. Then his eyes went wide as he speculated that perhaps she was a lesbian and just helping Austin out. What if the senator found out he was eating dinner with a gay woman? Ryan quietly chuckled at the thought.

"It's snowing!" said Tim as he came in the kitchen to help Bonnie carry more food to the dining room.

Ryan picked up a tray of food as well. "Yeah, I hope Austin makes it in. The wind has picked up and the radio said the temperature was down to twenty-one. That's cold!"

151

"Too cold for me," added Bonnie as she directed placement of the food. "The senator is on a conference call to Washington. He's expecting dinner in thirty minutes. I hope Austin makes it."

The senator arrived into the dining room in precisely thirty minutes, an annoying trait thought Ryan. However, he was glad the senator could fit the family in his schedule. The senator, smiling as he entered the room, waved at his family. Ryan thought the man's performance was like attending one of his fund-raising dinners. Everyone instantly wondered what he was up to. He kissed little Jasmine on the cheek, kissed Kathleen on the forehead, shook hands firmly with Tim who winced at the pain his knuckles felt, and nodded at Ryan from across the table. "Well, everything looks delicious, Bonnie. You've certainly outdone yourself. We are very lucky to be feasting inside where it is warm and cozy. Shall we sit down?" Ryan knew that last sentence was not really a question but more of a command. The senator had a habit of doing that. He was always in control, or at least he thought he was.

"Dear," began Bonnie, "Austin called from the car. He is due here any minute. Would you mind waiting just another minute or so? I would love to sit down as a whole family for a change. Would that be too much to ask?"

Bonnie had chosen her words very well, leaving the senator no choice but to be a gentleman and concede. "Why of course, my dear. The roads are getting bad out there. I hope he drives safely. Why don't we pour everyone a glass of that wine I brought home from Washington? It came to me via the Italian embassy." Ryan smiled slyly, as the senator just lifted himself up another notch on his self-worth podium.

Relieved, Bonnie and Kathleen quickly gave everyone a glass while Tim pulled the cork from the bottle and began filling the glasses.

Austin, forced to slow down as the snow picked up, felt fortunate the roads remained bare of other traffic. He grinned while noting the cops stayed off the highway as well. Ryan saw the headlights of Austin's car as he turned in the driveway. He couldn't help his reaction. "He's here!!" he exclaimed.

"Well, good, now we can eat on time," pronounced the senator, while letting everyone know they were running behind schedule. He checked his watch for emphasis. Ryan and Austin often thought he probably farted on a time schedule as well.

They all headed to the foyer to greet Austin. Just as Ryan turned the knob on the big wooden door Austin pushed through carrying his jacket over something in his arms. Snow peppered his hair and sweater, his shoes disappeared in the snow, but he grinned from ear to ear.

"Hello everybody. Merry Christmas!" Austin said merrily.

They all answered accordingly and in unison, "Merry Christmas to you."

"Where's your guest?" asked Bonnie, too expectant to wait. "Is she in the car?" she asked as she tried to look over his shoulder at the car.

Austin laughed and pulled his jacket off the bundle in his arms. "Mom, it's my favorite girl, Miss Bell. Sorry, to get your hopes up, but I couldn't resist teasing you!" The little dog sat up in his arms and barked mightily, as if she wanted to greet everyone with a doggie Merry Christmas.

Everyone laughed as Bonnie swatted at Austin playfully, and then gave him and Bell big hugs and kisses. Austin sat Bell down and the little cold dog took off immediately for her favorite place by the fire. Kathleen gave Austin a warm hug.

"I've missed you little brother. Say hi to your new niece, Jasmine."

Austin blushed as Tim shoved Jasmine into his arms. He smiled at Tim, and then looked down at the newly born baby in his arms. "Oh, my goodness she's so tiny. Look at those petite little fingers, but what big blue eyes she has. She is adorable. You did good Kathleen," and then remembering Tim he added, "and so did you, big guy. She is so beautiful."

Austin gingerly handed little Jasmine to her mother and turned to Ryan. "Hey, old friend."

Ryan had a big lump in his throat. He wished the rest of the family wasn't standing there. He wanted to grab Austin, swing him around in circles, and maybe even kiss him on the cheek, but that was not possible in the senator's house. He stuck his hand out like a businessman closing a loan on house. "I've missed you."

Austin glanced to see the back of the senator's head as he walked back into the dining room. He brushed Ryan's outstretched hand aside, and bear hugged him tightly and whispered in Ryan's ear. "I've missed you, too. I love you, you big dumb Yankee."

Ryan eyes immediately moistened, and in a whisper he replied, "I love you, too."

TWENTY-NINE

The dinner had been everything Bonnie hoped for. Well, almost. She was glad to see old Bell, and she gave her a fresh bone to show it, but she had prayerfully hoped that Austin was bringing home a future daughter-in-law. For a few hours after dinner, the family sat around the living room talking and catching up. The senator made it through about thirty minutes of such idle catch-up talk before dismissing himself to make a promised call to Washington. Ryan had planned to go for a walk with Austin, but due to the snow he cancelled his plans. Bonnie retired about ten thirty and shortly after, so did Kathleen and her clan. Ryan and Austin moved to the recreation room to shoot pool.

"I've got a bone to pick with you," began Austin suddenly, as he pointed his cue stick at Ryan.

"Yeah, what I'd do?" he responded Ryan in perfectly bad English.

Austin grinned and took his first shot, knocking a solid ball in the far corner. "I understand why you didn't call me, but did you ever stop to think that I might have needed to talk to you? What if I had needed surgery?"

Ryan cut him off. "You're as fit as a horse."

"What if I had a car accident? What if I got real sick?"

Ryan frowned. "You don't have AIDS do you?"

Austin stopped his next stroke and looked up at Ryan and frowned. "No, of course not. I'm careful. Hell, the only person I've had sex with in more than year is..." He stopped himself from saying what he thought, and then took his shot and missed. "Your turn," he said with a bit of an edge in his voice.

Ryan hadn't played pool in more than a year. He lined up his shot and missed an easy tap in. Austin continued as he lined up his next shot. "I'm just saying it was selfish of you to go and disappear on me like that. Do you still love me as your best friend?" he asked bluntly.

"Yes, of course I do."

Austin picked up his stick and suddenly pointed it again at Ryan's chest. "Then don't ever stop calling like that again. I needed you on a hundred occasions. You're my very best friend. I trust no one else on the planet like I trust you. And yes, I still love you even when you piss me off." Austin returned to the table, took his shot, dropped another ball, and then missed the next one.

"I'm sorry."

"You should be," shot back Austin slyly.

Ryan grinned. "You're not really mad?"

"Nope," smiled Austin. "I try to get mad at you. Life remains complicated for you and me. I don't want you to be gay. Hell, I wouldn't want anyone to be gay, but I am and I accept it proudly. Publicly my own father has denounced gays every chance he gets. He does this so he can raise support from the religious groups. In addition, you certainly can't be something you're not. I know that when we were young and lived on the island, well, it was the happiest time of my life. If I had to do it all over again, I would never have signaled to that helicopter. I spend all day working my ass off for this bank, and the harder I work the more they pile on me. I'm about to lose my mind. I have idiots working under me, and to fire one for improvement's sake is like trying to move a mountain. There is so much red tape, and so many stupid procedures and policies to follow. I'm sick of it."

"Sounds just the school system to me. Why don't you quit your job and do something else?"

Austin smirked. "And do what? What am I suited for? I certainly don't want to be a politician. I have no home life. No marriage. No kids. No partner. No..."

Ryan held his hand out like a traffic cop. "Stop, you're depressing me."

"Ryan, have you met anyone else? Someone to care for you as Jennifer should have?" asked Austin somberly.

"No. I've had girls flirt with me, but I don't know. It's like the drive has left me."

"I think you're afraid you might be hurt again," philosophized Austin.

"You're probably right."

"Listen, Bud," began Austin sarcastically as he recalled Ryan calling him buddy on the phone. "I know you better than anyone. You may have to lower your sights a bit, but find someone that loves you more than anything in the world, even if they're not as pretty or as smart as Jennifer. She was pretty but she wasn't smart to leave you. I would say that was the dumbest thing she ever did. Her loss..."

Ryan interrupted, "For a guy that lives alone, you seem to know a lot about love."

Austin sighed, and then looked intensely in to Ryan's eyes. "I had the best teacher in the world."

With that comment, he laid the stick down and went to his room. Ryan stood there, frozen in thought, bewildered by Austin's words, wondering what Austin was really thinking. He cut the lights out, replaced their cue sticks to the rack on the wall, and slowly walked to their room.

Austin had undressed and climbed in bed. Bell was sleeping at the foot of the bed. Ryan stood between the beds and undressed. Austin opened an eye and watched him, secretively. He couldn't help himself. It was like his video image battery had drained and needed replenishing. He knew every square inch of Ryan's body, but he could never look at it enough. He felt his manhood stiffen. He closed his eyes and turned his head away as he squeezed himself.

Standing in his boxer shorts, Ryan looked at Austin sleeping for the longest time. His mind was churning with thoughts and decisions, problems and solutions, but nothing surfaced. No great answer hit him between the eyes. He leaned down and patted Bell's head tenderly. He then leaned over and kissed the top of Austin's hair like a father kissing his child goodnight. He then turned to his bed, climbed in, and tried to sleep.

During the remaining days before Christmas, Ryan and Austin did tons of shopping for presents for the family and each other. On a warmer day they hiked and visited the camp, so Austin could see Ryan's house. On his last visit, Ryan mentioned to Austin about the offer from the camp to take over the promotion job. When he had returned from Raleigh, he immediately called the camp director and accepted. He had done well for the camp. Attendance went up and the camp's leaders became optimistic for the coming summer. When New Years Eve came, the senator and Bonnie were attending a republican holiday party in Asheville, while Kathleen stayed home with the baby who had developed a cold. Tim was trying his best to stay-out-of-the-way.

"We should go out tonight," began Ryan as he chewed on a piece of bacon.

Austin finished his breakfast and pushed the plate back. "I'm sorry, I was thinking of going out to a gay club in Asheville."

"Asheville has a gay club? I didn't know that."

Austin laughed. "You walk a different path. Didn't you know I have gaydar?"

"What? Are you taking anything for it? Is it like a rash?" asked Ryan in a suddenly serious, worrisome tone.

Austin busted out laughing. "No, stupid. It's this sixth sense that gays have. They can spot another hidden gay person as they walk down the hall of a mall, or eat at a trendy restaurant and so on. We also talk," he added sarcastically, "and several friends mentioned the club in Asheville. They said they had a great time there. I thought I would give it a try."

"It's New Year's Eve. The clubs are packed, aren't they?"

"Slammed yes, but the more the merrier. I think I just talked myself into going," announced Austin.

Ryan thought a minute. "Can I come?"

Austin smiled mischievously. "I don't know. You're getting pretty old and frail. I bet most of your plumbing is irregular now."

Ryan's face went askew. "What the hell are you talking about?"

Austin chuckled. "Boy, you're dense. You asked if you could come. I just assumed you were talking about sex, and I figured you were getting too old to get it up!" Austin cackled as he slapped his knee!

Ryan took a playful swing at him. "I beg your pardon. I'm still healthy, thank you very much."

156

"Yes, you can come," mocked Austin trying to stifle back another laugh, "but I must warn you because New Year's Eve at a gay club is party time. There will be a bunch of drunken folks in a party mood, and you're liable to get pinched, hugged, kissed, and groped."

"I know, but you'll defend me, won't you?" asked Ryan with a laugh.

"I'll be the one doing most of the groping!!" Austin busted out laughing. So did Ryan. Austin pushed his chair back and fled the kitchen as Ryan picked up the dishtowel and flung it at him.

They arrived at the club early but to their surprise, the line to get in was all the way out to the street. The cold wind did not stop the crowd from dressing up for the party. So far, Ryan and Austin had been standing in line about fifteen minutes. It was moving forward but with the chilly breeze it seemed to be too slow. Finally, they made the turn in the line from the street to the alley, when suddenly a car with a blaring bass stereo came around the corner, screeching their tires, and blowing smoke and loose stones high into the air. The car, filled with teenage rednecks, screamed obscenities at the gays in line calling them fags and queers, and then threw both empty and full beer bottles at them. The crowd scattered. Austin instinctively sheltered Ryan with his own body. The rednecks did hit a few of the gay men but no one was seriously hurt. Mostly the crowd remained pissed off. The car sped away as the patrons cursed and yelled at them, and then life went on as they returned to their places in line. Ryan realized that the gay people were far more used to being harassed than he was.

Once inside they found the club already packed, so they had no idea how all those in line behind them were going to get in. Austin told him mostly likely everyone would be squeezed inside like sardine in a can, as it was a big money night for the owners. They made their way through the crowd to the dance floor.

"I can't believe there are this many gays in Asheville," yelled Ryan over the music.

Austin grinned. "We're a minority, but more and more are coming out of the closet every day. Do you see anybody you know?"

"Oh jeez, I didn't think about that. Maybe someone will know me."

"You're safe. I'm sure the people you work with at camp are not here. Come on, dance the night away, or should I say, dance the year away!"

Austin and Ryan always did love to dance. They relaxed and began enjoying themselves. Austin soon had to pee, so Ryan made his way to the nearest bar and bought tall glasses of Long Island Iced Tea. Each glass contained double shots of five different of liquor.

Austin finally made it through the crowd and back to Ryan. He received a cold glass for his effort. "That's pretty stout," grinned Austin as he took a sip. His eyes went wide. "You are trying to get me drunk, right?"

157

"Precisely," shot back Ryan. "If I can get rid of you, then I can pick up some good-looking guy. I bet people all around me are wondering why a nice handsome dude like me is hanging around such an ugly troll!"

Austin poked a finger into Ryan's ribs. "You're going to pay for that!"

"Let's dance!" yelled Ryan as he took Austin's hand and still drinking their tea, they headed back to the floor.

Before the midnight magic hour they already had a strong buzz. Quickly the bar staff passed champagne glasses around. The horde began counting down the remaining seconds of the year. Together, the boys stood there with their filled glasses and yelled as well. When the top of the hour finally arrived a big horn sounded, and hundreds of couples began kissing one another. Ryan and Austin downed their champagne and stood there for a second or two as they watched the crowd all around them. Austin had turned in a circle and when he came back around, Ryan leaned into him, threw his plastic glass to the floor, stomped on it, dramatically bear hugged Austin, leaned him way back like a fancy dancer might do in an old movie musical, and then kissed Austin deeply. Austin felt stunned and at first didn't open his teeth to allow Ryan all the way in, but soon his resistance melted. The crowd around them began to clap and cheer. Blushing, they broke off the kiss, stood up straight again, and took exaggerated theatrical bows to the surrounding audience. Then they continued kissing for five or six long minutes before returning to the dance floor.

Shortly thereafter, Ryan had to pee so he excused himself and left Austin dancing with friends. Minutes later he returned to the dance floor with another round of Long Island Iced Tea. Austin was already seriously buzzed. So was Ryan. Those watching would have assumed they were the perfect couple. They spun each other round, flirted, dirty danced, and had the time of their lives. An hour later, they had yet another drink and continued to dance until the club closed at three in the morning. They knew they both consumed too much to drive, but failed to make a plan for this circumstance. They decided to walk to a nearby hotel and spend the night there. It was just two blocks away. Though they had drunk too much, they were still able to walk and talk, although they were not walking in a straight line.

They hung on to each other as they walked arm in arm. They were acting silly and laughing at most anything that was said. They had strayed but a block from the club when suddenly a car turned the corner racing directly towards them. The Shark Island survivors were oblivious to any street noise. The car slowed for a few seconds as the driver let off on the gas pedal, and then suddenly he slammed the pedal to the floor. The tires began spinning and squealing as the car leaped forward while leaving a vast trail of smoke and burning rubber. Ryan and Austin on a block that had no sidewalk or curb. The car shifted lanes and continued running towards them. Ryan glanced up as the headlights glared into his eyes. He tried to shield the bright beams so he could see what was coming. When Austin looked up, the driver suddenly switched on his bright lights, blinding their view of the car and the occupants. Ryan and Austin stood in the path of the car much like a deer might do on a highway. The friends were too frightened to move, too confused to run, and way too drunk to think.

The boys in the car began calling them faggots and queers out their windows while slamming beer bottles slammed against the nearby buildings. The drive continued heading towards them. The young hoodlums probably meant to just scare the obviously intoxicated couple. They felt sure the queers would leap out-of-the-way and run, but Ryan and Austin stood there like statues, frozen in time. Only a hundred feet of black asphalt separated the menacing car from the fragile bodies of Austin and Ryan. The driver was also yelling and screaming. He assumed they would run. The boys in the backseat were yelling for him to hit them. The driver thought they were playing chicken so he kept the accelerator pedal on the floor.

Just a second before certain death, Ryan suddenly came alive from his paralyzed state, and urgently pushed Austin towards the building. He then leaped into the air to get off the road. The front headlights of the car caught Ryan's heels smashing the lens. It spun Ryan around in the air. The car sped on with the driver now cursing the broken light, and already wondering what he was going to tell his dad.

Austin collapsed in a heap on the side of the road and no sooner had he hit the pavement on his back did he look up and find Ryan coming in the air to him like a fly ball to centerfield. Instinctively, Austin stuck out his arms, and Ryan fell onto him knocking the breath from both.

A second car passed and grumbled in disgust as they thought the two men were making love right there on the street. The boys didn't move for a long time. The air slowly returned to their lungs, and they were panting hard, much like Miss Bell does after running fast across the lawn.

"Are you all right?" gasped Ryan, still lying atop Austin.

"I will when you get off me. How much weight did you gain?" complained Austin.

Ryan, still buzzed, finally giggled, and replied, "Not a pound. You're just a wimp."

"Me, a wimp? I was ready to take on that car and knock the living daylights out of it. What did you go and knock me out-of-the-way for?"

Ryan got to a knee and then stood up. "Right, let me see if I have this straight, pardon the pun. Mister Gay Superman was going to punch out a car with his bare hands? You're drunker than I thought. The only defense you could have done would have been to use your hard head to put a dent in their door. Come on, get your butt up. Let's find that hotel and get off this street before they come back."

159

Austin and Ryan walked a bit and then the idea suddenly popped into Ryan's brain. "They thought WE were queers. If they had hit us, they'd only have hit one gay person."

"Maybe so, but they would have killed both of us," stated Austin solemnly.

Ryan replied, "We would have died together, like Butch Cassidy and the Sundance Kid."

"What?"

"Never mind. Come on."

They found the hotel, paid cash for the room, climbed the stairs, and pushed their way into the door. Once inside, Austin began taking off his clothes. "I smell like asphalt, beer, and smoke, none of which are very flattering. My gay membership card could be revoked for this stench. I'm taking a shower."

Ryan watched him as he walked naked to the shower. Austin soaped up and began singing softly in the shower. A minute later, he felt a draft as the shower curtain parted and Ryan stepped in. "Shut up. You're going to wake up our neighbors. Besides your crummy voice is making toilets flush all the way down the hall!"

Austin turned and faced a naked Ryan. "Who cares?"

"I do," said Ryan as he planted a kiss on Austin's lips. Quickly, he parted his lips, allowing Ryan inside. They made love in the shower, and then on the bed, and by dawn they were fast asleep in each other's arms.

Austin awoke about eleven, wondering if the night's events had been a dream and was Ryan still there. Thankfully, he was still alive. He tried to move but ached all over. He turned around after finding Ryan's arm draped around him and holding him close to his chest. Ryan was still asleep, but clinging on to Austin. They both were nude. Austin kissed Ryan's head and snuggled in closer. Ryan opened his eyes. He, too, ached, but he pulled Austin to him, and they drifted off to sleep once more.

They had to pay a late fee because they slept until four in the afternoon. Ryan didn't say much all the way home, and Austin already suspected that Ryan was about to disappear once more. Austin had begun to realize Ryan loved him, but could only make love to him when alcohol stifled his inhibitions. Part of him would say that if the lovemaking weren't true-blue and committed, then he should let it pass, but another part of him just couldn't. He loved Ryan so much that even making love twice a year and under the influence of alcohol was worth it. He thought if he couldn't have Ryan all the time, some of the time was better than nothing.

Nevertheless, he was wrong about Ryan disappearing this time. He never mentioned the New Year's Eve partying or the sex, but did talk about everything else. It was Austin who had to leave on Sunday afternoon so he would be ready to go to work on Monday morning. Ryan stayed at his adoptive parents' house until the end of the week, and then he was off to Florida on another promotion junket for the camp.

Austin's figured he could handle the months of no sex as long as Ryan called from time to time, but once Ryan hit the road, it was the same pattern as before. Days turned into weeks and weeks into months. Austin became bitterly disappointed. He couldn't understand Ryan, except to say that although he knew the love was there, the guilt and shame of what they did was still greater, and worst, it continued to rule Ryan's life.

It was April, two days before time to pay his taxes. Austin was at the kitchen table trying to figure out the Internal Revenue tax form. He soon realized that Uncle Sam was going to take about thirty-five percent of what he made this year, and that pissed him off. He loved America, but had grown tired of paying the high taxes of a single person. He felt it unfair that married couples received more deductions than gay partners. Suddenly, he said aloud to no one, "On Shark Island, we paid no taxes at all. Not even a coconut. Anything more than that is too much!" He laughed at himself.

He had left the television on, and after a while a Sunday morning evangelists began preaching. Austin paid little attention until he heard the word homosexual. The preacher was condemning all queers, stating they would be going to hell for their sins, and the Christians of the world should unite against homosexuals. He told them to send money to his church so he could fight the fags and queers.

Austin quickly reached for the remote and turned it off after telling the television bigot to go to hell. He knew that whenever the evangelists needed money, they played what they call the homosexual card, guaranteed to double their income.

Now he was in a terrible mood. All year the bank where he worked deducted taxes from his checks, but that wasn't enough, and he soon discovered he was going to have to pay two thousand dollars more. He couldn't get the reverend off his mind. He signed the tax forms for both federal and state returns, wrote the checks, licked the stamp, and laid the envelopes on the counter to mail. He decided to take Bell for a walk in hopes of changing his mood. He had dreamed about Ryan all night and woke up feeling horny, lonely, and unloved.

"Bell!" he called. "Let's go for a walk." He grabbed the leash and waited for Bell to come running from her favorite spot on his bed, but she didn't come. "Bell. Come on girl. Let's go!" He reached for his keys. The weather had cleared, and though the past weeks had been warm and spring like, today a cold front was coming through. Winter had not yet let go.

Austin walked to the bedroom. The moment he entered the room and saw Bell, he knew something was wrong. Bell was on her side, legs straight out, head down, and her eyes closed. At first, Austin thought she was in a

161

deep sleep, but then he noted her chest wasn't moving up and down. Gently, he knelt beside her and stroked her head. Bell was dead. She had gotten pretty old, but Austin thought she still had a few years left. He stroked her again as the tears in his eyes began cascading off his cheeks to the bed. Then he leaned down and nuzzled her. He kissed her head and then broke down sobbing. She had been his faithful companion since arriving on Shark Island. When Ryan married Jennifer, she did not want pets, and so Bell became his alone. He had played with her every day. She had been his link to Ryan. He talked to her about Ryan. He had hugged her when he felt sad, lonely, or depressed. What would he ever do without Bell, he wondered?

He sat there for more than an hour trying to figure out what to do about burying Bell, and what he was going to do without her. He didn't want to bury her at the condominium complex because that place would never be a permanent home. Ryan hadn't called in four months, and Austin didn't know how to reach him. Although the day had started off bad with the taxes and the preacher, he forgot all his problems once Bell died. Austin started packing his suitcases. He took more than he usually did when he went on a business trip. He took things that counted in his life. He took his picture album of Austin and Ryan that he had begun after they met at camp. He took his camera and his summer clothes. He packed the car, and then came back and gently bundled up Bell in her favorite blanket. He placed her in a box and put it in the car.

It had taken two hours to pack. He stood in the doorway of the apartment and stared back into the room for a full minute before locking the door and leaving the apartment. He made the five-hour drive to his home in Brevard in less than four hours. His mom was in Washington with the senator who was about to announce his bid for reelection. No one was home and Austin was thankful. He immediately parked the car and unloaded Bell. He picked up a shovel in the tool shed, and went behind the house near a big oak tree and dug a hole. He buried her and then knelt down, said his goodbyes, and cried once again.

After returning the shovel, he went in the house, found something to eat and wrote his mother a note explaining Bell had died, and that he had buried her in the backyard since that was not possible in his condo complex. He wanted her buried at home. He told his mom he loved her and that he loved his dad, and even his sister and her family. He signed the note and then returned to his car and drove off.

THIRTY

Bonnie frowned and sighed heavily as she moved her clenched fist to her lips. Reluctantly, she replaced the receiver to the phone cradle after ten rings and no answer. Other than intuition, she had no reason to worry, but deep inside she felt something must be wrong. She stared at the number written on the piece of paper, feeling frustrated by not finding him. Over the past few days, Bonnie called Austin's telephone number at his condominium on several occasions, but never caught him. She left numerous messages on his answering machine, but he hadn't replied, and now the full or broken machine no longer picked up her repeated calls. It was the same with his cell phone. Bonnie also left a few messages on his office voice mail, but still no reply. She tried not to agonize, assuming he was away on business. She tried not to think too much of it, perhaps he was away on a long vacation, she thought, but still she wished that he would call.

When Ryan returned from his winter trip and settled into his new camp house, he made a call to Austin, but found he could only leave a message on the machine. A week later, he also found the answering machine no longer picked up even though he let it ring ten times. He also assumed it was either broken or full of messages.

When Mother's Day came and passed without a word from Austin, Bonnie grew even more concerned. She tried to call again, but still no answer.

A week later, Kathleen called her mother to tell her that she was pregnant, and Bonnie was going to be a grandmother for the second time. Bonnie, thrilled at some good news, immediately called the senator to spread her joy. Then she hung up and dialed Austin one more time. The answering machine must still be full, she thought, as Austin wasn't getting her messages. She stewed over the situation for an hour or so, then looked up the number to the bank and called it. She had to go through several clerks before finally getting Austin's boss on the phone. She explained that she hadn't heard from him in a while, and wondered if she might call him where he was working, as he was going to be an uncle again.

There was a long pause on the other end of the line before the reply came. "Mrs. London, I'm sorry, but I'm afraid I am not going to be much help to you," began the man. "Austin hasn't come to work in over a month. We don't know where he is. Unless there is some plausible explanation, I'm afraid we'll have to fire him. He had many training sessions scheduled for him to teach but Austin didn't show up, and he has not left one single word of explanation. We do not know what is going on. This is not like him at all, and frankly, we were thinking of calling the police to report him missing. Please call me if you hear of anything, or if there something I can do. Until now, he did a great job for us."

163

Bonnie felt stunned at the banker's revelation. "Yes," she mumbled, "of course, I will. Thank you." She hung up the phone, paced the kitchen floor while chewing her lower lip. Suddenly, she grabbed the phone and dialed another number.

"Ryan? Ryan, darling, is that you?" asked Bonnie hurriedly.

"Yes ma'am," replied Ryan enthusiastically. Sensing the worried tone in your voice, he quickly asked, "How are you?"

"I'm fine. No," she caught herself, "I'm worried sick. I haven't heard from Austin in over a month, and he didn't call or send a card for Mother's Day. He has never failed to call on Mother's Day since he returned from Shark Island. The good news is Kathleen is pregnant. You're going to be an uncle again. I called Austin's office a few minutes ago, and they said he disappeared from work over a month ago, and no one has seen or heard from him. Do you know where Austin is?"

Ryan sat down on the stool by his kitchen counter absorbing all of Bonnie's words. His brow wrinkled. He involuntarily began bouncing his knee up and down on the ball of his foot. His palms became clammy and wet. "No ma'am, I haven't. I called him, too, but he didn't return my messages." He turned to look out the window as if wishfully hoping to see Austin walking up the stone path to his house.

Bonnie moved to the kitchen sink, looked out the window, and saw no humans anywhere. She moved to the left of her cabinets and gently ran her finger across the family portrait stopping when she reached Austin's smiling handsome face. "His answering machine is full, which I guess means that he wasn't listening to any of my pleas for him to please call me. Ryan, I fear something's wrong and I am afraid. This is not like him. He and I usually talk at least once a week or so. Honey, I'm…" Ryan heard her choke and swallow a bit, "scared." She couldn't hold it back any longer and began to cry.

A big lump formed in Ryan's throat. He had never heard Bonnie cry before and it broke his heart. His eyes filled with tears as well. His mind began to fill with all kinds of solutions. His biggest fear was perhaps Austin had committed suicide. This thought came up long before any thought of someone trying to kidnap, beat, or murder Austin. Then he thought maybe Austin did have that AIDS stuff, and was in the hospital, or he had died alone. Guilt overwhelmed him. Tears rolled down his cheek to the kitchen counter. His lips quivered. His heart was racing.

"Mom," he said. "I'm leaving right now, and I'll drive straight to Raleigh. I'll go to his apartment and find out what is going on. I'll call you from there."

"Thank you, dear. Please drive safe and please call me as soon as you can."

"I will."

"Bye, honey. I love you."

"I love you, too," replied Ryan.

Quickly, Ryan packed his recently unpacked suitcase, locked up the house, cranked the car, and drove to Raleigh. He made it there just before dark. He didn't see Austin's car in the parking lot, and discovered no lights were on in the apartment. He could not hear any music playing as he had found on his last visit. There were various notes on the door. He looked down at his feet and found the doormat littered with thirty or more newspapers. He found Austin's mailbox filled to the brim, and a yellow card from the post office stating they were holding the rest of his mail for him. Ryan read the notes. "Austin, call Al when you get in. Austin, your rent is past due, please call Sarah. Austin, where are you?"

Ryan turned the doorknob, but discovered the door was locked. He knocked on several neighboring doors, but no one had seen Austin. He found the manager's office and knocked rapidly on the door. The man opened the door while wiping his face with a napkin. Obviously, he was eating dinner. Ryan apologized for the interruption, but said the family was convinced something must have happened to his brother. That's who Ryan said he was. The man immediately went with Ryan to the apartment and unlocked the door. Quickly, Ryan went from room to room, and though he didn't find Austin, he was relieved he didn't find him lying dead on the floor. He also noted that Bell was gone. There were dishes in the sink, but the food stains on them were dry and hard. They had been there a long time. He found Austin's plants wilted and dying. Austin must have forgotten to get a house sitter this time, he thought.

"I'm sorry to trouble you," began Ryan to the manager. "I am relieved he's not hurt, but that still leaves us confused about where he is. Mom said he hasn't been to work in over a month, and she hasn't heard from him. Do you have any idea where he is?"

"No, nothing. He has been a good tenant. He usually paid me early because he did travel quite a bit. Now he's behind on his rent. I'll have to evict if we don't hear from him soon."

"Let me give you my number and mom's number. You can call us collect. If you hear of anything, please call. Give me a couple of days to try to find him, but if it comes down to evicting, call me. I'll pay his rent and collect his stuff, okay?"

"Sure, no problem."

"I'll stay tonight if that's okay with you."

"Go right ahead. I'll head back to my dinner," said the manager as he went through the door. Ryan thanked him as he left, turned and closed the door, and leaned against it, desperately trying to figure out where Austin could be.

Ryan ate a frozen dinner Austin left in the refrigerator. It tasted like cardboard. Some of Austin's mail was on the table. Ryan felt guilty for doing so, but he felt desperate for clues. He read Austin's mail, even his personal mail though there wasn't much to read. After he finished, he noted the postmark on this mail was early April, which meant that was approximately when Austin last brought the mail in the house. He quickly got up, went out to the mailbox stop for all the apartments, found Austin's, and brought in all the mail overstuffed into the box.

He dropped the pile on the table and began immediately sorting it. He threw the junk mail in the trash, pushed the bills to his left, and quickly found several personal items. He read them immediately. There was a postcard from a Steve, apparently a friend of Austin's and enjoying an end of the season ski trip to Colorado. He signed it, "Wish you were here." Ryan put the card down and read the next one. It was an 'I Love New York' postcard from James and Jeremy. They were on vacation in the city and sent Austin the card. Ryan recalled meeting them.

He then opened an envelope. It was from a Chris. Ryan read the letter quickly. "Dear Austin. Things are going well in Ft. Lauderdale. The new job is pretty cool. Yesterday I took members of the Kennedy family on a sailing charter. You should come down, and I'll get you a job with us. Give up the bank crap. You know you hate it. The men down here are hot. I'm sure you could find a Mister Right or at least a Mister Almost Right. Come get a tan. I miss you. Chris."

Ryan flipped the short note over. There was no address or phone. He picked up the envelope and in raised print in the upper corner was Thompson Sailing Charters in fancy lettering. He grabbed the phone and spent the next several minutes on the phone hunting for the telephone number for Thompson. He finally obtained the number and dialed it, but it was after hours, and so the phone rang unanswered. Reluctantly, he hung up but immediately dialed Bonnie and related what he learned, while leaving out any hint of Austin being gay. He told her he would spend the night in Raleigh and telephone Florida first thing the next morning. She felt relieved and hopeful Austin would be found, but completely confused as to what had happened in the first place.

Ryan hung up, and rummaged through the rest of mail, but found nothing of use. There was a knock at the door, and Ryan quickly opened it, hoping a friend of Austin's might have stopped by and could tell him about Austin. He found the manager standing there with two grocery bags of mail. "I thought you might want to give this mail to Austin," he said. "His mailbox was full."

"Thanks," replied Ryan. As the manager turned to leave, Ryan shut the door, dumped the mail on the breakfast table, and once again sorted it. He again found no clues to help him.

Feeling thirsty, he returned to the refrigerator. Suddenly his eyes lit up. There were several yellow notes stuck on the freezer door with telephone numbers on them. He saw one for Greg and immediately remembered the birthday party. He called Greg, but he had heard nothing from Austin. He promised to call around town, ask all their friends about Austin, and then would call back if he heard anything. Ryan called every phone number he found on the refrigerator, a wall pad, and even the cover of the phone book, but no one had seen Austin lately.

Ryan rumbled through the magazines near the couch, and went through the drawers in Austin's bedroom. He felt like he was invading Austin's privacy, but Austin could get mad at him for doing so later. First, he had to find his best friend. Austin had never disappeared before. Ryan soon realized Austin was giving him a dose of his own medicine, and that made him feel guilty for going so long without calling.

By midnight, Ryan had looked in every box, drawer, and closet, and even under the bed and inside shoes, but found no clues about where Austin might be. Ryan sat on the bed and feeling exhausted, he soon fell asleep. He awoke about four in the morning. He had been dreaming, and his dreams were back when the Cubans were chasing them through the cave on the island. However, this time his dream was different from reality. Ryan had made it over the waterfall as before, but seconds later Bell had sailed alone over the falls and landed safely in his arms. Then Austin came out of the cave with the sword sticking through his chest.

Ryan woke up sweating. He tossed and turned for hours thinking about Austin. He hugged one of the pillows as tightly as he could. He realized it smelled like Austin. He held on to it for the rest of the night. By eight o'clock the following morning, Ryan was busy dialing the number to Fort Lauderdale. A man called Max answered the phone.

"Sir, this is going to sound a little weird, but please hang on, okay? My brother's name is Austin London. Do you know him?"

Max was chewing on a fresh cigar and sipping his hot coffee. He spoke out the corner of his mouth not wishing to set his lit cigar down. "Sorry, can't say that I do. Is he a patron?"

"I don't know. He lives in Raleigh, North Carolina. He disappeared about a month ago. I am in his apartment right now and there is no sign of him. I got his mail last night, and there was a letter from a Chris mailed to Austin in an envelope with the name of your company on it. Do you have a Chris there?"

"Yes, Chris Patterson. He's one of our captains."

"May I speak with him?"

"I'm afraid not. He's been at sea for five days. Hold on, let me check his itinerary." The man put the phone down on the desk. Ryan could hear him flipping through papers. The long wait seemed to take forever. Finally, he picked up the phone again. "Here, it is. He's on the honeymoon cruise."

Ryan asked, "What does that mean?"

"Well, it's a two-week charter. They should have arrived in the Bahamas a few days ago, and spent the night before making their way to Turk Island and Caicos."

"Where are they now?"

"Hard to say, each trip sort of plans its own schedule based on the weather conditions, the wind, the mood of the guests, etc. Turk Island is a small isolated island. These are honeymooners who love to dive. That area is second only to Cayman in great diving spots. They may have stayed a week there, but most likely just a few days. Then they are going to head south through the Windward Passage and on to Jamaica. From there, they go to Cayman and then back here. I would not be surprised if they stay in Cayman and do some diving there, too. It's probably the best diving in the world."

"Is there any way to contact them?"

"Not that far out at sea."

"Do you have any contacts in the ports they come to?"

"Yes, of course. We've been in the charter business for twenty years. I have a bungalow in Jamaica and part owner in a dive operation in Cayman."

"Sir, it's urgent that I find Austin. Would you call and leave word at these places? Ask him to call home as soon as possible."

"Okay, sure, but Austin is not a passenger on the boat. I only show a Mr. and Mrs. Roger Callows."

"How about the crew? Could he be a member of the crew?"

"Chris and Bobbie is the only crew."

"Are you sure?"

"Yes, I'm sure. I write their checks."

"Okay. I'm flying down today. I'll come by your office this afternoon." Ryan gave him the instructions on how to call Bonnie in Washington and at home in Brevard. He then hung up and booked himself on the next flight out of Raleigh to Fort Lauderdale. He then called Bonnie and related the news. She had booked a flight home from Washington that would leave in an hour. She agreed to remain at her home in Brevard and become the person everyone could fall back on. She also had informed the senator. He was pulling some strings in Washington to see if they could locate Austin. Ryan thanked her, and then hung up, locked the door, and left for the airport.

168

THIRTY-ONE

On landing, Ryan immediately hailed a cab to Thompson Sailing Charters in Palm Harbor. The moment he stepped out of the air-conditioned cab, the heat flushed his face as the smell of saltwater marsh hit his nostrils. It had been a long time since he had stood at sea level. He paid the driver and walked immediately into Thompson's office, which he found to be nothing more than a cinder block building painted white and trimmed in blue. Behind the office was a small harbor filled with boats from small sailing crafts to shrimp boats and big yachts. The lady at the counter was busy with paperwork and didn't look up when he entered until he reached the counter.

"Excuse me, ma'am," Ryan began politely. "I'm Ryan Wilson. I spoke to a gentleman this morning and he..."

She lifted her hand like a traffic cop and stopped him in mid-sentence. She was a blond woman, who gave Ryan a slight pause with her hand while she abruptly spit out her gum in the trashcan. She looked like she might be an authority type so he decided to stay quiet and let her speak her mind. He surmised she was going to do so anyhow. She took a breath, which made her large breasts rise like the swelling of a wave as she looked up at him. Suddenly she spoke. "You're lying and you know it, and if you don't know it, I'm fixing to tell you. The man you spoke to is Rusty, and believe you me he IS rusty! Further, I'm his wife Pat, and I can assure you he ain't no gentleman!!" She winked at Ryan and smiled. "Now, as to where he is, he's gone out while teaching a sailing class filled with a bunch of blue-haired rich folks who want to learn to sail. The things we do for money around here. If they get their charter license the seas will never be safe again. Let's see, you're probably the fellow looking for Chris. Am I right or is my crystal ball fogging up?"

Ryan grinned as he sat down his luggage and shook a strong sailor's hand. He correctly surmised she was a tough likable broad. He began opening his wallet. "You're right, but really, it's not Chris I'm looking for. It's my brother, or half brother I should say. His name is Austin London." Ryan found a picture in his wallet of Ryan and Austin. He paused briefly to look at it once more and then showed it to her. "This is Austin. Have you seen him? He's missing and our family is sick with worry."

"Handsome lad, so he's your brother? My, good looks run in the family, don't they?" she added with a wet grin and big wink of the eye, which wasn't easy, as her false eyelashes were large enough to be mistaken for a bug. "But no, I don't think I've seen him."

"Chris wrote him a letter, asking him to come down here. Is it possible that Austin is aboard Chris' boat?"

"Better not be. We don't have visitors traveling with paying guests. Chris is on a two-week voyage, and they have many miles to cover, plus the party wants to do some diving in Turk Island and in Cayman. Rusty printed their itinerary for you as well as some contacts you can call."

Ryan took the computer printout from her. "Thanks. Rusty said that he thought they were already pass the Bahamas and on the way to Turk Island. Is there someone I can call there?"

"You could call the dive shop that we use. It's located at the local Ramada Inn, which is right on the water. Ask for Betty. She runs the place. Her number is on the printout. Are you staying overnight here in Fort Lauderdale?"

"Yeah, I guess so."

"There a cheap bed and breakfast down about a block called Pelican's Roost. The breakfast is great, the beds are lumpy, but it's clean."

"Thanks Pat. I appreciate the help. Let me write down our mom's phone number and please, if you hear anything about Austin please call."

"I will honey. I promise." She gave him another big wink and smile as he left. Without looking back, he was sure she was staring at his butt.

Ryan found the bed and breakfast, paid for a room, and immediately got on the phone to Turk Island and the Ramada Inn. The call eventually transferred to the dive shop. He was in luck because Betty had just finished a lecture for a scuba class. She took the call on a cordless phone. The static was bad until she turned around in a circle, found a sweet spot, and then suddenly she had a clear signal.

She was a bleached blond with a dark tan for a woman from Nottingham, England. She always hated the cold winters on the big island so she decided moving to the Caribbean was a smart move as she loved the water and the freedom. She had a swimmer's build and used to lifting heavy air tanks. She spit out her gum in a very unladylike move as she answered the phone.

"This is Ryan Wilson. I'm afraid my brother Austin London is missing. It is possible he is aboard Chris Patterson's sailing boat. Have they been there?" yelled Ryan over the bad connection that suddenly became clear.

"Yes, Chris came in yesterday. I can see the boat from here."

Ryan became excited. "There is a honeymoon couple aboard, and then Chris and the cook. Was they're anyone else aboard?"

"I don't know. The couple is out on one of my dive boats right now. They're due in a few hours. I don't know if Chris is on the boat or not. I will radio out and tell him to call you. What's the number?"

"Thanks." He gave her the number. "Please tell him it is urgent that we find Austin. His mother is most upset. He's been missing for more than a month."

"I will. I promise and out," she said with no emotion and hung up.

Ryan called Bonnie's cell phone and relayed the news, but she had news of her own. She had made it to their home in Brevard. She took a breath and said, "Austin has been here. There was a note on the counter. Seems poor Bell has died, and Austin came home to bury the little dog in the backyard. The note is signed 'love, Austin', but that's it. No clue where he went or what date it was written. I checked the backyard and weeds are already creeping back over the grave. Poor Bell, we'll miss her."

Ryan nearly cried. He lost his chance of keeping the dog when he married Jennifer. His wife wouldn't think of having an animal in their house. Austin had asked him to keep Bell on several occasions, but Jennifer would always decline. Now the little dog was gone forever. He hung up promising to call after talking to Chris.

He was afraid to leave the room fearing that Chris would call and he would miss his chance to talk to him. He finally ordered pizza and had it delivered to the room. He kept trying to recall if Austin ever mentioned anything about moving to Florida but couldn't recall anything. He didn't know this Chris, and wondered if perhaps Austin and Chris were an 'item.' He couldn't bear to say the word 'lovers' as so many couples often do.

Ryan had felt lonely on a many a night on the road for the camp, city after city, state after state, and always chasing the warmer weather and outrunning the snow. He would start way up north in the fall and keep working southward. After living on Shark Island in the warm Caribbean sun for more than seven years, all cold spells felt colder than he could ever remember as a child in Maine.

He ate but a slice of the pizza because he felt too worried and too deep in thought to eat. He sipped on warm beer and waited for the phone to ring. Nevertheless, it never did. He went to bed just after midnight, but had trouble going to sleep because just an hour ago a thought had occurred to him. Perhaps Austin did something that even he had wished for during many a dream. Maybe Austin went back to the island. Maybe Austin couldn't take the city life any longer. Perhaps he had given up on love and went away to live alone.

However, after he drifted off to sleep, he dreamed he could see Austin in the tree house, and he had grown long white hair and a lengthy beard, and he was starving. No, he was dying. He had a fever, and Ryan wasn't there to take care of him and nurse him to health. Then Ryan saw the wind blowing the tree house back and forth, and soon Austin was swept off the floor and out the door. Ryan suddenly woke up after seeing Austin's screaming body tossed head over heels as it skipped across the blue water and out of sight into a huge fireball.

Ryan's body was sweating even though the air-conditioning was on a maximum cold setting. Since Jennifer left, he had gone back to sleeping in the nude as he and Austin had done for seven years. He got up, wet a washrag, and wiped his face and then gently washed his whole body. Suddenly, a chill went up his spine, and he didn't know why. Chill bumps began forming from his ankles up his legs, past his groin, across his tummy, up his chest, and out to his arms. He looked in the mirror and his hair was moving as if an ocean breeze had entered the room. He was far across the room from the air-conditioner and yet his hair was moving. This was freaking him out. The chill bumps grew bigger. His eyes went wide. There was no explanation. His heart started pounding. The old fashion rotary dial phone abruptly rang loud and clear.

Ryan jumped. The washrag fell to the floor. The telephone rang again. The realization hit him. He dove over the bed and snagged the receiver from the cradle. "Hello?"

"Hi, mate! This is Chris Patterson. I got a message to call you. Listen, I'm sorry for calling so late. I went out for dinner, then off to a party, it's a Caribbean Holiday, you know, and well, time got away from me and when I got back, I found the message to call you. We're shoving off early in the morning so I figured it best I wake you rather than miss you. Sorry, old chap." Chris spoke with a thick Australian accent.

"Thanks for calling. I was at Austin's apartment the other day, and I saw the letter that you wrote him trying to get him to come down."

"Oh, you did."

"Yes, I'm sorry. I'm Ryan Wilson. Austin's..." he stuttered while searching for the right words. Chris cut him off.

"I know who you are. Austin told me all about you. I probably know your whole life story. He loves you, man. He really does."

The lump returned to Ryan's throat. His stomach churned into a knot. He softly replied, "I know."

"I tried my best to get him to fall in love with me and sail around the world. He was nice and honorable, said I was handsome and smart, and he was right of course," he laughed at himself. He paused a second in thought before continuing, "But no, his heart he gave to you, he said, and he had no more hearts to give out."

"I know. Listen, he has disappeared. No one has seen him for over a month. He just up and left. Have you seen him? His mother and I are panic-stricken."

"Yes."

Ryan's heart skipped a beat. "Is he with you?"

"I wish. No, he came to Florida weeks ago, stayed for a day or two, and then poof, he disappeared into thin air. He left a note thanking me for letting him stay a bit, and said he would miss me and that's it."

"Where did he go?"

"Don't know. He left no forwarding address. He told me he quit work. I assumed you knew. I'm sorry. I hope he's all right. He's special, you know."

"Yes, he is," beamed Ryan slowly while trying to think of his next question. "Do you have any idea where I might find him?"

"I don't think he is going back to a banking job. We were walking on the beach the day he got here. He had on an expensive three-piece pinstriped suit, but wrinkled like he had been wearing it a few days. He abruptly took it off right down to his boxer shorts and threw it in the ocean. It was hilarious. He was sober, too. He let the surf and sand flow between his toes. Instantly, an amazing peaceful look crept across his face. It was almost angelic. I know it sounds crazy, but it was as if he was in heaven."

"Let me give you Austin's home phone number in Brevard. Please call his mother if you think of something. I'll be checking in with her while I keep searching for him."

"Sure, mate. Please send word he's all right."

"I will. Thanks."

"I wish you well, mate. You're lucky to have his love, very lucky indeed."

Ryan couldn't respond. He choked up. He set the receiver down slowly as the tears flew down his face to his bare thighs. He checked the clock. It was two in the morning. He set the alarm and once again tried to go to sleep.

THIRTY-TWO

He now knew there was no point in flying to Caicos as Chris assured him that Austin was not there and he fully believed him. So that left the possibility that Austin was either somewhere in Florida, or somewhere in the United States, or somewhere in South America, or somewhere in the whole freaking world. He wondered if the dream was telling him where to look. He decided to fly to Cayman, as that was the closest democratic island to the Cuban controlled Shark Island. He made the flight reservations, after learning he could make the eleven o'clock flight if he hurried.

He rapidly packed and then drove immediately to the airport, got his boarding pass, found the gate, and then sat by a pay phone and began making calls. He called Bonnie and told her what Chris had said. He didn't tell her about the dream, but said he had a hunch. He asked her to call all of his and Austin's old friends, including Jennifer, to see if anyone had heard from Austin. He promised to call her when he got to Cayman. He then called the senator, something he had never done in eight years since their return from the island. While he was grateful for everything the senator had done for him, he hated him for the way he neglected Austin. His son was a wonderful, intelligent, beautiful man, and his father ignored him for the sake of politics. He vowed he would never vote for the man, but right now, he needed his help.

The senator's secretary, well trained in fending off calls for the senator in an ever so sweet charm school Southern drawl, while capable of softening even the most aggressive of lobbyists, took a breath to begin her welcoming speech. But before she got one second into her well-practiced pattern, Ryan cut her off abruptly and strongly. "Miss Mercer, this is Ryan Wilson, the senator's adopted son, put the senator on now. It's about his missing son Austin!"

She stumbled and swallowed hard before replying, "Yes. Yes, of course, dear. Please hold." She left her post, crossed the plush carpet with the design of the state of North Carolina on it, and entered the mahogany doors with the gold-plated handles and into the senator's private office. She found him in the midst of a meeting with several other senators. The senator from Brevard saw her coming his way and quickly tried to read her face. A second look told him something serious was up.

"Excuse me, gentlemen, just hold that thought a moment. My apologies," he said with a polite smile, and then leaned back away from the table.

She leaned into him and whispered that Ryan was on the line and why. The senator's face instantly turned pale. He sighed heavily.

He looked back at his guests. "I'm sorry, this is an emergency, fellows. I beg your indulgence. Please excuse me. I'm going to have to take this call. Miss Mercer would you show these fine gentlemen where the hot coffee is."

He had said it politely, but the conclusion removed them temporarily from the room. They nodded affirmatively and exited leaving their documents behind. The senator didn't wait for them to leave, but hastened swiftly to his desk and punched the red blinking line.

"Hello, Ryan, Senator London here."

Ryan sighed. Didn't the man have a first name? Of course, he knew who the senator was. "Sir, I'm sure Bonnie has spoken to you. I'm in the Fort Lauderdale Airport. I got in touch with Chris Patterson. Austin was here, but only for a few days, and that's been weeks ago. He didn't go with Chris on the sailboat so that rules out flying to Caicos to look for him. I don't have any other leads, but I'm flying to Cayman. I'm wondering if Austin is trying to go back to Shark Island."

The senator scoffed at the notion. "Surely, you're kidding. He spent seven years of hell on that island..."

The senator completely passed over the fact Ryan spent the same seven years with Austin, and they weren't hell at all. In his opinion they were heaven. Sure, they had storms and a few Cubans to outrun, but it was better than divorce, politics, crime, greed, and the bigoted, angry spirits from most people they encountered here. It was certainly better than any parent-teacher meeting he attended at the school.

"I know, but Austin wasn't happy with his job, and he wasn't happy with his life. The island changed him, and he hasn't been able to change back." Ryan heard the words coming from his lips, then the invisible sound waves hit the wall in from of him, and bounced right back in his face like radio signals from a satellite. He knew he had the same problem. He had tried to live a good life. He had become a noble teacher, only to be run in the ground by the system. He had done what the world expected and fallen in love, married, and wanted a child, but a child he couldn't produce, according to Jennifer, and a wife he couldn't keep happy. He wasn't doing any better than Austin. Life had been far simpler on the island.

"How can I help?" asked the senator finally, which is why Ryan called him in the first place.

"It's a long shot, but last night I figured Austin may have brought some money with him, but maybe not enough. Perhaps he's touched his bank account, or maybe he's used his credit cards. Do you have a way of checking on that?"

"Of course, I do," replied the senator without saying how he could. "He may have gotten a job down there and if so, he's paying taxes like every other red bloodied American. I will call the Internal Revenue Service and have them check on it. I'll also call the Social Security office, too. Can you think of any other possibilities?"

"Yes, sir. Call the Customs Office and see if he's used his passport. I didn't think to look for it when I was in his apartment. He usually kept it in his safe-deposit box at the bank. That's an idea. Also, get someone to open that box!"

"That's smart thinking, young man. I'll get right on it. Call me when you get to Cayman?" Ryan impressed the senator with his take-charge attitude. He made a mental note to get Ryan a job in his office. He needed aids he could trust. He wrote the idea on his pad after making notes on their conversation.

"Yes, sir," replied Ryan.

The senator hung up without saying goodbye, good luck, good riddance, or even good day. Ryan hated him, but he still needed him. He heard his flight called over the public address system, so he quickly gathered his stuff and boarded. He anxious sat on the plane waiting for it back away from the gate. He thought about search he was doing. A few days ago, he was showing the camp movie to a family in Georgia on his way home from the winter recruiting season. He expected to be fishing for bass on the camp lake this week, and now he was on a jet plane heading for Cayman, looking for the only man in the world he knew without any doubt loved him and that he loved in return. He prayed selfishly, asking God to bring him back. He had to find Austin. He had to.

Ryan spent three days looking for Austin on the British island. He spoke with every charter boat and scuba company, and even the police, but no one had seen Austin. The senator had indeed come through with his promises, and found out that Austin had used his Master Card in Fort Lauderdale and then again in Miami. The last charge was three weeks ago. At least he was still alive, thought Ryan, and then hated himself for thinking that perhaps Austin had committed suicide. He also found out that Austin had not used his passport to leave the country although the safety deposit box was empty. He had not worked anywhere or paid any taxes. In the senator's opinion, Austin could still be in Fort Lauderdale or Miami, or who knows where.

This put Ryan in an awkward position. His heart was telling him that Austin was on Shark Island. If he went back to Miami to start searching where the last credit card charge was the trail might still lead him to Shark Island. He explained to the senator his thoughts. The senator still felt that Austin would never go back there, but agreed to wire Ryan the money to charter a boat to find out. He also said he would fax the navigation coordinates for the island to him. Ryan caught a cab to the American Embassy office. When he arrived, a secretary held the door for him, escorted him down a long hallway, and through a secured door guarded by United States Marine soldier that lead him to a conference room.

"Mr. Wilson?" asked a man with a typical military haircut, white suit, wearing gold rings, a dive watch, and dark sunglasses. He removed the glasses. "Let's see, my name is Albert. Albert Einstein." The wink he gave Ryan told him that this was obviously a bogus name the man was using. Ryan didn't have the slightest idea why. Ryan almost laughed at the name the man chose as he leaned over and shook the man's hand.

The man smiled at Ryan's expected reaction. "The senator has asked me to assist you. Here's what you requested and a bit more. That duffel bag has ten thousand dollars in it." He tossed it to Ryan and then leaned over an opened map. Red lines had been drawn on it. "Here's Cayman," he pointed with a gold pen. "There's Shark Island. It's probably about one hundred and fifty miles from here. The Cubans were caught with their pants down the last time you were there. They've patrolled the island heavily since then. You'll need to meet a guy named Samson. He'll take you there. He owns a fishing boat of sorts."

Ryan had no idea what 'of sorts' meant. "Where do I find him?"

"He's expecting you. Just go down to Georgetown Harbor. Head on through town and on the right, you'll find a photography museum. There's a woman photographer there by the name of Cathy Church. She's famous. You may have heard of her. Tell her you're Ryan Wilson. She'll get you to Samson."

"What's the gun for?" asked Ryan as he gazed at the Uzi on the table.

"Leave your passport, drivers license, billfold, and anything else that says Ryan on it with me. I'll hold it for you. The gun is in case the Cubans get too close. I hope they'll think you're a refugee or a lost fisherman, and just shoo you off, so don't go brandishing the gun unless you have to use it. Wear a big hat, and try to look like a local. Try to obtain a darker tan and let your beard grow. Got it?"

"Yeah, I guess so," gulped Ryan. He had no idea how to do as the man in asked in the next hour.

"Let me show you how to lock and load the weapon, and then you stuff it in the duffel bag and head to the harbor. Samson's waiting on you." He gave Ryan a quick course in using the machine gun, then shook hands, and showed him the door.

Georgetown is in the heart of Cayman. It was the pinnacle point of the big harbor where the giant cruise ships dropped anchor. Almost everyone that entered the harbor of this tiny island took a picture of this typical tropical city. The odd thing about the island was that it had more international banks than most states in America. Both the South and North American financial institutions traded money with these banks. It was rumored that drug money was laundered here as well. However, it was a quaint little English island with streets that were still two lanes and always filled with tourists. Golden sunsets were a year-around tourist attraction. Currently, the harbor hosted two huge cruise ships. Fifty or more small boats ferried the quick spending tourists to and from town. Cayman was also the scuba capital of the world. The water around the island was clear to a hundred and fifty feet and the sea life exceptional. He passed at least a dozen or more dive shops as he made his way through town on foot. There was no need for a car. Everything was within walking distance. He was hot but didn't notice. He was focused on trying to remember everything Einstein had said to him. It was all too surreal. He felt a bit like James Bond. Einstein had to be military trained. The senator indeed had connections, he thought.

He found the museum, made his way around back and found a stairwell leading to the shop. A soft buzzer sounded as he pushed through the door to the photographer's studio. Inside he found hundreds of underwater pictures on every wall, all signed by Cathy Church. He discovered that she was indeed a very good, unusual, and extremely talented underwater photographer. Ryan was staring at a large picture of a young diver completely engulfed within a school of harmless stingrays.

A clerk approached. "That's Sting Ray City. Have you been there yet?"

"No, I'm afraid not. I'm looking for Samson."

Immediately the lady's smiling friendly expression left her face. "One moment," she almost whispered.

Ryan took the moment to look at another wall of pictures. He spotted a large moray eel, and shuttered at the sight of its huge jaws and rows of jagged teeth.

A tall woman walked up behind him. A reflection in the frame revealed a glimpse of her walking towards him. He turned to meet her. "I'm Cathy Church. May I help you?"

Ryan turned around to find that Cathy possessed a lean athletic build, sun-bleached hair, dark tan, smooth silky legs, and was wearing tennis shorts and pink blouse. Ryan even noticed the tiny gold sand dollar earrings she wore. Her wide, bright white, friendly smile made her even more captivating.

"Yes, I'm Ryan Wilson. I'm looking for Samson."

"Yes, you fit the description. We've been waiting for you. Please come this way."

She led him out the back of the shop, and then down a broken coral pathway and onto a dock. At the end of the dock, he spotted what he felt was the ugliest shrimp boat Ryan had ever seen. Mildew and slime covered the boat with some green moss growing on it.

"He's on that boat," pointed Cathy as she turned and left without waiting for a reply.

Ryan stood still for a moment, turned to watch Cathy go back to the shop, and then he turned around and walked timidly down the dock. He wasn't sure what he was getting himself into, but he would do this and more to find Austin. To Ryan, a successful end would justify any means to make it happen.

THIRTY-THREE

"Ahoy!" called Ryan before stepping aboard and feeling stupid for saying ahoy when yelling out for Samson would have made more sense.

A black head wearing a black, rolled up stocking cap, suddenly poked out of the engine hole on the boat, as smoke bellowed out around him. "Aye, aye! Come aboard Ryan. I've been expecting you. I'm just checking the engine to see if I can get one more trip out of it. I sure don't want to break down where we're going." The man began cleaning his oily hands on a worn red rag after closing the hatch to the engine room.

Ryan stepped aboard as the man walked across the deck to meet him. It was the first time he had stepped aboard a boat since boarding the ill-fated sailboat with his family and Austin. For the moment, words failed him, so he took another look at Samson. He was tall, six feet four inches, weighed about two hundred twenty pounds, and looked like he had been working out with weights all his life. His biceps were bigger than Ryan's thigh muscle. He had a small scar under his left eye and gold tooth in the middle of a top row of white teeth. He continued his attempt to wipe the grease from his hands onto the dirty rag before finally sticking out the big hand for Ryan to shake.

Ryan didn't hesitate. He had been shaking hands all winter with one parent and child after another who wanted to learn about the famous summer camp. However, this time was a bit different because it was the hand of the man he was putting his trust in, and a man who was willing to help him find Austin. He knew he must trust Samson, and he committed to doing so. His smaller, white hand immediately disappeared in the friendly but firm handshake of the smiling islander named Samson. "Glad to have you aboard. You can put that in the bait well."

He was pointing to the duffel bag. "I beg your pardon?"

"Sorry." Samson lifted the top section of the two-foot by three-foot tub of water filled with small baitfish, and underneath Ryan spotted a dry secret compartment for the bag. He placed it there. "That's just in case we are searched by the local authorities. I know what you're carrying, and if we're lucky, we won't need it anyway. Let's shove off. Have you been on board an ocean boat before? You got sea legs?"

"Yes, sir," replied Ryan without going into his story of being lost at sea. His gut told him Samson knew his life story anyhow.

Samson moved the bait tank back over the hidden duffel bag. "Good, get the bow line. I'll get the stern." Instantly, Ryan knew the request had been both an order for him to obey, and a test to see which end of the boat he went to. He passed on both accounts.

Samson turned the ignition key and the engine suddenly roared to life as the entire boat began to vibrate. The sun was about two hours from hitting the water. Smoke and noise bellowed out the stern, but once in deeper waters the boat picked up speed, more speed than he thought a boat this size should have. Samson scanned the ocean but didn't see any boats in the area. He then adjusted a hidden knob under the wheel, and the smoke diminished to just a slight trail. Ryan began to suspect the weather-beaten exterior of the boat was a mere camouflage to what this boat could really do.

Ryan asked, "Do much fishing?"

"Just enough to fool folks," he replied with a big white smile. You've probably figured that out anyhow. I'm an undercover drug agent for the United States of America on loan to Cayman. This boat has a two thousand horsepower engine, designed to look like it has only two hundred horsepower. I put the grease on here and there. I do my best to keep this boat dirty and smelly. How I'm doing?" He laughed.

Ryan smiled and nodded his head affirmatively as he looked around. "Do you need the map?"

"No, I memorized it. My fish finder secretly becomes a satellite navigational computer. I've already programmed in the coordinates. I'll put you right on the island at an hour before dawn. Then I'll head back out to sea and just outside the Cuban waters, and do a little fishing to keep up appearances. The next morning, at an hour before dawn, I'll pick you up. Got your watch?"

"Yep," replied Ryan.

"Let's agree that an hour before dawn is 4:30 AM. Don't be late or you'll miss your ride, and it's a long swim to freedom."

Ryan nodded slowly as worry lines began forming on his forehead.

"Can you search that bloody island in a day?"

"I don't have to. I'll know if he's been there, and I'll know if he is there."

"Good. If the Cubans approach then quickly hide. They must not know we're here. Don't fight them as you did last time. Hiding is safer. If they find out you're there I'll have a hell of time coming to get you. Do you copy?"

"Right."

"There's a couple of boxes of Kentucky Fried Chicken on the top shelf. One for you and one for me, don't eat both of 'em, or I'll have to feed you to sharks," laughed Samson. "Lighten up, kid. We'll find the senator's son."

Weary from trying to stay awake, Ryan finally dozed off about 3:15 A.M. The hum of the big diesel motor, the splash sound of the waves as they collided with the boat, and the gentle, uneven rocking of the boat as they made the crossing, all combined to make it easy for him to drift off. His mind immediately went to work replaying scenes of him and Austin on the island. Samson noted a slight smile on Ryan's face, and wondered what he was dreaming about, and how such a nice kid ended up attempting to breach Cuban territorial authority. It made no sense to him, but orders were orders.

181

For over twenty years, he had run covert missions in and around the Cuban islands, but this one felt different. He deliberately didn't mention those operations to Ryan. He almost hated to wake the kid but timing was crucial on this run. He bumped the boy slightly with his boot.

"Ryan? Ryan! It's time."

"Huh?" mumbled Ryan, and then seeing Samson's bright white smile brought him back to reality. He stood up and stretched.

"I'll almost run us aground. When I say jump you do so. Don't hesitate because at the same time I'll be thrusting the engine in reverse and getting out before the next wave. You got it?"

Ryan gulped. "Got it?"

"The duffel bag is up at the bow. If caught, immediately offer the soldiers a bribe before they report to their superiors in Cuba. I kept five thousand on the boat. Make a deal with them. You'll give the Cubans five thousand up front, and the rest when you're safe on my boat. The chance to get more money will keep you safe from harm. If the worst happens then use the gun. Of course, your best bet is to try very hard not to be seen. If you see any aircraft, get under the cover of the trees. I repeat. They must not see you." He didn't wait for a response. It had been another important order. "Get ready."

Ryan moved to the front of the boat. Samson had been navigating by computer. The moon was almost over the horizon, but still afforded just enough light for Ryan to see the island. It felt eerie to see the island from the ocean. He had never been out this far from Shark Island's shore. They had just two hundred yards to go. His heart was beating rapidly as he bent down, grabbed the duffel bag in his left hand, and waited eagerly to set foot on the island. Though desperate for help, Ryan knew he his decision to trust this stranger with his life was a good choice. He hoped Samson knew what he was doing. He even hoped he knew what he was doing. He took a few deep breaths to try to calm his nerves down while staring intently at his former island home.

The boat crested the top of an inbound wave. Samson gunned the motor and road the wave like a surfer. The chop settled in and Ryan held on tightly as the boat rocked rapidly left and right. It was just a few more seconds to shore. He could feel his pulse beating in the temples alongside his face. His mouth was suddenly dry.

"Go!!" yelled Samson as he thrust the shifter into reverse and barely looked up to see Ryan leap through the air and land in knee-deep water, and then ran up the shoreline. Samson grinned, as Ryan had never hesitated but leaped out like a runner on the trail of an Olympic record. Ryan waved that he was okay, but Samson didn't see him. He was watching the waves as he was backing away, and when the timing was right, he spun the boat around and gunned it to keep from getting hit broadside. Once over a big, oncoming cresting wave, Samson turned and gave Ryan a big thumb up sign indicating he was wishing him good luck.

Ryan waved and then turned to study his position for a moment, instantly noting that he had landed on the southernmost tip of the island. It would take him about an hour to hike to the tree house. He quickly began moving across the beach. He stopped to remove his shoes and tied them to the duffel bag. He doubted if Austin heard the boat approach from this far away, and wondered how surprised Austin would be, if indeed he were here. He also realized how vulnerable they had been to anyone that landed on this end of the island. Their security had been weaker than they thought. Their salvation had been the ease in which they could move about on the island, beginning with the ropes in the trees and the secret cave. However, their main weapon was their isolation. No one knew they existed, so no one would have been looking for them. It had only been chance that caused the Apollo spacecraft to land off course and closer to their island. The reporter that saw their signaling became pretty close to being a miracle encounter. Unfortunately, the incident led the Cubans to them.

His heart was pounding as the sun seemingly burst through the water and began its long golden ascent into the sky. The island lit up beautifully with the lush greens, the birds, the white sand, and the deep blue water surrounding it all. It was a glorious place, a peaceful oasis in a world full of hate, thought Ryan. He hadn't found anything in America that compared with their spectacular Shark Island. He spotted the tree house. He stopped and sighed heavily. He was home, a special home. He had missed it more than he imagined he would. It seemed bigger than he remembered. He could still see the perch in the top of the tree. He left the beach and moved inland, noting how well the tree house remained camouflaged, and after eight years, it still swayed in the breeze just fine. No hurricane had blown it away. He flung the strap of the duffel bag over his shoulder and began making his way up the tree. He felt he was getting old, but not too old to make the climb. He grabbed a rope, shook the cobwebs from it, and began making his way to the deck. He wanted to yell and announce his homecoming to every creature, but was still afraid someone else might be on the island. Then suddenly, it occurred to him the Cubans could have set a trap for him. Maybe the island now had guards patrolling it.

He paused briefly just across from the deck. He heard no sounds. Saw no one moving. He checked his watch. It was a little past six. He swung across to the deck while dropping down safely onto the dried limbs. He didn't let go of the rope until he was sure it would hold. Filled with apprehension, he took a breath, and then quickly moved inside and immediately felt disappointed. Undisturbed dust was everywhere. He found no footprints. The Cubans had shot up the place on their last visit to the island, but nothing had been touched since their departure. Carefully he moved around the tree house, checking everything. He picked up a bowl he had carved and put it in the duffel bag, then laid the bag on the floor, and made the climb to the perch.

The view was magnificent and he stood very still for a moment taking it all in. He was in awe of the splendor of the island surrounded by the gorgeous blue crystal waters. He wondered why had they left such a paradise? Everything after their return led to a bit of heartache. He turned slowly in a circle. He spotted no boats, not even Samson, and thankfully no helicopters as well. The floor in the perch was a bit creaky, but other than that, it was intact. Oddly, he found his first hint of visitors to their home. On the floor in the corner was an empty six-pack carton of beer. The bottles had Spanish writing on them. He assumed a Cuban soldier might have been left here to watch after the island or watch for returnees. A wild thought went through his head that perhaps Austin had landed, and was immediately captured and hauled off to Cuba.

However, as he analyzed the beer bottles and the carton they left years ago, he knew Austin had not returned. On his arrival, he hadn't found footprints under the treehouse, and so he knew that time, wind, and sand had returned the island to its natural state. He made his way down the old rope ladder to the deck. He placed his bag over his shoulder, and walked to the deck where they had swung to get away many years before. He took the rope in his hand and hesitated to swing. He didn't remember the ground being so far down or how risky they had been. The island kids were too naïve to be afraid, but now he was a bit intimidated, but still unwilling to back down. That part had not changed in either of the boys. He took a breath, clung tightly to the rope, and swung across to the next big limb. He almost yelled out with glee when he made it. He had to steady his balance. It seemed easier when he was a teenager. He swung to the next limb, and then continued until he reached the hill and finally the ground.

THIRTY-FOUR

The path to the cave was now almost invisible, but it didn't matter to Ryan, as he knew every step of it by heart. He spotted some goats and noted more rabbits than he could remember. As he came closer to the cave, he checked the ground for footprints but found nothing more than animal tracks. He entered the cave and waited on his eyes to adjust before advancing, but after twenty feet he felt convinced no on had entered, as the cobwebs were thick and full, and still no footprints.

Once outside, he climbed over the hill and down to the pool. He hiked over to the waterfall, and then to the other side of the island. Once again, he couldn't find any sign of Austin. His emotions bewildered him. He sighed hard, felt dejected and confused, as well as disappointed, and yet also relieved. He had been afraid that he would find Austin, but discover that he was dead. He had been wrong in assuming Austin had retreated to their island paradise. He knew the senator would not be happy with his mistake in judgment, and his waste of government resources and their time.

Nevertheless, the worst part was that if Austin was not on Shark Island, then where was he? Where would he go? Would he go stay with someone, and if so, who? Ryan knew little of Austin's friends outside those he met in Raleigh. What other jobs would Austin do? What else was he suited for? How would he live without money, and where would he work when he needed it?

The questions revolved over and over in his mind as he made his way back to the tree house, and then climbing it again for one more look around. He found the pole where he read the date and initials that he and Austin had carved together. He smiled down at the place where he and Austin had slept together for so many nights. He noted little Bell's pile of bones only slightly hidden behind a pile of rope. Every step he took brought vivid memories as they replayed like videos in his head. The flashbacks brought a smile to his face and a measure of peace to his heart. This had been a magical place to them, and they felt there was nothing else like it. He felt the gentle breeze on his face as he walked out to the deck. The house swayed in the breeze, and it felt good and right to him. He climbed the perch one last time to scout around. He checked his watch. He had covered much ground, but it was already two o'clock. Nightfall was five hours away, and Samson would be here early in the morning. He still had time to search the rest of the island.

He began turning around in a long slow circle of the island, taking in the view and remembering everything they had seen and done for those seven plus years. He had just about finished his loop when something way out in the ocean sparkled towards him from far off to the northeast. He spun the old telescope around, removed his handkerchief, and quickly cleaned the dirty lenses. He knelt down to look through it. He scanned the horizon of the ocean until he found the source of the twinkle. It was a boat and to his surprise it was coming towards him. It was probably an hour away. That would be too soon for him and too late for Samson. He stared at the boat and wondered if it was just a patrol boat cruising by, or perhaps a mere fishing boat that was trolling for marlin.

He pulled his eye away and checked his watch. Ten minutes passed, and then he spotted the boat once more. It was much closer. It was making good time and probably not a fishing boat. He could see a flag but couldn't tell which country the flag belonged to. He checked his watch again.

Ten more minutes passed, and then he scanned the horizon until once more he found the boat in the lens. He slowly turned the focus ring until he could make out the flag. It was the dreaded Cuban flag. The boat was about thirty-five feet long and painted gray, which was pretty standard with the military for most countries. There was huge gun mounted on the bow. He could see soldiers running around preparing to land. He guessed there must be at least twenty of them. The worst news of all was they appeared to be heading directly for the island.

He wondered aloud. Why were they coming? Had radar or a Russian spy satellite picked up Samson's boat and a warning sent to the Cubans? Okay, what's the worst that could happen? They land on the island, they find nothing, and then they leave. "Oh jeez!" exclaimed Ryan. "My footprints!"

He swung the bag over his shoulder and then rapidly descended the ropes, not once thinking of the fear of falling, but rather how fast he could get to the ground. He landed with a thud, broke off a nearby palm, and began brushing the ground all around the tree house. Then he made his way back to the beach, retracing his footprints right down to the beach. He became relieved to find the midday tide had come in and washed off the remaining footprints towards the southernmost point. He worked his way from the beach wiping the footprints while hoping no one was watching him. Once in the underbrush he made his way into the jungle to hide but not far from the tree house. He assumed if this boatload of soldiers knew anything about the island, they would know about the tree house. If they were looking for someone, he surmised they would come there first. He sat down to nervously wait.

He spotted the boat as it crested a wave, but couldn't hear it just yet. He checked his watch. It was almost three. Four hours to darkness and then he could creep down to the southern point and wait for Samson. He moved back farther into the brush, hiding himself as best he could, but being careful to make sure he could still see the tree house through jungle plants that hid him.

He finally heard the boat's big engine, as it approached the shore. He moved a bit to his right so he could see it. It had stopped just offshore. A Zodiac inflatable craft with an outboard motor attached was lowered to the water. Six men climbed in and all were armed with automatic rifles. Ryan gulped and moved deeper into the forest. When the launch landed, a captain leaped onto shore and quickly began barking orders rapidly in Spanish. Ryan had minored in Spanish at UNC, but he couldn't keep up with the swiftly speaking captain and only make out about every fifth word or so.

The captain sent an armed man in each direction on the beach. He noted the soldiers not only had a weapon, but a radio to communicate quickly with their captain. The remaining three men followed the captain as they moved quickly to the tree house. They studied the sand carefully so Ryan knew he had been right to take the time to remove his footprints. The man heading south passed down the beach right across from Ryan, but he was not visible to him. When they reached the tree house, the captain began issuing orders once more.

One of the soldiers strapped his machine gun over his shoulder and began making his way up to the deck. Ryan tried to recall if he had left anything there but was pretty sure he hadn't. He had only brought the duffel bag, and he only took the bowl. Oh jeez, he wondered silently. Had they taken an inventory? Would they know the bowl he had carved was now missing?

Ryan could see the soldier moving throughout the tree house, he then climbed partially up to the perch until satisfied no one was up there. He yelled back down to his captain there was no one there. He then reentered the tree house and walked through it more carefully, but found nothing. He returned to the ground.

The captain radioed to his men on the beach, but they, too, reported no sign of visitors. The foursome then moved into the jungle, searching for clues. Once out of sight, Ryan sighed heavily. He wondered how long would they stay? He checked his watch. It was almost four.

It was two hours before the captain and his men met each other. All six were now together, having met up on the backside of the island. They decided to cut across the island towards the tree house. Ryan watched them while carefully moving through the big leafy jungle plants. The Cubans reached the pool of freshwater that Austin and Ryan had discovered their first day on the island. There the soldiers stopped to rest and cool themselves off by dipping their helmets into the cool water and pouring it over their heads. They passed around cigarettes while the captain remained busy radioing a message to the boat that would forward to their headquarters in Cuba. Ryan was able to translate the message. The captain had reported the island was empty.

One of the men needed to potty and slipped away from the group, found a good spot, removed his backpack, retrieved some toilet tissue from a side pouch, pulled his pants down and squatted down. A few seconds later, he heard a grunt in the brush not far from him. His eyes went wide. He tried to hurry his bowel movement. The grunt came again, but a bit braver and louder. The soldiers heard it this time and quickly picked up their guns, pulling the metallic cocking hammers.

The grunt came once more accompanied by a loud snort. The man quickly wiped himself. Then he heard not one but four grunts. The brush began moving. He jerked up his pants, grabbed his pack and his rifle, and ran to the others. One of the men almost fired at him, but pulled his barrel up abruptly. Limbs cracked, leaves fluttered, the swish-swish of the brush grew louder. Something big was coming their way. The usually brave soldiers became frightened of what they could not see or identify. Their training did not include fighting wild animals.

Suddenly, there was a loud growl, and then a large wild boar burst from the brush and butted the nearest man, knocking him into the water. His arms were wailing about in the water as he screamed rapidly in Spanish because of his injury by the boar's tusks piercing his legs. The men swung their guns around, firing wildly and repeatedly at the boar.

Ryan flinched at the exploding sounds of the guns shook the silent jungle paradise. He feared they might have found what he had come to look for, but the moment he spotted the brown hairy back of the attacker, he knew immediately, it had been a big boar that attacked the soldiers.

All the men had swung to the left to fire at the charging boar. However, the brush on the right broke free and another boar charged hitting the man nearest him, knocking the man to the ground, and then attempted to gnarl him to death. Panic stricken, the man quickly scampered into the water. The soldier turned to fire at the boar while falling back deeper into the water. The men aimed at the second boar and pulled the triggers on their rifles rapidly.

Three more boars charged, but they gunned them down as well. The captain yelled for them to cease-fire. They had fired hundreds of rounds of ammunition. Six boars lay bleeding on the ground. Some of the poor animals' legs were still twitching as blood spurted from their wounds. Two of his men received injuries. He ordered his men to reload, and then cautiously they left the area, making their way towards the tree house.

Ryan hadn't been able to see everything, but he knew the sound of the boars. He watched the wounded soldiers retreating from the watering hole, but couldn't imagine what had happen. They helped the wounded across the sand as they bled freely from the legs. He heard a soldier say boar in Spanish, and then he realized the boar population must have grown since the days of Boary Boar. The men quickly scrambled aboard the launch, pushed off, and returned to the big boat.

Ryan was relieved they had left the island. He had counted the men in the launch carefully to make sure they had not left even a single one behind. He nervously watched as they unloaded the launch and stowed it away, while Ryan waited anxiously for the soldiers to raise anchor and leave. He hoped they would return to their base, but to his dismay, they didn't.

Ryan checked his watch. It was 5:30. Several times the glare of the sun reflected in the glass lens on a pair of binoculars used by a soldier on the bow. Ryan remained hidden in the vegetation for several hours, afraid to move during daylight, fearing they would spot him. Having no choice, he stretched out and took a nap. The stress was catching up with him. The rush of adrenaline left him spent. He woke briefly. The sun appeared to be dipping into the water. The shadows were getting longer. He checked his watch. 6:15. The Cubans were still there. He wondered what were they waiting for?

Samson could see the vessel as he floated silently near the southern point. The radar mounted on his mast looked like a typical day sailor unit, but in fact, it was an extremely compact highly amplified unit designed by NASA. He knew the boat waiting offshore was a Cuban patrol boat. These boats were usually out for a shift at a time as there were no sleeping quarters on-board. He hoped the end of their shift was approaching so they would retreat before he had to make his run to the island. Painted with a special anti-radar paint, he knew his ugly boat should not be detectable. It was the very same paint used on the stealth bombers. He could see the Cubans on his radarscope, but they couldn't see him. He checked his watch again. 6:40. He would soon lose a visual on the ship unless they lit up the boat for night travel.

Ryan looked up to the sky. There wasn't a cloud in sight. He knew if the boat stayed where it was, he would not be able to move forward to the beach. When the moon came up, he would become an easy target. This meant that he would have to retreat, cut across the island, hit the beach on the far side, and then hike south. He had waited too late. The sun was almost gone, and it would be hours before the moon would be high enough to provide light. He was going to have to cut through the jungle in the dark. He searched the bag, but there was no flashlight. It was just as well, he thought, as the light of the beam would betray his location. He laughed to himself when he realized that he had five thousand dollars in his bag and not one single flashlight, nor a match to even light one dollar at a time to light his way.

He unzipped the bag and carefully removed the Uzi from the duffel bag in case he ran into more boars. He hoped he didn't accidentally fire the powerful weapon. His camp rifle training was on a .22 long rifle or skeet shooting with a shotgun. He crept down low and moved slowly until he was out of sight of the boat, crossed under the tree house and paused briefly as he gave it a good long look, and silently said goodbye to his old home for a second time. He began making his way through the jungle, using the same path to the pool the soldiers used. As he moved closer, the stench of the dead boars hit his nostrils and nearly made him vomit. Birds of prey flew to the trees. Ryan had temporarily interrupted their feast. He prayed there were no more boars to chase after him.

189

Darkness had overtaken him. The thick tree limbs over his head sheltered even a hint of moonlight from the path, but relying on his memory he was still able to make his way through the jungle. He could almost close his eyes and see it, though he stumbled on roots and loose rocks while trying to calculate how much farther. He checked his sports watch, thankful the dial glowed in the dark. It was nine thirty by the time he hit the beach on the backside of the island. He sat down to rest feeling relieved. His stomach growled, but eating fell far from his mind.

A light sparkled offshore, straight out from the beach. He watched it while he rested then sighed heavily. It was at least a mile or more away, but he knew it was probably another Cuban boat. The boat moved rather slowly along while patrolling the waters on the backside of the island, the area of water directly between Shark Island and Cuba. The boat was moving southward and Ryan feared it would stay in the area where Samson was to return.

Samson also knew about this boat thanks to his satellite phone, which remained hidden in a fake panel. The agency Samson worked for had the best military and spy tinker toys in the business. He flipped a switch on his fish finder and was instantly looking at a satellite view of the island. The red dots on the screen were the Cuban boats. He sighed. This mission was getting tougher, plus the disadvantage of working with an amateur without a radio and without experience. He told himself he would give the kid one shot to get on his boat and not a second longer.

Fortunately, the second boat was a lot farther from shore and so Ryan took a deep breath and began walking down the beach. For a while, he felt like the patrol boat was following him south, but after about an hour, the boat turned around and headed back in the opposite direction. Ryan felt reassured that it was just patrolling a section of the ocean and not looking for him. He finally made it to the southernmost point at roughly two in the morning. He checked his watch to be sure of the time, then settled down between two sand dunes and began nervously waiting.

THIRTY-FIVE

Two hours later, the distant patrol boat returned. Ryan had calculated about where the boat last turned around, hoping it was following a preset route, but this time it didn't. It just kept coming south. He sighed hard.

"Damn!" exclaimed Samson as he watched the satellite picture. Then to no one he said aloud, "Turn you commie bastards. Turn!"

The moon was nearly at its peak in the sky, causing Ryan and Samson even more concern. It was almost a full moon that brightly lit the beach almost as well as the sun. There was not a cloud in sight to help them. Samson knew that Ryan would be forced to cross the white sand with the moon following like a natural spotlight.

Samson checked his watch. 4:00. Just thirty minutes to go. He downed another cup of coffee.

Onshore Ryan took a much-needed piss. As he stood up, he was even more frustrated to still see the patrol boat as it continued heading south. Thankfully, it was still a couple of miles out. He decided to round the point just enough the other way to see if the captain and his boat were still hanging out near the tree house. He grabbed the duffel bag and began the final half-mile walk around the bottom of the island.

He had just made the last curve when a flashlight beam shone on a breaking wave not fifty yards out from him. Ryan quickly ducked down. He heard Spanish voices. Staying low to the ground, he ran behind a sand dune, and crouched down on the ground. Filled with fear, he once again retrieved the Uzi from the bag. He heard more voices. Carefully, he rose just a little and spotted two soldiers coming down the beach towards him. Ryan glanced out at the water. His footprints were everywhere. They were too close. No time to remove them. He cursed his mistake.

His mind was racing. The captain must have put these men back on island after dark thinking that if someone were hiding they would surface after the sun went down. The armed soldiers had less than seventy yards to go until they reached the spot where Ryan was hiding. He knew his fresh footsteps would lead them right to him. He belly crawled through the sand to the edge of the jungle and then moved from bush to bush heading south. He checked his watch. 4:20. He was in trouble. He had only ten minutes until Samson hit the beach. Now forced to waddle and crawl along in the sand, it would take twenty minutes or more to get to the landing site. The men were still coming. Ryan's heart was racing. His mind began running through a bevy of improbable solutions.

Samson slowly began moving towards the island. He checked his watch. 4:25. He almost held his breath. Suddenly, the thing he had worried most about, happened. The patrol boat on the backside of the island suddenly came to life. All their lights came on. The helmsman pushed the throttles forward to maximum power. Alarm bells sounded. Machine guns cocked. They had somehow spotted Samson's boat and their bow was now turning in his direction. They were heading at top speed right for him!

Ryan glanced up from the bush he had just hidden behind. The men on the beach were but twenty yards from his tracks. Ryan glanced south to where Samson would be coming. He couldn't see him, but he knew Samson wouldn't have left a light on. He checked his watch. 4:28. He was sure Samson wouldn't be late to arrive, and he certainly wouldn't be late on leaving. Ryan realized he would have to make a daring run for it.

Suddenly, the radio the soldiers carried on their walk along the beach sprang to life. The captain urgently told them the other patrol boat had spotted an unknown vessel. While talking with the captain the men instinctively turned north and facing their own boat. Ryan took advantage of that brief moment to run over a dune and on to the beach. The roar of the waves drowned out the swish-swish of the sand as he ran. It was 4:30 sharp.

Samson hit the beach with the bow of his boat and found no kid waiting for him. Indecision ran through his brain. He checked his watch. He had landed right on time. One minute he told him. While his heart felt sorry for the kid, he was a well-trained soldier who stuck to orders, plans, and objectives. He checked his satellite scan. The patrol boat was but a mile and half away. He flipped the screen to radar. To the north the captain's boat fired up its engines and was moving south towards him. The second boat was still coming. Thirty seconds, he said to himself, and not a second more. There was no way he was going to a Cuban prison for the likes of an unknown kid. He removed a hidden Uzi from under a floor panel and cocked it. "Come on, kid!" he said aloud.

The soldiers on the beach turned around while turning on their flashlights. Instantly, they spotted Ryan sprinting across the sand. One of them began chasing him, firing his gun wildly at him. Ryan heard the sing of the bullets as they whizzed passed his head. The other soldier got on the radio to the captain speaking rapidly in Spanish. The two boats were now less than a mile and closing. Samson slammed the gear into reverse. He saw and heard the gunfire. He counted aloud. "Five, four, three..."

He spotted Ryan about the same time that Ryan located him. "Run boy, run!" yelled Samson.

However, Ryan suddenly stopped. Samson's heart sank. He paused in awe of the boy. Ryan had dropped his gun to the beach, unzipped the bag, reached in, and grabbed a thousand-dollar stack of one-dollar bills. He ripped the band from the bundle, faced the soldier running towards him, and flung the money into the air. He then snatched up the bag and the gun once more, ran through the surf to the bow, and leaped over it just as Samson hit the throttle.

The flying dollar bills flew into the face of the nearest soldier. He recognized the money immediately, dropped his rifle, and got down on his hands and knees and began grasping the air to catch all the money he could. The second soldier caught up with him, and though shocked at the sight of the money, he began stuffing his pockets with the cash as well.

"Good move, kid!" laughed Samson. "Hold on and get your head down. We'll be shot at for sure!!"

Samson raced the boat backwards while watching the white crests of the wave. Ryan could see the two boats rapidly racing towards them from opposite directions. Samson suddenly swung the boat around while shifting the gear to forward. The sudden abrupt change of motion nearly flung Ryan overboard. A spotlight lit up the side of their boat. Samson slammed the throttle all the way down. They raced over an upcoming wave, briefly catching some air before crashing down the backside of the wave and hurtling towards the next one. Machine gunfire began spraying the water from both sides of the boat.

The Cuban vessels were racing from the north and south respectively towards each other at a high maximum speed. Samson had turned his craft and was now heading east to quickly get out of Cuban territorial waters. Bullets sprayed the side of the boat. Ryan had fallen flat on the deck. "Turbo charge time!" laughed Samson as he pulled a secret lever under the wheel housing. The boat suddenly began vibrating even more heavily, as if they were sitting on a rocket launcher, and then boom, they triple timed their speed through the water.

The Cubans, stunned at the rapidly fleeting vessel, desperately kept firing. The captain turned his boat away from shore to avoid the barrage of bullets from the other patrol boat. They attempted a chase, but their outdated, Russian built patrol boats were no match for Samson. A few minutes later, they happily crossed out of Cuban waters.

"You're safe now, kid. You hungry?" Samson said so easily and calmly, as if nothing had just happen. Ryan was still shaking and his heartbeat was pounding in his head.

He stood up, brought his duffel bag into the wheelhouse, and grinned. "I'm starved."

193

"I take it he wasn't there?"

"Nope, not a sign. How'd the Cubans find out we were there?"

"Don't know. I can't tell you about this boat, but I suspect they were looking for someone else, or perhaps someone tipped them off about you?"

"By whom and what for? Who cares that Austin and I were on this island in the first place? We did them no harm, at least not until they came after us. We killed one of them that tried several times to kill us."

"Maybe some officer was kin to the dead soldier. Revenge can be a mean mother. Who knows? Let's go home!" he grinned, as he handed Ryan a bag of sandwiches and two cans of beer.

THIRTY-SIX

Once onshore, Ryan planned to immediately return to the embassy. Carrying that kind of cash made him suspicious of anyone and everyone he encountered. The old worn out engine of a Cayman taxi backfired while Ryan was crossing the street, causing him to spin around and start fumbling for the zipper on the duffel bag. Fortunately, the realization of the sound registered in his brain so he re-zipped the bag shut. He sighed heavily as he regained his composure and walked even faster to Albert's office. He carried the balance of the money to the anonymous Albert Einstein, and the unfired Uzi, while feeling glad to be rid of both.

Later than day he caught a flight to Miami. He called Bonnie and the senator and reported in. Bonnie had no suggestions to offer. Ryan hadn't told her of his escapade on Shark Island. The senator on the other hand felt impressed with the way Ryan had handled himself. Samson had personally briefed the senator on the mission earlier that morning by satellite phone. By ten o'clock that morning, the senator was perusing satellite photographs of the entire operation courtesy of the CIA. He laughed aloud at the picture of Ryan throwing his money in the air during his escape.

Nevertheless, the senator was still worried about Austin. He began working another angle for the search. His staff informed the city and county police forces in both Fort Lauderdale and Miami that his son was missing and last seen in their area. He was continuing to monitor for credit card, ATM, and IRS transactions. The FBI Director received a personal visit from the senator by eleven o'clock. The senator also hired private detectives in both towns to start an independent search. Like an organist playing the Messiah, he was willing to pull out all the stops and favors he could. By two in the afternoon, the senator had flown down to Florida and held a press conference in Fort Lauderdale offering a fifty thousand dollar reward for information about his son. He did the same in Miami at 4:00. The media coverage was phenomenal. Austin's picture was on every newscast and by morning, it would be on every newspaper in Florida. It was the cheapest and best media exposure he had ever purchased.

By six that evening Ryan was at the airport sitting across the table from the senator. He had relayed his own account of his adventure on Shark Island. The senator said nothing about the information he already knew. He congratulated Ryan on his guts and his quick thinking in the presence of danger. He then asked Ryan if he had any clue about where his son was.

"No, sir, I don't. I've thought of nothing for days now. I've rehashed over and over all our dreams and stories. The island was the only thing I could think of. I really don't know where to go next."

"I'm heading back to Washington in an hour. Maybe you should stay in Miami a day or two, and see what develops from my publicity efforts and my contacts. I've arranged a room for you in the Radisson Hotel. Get some sleep. You look beat. I'll call Bonnie and bring her up-to-date. Call if you hear anything."

"Yes sir, I will. Thank you for your help."

The senator had been right. Ryan was too emotionally and physically tired to do anything. Ryan took a cab to the Radisson and found the ride from the airport to the hotel to be reminiscent of the ride he and Austin had taken with his parents as they drove to the port to leave on the sailboat almost eight years ago. On entering his hotel room, he dropped his bags, turned the air-conditioner down a few digits, stripped, and then soaked in the shower for nearly a half hour. Five minutes later, he fell in the bed and was asleep in seconds. Hours later his dreams were of Austin on Shark Island, then dreams of them making love in the States, and more dreams of all the things they had done together.

He didn't wake up until almost noon when the phone suddenly jarred him from his peaceful bliss. Ryan was groggy, hungry, and not amused at the phone ringing so loudly in his ear. He reached for it, but knocked it off the nightstand to the floor. "Hold on! I'm sorry! Hold on!" he grumbled as he spun around on the bed and stretched his hand out for the phone.

"Ryan? Ryan, darling, is that you?" said the sweet voice.

"Bonnie! How are you?" Ryan quickly sat up in bed. His second mother was on the phone and he was sitting there naked. He instinctively covered himself with a pillow and then pulled the sheets around his waist as if she could somehow see him over the telephone.

"I woke you, didn't I?"

"What time is it?"

"Ten past noon."

"I missed breakfast. Thanks for keeping me from missing lunch. I'm starved. I didn't eat much on Cayman. I had no time and no appetite. I'm so sorry I didn't find him. It would have been so much better if I had. I am worried sick about him because now I have no clue as to his whereabouts."

"I know, dear, but listen. I got a call this morning from Cayman. From Chris..."

Ryan interrupted her, "Patterson? What did he have to say?"

"He said on the sail from Caicos, he remembered Austin talking about a Bill Bolt. He said Bill went to camp with you, and that he and Austin were friends. He said he thought Bill lived somewhere near Miami."

"So maybe Austin went to see him. Thanks Bonnie, that sounds like a good tip. I think I know how to find Bill Bolt. If he went to camp, I can get his application faxed to me, phone number, social security number, or something. I'll get right on it and call you later. Thanks Bonnie. I love you."

"I love you, too, dear. Please find our Austin. You be careful now. I miss you both."

The lump returned to Ryan's throat as he hung up. He swiftly shaved and dressed, ordered lunch from room service, and while waiting for it, he called the camp office. Nancy Galloway had been the camp's secretary for over thirty years. She was in excellent health, could hike five miles without breathing hard, and swam from early spring to fall in the camp's freshwater mountain lake. She was also a strict vegetarian, possessed both a sharp wit and an amazing photographic memory. She could literally recall every camper and staffer, and even what year or years they attended camp. She was a walking encyclopedia and faster than the Internet.

"Nancy, this is..."

"I know who it is. I'm no idiot you know!" He had insulted her without trying to. He rolled his eyes while he waited for a chance to speak again. "Where are you, Ryan? Moreover, what's this I hear about you taking an unexpected vacation? We got work to do around here, young man. You'd better get your..."

"Nancy! I'm sorry to interrupt you but this is important. First, Austin is missing. Has been missing for over a month and no one has clue about where he is. I've just returned from Cayman, thinking he was there. I'm in Miami tracking down all possible leads. A friend told me that Austin knew a Bill Bolt that went to..."

"Yeah, I know. He was here three years before he got..." she paused unexpectedly.

"What's the matter, Nancy? What about Bill?"

She sighed heavily over the phone. "His last year was the first year you and Austin became staffers. You know, after your return from that ocean island. Bill was a lifeguard and a cute fellow. He had the biggest smile and the deepest chocolate brown eyes I've ever seen, except for the little Mexican seven-year-old that came to camp last year. You know him, Paulino was his name..."

"Nancy, please. Tell me about Bill," exasperated, Ryan had to butt in again.

"Oh, I'm sorry. Well, it was the eighth week of camp and Bill's cabin and Robert's were camping out together. You remember, Robert, the rock-climbing instructor. Well, apparently after the kids went to sleep, those two shacked up together, if you know what I mean..."

Ryan blushed even though she couldn't see him.

"A kid had a tummy ache and went to tell Bill, and found the two of them having sex. The boss fired them on the spot."

"Oh," replied Ryan softly. "Do you have an address and phone on Bill?"

"Sure, I do. Hold the phone." Nancy walked to the far side of her office. There was a long line of twenty-three file cabinets. She didn't have to read the labels. She knew exactly which file drawer her staffer forms were in.

197

She pulled the file and walked back to the phone while flipping through it. "Here it is. You got a pencil?"

"Yes, ma'am."

"His address is 132 Oakdale Road, West Palm Beach, Florida. The zip is..."

"I don't need the zip code. I'm on the way to see him. That's not too far from here. Do you have a phone number?"

She read the number out to him. "Ryan, you know I'm not prejudiced. I'm straight as they come, but will you tell Bill, old Miss Nancy misses him, and that I wish him a long and happy life."

"I will."

Then she added quickly, "Tell him to practice safe sex, or I'm going to kick his cute little behind!" she giggled. "Now, you be careful. You're in the land of the nuts down there in South Florida. That's where all those blue-hair Yankees end up when they retire. I wouldn't live there for a million bucks. Call me when you can? Bye, 'hon."

"Thanks for all your help, Nancy. Bye."

He hung up just as the room service clerk knocked on the door. Soon he was eating a burger while dialing Bill's number. He had just completed the last digit when a recording came on the phone explaining the dialed number was no longer a working number. Ryan hung up and quickly dialed again in case he had dialed incorrectly. He got the same recording.

"Damn!" he said aloud. He called the senator and gave him the details on Bill, but most certainly left out the camp's firing of Bill. The senator agreed to track Bill down from his land of computers and spies. Ryan immediately checked out of the hotel. He rented a car in the lobby and headed north from Miami on Interstate 95 to West Palm Beach.

The drive up was uneventful. He checked his watch. It was 3:10 and the sun was hot. He took the exit to West Palm Beach and pulled into the first convenience store he came to. He went in and bought a city map. He came back to the car, unfolded the map, looked up the coordinates for Oakdale Road, found it on the map and circled it. Then he found the road he was on. He took the small pad he had brought from the motel room and wrote down the directions that would get him there. He refolded the map so he could easily see Oakdale, got back in the car, and headed east.

Ryan passed through what he felt was the middle of the city, and then began counting streets until he reached 51st Avenue North. He made a hard right, glanced at his notes, and went six blocks to Hudson Boulevard. He then made a left on Pier Point, two blocks down, a right, and presto, he was on Oakdale. He immediately noted the run-down look of the neighborhood. There were junk cars on the side of the road. Scattered broken glass covered the roads and sidewalks. A group of Cuban-Americans stood on the corner

198

hanging out with a loud portable stereo blasting away. One of them spat at his car. He frowned, locked the doors, and drove on.

He crossed a side street that immediately put him in the hundredth block. He started counting houses. Most of them had no identity numbers. He glanced down at his notes to verify the address one more time. Just as he looked back to the road a little girl about four years old darted between two cars and ran across the street right in front of him. Ryan slammed on the brakes, just barely missing her. The child ran on completely undaunted. Ryan's heart was racing. He drove about another hundred feet before finding the house on the right, or in reality the remains of the house at 132 Oakdale Road.

THIRTY-SEVEN

Ryan pulled in front of the house and shut off the engine. The grass was overgrown in the yard. Trash was lying everywhere. The front door had been yanked off its hinges and propped against the side of the house. Ryan felt horrified to see emblazoned in bright red paint the words 'DIE FAGGOT' on a wall. Nearly every window across the front of the house was shattered. A big hole in the siding exposed blackened charred timbers. He realized a recent fire had nearly gutted the inside of the house.

Reluctantly, he got out of his car and walked to the house. He had never seen a house so demolished. Inside the front door on the wall was more anti-gay graffiti. Most of the sheet rock walls were kicked in. The carpet was ripped and burned. Bill's record collection was smashed and most of it melted by the blaze. All his ceramic flower vases were crushed. A television screen was kicked in. He found the remains of a couch covered in human excrement and swarming with big flies. He looked up through a charred hole in the roof and could see the sky. He stepped through the door into the kitchen and immediately noted the chalk outline of a body on the floor. The linoleum was stained with dried blood. He gasped at the sight and prayed it wasn't Austin's blood or the outline of his torso.

Desperately, he went from room to room searching for clues of any sign of Austin or a clue about Bill. He found nothing. The vandals had destroyed everything. He found a mostly half-charred rainbow flag in the bedroom and a melted sex toy, but absolutely nothing of use in his search for Austin.

He began making his way back to front door when something small on the floor caught his eye. He knelt down on the filthy carpet. It was the remains of a section of a beaded bracelet. Four white beads and single blue one, a familiar pattern he recognized. He picked it up carefully noting the remaining tiny beads scattered down the hall. He looked at his wrist. He was wearing the identical bracelet. Austin had made two such bracelets their first summer at camp after their return from Shark Island. They both had worn them ever since. Jennifer had tried to get him to take his off, but Ryan never would. It was like keeping a part of Austin close to him no matter where he went. Whenever a stressful situation occurred, he would finger the bracelet and think of Austin. He had never seen Austin without his matching bracelet.

He put the remaining pieces of the strand gingerly into his pocket as his eyes moistened. He now knew Austin had been there, but what had happened? He stepped into the yard and thought he saw a neighbor across the street peeping through curtains at him. He decided to walk to the house and ask. He knocked several times before someone answered.

Slowly the door opened. Behind it was a small, frail, very old Jewish woman wearing a small, gold Star of David on a gold chain around her neck.

"What do you want?" she said through the locked security rails that gave the appearance of her house being a jail. She seemed very fearful of Ryan.

"I'm sorry to bother you, but I was wondering if you could tell me what happened over there?"

"Why?"

"I'm looking for my brother. His name is Austin London. He might have been visiting a Bill Bolt. Is that Bill's house?"

"Yes, it was." Then she asked boldly. "Are you a queer, too?"

Ryan blushed a little. "No, ma'am. We worked at the same summer camp."

Her expression softened a bit. "It's a sad thing. Jews were persecuted, too, you know. Bill was a sweet neighbor. He always checked on me, and made sure I had something to eat. He was always bringing me plants for my backyard. However, a rough gang now controls the neighborhood. The streets aren't safe anymore. I don't know how, but they found out Bill was queer. They beat him up on several occasions, and those stupid cops just laughed when he reported the incidents. They said he deserved it for being queer. No on deserves to be the end result of a hate crime."

"Did you see my brother?"

"Bill did have a visitor a few weeks ago."

Ryan quickly fumbled through his wallet and pulled up a picture of Austin. "Is this the guy you saw?"

She studied it carefully. "My eyesight isn't much any more, but I think so."

Ryan felt excited. "Do you know where he is?"

She dropped her head and sighed heavily. "A few weeks ago, on a Saturday night, Bill and your brother, uh, what was his name?"

"Austin."

"Well, they had been out and came home around midnight. There was a gang hanging out on that corner there." She pointed to where Ryan had seen the men hanging out before parking his car. "They threw bottles at Bill's car, but Bill ignored them. I saw 'em throw them because I've been having trouble sleeping at night. I'm frightened most of the time since my husband died a year ago. Bill parked his car and together they ran into the house. I bet he called the cops, but they didn't come, at least not for a long while. The punks came on down the street and took baseball bats to Bill's blue Honda. In less than twenty minutes, they had totally destroyed that cute little car. Bill came running out the front door when he saw what they were doing, but they must have figured he would. Just as he came across the lawn, a man came out from the corner of the house in the dark. He hit Bill as hard as he could in the back of the head with a baseball bat. It was an awful, sickening sound. I called 911 and gave the cops hell until they promised to come.

"The kids laughed as Bill's head came apart, and he went down on the ground face first. Austin ran out, grabbed Bill, and dragged him back into the house. Once the gang was finished demolishing the car, they started chanting, 'Kill the faggots! Kill the faggots!' They spray-painted his door, walls, and then kicked it in. I could hear loud cursing and yelling inside the house. They started tearing the place apart with baseball bats. Then a fire started. I could hear the windows breaking. I could tell the gang savagely destroyed the house. I am sorry but I don't know what they did to Bill and Austin. I called the cops again and an ambulance as well. It took thirty minutes for the cops to arrive. The gang scattered. They didn't catch a single one of them. I saw the EMS boys bring two stretchers out of the house. One carried a zipped body bag and the other a body on an open stretcher. The paramedics were busily working on the latter.

"The cops never questioned me, so for two days I didn't know what happened. Then I spotted a small clip in the paper stating that another hate crime had happen in West Palm and Bill Bolt had been killed. It said another man received injuries but was released. No suspects were in custody. Those mangy brats got away with it. It scares me to death."

Ryan sighed heavily. The story had almost been too much for him. He assumed and hoped the released person might be Austin. He thought long and hard before asking. "Ma'am, do you know which hospital they would have taken Austin?"

"Regent. It's the closest county hospital."

Ryan asked where it was. She gave him directions. "Where is the police station?" She again gave directions. He smiled at her as best he could. "You've been most helpful. I hope I can find my brother. I'm so sorry about Bill. Are you going to be all right?"

"Yes, my son is coming down from New York next week and moving me out of here. I'll be fine. Go find your brother. You're a good lad. Tell him I miss Bill." She turned and locked the door. Ryan started down her porch and heard someone yell. He looked up and saw the gang on the corner coming down the street at him.

"You a queer?" one yelled. "We'll nail your butt, too, you freaking faggot!"

Ryan moved quickly towards his car. He jumped in and turned the ignition. He looked up in the rear mirror and saw them running at him. He slammed the transmission into drive and stomped the accelerator to the floor. A thrown bottle shattered across the back of the car. He made a quick right turn at the first intersection, and then another left at the next in case they were following him. After ten blocks he finally caught his breath and began to relax. He had never experienced gay prejudice like this. He recalled the treatment he and Austin received after coming home from Shark Island, but he was innocent then. Now he knew that someone might kill his best friend because of his sexual orientation. His palms became damp with perspiration. His upper lip was wet, too. He turned the air-conditioning on high and began making his way to the hospital.

202

"Ma'am?" Ryan almost yelled for the fourth time through the thick glass surrounding the information booth in the lobby of the colossal county hospital. Patients were impatiently waiting in line while clerks were frantically trying to stay under control. He watched as doctors, nurses, and aides ran from room to room trying to help everyone. He thought the place looked like a human zoo. He yelled again.

A large fat lady, sucking on a lollipop, finally opened the sliding door. She already seemed aggravated that Ryan was even standing there. "What do you want? I'm busy you know."

Ryan had met many a temperamental parent that was fired up and ready to berate him for some insignificant problem her child had with his counselor last summer, so he slowly repeated the magic words that always diffused an argument, "I understand. I know you're working hard, but my brother is missing. They brought him here about two weeks ago. They killed a friend of his, Bill Bolt, and Austin was badly beaten. Bill died. Could you possibly tell me if Austin London is still here?"

She looked up over her gold rim glasses. She saw his earnest, soulful eyes. To her, his eyes looked sad and pitiful, and yet somehow, they were still filled with hope. She studied them a bit more. She soon saw love in those eyes. "Let me check. London did you say?"

"Yes, Austin London," replied Ryan hopefully. "Thank you for helping," he added as icing on the cake.

She punched some well-worn keys on her computer and a few seconds later Austin's file popped up on her screen. "Yes, he was here. Seems he had stitches and x-rays done. Apparently he received stitches to his head, and he also had some broken ribs and many bruises. They kept him overnight."

"Where is he?"

"Don't know. He checked out the next day."

"How'd he pay? He didn't call home. Our mother is frantic." He had said that tenderly, but he was also pouring on the pleading. He needed a clue, a lead, and a place to search, a direction to go, a window of hope, something.

"He showed us his insurance card and that was that."

Ryan wondered why the senator hadn't found the claim. It was one of the things he was checking on just in case Austin had been in an accident. Even though grown and both had camp or bank insurance, the senator still managed to keep them on his government policy.

"Did he list a forwarding address?"

"No, let's see. Let me read this long chart. Here's his next of kin. Maybe they can help. It's Ryan..."

He interrupted her, "Wilson. That's me."

"Oh," she smiled. "Well, he can't check out unless he gives us some kind of address. He listed Big Ruby's on State Street in Key West. No phone."

203

Ryan muttered, "Big Ruby's? Anything else?"

"No, sorry."

"You've been most helpful. Thank you. Thank you very much," he said earnestly and politely. "I hope you get some help around here. You are swamped."

"Thanks."

He smiled, nodded courteously, and returned to his car. He had planned to go to the police station, but with the new lead he no longer thought it was necessary. According to Bill's neighbor, they seem to care little for people like Bill and Austin. He drove about ten miles until he found the entrance ramp for Interstate 95 south. He pulled into the last gas station just before the exit, filled up, found a phone, and called Bonnie and related the news. He then called the senator and told him about the insurance claim. The senator surmised that a county hospital was probably months behind in filing claims. Ryan told him he was heading to Key West to Big Ruby's. Ryan hung up, bought two overcooked hot dogs, a big Snicker's candy bar, and a large Mountain Dew. It was a pitiful meal, but it would keep him awake for the long drive southward to the tip of Florida and Key West.

THIRTY-EIGHT

The sun was setting off to the west as he passed through Miami. It had been a bright, beautiful, blue-sky day with mild temperatures. The gorgeous scenery escaped Ryan's eyes as his mind focused on but one thing, Austin. Even his peripheral vision would not allow the spectacular sunset on his right to enter his thoughts. Finding Austin became his mission. Nothing else mattered to him. He went around a curve and spotted a big green Interstate sign displaying it was a hundred and fifty miles to Key West. Ryan thought he could do it in three hours, but an hour south of Miami, the four-lane expressway he had been doing 80 MPH on, suddenly became an old, two-lane highway. Traffic immediately slowed because of numerous freight trucks making the slower pace almost unbearable. He began to count the bridges that he went over. He tried listening to the radio. He tried to think of a peaceful time on Shark Island, but everything he tried to consider, brought him back to worrying about Austin. It was two in the morning when he saw the city limits sign for Key West. He had no idea where the bed and breakfast called Big Ruby's was located, but he knew that was his destination. Feeling exhausted, he stopped at the first motel he came to with a vacancy sign lit up in pink neon and checked in. He looked up the address for Big Ruby's in the phone book and wrote their phone number and address down on the pad by the bed. He stripped down, flopped onto the bed, and fell asleep in seconds.

Ryan had no idea Key West was as gay friendly a town as San Francisco or Amsterdam. He woke up at eight, showered, dressed, and checked out of his room. He threw his luggage in the rental car and walked across the street to a pancake house. Mounted to the outside wall was a rainbow flag gently flowing in the breeze, and on the glass entry door was a rainbow decal right next to the window stickers for Master Card and Visa. The rainbow gave him a peaceful feeling, so he thought perhaps Austin had eaten here. He assumed the flag meant this was a safe place for gay men to dine. Though he wasn't gay, Ryan felt safe in gay friendly places. His excessively cheery waiter must have been Key West's best morning person, thought Ryan. He knew the man acted a little too queenie to be straight. Ryan used to be bothered by a flippant person, but not anymore, and certainly not after going out with Austin and meeting his friends in Raleigh. He had never known a man to be so perky and cheerful in the morning, but this guy was definitely wide-awake and happy. Ryan, on the other hand, was not even close to being fully awake. The stress of the previous days had taken a toll on him. Ryan tried to show his support by tipping the waiter generously, and then as the guy cleared away the dishes Ryan asked him, "Do you know of place called Big Ruby's?"

The waiter's face immediately displayed disappointment. He had hoped handsome Ryan might be asking him out, but he smiled, rolled his eyes, and replied, "Of course. It's a bed and breakfast right off Duval Street. A gay bed and breakfast," he added proudly, testing Ryan. "Are you family?"

A year or so ago, Ryan would have answered yes, Austin is my family, but now he knew that family meant another gay person, or a member of the gay crowd, so to speak. "No, I'm not. My brother is. His name is Austin London. Do you know him?" he asked hopefully.

"No, he lives here?"

"Well, I'm not sure. He's missing and Big Ruby's is the last lead I have in finding him."

"Oh, I'm sorry. Let's see, go straight down this highway to the center of town. Make a right on Duval Street, its like main street USA. You'll know it when you see it. You'll go about six blocks until you see an old theater marquee on the right. Take the next left. It's a very narrow small street, but Ruby's will be down about forty yards on the right. You can't miss it. Tell Jim and Larry hello."

"Who?" asked Ryan while trying to remember the directions?

"They're the owners, and they run the best bed and breakfast in town. They're great people. They've also raised a ton of money for various gay causes, especially AIDS research. Tell them Alan said hi." The waiter went back to clearing the table.

Ryan stood and shook his hand. "Thanks."

"You're welcome," smiled the waiter as he watched Ryan turn and begin walking down the aisle to leave. He had momentarily stopped cleaning so he could watch Ryan's butt as he left the restaurant for his car.

Ryan knew he was watching and didn't care. It actually boosted his ego a bit, and for the first time in a while it also made him smile a little.

He counted the street blocks aloud until he spotted the theater. He made the left turn, and soon passed the entrance to Big Ruby's. Finding it had been easy, but finding a parking place in busy downtown Key West was another matter. He rounded the block twice before he found a tight spot a block away, but somehow managed to get the rental car parked. He walked briskly up Duval Street, noting every store window hung a rainbow flag in the window. He saw men holding hands as they walked down the street in daylight, and no one cussed them out. He spotted two lesbians kiss playfully at a coffee shop. The freedom gay people experienced here astonished him. It felt as if he had driven so far south that he had arrived in a foreign country. He found it hard to believe that Key West was a part of the United States. Just yesterday, he saw the results of bigotry and hatred in West Palm Beach. He discovered a former camp friend killed simply because of his sexual orientation, and learned his dear Austin had been hurt as well.

As he walked down the small street in front of Big Ruby's, he wondered if Austin was behind the light green fence surrounding the place. He silently prayed he was. He paused to stare at the quaint old two-story house converted and restored into an exquisite, gorgeous bed and breakfast inn. He noted the additional rooms added along the exterior walls in the back and around a beautiful swimming pool. Tropical plants filled the corners. He could hear the sounds of music and people swimming. He heard laughter and heard someone yelling for Jim to come to the kitchen. He read the sign that said welcome to Big Ruby's and pulled the latch to the big gate. The locked door surprised him. He tried again before noting an intercom button off to the right. He pushed it.

"Welcome to Big Ruby's. May I help you?" A quick reply came from a pleasant voice, even though the sound on the little speaker was a bit tinny.

"Yes, I'd like to speak to Jim or Larry."

"Larry's in the kitchen. Are you a salesman?"

"No."

"A preacher?"

"No."

The voice sighed with relief. "That's good, honey, because I ain't in the mood for either today. I'll buzz you in. Come down the deck walk and turn left at the glass door."

Ryan heard the electric buzz of the door lock click so he quickly opened the gate. Inside, he found a lush, tropical paradise setting surrounding the kidney shaped swimming pool. He heard and then turned to see a small waterfall splashing down a cascade of rocks and into the pool. This garden was nothing like the hot, dusty streets of Key West. Big Ruby's had created an amazing oasis in the middle of Key West and Duval Street. The huge palm trees provided shade from the hot sun. Hundreds of tropical plants and bushes, and thousands of flowers gave the area a fragrance that immediately reminded him of Shark Island. Altogether, the scenery and the scent mesmerized him. He noted that everything he saw was precisely arranged and planted. The yard and walkways were trimmed to perfection. There wasn't a piece of trash anywhere.

He noted a long two-story motel unit on the right. He heard some conversational laughter and glanced over a big fern to discover the nude bathing area. He spotted at least a dozen men dripping in suntan oil, lying on thick towels and lounge chairs. While finding them nude a mild shock, their being nude wasn't. He and Austin had lived for seven years in the nude and felt it was very natural. He quickly scanned their faces. Ryan could hear music from the almost hidden Bose speakers mounted in the tops of some of the palm trees. He could see the edge of the pool ahead of him and more men, but not one of the guests was Austin. He came up to the glass door marked office on the main house and stepped inside.

"Hello," said the good-looking young man behind the counter. He was wearing a red, Hawaiian flowered shirt, with sunglasses hanging on his chest by a beaded lanyard around his neck. He had said hello in an upbeat, friendly voice. Seeing the beaded lanyard made Ryan reminded him of Austin's broken, beaded bracelet he had found and still carried in his pocket.

"I'm looking for Austin London. Is he here?"

The clerk seemed taken back for a moment. His once radiant, welcoming smile fell from his face. "Oh, uh, uh, uh?" he stuttered, "Let me get Larry. Stay right here." He disappeared out the back of the office before Ryan could question him. Ryan leaned over the counter to see if there was a guest register, but they used computers and so there wasn't a guestbook for him to check. He could see through the kitchen out to the pool. The men seemed happy but again none were Austin. Ryan waited a full minute but could not wait any longer. He stepped out the glass door and made his way to the pool area. He studied everyone's face for a full second before moving on to the next man. All the men stopped what they were doing and studied him for much longer than a second. Ryan was good-looking, as well tall and handsome. He was certainly handsome enough to catch their eyes.

"Welcome, honey," said a man sitting in the shade sipping a cooler. "Where are you from?"

Ryan decided to be polite. "North Carolina now, originally from Maine."

"Michigan myself. I'm Ralph."

"I'm..."

An older man, with mostly white hair, as well as a tanned, lean body, suddenly tapped him on the shoulder. Ryan turned around. "I'm Larry. My partner and I own this private bed and breakfast. How may I be of help to you?"

"I'm looking for Austin London. He's been missing for more than a month, and his parents and I are fearful something may have happen to him. Though injured in West Palm Beach, he left your place as his forwarding address, so to speak. I drove immediately down here last night. Is he here?" Ryan almost demanded, and then regretted his tone. "Is he okay? Is he hurt? Where is he?"

Larry listened to the multiple questions carefully, while rubbing his chin, obviously thinking deeply. Everyone around listened intently. Larry noticed that. "Please, step into my office." Larry pointed through the kitchen. Reluctantly, Ryan walked back to the privacy of the office. "I'm sorry. I must protect the pleasant atmosphere of my clients. They pay handsomely to enjoy solitude and serenity. May I ask your name?"

Ryan tried not to become annoyed, but the answers to his questions were taking too long. "I'm Ryan Wilson, from Brevard North Carolina. I'm..."

"You're Ryan?" quizzed Larry almost disbelieving.

The fact Larry knew his name instantly told him he was on the right track. He answered quickly, "I am, in the flesh. I'm here. You know me. Now tell me about Austin."

"He told us you were the only one that we were to acknowledge that he is here."

"He's here!" shouted Ryan gleefully while pumping his fist like a basketball player who had just scored a 3-point shot. His face displayed a bright strong smile.

"Yes."

"Take me to him."

"I will of course, but first, let me explain."

"Explain what? Is he hurt?"

"Yes and no. They killed his friend Bill Bolt. They beat Austin badly, but the stitches are out now, and the ribs are doing much better, though ribs don't heal quickly. Jim and I have been trying to get him to eat. He's an old friend. He stayed here two or three times a year. He often said it was the only place in the States where he felt free and uninhibited. My lover and I have been together twenty-eight years. We have almost adopted Austin. He's special, but you already know that. The problem is..." Larry sighed before continuing. "Several incidents snowballed on him so he has fallen into a funk or depressive state, and well, a few nights ago, he tried to kill himself."

Ryan's smile fell away. The words stung his ears like a spear thrown to his chest. He gasped at the words Larry said. Chill bumps raced up his back. The hair stood up on his neck. His heartbeat began beating so loud he thought surely Larry could hear the thump-thump, too. His face went white. "What?" he muttered softly.

"He took two bottles of pills. I had gone up to his room to see if he wanted to come by the pool to eat dinner with Jim and me. If I hadn't done that, he would have been gone. We rushed him to the hospital, they pumped his stomach, and he came home yesterday. He's in his room. Now he remains stone silent. He won't discuss it with us. I have a therapist coming to see him. We're terrified. He's too good a person to lose. I'll take you to him now. Maybe you can bring him back. He loves you with all his heart and more. He's told us that over and over again. He says he has never loved another man in his life. In the hospital while he was coming round, he repeated your name many times. Come, it's this way."

209

THIRTY-NINE

Larry's words made Ryan's eyes tear. Larry took him by the arm at the elbow and immediately felt that Ryan was trembling. Ryan's stomach had tightened into a huge knot. He could feel his pulse in his temples. He climbed the stairs with Larry, but the higher they went the more he thought he was going to faint. Larry knocked timidly on the door and then slowly opened it. He decided not to announce Ryan, but just to let him step in and see Austin. Perhaps that would jolt Austin back to reality, back to this world, and he hoped back to his friends.

He opened the door and motioned for the ashen-faced Ryan to go on in. After such a long trek to find him, it hadn't yet sunk in that he finally found the person he loved most in this world. The room, trimmed in white decorative shutters that were left slanted to prevent the hot sun from entering too strongly, felt more like a home than a guest room. He liked the soft, pale blue walls that remind him of the sky. The tweed rug was a mixture of gray and blue. Ryan noticed these things because he was almost afraid to look at the figure in the bed. He stepped quietly into the room, turned his head to the right, and heard the door respectfully shut behind him. Now alone with Austin, he slowly allowed his eyes to travel across the carpet to the edge of the bed, and up the side of the bed and eventually to Austin's face.

Austin lay in the bed beneath a single white sheet. He was staring at the ceiling. A bit curious and mystified, Ryan looked up to see what Austin was looking at, but he found nothing but an off-white sheetrock ceiling. He thought Austin's face looked very pale, and his lips were dry and cracked. He noted the hospital identification strap around his wrist. Ryan couldn't hold back his emotions any longer. Tears began cascading slowly down his cheeks.

"Austin?" he whispered, but Austin didn't look away from his gaze at the ceiling. "Austin!" Ryan said stronger. Still there was no change. Ryan quickly took the remaining steps separating him from his best friend in the whole world. He fell onto the bed and wrapped his arms around Austin. He leaned up and kissed his neck, and then gently kissed his cheeks, his face, and all the while saying Austin, Austin, Austin repeatedly.

The tears fell from his red weary eyes onto Austin's face. The drops were like a magic potion that gently broke the spell his friend seemed to be under. Austin sighed loudly and then turned his face towards Ryan. He stared at him intently, as if he thought he might be dreaming. A minute passed with no words spoken. Slowly and tenderly, Ryan kissed Austin's forehead again and leaned down to allow the tip of his nose to touch Austin's lightly. He felt the stitches in Austin's scalp. He kissed his hair. Austin kept staring at him.

Ryan did not know what to do. He squeezed Austin once more and then looked into Austin's glassy eyes. They seem to be like windows he could look straight through and into a vast darkness. As the next few seconds ticked by, he saw life slowly return to those piercing eyes. Now Ryan felt like he was looking right into Austin's heart, a feeling he had never experienced before. Austin's lips slowly parted as he muttered, "Ryan?"

"Yes, Austin, it's me. I love you." Ryan kissed those precious lips. He squeezed Austin tighter, momentarily forgetting his wounds and wanting to never let go again.

Austin whispered again. "Ryan?"

"Yes, I'm here. I'm here. Are you all right?" Ryan asked rapidly.

A slight hint of a grin came across Austin's face, his lips parted, but no words came. He swallowed hard. Ryan waited patiently. Ryan kissed him once more. Austin sighed and said strongly, "You're killing my ribs!"

Alarmed, Ryan quickly pulled back from the hug. "Oh, my gosh, I'm sorry. I forgot about the ribs. I'm sorry, I'm sorry," Ryan said over and again, but a smile came to his face, too. He kissed Austin repeatedly, and each time he could slowly feel Austin kissing him back.

Instinctively, Larry opened the door and entered the room carrying a food tray with a steaming bowl of chicken soup. "I knew you would be his Prince Charming. You've kissed that Sleeping Beauty back to life. Would you mind seeing if you could get him to eat? He hasn't eaten for days, but now that you're here he's looking better all ready. I bet you were a sight for sore eyes," smiled Larry as he patted Ryan's shoulder and squeezed it gently. Then to Austin he added, "We missed you, Austin. Welcome back!" He gave a playful tug to Austin's foot.

As Larry left once again, Ryan picked up the bowl and spoon, and carefully lifted the spoon of warm soup to Austin's lips and cautiously, Austin began to eat. After the last spoonful, Ryan used a warm washcloth to bathe Austin's bruised and battered body. He led him to the sink where he gently and lovingly washed his hair. He even managed to shave away Austin's scraggy beard without nicking him. After drying his hair with a towel, he carried him back to bed and let him sleep a while.

Four bowls of soup scattered over several hours, and then Austin could sit on the edge of the bed on his own. Ryan helped him to the bathroom. With Ryan holding his penis for him, Austin took a much-needed pee. No matter what they did, Ryan always touched him. When Austin drifted off for a nap, Ryan curled up beside him and cuddled as they had done in the tree house so long ago. He slept with his arm encircling Austin's waist. He took care of him just like they took care of each other on Shark Island when he was sick.

It took another day before Ryan got some solid food into Austin. Hour by hour he improved. After finishing a bowl of beef stew, Austin suddenly spoke out, "Ryan, I think I'm going nuts."

"There's no thinking to it," shot back Ryan quickly. "You are nuts. You are certifiably nuts! You've always been nuts since the first time I met you at camp many summers ago. Moreover, worst than that, I'm nuts for loving you. Maybe we ate too many bananas when we were young!"

The joke had been a simple reflex, but it was those uncomplicated words that broke the dam of Austin's depression. They both busted out laughing. As he was returning from ushering new guests to their room, Larry heard them in the hall and sighed with a twinkle in his eye, and then a look to heaven mouthing the words 'thank you.' He went immediately to tell Jim and the rest of the staff. The news thrilled them.

Austin said, "I mean, it got where I just couldn't take being in the closet at work, or having to lie to my parents, and especially having to lie to you."

Ryan frowned. "You lied to me?"

"Well, not directly, but indirectly. I didn't even tell you about my visits to Key West. I didn't tell you that I had called Bill Bolt. I couldn't tell you about the men I met. A couple of times, I thought I met someone I could spend a lifetime with, but they never could measure even closely to the man I almost did spend a lifetime with on Shark Island."

"You shouldn't try to measure them. Everyone is different. Humans aren't a suit a clothes. They all have other traits greater than mine." Then he added with a grin, trying not to let Austin get too emotional or serious, "Of course, they probably weren't as good-looking as me."

"Not even close," shot back Austin. "I was afraid the love we had between us was ending because of our desire to be together sexually. Hear me out," said Austin quickly because Ryan was about to correct him. "Ryan, you use alcohol to put you back on the island and when you're in that state, you put your environmentally trained inhibitions aside, and for a few hours, you and I reach cloud nine and beyond. We're exuberant. We don't just do sex, we push our love to the max! Now, I know you're straight. I wouldn't wish for you to be gay. That would be selfish, somewhat tempting, but selfish nonetheless," he grinned.

Austin continued, "I know you felt guilty after we had alcohol enhanced sex, and you would brood for months before you would call. I kept thinking you would get over it, or used to it, or something. However, those long periods of silence made me hate myself for my selfish moments of making love to you, knowing those acts of love were driving you away. I can't imagine what would happen if the senator's critics found out he had a gay son, and what would they now say about the gay son and his best friend on an island alone. Rumors would fly, my mother would be hurt, and so would you."

"I decided I couldn't let you see me anymore. I had to move away to where I was no longer the banker, the senator's son, my mother's child, and your best friend."

"You were going to give up our friendship?"

"I was going to give up for the sake of our friendship. I had been hoarding cash for years in my safe-deposit box. I had once planned to buy a boat and head back to Shark Island. Bill had asked me down to Florida many times, and so I decided to drive down and stay a few nights with him before heading on to Key West. I was going to sell my car and get a boat here, pack up and sail to Shark Island. Hide the boat if I could or sink it if I couldn't."

"You were going to live on the island alone?"

"At least I would be free. No one would call me names, no one would be embarrassed because of me, and no one would run from me." Austin looked squarely at Ryan. "I don't blame you for feeling guilty, but it hurts me all the more, to know I hurt you, the person I am still in love with. Please, get me well, get me strong, sell my car, help me get the boat, put together some supplies, and then say goodbye and wish me well."

Ryan responded instantly. "Can't do that."

"What?" His quick and steadfast response caught Austin by surprise. He expected his support.

"We can't go back to Shark Island. I was there a few days ago."

"You were there?" His ears heard the 'we' Ryan had used, but it didn't register in his brain just yet.

Ryan replied, "I had these weird feelings that when I couldn't find you anywhere else, Shark Island is where you would go. I guess it turns out I was right, just early in my prediction like Nostradamus. Therefore, the senator arranged for an undercover agent to help me get on the island. The Cubans are now patrolling the place. It's as if they expected us to return, and then they were going to kill or imprison us, or something. They almost caught me. They shot at me. I'm sorry, but I am afraid the Cubans don't like us very much."

"Oh," sighed Austin as if the wind had fallen from his sails.

"You'll have to find another island."

"How will I do that?"

"You won't. We will."

"We?" asked Austin.

"Yes. Look at you. You can't take care of yourself and I was only out-of-town for a few days..."

"A few days," chided Austin.

"Okay, a few weeks."

"More like a few months!" corrected Austin.

"Okay, for a short while, and our poor Miss Bell dies, you leave your job, you leave me and your mom with no way to get a hold of you, you become involved with a hate filled rampage in West Palm Beach, and after surviving that you nearly kill yourself!"

"I was having a bad decade," shot back Austin slyly.

"I'll say. Listen, my friend, you're my anchor," began Ryan seriously. "If you cut the chain, my boat drifts off course, too."

"Is that sailor talk for..." grinned Austin.

213

"That's me talking and telling you that you will never, ever check out on me. Do you understand," he paused, "and in conclusion, I love you. Love is a precious thing, very precious indeed. I learned that from you. Sure, I'm having trouble with my inhibitions, but I am having no trouble at all with my love for you. You're asking a lot to have me go through the rest of my life without you. I've learned what life is like for a gay person in this world, especially in America. I know that means cruel people beat homosexuals. Some gays are fired, kicked out of their apartments, and even their houses burned, and others, like poor Bill, die as a result.

"I will not let any of those things happen to you. You are a wonderful, bright, intelligent, sincere, caring, witty, and exciting person. It should make no difference to anyone what your sexual preference is.

"You must promise me you will never attempt to kill yourself again. I mean it. Promise me!" exclaimed Ryan almost shouting.

Austin's heart pounded in his bare chest. He took in several long breaths before answering. "I promise."

"Good, because you were this close to getting a spanking!"

Austin grinned. "A what?"

"A spanking. I was just about to turn you over my knee and whip your pitiful skinny ass."

"My butt is cute."

"Says who? When's the last time you looked in a mirror? You need a tan, too. You're thin and where did your muscles go? Did they fall under the bed?" he lifted the bedspread and pretended to look for the lost muscles.

Austin bent his arm up at the elbow to display his arm muscle. Ryan laughed. "You call that a muscle. I would call that little bump a very bad mosquito bite!" Austin busted out laughing.

"I'm going to nurse you back to health, well not literally, and then we'll start planning. Now take a nap while I'm going down to call your mom."

"Our mom," corrected Austin.

"Our mom," smiled Ryan as he leaned over and kissed Austin lightly on the lips.

"Tell her I'm sorry," he paused before adding, "And that I'm gay."

"I'll tell her you're sorry, but you'll have to tell her you're gay."

"I don't think I can."

"You don't have to right now, but you should. All right, lights out camper, it time for you to rest. I'll be back in a while. You get some beauty sleep because right now when people see you with me, they are going to be asking me why I'm walking around with Mister Ugly on my arm!!"

Austin laughed. Ryan laughed and winked at him, turned the lights off, and left the room. Outside the room he jumped like he had just scored the winning point of a ballgame. His heart was pounding. It was the happiness moment for him in a long line of disappointments.

214

FORTY

Four days later, Ryan had Austin up and around, and sitting by the pool with the rest of the guests while waiting on Larry to serve their breakfast.

"Why good morning, dear, you look marvelous today!" beamed Larry as he gave Austin a hug and poured him some fresh orange juice. "I can't believe what Prince Charming has been able to do with you." He gave Ryan's shoulder a playful hug.

"Thanks, and Larry, thank you and Jim for keeping me here when I was sick," began Austin. "I'm sorry I was such a burden."

"You're no burden, a pain in the butt perhaps, but not a burden," he replied by changing his playfully tone from sweet to sour to sweet again. "I'll fetch Jim from the kitchen. He's dying to see you, whoops, sorry about that, bad choice of words. Ryan, you're a godsend," he added as he gave him another hug as well.

"Thanks for helping us. We appreciate it," replied Ryan.

"You're welcome. Okay, enough chitchat. Two hot breakfast plates for this table. I'll be right back."

Larry turned and made his way to the kitchen by pouring juice to any guests who wanted more.

Austin smiled. "Isn't Key West beautiful?"

"Yes, and I must say, I never imagined that a city in the United States could be so gay friendly," stated Ryan. "I mean, I knew San Francisco has a large gay population, but I guess the whole town is not gay, so that means there's probably prejudicial problems there as well."

"All the large cities have a section of the town where the gays roost, so to speak, or at least where they feel safer in numbers. Key West is the exception. I'm sure there are people here that are big old bigots, but in this town they're in the minority. And make no mistake, the mighty gay dollar speaks loud and clear, too."

"I noticed. Every shop has a rainbow sticker in the window and rainbow flag flying overhead. When I go out shopping, people assume I'm gay. That usually bothers me, but not here. I feel even though they're wrong, they're not going to belittle me."

"Tolerance is the key. I'm sure many don't approve, but they tolerate the difference."

"Austin!" screamed Jim at a high pitch as he made his way through the tables, and then bent over and gave Austin a big hug. Ryan knew the hug had to hurt Austin's ribs, but Austin never complained. He planted kisses on Jim's cheeks. Jim continued, "You look wonderful. Is this Prince Charming?" Ryan noted that Jim was a short man, with white, perfectly combed hair, and a medium tan. He had a prodigious friendly smile. He wore gold-rimed glasses, bright yellow shorts, and a white tank top that had "Free the Gays" emblazoned across the front. Around his neck, he wore a small thin black cord that held a set of rainbow metal rings. Even the sandals on his feet had pink triangles on the woven straps. His smile was genuine and huge. While he dressed casual, everything about him displayed a very clean, well-mannered, classic gentleman. Ryan liked him instantly.

Ryan blushed because Jim made the comment loud enough for all the guests that were eating by the pool to hear. Austin laughed. "Yes, this is my Prince Charming. The only man I've ever loved," he paused for a second, "and the only one I could believe loved me."

"Loves," corrected Ryan as he reached out to shake Jim's hand. "Jim, it's a pleasure to meet you. I can't thank you enough for all your help. You and Larry have a wonderful place. An oasis surrounded by a cruel world. It is truly a paradise."

"We think so. I can't imagine why Robinson Crusoe here," Jim pulled Austin's ear playfully, "would ever want to leave Key West for some shark infested island."

Austin and Ryan laughed. "It's not shark infested, it's just called Shark Island."

Jim grinned. "Well, they don't call it Shark Island because it's full of turtles, now do they?"

Everyone laughed including the nearby tables. Austin looked straight at Ryan. "I'm sorry, Ryan. I forgot to tell you that Larry was having trouble with his hired help."

"I beg your pardon," whimpered Jim. "I cook and clean for a good-looking man and all I get is grief. It's the story of my life!" laughed Jim as he set his cup of coffee down at their table and sat down. "It's so good to have you back."

Austin grinned. "Thanks. What's for breakfast? I'm starved."

"Good, it's scrambled eggs, fresh homemade orange muffins, lean bacon, and in your honor, GRITS. However, the other guests haven't figured out what to do with them just yet."

Ryan laughed. "I know what you mean. When I travel up North all the wait staff just laugh at me when I order them. I must say, until they learn how to cook them, they ain't gonna like eating them!"

Jim suddenly turned serious. "Listen, you two." He lowered his voice. "It's the off-season though we're almost full right now, but in a few weeks it'll thin out some. So you are just going to keep staying with us for a while, so don't you even think about going out looking for a place."

"Thanks, Jim. That's sweet. However, I still plan to make my journey. I may have to find another island, but I'm going. Ryan will help me get ready."

"You're a stubborn boy. Just look around. Paradise is right in front of your nose." He winked at Ryan. Ryan smiled in return.

Larry set hot plates down on the table. "Eat up you handsome gents. It takes good food to make a good body. Just look at me!" he shrilled as he spun around like a ballet dancer, and then danced his way back to the kitchen to the applause from the laughing guests.

"You're right about the help," smirked Jim. "I must have hit him in the head with my elbow last night!"

Everyone laughed but Ryan. He was thinking about Austin's determined goal of going home, only on to a new island. Part of him wanted to go with him, but a bigger part wanted Austin to stay. He knew there would more discussion on the subject, but he would bite his tongue for now. The immediate goal was getting Austin well and strong, and that included his attitude, his mind, and definitely his body.

Three weeks passed by quickly in Key West. Austin sent Ryan to the office with cash to bring his bill up to date. Jim refused but Ryan insisted, while apologizing they had yet to think of a way to show their appreciation for the help they gave to both boys. Just yesterday, Austin and Ryan went sailing with two friends they had met at Big Ruby's. The couple was from New York, who spent ten days a quarter, sailing out of Key West. They owned a men's clothing store on Fifth Avenue. They had been together as a couple for over twenty years, founded the business together and made it a huge success. Their clientele knew they were gay, but neither man acted effeminate. They felt accepted. They worked out at a health club, ran in a marathon, attended the opera, and had season tickets at Yankee Stadium. The couple was as well rounded and active as they could be. To most anyone, they were just average, hard working, and very well educated men who just hadn't met the right woman. In the eyes of their friends, and hopefully their God, they were loyal, devoted and married to each other in every possible way. Jerry and Terry made friends easily, but they chose Austin and Ryan because they shared a special bond.

Ryan didn't know it yet, but Jerry and Terry knew Austin and Ryan loved each other before their introductions. They had watched them from across the pool. It was a combination of the way they looked at each other's eyes, the playful way they touched the other, the teasing manner of speech, and a dead ringer was the way they looked after each other, demonstrating a caring bond that exceeded explanation.

Jerry asked Austin and Ryan to join them for dinner at a new restaurant they were going to try that was known for the best crab legs in town. The boys couldn't resist and so at seven, then loaded up in Ryan's rental car and headed over for a night of feasting. The restaurant lived up to their expectations and everyone ate more than their monies worth. Over the course of the meal the foursome bonded well and became more than the usual meet someone quick acquaintance friends. Jerry and Terry understood Austin's desire for total freedom, and they assured him that was the very reason they stayed forty days a year in Key West. Nevertheless, like Noah in the Bible, they often joked, they eventually have to go back to dry land.

217

The next day, they took Austin and Ryan for a day of sailing in the Caribbean. It was their first time back on a sailboat since they were ten years old. They loved it. It was a picture-perfect day. Ryan and Austin took turns manning the helm. Austin sat in the cockpit, smiling with enthusiasm as he watched the sea work its magic on Ryan while he was commandeering the boat. Jerry and Terry couldn't have been smarter. They disappeared to the bow to sit in the sun and let their friends do the work for them. Ryan was busy checking the compass, and glancing up at his sails and trimming when needed. Austin soon assumed that by birth in the great state of Maine, and more precisely in Portland, the sea must have indeed been flowing through Ryan's veins. After an hour or so, Ryan realized that he was hogging the opportunity to sail the boat, so he called for Austin to join him.

Austin took the helm with Ryan's hand on his shoulder while pointing out the details of the boat. He gently offered suggestions and lovingly squeezed Austin when he did things correctly. They laughed and told stories while they sailed. More than once Ryan slapped Austin on the butt. Jerry and Terry knew they were more than just friends, but they said little.

About four, they dropped anchor in a scenic Caribbean cove, and the boys became surprised when Jerry and Terry broke out scuba gear from the forward sea locker. They spent the next half hour educating the boys about diving. Soon they submerged into the sparkling clear water. Jerry took Austin by the arm and led him on a journey beneath the surface. Terry took Ryan just ten yards a way, but the lovers were acting as supervising instructors, making sure the boys kept breathing properly while taking their time to point out all the marine life. They spotted sponges, lobsters, pirate fish, a barracuda, a big turtle, eels, and even a small stingray. It was an exciting time for the boys. Jerry and Terry took great pride in sharing the opportunity with them.

As the sun dipped into the water as far west as their eyes could see, they feasted on fresh lobster and steak, red potatoes and corn, and all so aptly prepared by Terry. Ryan noted Jerry and Terry were amazingly harmonious. The couple rarely asked the other to do something. They never fussed about who did the most work, but rather aimed to provide as much comfort for the other as possible. It was a shining example any couple could benefit from. Over wine they made wishes as the last of the bright orange sun fell beneath the horizon. It was a magical moment.

Jerry and Terry sat hand in hand, sharing a glass while lightly kissing from time to time as if this was their first date. Ryan slipped his hand in Austin's and squeezed it tightly. He felt free on the boat as he once did on Shark Island. Free on the ocean. He felt alive with each beat of Austin's heart that pulsed from his hand to his own. Austin didn't encourage him, but neither did he discourage him. After all, they were with guests, even though the guests were gay. Ryan had never shown affection in public as he had done during their stay at Big Ruby's. In the past weeks, he had kissed Austin on the lips on more than one occasion in daylight. They swam nude in the pool and then dried in the sun as they had on Shark Island. They slept in the same bed as they had on the floor in the tree house. In a just a few short weeks, they had gone back in time to when they were carefree, happy, and in love.

FORTY-ONE

The next day after their sail, Ryan and Austin decided to stroll down Duval Street to the Wyland Museum. Wyland was a famous marine wildlife artist. Known not only for his highly dramatic giant murals that graced giant outdoor walls around the globe, Wyland was also known by his fans for his immensely detailed paintings of dolphins, turtles, and manatees. He also did bronze and glass sculptures carved into large coffee tables. He was an extraordinary artist. Ryan and Austin stopped in the museum by accident on their way to meet friends for dinner. This time, however, they had set aside time to view each piece and to store it in their memory banks.

Leaving the hot sun and entering the air-conditioned exhibit area felt like the boys had been transformed beneath the sea. The decor was classy, the lighting modern, and the works of art on display literally blew them away. They had been in the shop about an hour when they spotted a scene of a fantastic killer whale, leaping in the air while turning and then crashing into the water. Exquisitely framed in a hand-polished teakwood, the scene divided into one large center section and two smaller sections. It was a marvelous painting. Strategically placed viewing couches surrounded the room. Ryan and Austin decided to rest their legs and sit for a spell. The picture overwhelmingly mesmerized them. Ryan reached over and held Austin's hand while they stared at it.

So intently were they devouring the beauty of the artist's rendition of the whale, they hadn't noticed what seemed like a sweet old lady, that was perhaps a retired schoolteacher or a pastor's wife, had quietly entered the room. Her husband sucked on an unlit cigar a few feet behind her. She wore a light green pastel dress, with a darker green scarf tied classy-like around her neck. She held a pair of sunglasses in her left hand along with a light straw hat to protect her from the sun.

She, too, felt mesmerized by the painting and studied it intensely for a few minutes before letting her eyes wonder the room at other smaller paintings. After finishing the first painting her eyes fell on Ryan's hand surrounding Austin's as they sat there quietly minding their own business.

"Damnation!" she blurted out so loudly the entire throng of viewers in the museum turned to see what had happen. Ryan and Austin turned to look up at her with their hands still engaged.

"Ralph! Look, they've gone and allowed queers in here. Damn you boys to hell. You ought to know the Bible says you will go to hell for this sin. Ralph!" She rapidly shook her fist at them.

The husband rushed into the room to comfort his wife and then looked down at the boys in disgust. He didn't say anything right off, but the boys noted the veins in his neck were growing larger. His face turned red, and it looked like his eyes were bulging and might actually pop out of his head. They thought he was going to explode right in front of them. Ryan slipped his hand from Austin's grasp. At that precise moment, the man exploded with anger. "Don't try to deny it now, you fairies! I saw you holding hands. Why don't you just wear a dress, too? You don't deserve to live. I hope you both get that AIDS stuff. Queers are abomination of God. You're going straight to hell boys. Straight to hell!" he repeated.

"Let's go," said Ryan. Austin nodded affirmatively so they stood to go.

Just as they made their way past the lady, the man abusively spat vile phlegm on the side of Ryan's face. Not once in his lifetime had he ever been spat on. The shocked of it stunned him cold. He froze where he stood while Austin completed another step or two before turning back to see the disgusting spittle sliding down the face of the man he loved so dearly. Ryan had been taking the abuse far calmer than Austin was, or perhaps his rage was slower burning, but not Austin. He unexpectedly lunged at the man while swinging his fists wildly. The man had been in the army in his earlier years, and out of pure reflex he ducked. Austin missed him as he rolled into the lady that started it all, knocking her squarely on her butt.

"Ha! You stupid fairy can't even hit an old man like..."

He never finished the sentence. From that second on he wouldn't be able to utter a word for three months. Ryan had turned and swung his right fist with a force he never knew he possessed, hitting the man under the left side of his lower jaw like a boxing champion. The bone broke so loudly the rest of the patrons of the museum flinched and cringed at the sound of it cracking. Various teeth sputtered and fell across the marble floor. The man went down like a rock. Ryan calmly helped Austin up, and then took him by the arm and led him out the door. The patrons and salesclerks cheered, but the boys never heard it.

"Slow down," said Austin. "You're killing my ribs."

"Sorry," said Ryan curtly, as he slowed down slightly while letting go of Austin's arm.

"Where we going?"

"Home."

"Home, you mean Big Ruby's?" asked Austin as they crossed Duval Street.

"No, I mean home to North Carolina. That's where we belong."

"That's where you belong. I belong where I can be free."

Ryan stopped on the corner and looked back him. "If you don't come home with me then I guess we're not friends."

"What are you talking about? Calm down. The man was a jerk. You put him in his place. Life goes on. It is his kind I want to get away from. Going back to North Carolina would put me in the middle of the Bible belt for Pete's sake. They wear that belt like they were the heavyweight wrestling champions of the world, and they love to hit you with selected scriptural

221

punches until they knock you to your knees. They'll stuff the Bible down your throat until you choke on it. If you don't repent, they count you out!"

"That's nonsense. I'm going home."

Austin felt stunned, angry, confused, and devastated. He never thought of Ryan leaving. He assumed that perhaps he had accepted the idea of returning to the Caribbean and maybe he would join him. He hadn't felt so much a part of Ryan, so close to Ryan, so in love with Ryan, as he had these past few weeks. Every day had been better. He was stronger. He didn't know what else to do but follow Ryan to Big Ruby's.

Jim said hello to Ryan as he entered the gate, but in a way very unlike Ryan, he stormed past him and ran to their room. When Austin got to the room, Ryan had already packed most of his stuff.

"Wait, Ryan. Please. Wait. Just stop a minute. Talk to me. I can't take this. We were doing so well," pleaded Austin.

"Hold it! Hold it right there. We were doing well? What is that supposed to mean? You thought I was coming around. That I was going to turn gay? That because I loved you, I was going to fall in love with you? Not true. My job as I see it was to get you healthy, get you strong, get you well, and I've done that. My job is over."

"You don't love me?"

"I said I loved you and I do, but not gay love. You're healthy. You can take care of yourself. Just promise me you'll stay in touch."

"I've only been untouchable once, you're the one that keeps leaving just as you are now. We could leave Key West. We could leave America, even the whole continent, and we could be free."

"Where would we go?"

"We'll find a place just as we found Shark Island."

"Yeah, right," replied Ryan with a smirk.

Austin was breathing and sighing hard. Ryan was still packing. "Ryan, please. I'm hearing you loud and clear. Just don't go like this. It's Wednesday. Make a plane reservation for Sunday. That'll give us a few days to say our goodbyes and leave on a good note instead of like this. I may never see you again. Will you do that for me? Please."

Ryan abruptly stopped throwing his belongings into his suitcase. He turned and looked up into Austin's eyes. Silent tears were sliding down Austin's cheeks. Ryan's anger fell away. His pulse slowed down. He nodded affirmatively. "Okay, but I'm sleeping on the floor."

Austin grinned. "Well, I guess I'll take the soft, warm, cozy, bed."

Ryan smiled. "You don't play fair."

"I don't want to play at all. I wish I could rewind the day and leave out the part where we went to town. Until then, I was the happiest guy on the face of the earth. Now, I'm counting my final minutes with the person I love most in the world and yes, I know I'll have to find the courage to soon say goodbye. I love you. I'll always love you. I'll love no other but you. I love you, you big lug."

"And I love you, but I'm not gay. I'm..." He let the end of the sentence fade away. No more words would come. He felt drained. He took a wet washcloth, washed his face twice, and then fell on the bed, rolled on his side and soon fell asleep. He had already forgotten his threat to sleep on the floor.

Austin sat in the chair still watching him, still trying to wish this all hadn't happen, and then wondering was there anything else he could do to keep Ryan with him for the rest of his life. He knew that for him to do anything while attempting to persuade Ryan to stay would be wrong. Ryan must want to stay, or he might as well leave. He sat there thinking for over an hour before finally lying down on the bed beside Ryan and stared at the ceiling still searching for answers.

FORTY-TWO

The next day Austin watched through a corner in the blinds as Ryan walked to his car. This caused his stomach to feel very tense. Ryan drove to the airport and purchased a ticket home for Sunday. That was just three days away. Austin started to leave his room for breakfast with the rest of the guests, but his appetite failed him. He sat nervously at the table near their balcony window, waiting eagerly but also apprehensively for Ryan to return. He felt so anxious he could feel his heart beating in a spot just above his jawbone. He took a deep breath and sighed heavily. He did it again hoping to relax a little. He temporarily looked away from the green garden gate he hoped Ryan would return through and looked up at the sky. He noted the color of the sky today was a deep blue. He looked left and right, but there wasn't a cloud in sight. A casual tropical breeze cooled his face. His nostrils smelled the fresh and clean air from the gardens in the grounds of Big Ruby's. An early morning Key West shower had rained for about fifteen minutes and disappeared, leaving the vegetation damp. A day like this is what the locals called another beautiful day in paradise. He had to agree. A single bluebird that was chasing crumbs thrown by the other guests caught his eye. Finally, he broke his mood and went down to the breakfast area and sat down alone.

Austin was leaning back in his chair so he could watch the bird take flight. He watched the bird soar into the air, as it flapped it wings to gain speed and altitude, but tiring, it began peacefully floating on the warm air rising from the earth below. It looked so calm and confident. It was a glorious moment for Austin, and the event made him wonder what it would be like to be as free as a bird.

Jerry cleared his throat loudly. "Hey, we're a tribe on this planet, too," he teased. "May we join you for breakfast?" He and Terry set four plates down on the table.

The comment brought Austin back to reality as he turned and gave his friends a slight smile. "Oh, I'm sorry. Sit down. How are you?"

"We're fine, but you don't look so good. Where's Ryan?" asked Terry.

"He went to buy a plane ticket home," replied Austin somberly.

"Oh no, so soon? I just about had you retrained into a respectable gay man. When are you fellows leaving?" asked Terry between Austin's bites of the orange muffin.

The smile left Austin's face. "He's going home. I'm staying here."

"Uh oh, trouble in paradise," muttered Jerry with a heavy sigh as scratched his head.

"Hush, that," scolded Terry with a playful wink to his partner. "It is absolutely none of our business what they do." He paused to let the sincerity of what he said dwindle, and then added with a smile, "Do you want to talk about it?"

Jerry gave Terry a playful poke to his ribs while wagging his index finger at his partner in a no-no fashion. Terry rolled his eyes and shrugged as if to say 'what's the harm?'

"No. Yes. I don't know," replied Austin as he fretfully twisted a paper napkin into little wadded bits and dropped them on the table one by one.

"Planning a parade?" teased Jerry.

Terry bumped Jerry's knee with his own while giving him the shut up sign by raising his eyebrows. He turned back to Austin. "I don't know what's going on, but let me tell you something. Jerry and I have met thousands of gays in love, and thankfully, hundreds of couples that made it past the dreaded sophomore slump in their second year. I've seen some marvelous examples of romance, but let me tell you this, and I'm sure Jerry will agree, watching you and Ryan, well, I've never seen any two people more in love, and more fit for each other in my entire life. We've traveled the globe for many years. We have seen lovers in almost every country. However, when the two of you walk down the street, glancing at each other, touching here and there, speaking with silent eyes, feeling and thinking thoughts without touching, it is amazing. I swear to you, flower buds bloom as you pass by, birds sing, and people turn and stare. The two of you are a walking Broadway musical for Pete's sake. You have something special."

"Yeah, but one thing is missing," replied Austin sarcastically.

"What's that?" asked Jerry and Terry in nervous unison, and then catching their anticipation, they fretted at being so eager to know. Their soap opera genes just kept surfacing uncontrollably.

"I'm gay, and he's not."

No one in Big Ruby's had known that. Whenever Austin described Ryan, everyone just assumed he was gay, too. Austin never corrected their assumptions. The way Ryan cared for Austin, their gentle caressing, and their love blew away all doubts they were not in fact a couple. No one would have guessed Ryan was not gay. His love for Austin surpassed a level others only dreamed of. They felt each partner of the couple was the lucky one.

"But I know he loves you," said Terry.

"Yes he does, and I love him. We had sex all the time on the island and we've been intimate some in the States, but the bottom line is he's straight."

"No, can't be. He's probably bisexual," added Jerry.

"No, he says he's straight. If he was bi then perhaps we could work this out. I want to live where I'm free. He wants to go home to North Carolina."

Jerry frowned. "Wait a minute. I know things were going so well between you. What happened?"

Austin related the incident in the Wyland Museum. They felt horrified.

"The bitch!" pronounced Jerry. "Where is she? I want to claw her eyes out and feed them to the birds!" Terry sensed it was the wrong time for them to talk, and politely touched his index finger to his lips, as he nodded at Jerry and winked. Jerry calmed down and squeezed Austin's hand to assure him they were still here for him.

Austin continued, "Oh the island, Ryan had no inhibitions. We lived only as we knew, and I can tell you the love we shared there was far greater than anything I have ever experienced with another soul in America. I have never been happier, more confident, and neither has Ryan. We made love, we felt love, and we were love. Everything collapsed when we came back to civilization as grown men and discovered the difference between being straight and being gay. On the island, there were no boundaries, just pure love. I know I am gay, and I know he's not, but I swear to you, when he's with me, there is no gay or straight, only love."

Jerry and Terry had fallen silent as they listened to Austin pour his heart out. They did not know what to say. Jerry took Austin's other hand to comfort him while Terry continued to hold on, too. A slow tear fell across Austin's cheeks. Jerry and Terry sniffled as they fought to hold their own tears.

"If there's anything we can do, just ask," said Terry.

"Thanks guys. I will be okay. Thanks for being such good friends to both of us. Please don't be mad at Ryan. He can't help what society has crammed down his throat. I believe genetically gays are different from straights. Maybe it is something else. Perhaps the reason man has survived since the prehistoric time is because man learned to adapt by educating himself. Man made a few errors, but he adapted. On the island I felt like we successfully grew up from kids to teenagers because we adapted and our love for each worked. It wasn't until we came home that it all fell apart."

Austin picked at his food for a while, and then the three friends sat back in their chairs to finish their coffee in an eerie silence. No one knew what to say.

A few minutes later, as if on cue, the gate to Big Ruby's opened. The patrons all turned to see who was arriving, as if they were all waiting on Mister America to walk through the door. Some thought their hopes had been achieved as Ryan pushed through the gate. With their curiosity satisfied, the sunbathers smiled and waved a hand or offered a polite nod and smile. Jerry and Terry sighed, too. They waited for Ryan to walk over and join them. Ryan sat down stiffly, laid the ticket down beside the silverware, nodded politely at Jerry and Terry, but words failed him. Jerry retrieved the cover from Ryan's plate and smiled at him. He thought Ryan should eat. Ryan expected an argument to start, but when none came, he picked at his food. He was too stressed to eat.

"Well, excuse us, fellows. We've got some work to do," said Terry as he bumped Jerry's elbow to get him up.

"Work to do?" What work have we..." protested Jerry, but Terry cut him off with a nod towards the entrance. Jerry frowned, as he wanted to hear what Ryan had to say.

"Just odds and ends," added Terry as he pushed Jerry ahead of him. "Come on. Let's leave these two handsome gents to a quiet breakfast together. We'll see you later."

Austin and Ryan watched them head out the green gate. Soon Jim arrived from the kitchen. He brought Ryan a second plate of hot food. "Let me get that cold stuff out of your way. These omelets are hot and ready. Both of you need to eat so get to it." Jim gathered the cold breakfast and disappeared. Ryan tried to take a bite or two, but nothing went down.

"I see you can't eat either," smiled Austin.

"Nope," he paused before adding, "I've got to tell you, buying that ticket was the hardest thing I've ever done. I will not leave you in anger. I wish you would come back with me. We are best friends, isn't that enough?" asked Ryan.

"No," started Austin as his temper almost flared, and then he caught himself, "yes, of course it is, but I'm like a bird that dares to fly and feel free. You're like the rock, ever steady, and always strong and yes, stuck on ground with the rest of the stupid straight people and their prejudices. I guess when that helicopter rescued us they saved and doomed us at the same time. Had it not been for Shark Island, maybe, we would have just remained the best friends we were during our camp days."

Trying to change the subject, Ryan said, "I spoke to Bonnie. She wants to talk to you. Will you call her?" he urged.

"Yes, I will. I'll call her tonight."

"That's good."

During the next two days, Ryan and Austin noticed the other patrons whispering when they came around. It was as if they were talking about them. It confused them because the guests of Big Ruby's had been so friendly and polite to them. They felt a bit like outsiders or perhaps because they weren't the perfect couple everyone had hoped for, the boys felt like somehow let them all down. Jim and Larry were always in a hurry. Their new friends Jerry and Terry must have left without saying goodbye, as they hadn't seen them at all. Austin and Ryan had hoped to talk them into one more sailing adventure before Ryan's Sunday morning flight out of Key West.

Ryan slept on the floor the remaining nights, almost cursing himself for shutting Austin's affection out these last days. He could not sleep Saturday night, so he decided to take a late night walk well after midnight. Most of the guests had gone dancing, and so Big Ruby's tropical courtyard was quiet except for the chirping of the crickets and the hollow throat sound of a big frog. He took the path that led him by the pool. He felt so restless that he slipped out of his shorts and dove in the sparkling water. He swam a few laps and then just casually floated on his back in the middle of the pool. He didn't know Austin was watching him from their window. Austin thought Ryan looked so beautiful in the water. He wanted to join him, but he knew he mustn't. If they couldn't sleep together, they certainly couldn't swim together in the nude.

Ryan drifted off to the side of the pool when he suddenly heard the green door open. Austin and Ryan's eyes followed suit as they both looked at the gate to see who it was. From his view from the balcony, Austin spotted Jerry and Terry first as they walked along the ramp. Ryan did not want to talk to anyone so he ducked down behind a palm plant around the curve of the pool. Ryan soon discovered it was Jerry and Terry who had entered, but though they were friends, he still did not want to speak to anyone so he remained hidden.

The kitchen door opened and Jim and Larry came out.
"You made it," said Jim. "How was it?"
"It was perfect," giggled Jerry.
"It is just what they need," added Terry.
"I hope you're right. This is going to take a big miracle," stated Larry. "Come on in the kitchen, I've got some coffee brewing."

Austin heard none of their comments, but Ryan heard it all, but not one word made sense to him. He floated a while longer, then grabbed his shorts, and walked back to the room while still dripping. Austin quickly returned to the bed. Ryan tried to creep in the room silently. Although Austin pretended to be asleep, he could only mange to close eyes, but not his brain. Ryan toweled off, lied down on the floor, and stayed there for almost twenty minutes, before abruptly getting up and climbing beneath the sheets with Austin.

Austin remained still, afraid to breathe, afraid to hope, and afraid to move. Ryan remained still for a few more minutes before sliding over and cuddling Austin. Austin started to sob silently. He knew this would be their last time forever. He silently thanked Ryan for giving of himself to him. He pushed back into Ryan and Ryan pulled him in closer, and then pulled at his shoulder until Austin faced him.

"Don't say anything, not a single word. Just love me with everything you have and more," whispered Ryan before planting deep wet kisses to Austin's tear drenched lips. They made love repeatedly, passionately, desperately, and when the alarm clock went off, they felt spent, sore, and delirious.

228

They had said goodbye in their own special way, without words, without promises, without anger, but not without love.

FORTY-THREE

They came down the stairs a bit late for breakfast, and immediately surprised to find almost every table filled with Big Ruby's guests. That was rare on any day, but especially the morning after a big Saturday night of partying while celebrating the end of the week. Everyone seemed happy and chatting, at least until they arrived, and then suddenly it felt like they were whispering about Austin and Ryan once again. The boys looked at each other quickly, checking to see if their zippers were open, or perhaps they had a bugger in their nose. They wondered why they were receiving the silent treatment.

With great flurry, Jim quickly led them to the only bare table, and set down their breakfast plates. He chatted about nothing, but oddly kept rushing them to finish eating by pretending he had somewhere to go. He had never done that before, but they obliged him anyhow. Jim took away the plates just as they both stuffed the last bite of pancakes into their mouths, and quickly downed their fresh squeezed juice. He took their napkins and quickly wiped their faces before they could protest, as if they were his children. They were too stunned to react.

Larry suddenly entered the pool area. "Ladies and gentlemen, this is a special day because two of our most prized guests are leaving today. Yes, I'm sorry to say it, but Ryan and Austin are leaving today."

"I thought I was your prize?" asked Jim as he returned from the kitchen faking surprise and walked up next to Larry. The audience chuckled as he placed his arm around his longtime lover.

Larry grinned. "You are, my dear. My prize bull!!"

"Oooo," echoed the crowd.

"You thought he kept me happy with his coffee?" added Larry as he lifted his cup to his lips for a sip. The crowd laughed again. "As I was saying, the two of them are indeed leaving today."

Austin and Ryan were listening but remained confused. Ryan was leaving, they thought, not Austin. What is he talking about?

Larry finished his little opening comments and then said, "I'll now turn the floor over to our dear friend Terry, one of our supermen of the day." Everyone clapped as Terry came to the front of the group.

"I've met many gay couples since coming down here three weeks ago..." he began.

Jerry jeered, "Make that three DECADES ago, dear!"

The crowd laughed and cheered. Terry blushed. "Uh, yeah, that's probably right. Time sure flies by. Let's see as I was saying. I can tell you with all sincerity, I have never met two men so suited for each other, so perfect, so blessed as they mirrored their compassion for the other. I will also tell you if everyone could emulate what these two men so naturally possess we would be among the greatest lovers of all-time."

230

"I am the greatest lover, and it's time you lied and admitted it!" broke in Jerry.

"Right dear," with a mock salute and grin, then added politely, "now shut up or no nooky for you tonight," shot back Terry. The patrons laughed again. "As I was saying one more time before my sweet thing interrupted me," Terry winked at Jerry to let him know he was just teasing. "Ryan and Austin are very special to Jerry and I, as well as to Larry and Jim, and I'm sure to all of you as well. We have all seen what Ryan was able to do when poor Austin was down-and-out. He was a real Prince Charming, and we thank him ever so much for bringing our Sleeping Beauty back to life."

"This is getting deep," said Jerry to the crowd as he feigned drying his eyes with a napkin.

Terry rolled his eyes at Jerry and frowned.

"I'm sorry, I'm sorry. I'll be quiet," added Jerry quickly.

"On an island not too far from here, these two boys spent seven years in exile there. Exile is what we land lovers would have called it. They called it paradise. It was a special place. They landed there at the age of ten. They knew no prejudices. They had no vain reasons to lie. Felt no effects from political attitudes or wars. They lived each day happily while feeling loved and nurtured. Society had missed its chance to ram its inhibitions down their throats. They experienced no Bible-thumping television evangelist threatening their souls, nor were they mocked or scorned. No stuffed shirt generals could threaten to kick them out the military, and thankfully, no Sunday schoolteachers spat at them. They felt contented. They were in love. They were special.

"That utopia crumbled at the moment of rescue, and unfortunately, they have not been able to put it back together again. Austin dreams of going back to that paradise, to live free, and happy, but the only thing that could really make him happy would be if Ryan were to join him. However, don't be mad at Ryan, for you see, Austin is gay, and Ryan is not. There, I said it. The secret is out. How God makes anyone warrants no shame. It is just a biological fact.

"But I believe these two men love each other anyhow. I have seen it with my own eyes, heard with my own cute little ears..." the audience giggled, "and felt it with my heart. I pray I can learn how to love my dear Jerry as much as they love each other. Society has thrown them a curve and the dilemma is magnanimous.

"Several of us have been working for days to find a solution to their problem. We made calls all across the country and around the world. We could not just idly sit by and let such a perfect love go down the drain. They represent what we all seek, search, and yearn for. They became the example and they have the goal we should all seek. Surely, we thought, someone must have a solution somewhere to their problem. That's the way it's supposed to work, right?

"So raise your hands on this question, how many of you have heard of an island called Elysian?" Several hands went up. Austin and Ryan had never heard of it.

"Let me bring everyone up to speed on Elysian. It is a small island just east of Barbados. We know that France sent many of its prisoners to places like Devils Island to live in exile, but there was another group of people purposely marooned on an island. They were the outcast homosexuals. There was a period in history when France frowned on anyone gay. The prisons soon filled with men caught in the act. France sent hundreds of these gay prisoners to the island of Elysian. France thought they had sent them there as punishment, but little did they know the gays suddenly found themselves free to be themselves. On the island, they could wear what they wanted to, they could hold hands in public, they could kiss anytime and anywhere, hell, they could even do the 'nasty' in public!!" The crowd laughed.

"You see they had found their own paradise. For fifty years, Elysian was heaven on earth to these men. However, word of their bliss traveled back to Europe from the trading ships that stopped off to sell their goods to the homosexuals, and soon the priests came to convert them from their heathen ways. The priests made little success, but unfortunately, their entourage brought with them germs from the disease called smallpox. They suffered like many of our American Indians. Because of their deep affection to one other, while often experiencing open and free sex, the disease spread rapidly. Soon the entire population of Elysian became infected before anyone discovered why they were getting sick.

"Within a week after the first person fell sick, they all became ill. Horrified, the priests left the island. They lied and said God had punished the homosexuals. The traders stopped coming. It was as if the island was a leper colony. At first, one died, then three, and in less than a month, they all died except one couple. Many years before the arrival of the holy clerics, this couple had fallen in love and made themselves a married couple. They had sex only with their partner and no one else. They had chosen to live life their own way. Not long after landing on the island of Elysian, they had packed up their belongings and hiked to the far side of the island. This meant they had to climb over a steep, rugged, rocky mountain most assumed impassable, but it wasn't. In a beautiful valley on the other side, they lived quietly, successfully, and alone, and the lovers never knew they were the only ones to survive. They died about the turn of the century, leaving the island vacant of all human life.

"I have a longtime friend in New York. His grandfather was in the shipping business. He was traveling on one of his family's merchant ships in the Caribbean when a huge hurricane hit them broadside and tumbled the ship over and over again, and smashed it on the shores of Elysian. The man and twenty of his crew lived there for six months before a rescue party found them. He loved the island so much that twenty years later when he became filthy rich, which is my favorite kind of rich," the crowd chuckled, "he arranged to buy the island. Sadly, not long after he bought the beautiful island, he became sick and died, and so it passed down to his heirs. His only son held the land for forty-eight years and did nothing with it. He never once even bothered to set foot on it.

"My friend is called Arthur. He then inherited the island from his father. When Arthur became the owner in the sixties, he decided he wanted to see the island. He charted a sailboat, and with several of his gay friends, he visited the island and fell instantly in love with it. As the years went by, he had a close friend die of AIDS, and saddened by the lost, he and his partner decided to move to the uninhabited island of Elysian. He was quite the entrepreneur. He began by building a unique gay bed and breakfast there, that is only second to the fabulous Big Ruby's." Everyone cheered. Jim and Larry took a bow.

"He began to teach sailing, and then added scuba diving. He improved the cuisine by hiring an incredible chef. Over the decades the place has truly blossomed. Gays now come from all over the world to feel that freedom the original homosexuals felt when they came from the prisons of Paris over a hundred years ago.

"Jerry and I have just returned from there. We flew out the other day for a quick visit. We met with our friend, toured the island once more, and I tell you, there is still nothing like it in the world. Nevertheless, I am afraid our journey was a sad one as well. You see Arthur has been HIV Positive for a long time. He thought perhaps he had beaten the disease by eating certain tropical fruits and taking the latest prescriptions, but last year it flared up with great intensity. He is now too sick to run the place. It is his dream that what they started on Elysian continue after him, but alas, there's a problem. He has no children to pass it on to.

"Three months ago, he asked Jerry and I to take it over and run it. We felt flattered, and though we love to visit the island, we both remain smitten by fashion. It still excites us. But Arthur made us an offer we couldn't refuse, so we told him we would visit while we were in Key West and make up our minds."

With great flair, Terry continued boldly, "Well, I'm proud to announce that Jerry and I have turned down the offer to run Elysian." He paused for the expected hisses to expel and then added, "However, we did buy the island. Actually, Jim, Larry, Jerry and I now own it, and sadly, my friend Arthur will probably soon die there. However, we bought it not for us, though sorely tempted, but instead we bought it for two people who have the perfect expertise to manage an island. We chose two men who know how to make happiness flourish where others might just feel stranded, and who know how to make dreams come true. They know how to care for each other, and how to produce love on a higher plane I can barely dream about. Can you just imagine how much better our world would be if they could spread their devotion and love to the thousands of gay pilgrims that will spend their vacation time with them? Wouldn't that be a heavenly paradise?"

He turned from the audience, paused, and stared with a smile at the boys. "Austin and Ryan, we purchased this island for you!"

The audience stood and cheered, and some even yelled and screamed. They whistled and whooped. It was instant pandemonium. Tourists stopped on the street and wondered what was happening behind the big green fence. Austin and Ryan were far too stunned to speak. Terry waited for the crowd to settle down before continuing.

"Now, Ryan, I know you're planning on leaving our paradise in Key West, and Austin, you planned to stay behind. To Ryan's credit, I know you have begged Austin to come home with you, but he wouldn't. On behalf of everyone here, I want to ask Ryan to do this one last request, or I should say this one last favor. Would you honor us by flying down to Elysian, and staying there as our guests for two weeks? Talk with Arthur, and if at the end of two weeks you wish to come home, I will have a ticket prepared in advance for you. Everything will be at our expense. We hope you will love it. I know Austin will like it, but Ryan, you are the one that has to find his own peace, and your own place in this world. Will you say yes? Will you at least go down and take a look at this special place?"

The crowd began to chant, "Yes! Yes! Yes!"

Ryan looked at Austin. Austin shrugged. "What's the harm?" he said as he leaned into Ryan.

Ryan chewed his lip. The crowd kept chanting. He finally nodded his head affirmatively, finding himself overwhelmed at the magnificent offer. He couldn't say anything, however, the crowd cheered.

"Ah, yes, wonderful!" exclaimed Terry. "I must be honest, Ryan. I was afraid if I had offered you this while we were alone, you would have thought me a fool and turned me down, but I didn't think you could turn down forty of your new best friends!!" The crowd clapped and cheered as Terry extended his hand to the audience.

"Larry has already packed your stuff while you were eating. Here are the tickets. Your flight leaves at ten o'clock, which is forty minutes from now. I think everyone would like to send you off with a big hug. Am I right, fellows?"

The meeting broke up instantly. Larry and Jim loaded Ryan's rental car. One by one, the guests gave the suddenly shocked couple their hugs and best wishes. Jerry gave them a long hug and kissed them both on the cheeks, so did Jim, and then Larry. Terry would be the last. He placed a thick envelope in Ryan's hands.

"In this you'll find your flight tickets as well as a ticket for your return flight as promised. There is spending money in there and I expect you to blow it all while traveling. Have a great time. One more thing, if Jerry and I

234

could have had sons, if we could have imagined perfect sons, intelligent, bright, gifted, beautiful, loving sons, we would still have wished they were as much like you and Austin as possible. We cherish you both as friends, so please go with our best wishes, our blessings, and our hope you will find a place so special, your love will grow despite any misfortune. I love you." Terry hugged them. Ryan and Austin were so overcome at the support and love offered, they both just starting crying. Jim cried. So did Larry as he wiped his eyes with a dishtowel.

"Jeez, this is getting mushy on a Sunday morning. Would you two hurry up and drip-dry, and get the hell out of here, I have to work on my tan!" teased Jerry.

They all laughed, hugged once more, and then finally Ryan and Austin got in the car for the ride to the airport.

FORTY-FOUR

They flew back to Miami, and then waited about two hours to catch a flight to Barbados. As they flew over the blue waters of the South Caribbean Islands, they became fascinated at just how beautiful it was from the air. For many years, they had seen the ocean from just the view from their island, but at fifteen thousand feet, the sight was spectacular. Ryan awoke that morning planning to leave for North Carolina, however, a few hours later he was on a flight due south to Elysian. At the start of the day, Austin expected to lose the person he most loved, leaving him with no future plans in sight, no new dreams, and no more hopes. Now he sat by Ryan staring out the window and looking for the island Terry described in his presentation.

In Barbados, they caught a cab from the airport to the seaplane dock on the edge of the island. It gave them a chance to see a little bit of Barbados. From the brochure, they learned Captain Powell had developed the island, and though the once mighty Arawak Indians lived on the island centuries ago, the Portuguese drove away the warriors. However, it became an English colony in the late eighteen hundreds, but gained her independence in the nineteen sixties. Tourism is the island's main source of income followed by the sale of sugarcane. The islanders are mostly descendants of African slaves. It was a gorgeous island, and the people were so friendly and helpful. They gave Barbados a score of nine, but doubted Elysian would be able to beat the high score. The cab took the boys right through the center of Bridgetown, down the narrow streets filled with shops for the tourist trade, and then out to the small seaplane port.

Neither Austin nor Ryan had ever flown in a seaplane. The small seaport had just one waiting plane parked before them. To the boys, it looked like a fat duck with wheels and skis. Twenty minutes later, they saw another plane land on the water and coast up to the cement landing, much like the boat ramp at the camp. The pilot then gave the engine some gas with a slight push on the throttles, and to their surprise, the plane easily moved up the ramp on the wheels hidden below the waterline in the bottom of narrow pontoons. The pilot spun the craft around and then shut down its engines. The seaplane was the modern way for people to get from the smaller islands to the bigger hubs for jet service. They tossed their bags into a compartment in the tail. The pilot told them to climb in and buckle up. No one bothered to check their tickets. It was a primitive and simple airport.

Three minutes later, they found themselves sitting on a long bench hugging the interior wall with a man holding a goat, another with two prize chickens in a small cage, a screaming baby, an exhausted mother, a priest, and a well-dressed European. They were all going to other islands. The pilot closed the hatch and went immediately to his seat, where he fired up the engines, and minutes later, they skimmed across the water and rose quickly to

236

just a thousand feet above the water. The view was stunning. Ryan checked his watch. It was already four in the afternoon.

The flight was about an hour in length before the pilot circled the island for the benefit of the passengers. He announced over speakers that the beautiful island below was a private island called Elysian. Ryan and Austin kept their eyes glued to the windows. It was an island about twenty times the size of Shark Island with deep valleys and tall mountains. They pointed at a large waterfall. They note the sparkling sandy beaches that circled the most of the island, as well as the dark green jungle-like vegetation. Just as they were about to land, they spotted the pier and guesthouses. As they glided closer, they saw the large main home set back from the shore. To them, it was like going on a sailing adventure to the South Seas and discovering a Polynesian village.

At the end of the pier was a set of steps that went down a ramp leading to a lower floating dock a few inches over the water. The plane gently coasted up to it. The pilot shut off the engine, then expertly exited the plane by leaping to the dock, and tied off the plane with a coiled rope. Ryan and Austin were anxious to get off the plane. After stepping onto one of the pontoons, they tossed their bags to the deck. They bid the pilot good day as he untied the rope and jumped back to his plane. They stood still in awe of the beautiful island though they were still in shock of the opportunity that resulted in their arrival.

"This seems like a dream," said Austin.

"It's more than that!" boomed a strong voice from the pier above them. "Come on up and welcome to Elysian, my own special paradise." They glanced up and spotted a well-tanned man wearing a white suit with a wide brow hat. He carried a cane. As they climbed up, they thought he looked eighty, but they knew from Terry that he was only in his early sixties. "I guess you two handsome gents are Ryan and Austin, or is it Austin and Ryan." He smiled as he shook their hands warmly. They regretted noticing the purple lesions on his neck and arms.

"I'm Ryan and this is Austin. You must be Arthur Kingsley," stated Ryan with a warm smile and excited eyes.

"Yes, I'm afraid I am. Welcome to my paradise. I am sorry I am too weak to carry your bags. Do you think you could manage?"

"Yes, of course, we can."

"Well, I should give you the short tour before dark. Let's start here. We are an hour by air from the nearest island, which is Barbados. The island is about twenty square miles. It sits pleasantly on top of an inactive volcano. There are tall mountains and valleys that are spectacular. You will love the waterfalls and of course, there is always plenty of fresh water around. Water has never been a problem here. You are looking at the only village on the island. There are twelve guest cottages, a dining lodge, and of course, my home and office on the slight hill to the back of the clearing. We placed the cottages in the shade of the trees, but close to the ocean so they enjoy a constant breeze. Come on, let's take a closer look."

Ryan and Austin were all eyes and ears. They stepped off the pier onto the white sand. They found no signs of any trash. The island was immaculately clean and pure. Arthur led them to the nearest cottage, which was a twenty by twenty foot cabin. It was built with salt treated pine lumber that had to be shipped by boat. The cottage was covered with palm shakes to give it a natural look. To their surprise, each cottage featured running water with a toilet and sink. There was no electricity. Kerosene lamps and candles provided light at night.

"As you can see it is cozy and yet private. The windows are just tall enough that if you were making love to your companion, you would still feel the gentle wind without observation from other guests. Each guest cottage is just like this one. They all have a front porch, a double swing and hammock, and their rooms are stocked each morning with fresh fruit and flowers. Our guests value their privacy, but when they want company, they are just a few minutes away from the lodge and the dining room. The lodge is our gathering place. We can make our way to it while we talk. As you can see we offer a variety of sports. On the beach is our volleyball net, and there are native canoes to take out on the water. If you look way out at across the ocean, you will see a boat heading this way. That's ours, too. They took six men out for an afternoon scuba dive. There are dive sites nearby that are the best in the world, only we don't tell people about them. We allow no reporters, photographers, or travel agents here. Only our guests enjoy our amenities.

"We also have shuffleboard, tennis, hiking, horseback riding, as well as simpler games like chest or checkers, good books to read in our library, card games, and special events."

"Jeez, this is a lot like my summer camp," said Ryan.

"Precisely, but it's only for grown-ups that are gay or friends of gays. There is no bigotry here, nor crime, and no police force. There's also no hate. I carefully control how many guests are on the island. Elysian will never become a tourist trap, so I guess it is my version of Utopia. Except for a few weeks a year, our guests have to live in the harsh world. Some are still in the closet except during their vacation here. They come here once or twice a year to gain both an inner peace, but also to build a more determined strength to endure the cruelties of their homelands. Many of our repeaters struggle to survive bigotry in their hometowns, but they can't wait to get back here," he said with a chuckle. "It must be something we put in the food."

They stepped into the lodge, which featured high ceilings supported by exposed beams. At one end was a large rock fireplace, and along the walls were pictures and paintings that furnished by previous guests. Ryan and Austin saw pictures of divers swimming near big manna-rays, pods of dolphins, and guests exploring giant lobsters on a night dive. They saw pictures of couples swimming in the pools at the bottom of the waterfalls.

Others were riding horses along the upper mountain trails. The unique feature the pictures had in common was the genuine smile on everyone's face. The lodge was a cozy commonplace for all guests to sit and enjoy the company of others.

Arthur said, "The guests can listen to music in the lodge. As you can see, we supplied it with big overstuffed couches and chairs, ceiling fans, and a compact disc player. There are no electronic gadgets in their cottages. I want them to sleep listening to the ocean breezes. I want them to listen for the sweet sound of their partner's breath. I want them to hear each other's heartbeat and attempt to touch their soul with their thoughts. My married guests stay married after visiting with us. My guests have a higher successful marriage rate than other gay couples that have not experienced the magic of Elysian. In this environment, everyone is on the same playing field with no pretentiousness or lies. They discover what they really like about their partner, and learn to accept things they cannot change, while enhancing the traits they love most. It sounds corny, but it works. Nature can heal even the most complicated problems.

"This place is miraculous for lovers. It was for Paul and I." The boys noted a bit of sparkle in Arthur's eyes as he spoke of his lover. It touched them because they knew personally the anguish and fear of possibly losing the person they loved most in the world. Arthur paused and swallowed before continuing. "When AIDS took him we felt stunned. We thought we escaped the world, and for a time that was true. We did not know the stupid disease was like a time bomb ticking off inside us just waiting to go off. It killed him ten years ago.

"Now my turn is coming. I will be honest; it will be hard to leave this place. I cannot imagine going back to the States to die. I would rather die here, but for now, Elysian still needs me, and so I am here. I must find new caretakers for thousands of lost souls that visit each year, searching for a renewed spirit. It is not an easy job keeping this island running, but the reward is greater than you can imagine. It is a wonderful feeling because you actually can make a difference in someone's life, a difference that can last a lifetime. You will love the joy it gives you. I suspect you experienced the same reward when you took a rebellious kid at your summer camp, and turned him on to the great outdoors, or perhaps the thrill of rock climbing. However, let me also tell you I have been shopping for the perfect new owners for more than a year, and no one has met my criteria. My good friends Jerry and Terry tell me you will, and so I agreed to show you our world. When you are ready, you can tell me if you can picture yourselves staying here, then I will tell you if I can picture it, too. Fair enough?"

They both smiled and nodded affirmatively. They instantly liked Arthur. He was kind and generous, and yet strong and forthright, despite his losing battle with AIDS. He had wit and grace, and most of all he had style and a magnetic charisma.

"Let's go up to my house. I have a special guest wing I have reserved for you." A tall dark Brazilian man came down the steps to help Arthur with the short climb. "Gentlemen, this is James, but that's not his real name. We call him that as a mild attempt at a joke. He is my butler, my helper, and my friend. No, we are not lovers, in case you are wondering. He has a lover called Smitty. His real name is Jim, so you will hear me call him James or Jim, and fortunately, he answers to both. I found this poor couple on the street of Rio de Janeiro. Because they were lovers, they became outcasts in their own country. There are mobs of straight folks, church people, and citizens who beat and kill the gays when they find them. I rescued these boys from a mob by hiding them in my jeep. I brought them back here when they were just fifteen years old. That was eighteen years ago. They have special quarters away from the guests and my house. Smitty takes cares of the horses and the grounds. James takes care of this old horse," added Arthur pointing to his chest and grinning.

Jim opened the door as Arthur, Ryan, and Austin entered the magnificent post and beam home. Stout bamboo poles supported the high arched ceilings. The beautiful floor featured aged oak that was well polished. Like giant lily pads on a pond they saw various woven rugs that covered the floor randomly. Ceiling fans hung down from long poles over a large sitting area that contained a slow curling couch over twenty-five feet long. Tropical colors were everywhere, and remarkably, the house was spotless. They didn't see a spot of dust anywhere. James was an excellent housekeeper, thought Austin.

"James, please lead my guests to their rooms so they can freshen up. Please fix the fellows some of our famous tropical coolers. Dinner is at six. If you don't mind boys the excitement of your visit has tired me just a bit. I think I will enjoy a little nap before dinner. Wake me before dinner, James. I'm okay, just little tired," added Arthur anticipating everyone's concern, as he gave Jim's elbow a reassuring squeeze and then a smile. "Welcome Ryan and Austin. Please make yourselves at home."

They passed by a well-equipped kitchen, a beautiful bathroom with a Jacuzzi tub in it, and then into their area, which consisted of a sitting area with another large couch, a fireplace, and their bedroom. Jim made his exit while they unpacked. Ryan strolled over to look out the window and soon realized the guest wing possessed a breathtaking view of the ocean. The sun was setting. He felt it was a special time of the day. He saw guests gathering at the pier and soon realized they were all there to watch the sunset just as folks did in Key West.

"This place is just too much. It is heaven. It's amazing," began Austin as he bounced on the bed.

Ryan walked quickly from the window, grabbed Austin's hand just as he was about to sit on the bed. "Come on, we're getting out of here!"

Austin's heart sank. He thought sure Ryan would at least stay and enjoy the vacation. "What's wrong?"

"Nothing's wrong. The sun is going down. The guests are gathering on the pier to watch. Get your ass up. We're going, too!" He smiled as he winked at Austin.

FORTY-FIVE

Jim met them in the hallway with their drinks. He nodded his approval when they said they were going to watch the sunset. Ryan counted heads as they made their way down the grassy hill, and then across the white sand and onto the pier. The rest of the guests were at the end of the pier and looking at the sunset. A big black fat man stood behind a cart fixing drinks. He was almost as big as the cart.

"Let me guess," he said to the new arrivals as they came his way, "You must be Ryan and Austin. The boss said to treat you good, so how about a nice fruit punch, no pun intended," he laughed at his own joke, which he used on every new guest. "Just hand me your empties, and I will replace them with my special magic drinks. I'm Tomas. I'm the cook and bartender around here. Do you see how happy the guests are? Well, they are happy because my food is in their tummies, and my alcohol is swirling around in their cute little heads. Just look at what my good cooking did to me!" he laughed again as he handed them two tall glasses filled with a red punch and rum, and a long one-inch sleeve of juicy fresh pineapple. The boys liked him immediately.

"Now come with me and I'll introduce you to everyone." He led the way to the end of the pier. "Gentlemen," he said loudly and then with a sly grin he added, "and lovely ladies." A few gay men curtsied and then giggled. "It is my distinct pleasure to introduce Ryan and Austin. They hail from North Carolina, or least I know Austin does because I would recognize his accent anywhere. Am I right?"

"Yes, you are, and thank you. It's a pleasure to meet all of you."

"And Ryan, I hear a Maine accent, but it seems sort of messed up. You must have been eating some of those Southern grits we hear so much about. Where are you from?"

"You're right I am from Maine, but now I live in North Carolina. I have been there most of my adult life. I guess all those grits are making a change to my voice."

"And no doubt to the rest of your body!" laughed Tomas. "Anybody need refills? We've got about ten minutes until the old mother sun drops into the ocean to cool off for the night." Several guests handed him glasses, and then politely they came over and shook hands with Ryan and Austin. In minutes, they met bankers from Chicago, a contractor from Georgia, a couple from Sweden, another from Australia, and two lawyers from Portland. They were a mixed group, but they all had at least two things in the common: they were all gay, except for Ryan, and they all found paradise on Elysian Island.

Arthur could not have planned a more magical time for their visit. The sun quickly fell into the ocean while providing a spectacular array of colors, especially bright shades of orange and purple lighting up the skyline. They noted the clear blue water under the pier, and of course, the white sandy beaches. Big fish were casually swimming under it. They stared a moment at the scuba boat tied up on the south side. As they walked back to the village, they spotted Jim lighting torches on the front of the cottages like streetlights in the old colonial days. Tomas had disappeared when the sun fully set, but soon he came out onto the veranda of the lodge. He took a large stout piece of iron and began swinging it back and forth inside a triangle steel bar. Tomas rang the dinner bell like a ranch hand.

Bob and Steve made easy friends with the new fellows. Bob grinned as he stated, "That is the best sound on the entire island. I have gained ten pounds since arriving. If it wasn't for all the fun activities I bet I would have doubled even that amount."

Ryan asked, "How long have you been here?"

"We can only come for two weeks a year. We have just three more days. It is so hard to leave," added Steve. He was a landscaper and his partner Bob a contractor. They had not met in a bar, but met on a construction job. "I know many people don't believe in gaydar, but we do. Something inside us just clicked when we met, and instantly, we knew the other was gay, and so we weren't afraid to ask each other out for drinks, dinner, and finally dancing." They dated for a whole year before committing to each other. This trip was a celebration of being together for eleven years.

"I hope you are hungry because Tomas is unbelievable."

Arthur greeted the resort's guests at the door with a smile while offering his hand. Most of them skipped his handshake by giving him a hug. Everyone knew he was sick, but he would not allow anyone to ask him how he was feeling. He wasn't being rude, but strongly felt that the guests were here for a vacation, not grief, he had stated firmly to his staff. "Come, gentlemen, the feast begins. It is pork night and no we're not serving Tomas!" it was his turn to make a joke. Tomas responded with a huge grin, and the tap of a metal spool to the lid of a plate like a drummer hitting a cymbal.

"Ouch! I'm hurt, only I don't feel it as it'll take a week to get to my heart through all this pork!" he laughed at his self-deprecating humor. He quickly began serving the dozen dishes he had prepared.

Ryan and Austin noted the food was expertly displayed, spectacularly decorated, and easily world-class and plentiful. They had no idea how much it cost to stay here, but they were thankful their visit had been a gift. Guests could take their meals out to the veranda or sit around a large round table. Arthur explained the old table once had been used in a castle in Europe for the heads of the local city to sit around and govern. He shipped to the island twenty years ago.

On this night, all the guests chose to sit inside while chatting and eating, and of course drinking, and then eating some more. The comments by the guests had been right, as Austin and Ryan agreed the cooking by Tomas was unbelievable.

Ryan and Austin stuffed themselves, and though a little tired from their journey, they stayed and talked with guests and staff while Arthur made an early retreat to his bed. A few wanted to know if the Atlanta Braves were winning in baseball, and what was happening at home, but no one wanted to hear any bad news. Bob and Steve invited them to a white whale party. They thought they had pulled a joke on newcomers Ryan and Austin, but white whaling was a common practice at their old summer camp, and so they agreed to meet them at the pier at nine o'clock.

They left the lodge, went to their room to change out of their traveling clothes, and put on loose nylon shorts. Leaving the rest of their clothes in their room, they walked down to the beach to stroll along its sandy shores. They could see a few birds flying overhead as the moon began its long climb into the sky. The white sand reflected the light. It was beautiful place to walk. The waves crested quickly, signaling the shore must drop off sharply and deep.

"Breathe that air," urged Austin as his nostrils flared with each deep, lung filled breath.

"I know. It has been a long time since you and I have walked on a beach like this. It is so quiet. Just listen. You can hear everything."

"And you don't hear sirens, car horns, or people yelling at us."

"Yes, it is peaceful. Do you think people become bored here?"

"Did we get bored on Shark Island?" asked Austin.

"We didn't know you could get bored. We did not know a lot of things.

Austin pinched Ryan ribs. "We figured out how to have sex, and we did it without magazines, movies, and without some anal retentive, old maid teacher's health book."

"Yes, I guess we did. This place does have the magic of Shark Island."

"But it also has a lot more. There are people, but not too many, and there are creature comforts, like electricity when you need it, freshwater, and Tomas!" grinned Austin, as he patted his bare but full tummy.

"Yeah, a fellow could get fat here if he wasn't careful."

"I assume they are painting a pretty picture for us, perhaps wanting us to take over the place, but I bet there are chores to do, and they probably weather storms just like we did on Shark Island."

Ryan nodded, and then surprised Austin by slipping his hand in his as they walked along. "I imagine there are boatloads of food to haul to the kitchen, supplies, and where is the laundry? They must use lots of linens and towels."

Austin squeezed the hand that held his. "You know you didn't have to come here. You could have said no. I am thankful you came, no matter what. Treat this as our last vacation together if it makes you more comfortable. Do whatever you want, just please, do it with me?"

They walked in silence for fifty yards or so. Ryan suddenly stopped, but did not let go of Austin's hand. He spun him towards him. He said nothing. He looked intently into his eyes. He felt the freedom of being on an island. There was no one on the beach but them. There was no one to condemn them, and thankfully, no one to curse or spit on them. He felt alive and relaxed. He wasn't tense and nervous, and yet, he could feel his heart beating in his chest.

Austin was afraid bad words were about to come from Ryan's mouth so he said nothing, but looked intently into his beautiful eyes. Ryan reached slowly upward with his free hand, and with a gentle touch, he brushed the windblown hair from Austin's forehead. "Did I ever tell you just how beautiful you are?" he whispered.

"Not in this century," shot back Austin.

"I'm serious," replied Ryan in almost an urgent, but still playful tone. "You are. You are perfect. I love to watch you walk naked to the bathroom or to the beach. I used to watch you walk on Shark Island. Your cute little buns just bounce like jelly as they swish back and forth."

"They were swishing because you drilled them loose so much," laughed Austin.

"Come here," said Ryan as he put his arms around Austin and pulled him in closer. They each felt the sudden tightening in their shorts. Slowly and gently, Ryan kissed Austin. First, a light tender kiss on the forehead, followed by butterfly kisses to each closed eyelid, and then softly he kissed Austin's temples. He smiled as he kissed his cheeks, one kiss after another down his neck, and then moved upwards to his chin. Then a kiss to the left and right of his lips, the tip of his nose, and then after a slight pause, he kissed him lightly on the lips at least ten times. Ryan gently parted Austin's lips and entered his delicious mouth with his swirling warm and wet tongue.

Austin reached and squeezed Ryan's buns. Ryan slipped his right hand into Austin's shorts, and gently rubbed them across his buttocks. The kiss was long and deep, and long in coming. It was a special moment between them. They knew they had not kissed like that since leaving Shark Island over eight years ago.

When they returned to the pier it was at least 9:15. All the guests were swimming off the pier in the nude. When they spotted the new guests, someone yelled, "White Whales Are Up!" Everyone quickly did a surface dive while allowing their white, tan less butts to remain on the surface for a few moments. Ryan and Austin broke up laughing, then without hesitation they dropped their shorts on the pier, and ran and dove off the edge, while simultaneously doing what they called a watermelon dive, which is like an upside down cannonball dive. The result sent twin geysers of water high into the air. Everyone cheered. They played, talked, and swam in the water for over an hour, and then as time ticked by, couple by couple began to disappear.

245

After returning to their quarters, Ryan and Austin soaked together in the hot tub for another thirty minutes. Jim entered the bathroom surprisingly unannounced, bringing tall rum punches and bidding them goodnight without even a hint of a problem seeing two naked men in the tub. They thanked him and drank deliciously. They dried each other off with the thick white towels, and fell onto the sheets while still nude. Beside their bed was a basket of condoms and a lube dispenser. After much kissing and playing, Ryan entered Austin with such ferocity that it ignited a ravishing passion between them. They made love long into the night.

They heard Tomas ringing the breakfast bell at precisely eight o'clock. Reluctantly, they rolled out of bed and struggled through aches and pains to find some shorts and shirts to put on, and still barefooted, they made their way to the dining lodge. All the guests were already there and clapped when Ryan and Austin finally arrived, knowing what had happened on the first night, and laughing at Austin's slow, but steady cowboy walk. The boys both blushed and gladly accepted the pineapple-topped pancakes Tomas dished out in large quantities to everyone.

Tomas grinned. "Austin, I know how you feel. I can't keep my man off me either!" Everyone laughed heartily at old Tomas. It was the perfect beginning for another beautiful day in paradise.

FORTY-SIX

After breakfast, Arthur told them he was sorry, but he was not feeling well, and politely asked if they would mind if Smitty showed them the rest of the island. After offering to stay with him and Arthur saying no that he would be find, they wished him well and eagerly followed Smitty on his behind-the-scenes tour. He began by taking them to the back of the house and then up a path, which ended after a steady climb of about forty yards before continuing to the side of a mountain. When they reached the top of the path, they looked by and realized they were not looking down on the house and the rest of the village. Through the tree limbs, they could see the glorious blue sea surrounding the pier they arrived on just yesterday. To their surprise, the path led into a large opening in the mountain and a large natural cave.

Smitty gestured with his hand to the boys to come deeper into the big cave. "This is where we store our supplies, get our drinking water, and can hide from serious storms like hurricanes and such. There are rivers, waterfalls, and many creeks and brooks throughout the island, but the drinking water is filtered through layers and layers of sand and rock before bubbling to the surface. Nature has created a large water system for us, which is more efficient than the chlorine systems found in cities in America, and our guests tell us it is the best tasting water in the world. However, the best news is it doesn't cost a penny to operate. Inside the cave, they found a large clear pool of water serving as the island's water reservoir. It also created the water pressure to supply the showers, bathroom, and faucets on the island. The boys recalled seeing a large, six-inch diameter, white pipe paralleling the path they had taken to the mountain. The pipe went under ground about twenty feet before they reached the cave. Smitty told them the pipe lay under the floor they were standing on, and ended about a foot from the bottom of the pool of water, at a depth of six feet. He estimated it held about twenty thousand gallons of water, and it had never run dry. "Feel and taste it," he said simply as he helped himself with a scoop of water.

The boys knelt. "It's cold," stated Ryan.

"Very," added Austin.

"Yeah, we are lucky because not all islands have freshwater, and we use this water in many ways. The water flows by gravity down the mountain, building pressure as it goes. All the toilets and sinks in the cottages and house feed off the big white pipe. It also provides water for the kitchen. The pressure is so strong that most guests assume we have a huge pump somewhere. Like most tourists, they arrive with backpacks of bottled water to drink like they were in Mexico, but soon learn that our water often taste better, and so they leave with bottles of our water to take home. In this cave, we have a series of cool rooms that help us keep our food cold. We have a freezer in the kitchen but not a large one, so keeping food cool is important. We do have an ice machine, but mostly for rum drinks. Tomas makes a good drink, no?"

"Very good," echoed the boys.

Smitty led them to a big room on the other side of the pool. He flipped the switch on the wall. "See, electricity. It's magic, no? I'll show you later how we make it, but on these shelves we store our supplies. We warehouse everything here because storms come quickly to the island. There would be no time to move everything to higher ground." Bamboo poles tightly laced together created the raised floor. A kitty suddenly sprang to Smitty's open arms from a shelf. "This is Cat. She keeps the mice and bugs out of here. She does a good job," he added as he stroked her back.

They turned to leave the room. Ryan spoke up, "How often do the storms come?"

"Not often. Thunderstorms come quickly and then are gone, but they are usually harmless. We get rain for about twenty minutes and that's it. Those mini-showers appear three or four times a week. The rainwater begins their journey through the rocks and crevices high above us and eventually into our water tank. Tropical storms come about three times a year. Mostly there's just some rain and wind. We just have to batten down the hatches so to speak, and pray the waves aren't too big. About every two or three years, a hurricane-size storm visits near us, creating large waves. It has been decades since a hurricane hit the island directly." They exited the cave into the sunlight and looked back over the village. "You can see the back of Arthur's home from here. Do you see the satellite dish and other antennas?"

"Yes, I never would have guessed they were there," replied Austin.

"Precisely, Arthur made them impossible to see from the beach and the village. He wants everyone to feel like this is their personal paradise, faraway from the news of the world. Nevertheless, business is business. He has an office in the house. He keeps the door to it shut. The office has all the modern pieces of equipment from computers and fax machines, to satellite telephones, Internet, and email. There is no checking in or out, as our guests prepay their stay here with a credit card on our website. No cash is ever needed, as everything is included. However, the cottages have small safes to protect their valuables.

"We get the weather news from the satellite. Arthur often tells the guests he can forecast the weather with his bum knee, which isn't exactly true," Smitty grinned slyly. "When Arthur sees a storm coming on the computer screen, he rearranges scuba trips and hikes, and keeps everyone close in. In an effort not to alarm our guests and perhaps spoil their vacation, the staff quietly moves perishable food to the cave. If the storm passes by, we move it back without a single guest knowing anything about the procedure. He just doesn't want anyone to worry needlessly.

"If a storm is going to hit us, then he throws what he calls a 'prehistoric' cave party, complete with food, wine, and costumes." Smitty laughed. "Many of the men want to dress like 'Conan the Barbarian,' but alas most of them are short a muscle or two!" The boys laughed.

"Arthur is really something, isn't he?" stated Ryan.

Smitty smiled, and then a lump came to his throat. "He's the only father I've ever known. He is special, very special. He will be missed. Come on, there's more to show you."

They hiked down to the back of the kitchen by veering off the main path. They arrived at an area surrounded by tight, thickly grown bushes and plants. They followed a single, wider, and well-worn path. Twenty steps later, they abruptly came to a building they had no idea existed. The brush blind was well done. Immediately on stepping inside, they met a strong black man called Alley. The room had a long row of washing machines running down one side.

"My gosh, it's a laundry! I wondered how you got all the linens done," stated Ryan.

"It's a pretty clever creation by Arthur. Behind this building is a large water trough. From another section of the mountain, we tapped into a large water stream. The funneled water falls into the trough, as it goes down the mountain it feeds into a twelve-inch pipe. In line with the end of the pipe is a wheel, a big waterwheel. The pressure of the water turns the wheel, which turns a big belt feeding into the back of this building, and attached to a series of pulleys and wheels that spin the clothes inside the washers. They are not electric, they're hydro washers, and it works very well. In just two hours, Alley can wash everything in the laundry for the day."

"But how do you dry them?" asked Austin.

"This way," pointed Smitty, as he led them down a hall to another room that looked like a tall tobacco barn. There they found linen hanging everywhere. It was like a giant, indoor clothesline. The lines ran back and forth across the room just six inches apart. Each line looped on a pulley so Alley could wheel a cart of wet stuff to the end of the room. This allowed him to stand in front of his cart hanging out the linen, pulling on the line, and adding more to the next free space until the row filled. "He does the laundry early in the morning. It is usually dry by afternoon. On wetter days, he has a big blower hooked to the same belt system for funneling outdoor warm air through this room until they are dry. It costs nearly nothing to run this laundry for the whole village. The only item we have to purchase is soap and bleach. Arthur insists we do all we can to kill any germs."

Austin laughed. "Ryan, these systems would have made Swiss Family Robinson proud!" He marveled at Arthur's creativity.

Ryan responded, "I wish we had thought of that on Shark Island."

"You dummy! We didn't have any clothes to wash on Shark Island!" laughed Austin, as he playfully poked at Ryan. Smitty laughed as the fellows pretended to box each other.

They hiked over to the stable. There were at least twenty horses in a large field. "Each horse," began Smitty, as he petted a beautiful red mare, "was born on this island. There are no fences, but they know where their home is, and they know this the only place they'll get great feed. Each year a new horse or two is born. No need to buy 'em, and they're fed off the corn and apples we grow."

"Corn?" asked Austin.

"Yes, come, I'll show you."

Smitty led them out the back of the horse barn into a valley they hadn't noticed from the air. Here they met a man called Johnny. He was tall and lean, but possessed powerful arms. He had a horse hooked to a plow, and he was tending to a five-acre field. Alongside were smaller fields. Plants were growing everywhere.

"We grow all the vegetables and fruits you eat on this island. Everything is fresh. Hidden on the edge of the field near the back is a pig and chicken farm. We eat well here, too well," added a grinning Smitty as he patted his stomach.

"No, I stay fit. You're the one that eats too well," chided Johnny. They all laughed.

Smitty continued, "Along the edge of the jungle are apple, pear, and banana trees. The rows in front of the trees are pineapples. Johnny works in the field every other day. On his off days, he's out in one of our boats fishing. Jim often goes with him. They catch most of the fish we eat, including lobsters and shrimp. We buy as little as we can."

"I am overwhelmingly impressed and surprised," stated Ryan.

"Very efficient, I would never have dreamed all these amazing assets were here. This island is like a modern day paradise, isn't it," added Austin.

"Very much so," replied Ryan.

Smitty said, "Come, let's take this path. We have to hike around the edge of the mountain. The path we take is a filled in ditch. It has a pipe running through it. I'll explain when we get there." He led them up a steep hill, and helped them maneuver their way around the ledge. Ryan and Austin began to think they were going on a rock climbing expedition. When they reached the top, they crossed over a mountain peak and immediately caught a glimpse of the ocean nearly fifteen hundred feet below them. The air felt cooler, and they heard water falling. They carefully made their way down a series of wet and slippery rocks. They continued climbing down for a while. The sound of crashing water became louder and louder until they could hardly hear themselves speak. Smitty took a sharp curve and led them through a huge cave. They had gone only twenty yards when the cave ended. To the right was the waterfall, and they were behind it. It was an exhilarating experience. Thousands of gallons of water rushed downward as fast it could go.

"This is our biggest waterfall. Follow me, but be careful and don't slip," he warned as he led them around the edge of the waterfall.

250

They walked into the daylight on to a cliff so they could see it. It was spectacular to say the least, thought Ryan. Amazing was all Austin could say. Then Smitty led them down another hiking trail. They started seeing a large wooden trough near the bottom of the waterfall. When they were closer, they realized the waterfall crashed into a huge natural pool, and then the water rushed out of the pool in two directions. Off one side, the river continued down the mountain. The channeled water went out the other side and into the large trough placed along the side of the mountain and yet dropping downward at the same time. They rounded a series of switchbacks and suddenly spotted a two-story barn. Attached on the side of the big barn was a huge, old fashion waterwheel. The rapidly flowing water in the trough led right up to the top of the wheel forcing it to turn. Smitty led them across a wooden bridge and into the barn.

They could hardly hear once inside the building. They could see the wheel spinning out of an open window. After turning the wheel, the water cascaded down the hill into a small lake. The wheel was turning fast. The shaft from the center of the wheel came through the wall of the barn, and once inside, it ran the length of the room to the other wall. Looped around the shaft were a series of belts and pulleys that went all the way down to the floor level. One of belts turned a large stone. Smitty reached alongside the stone and held out a handful of naturally ground flour for the boys to see. "That's why our breads are so good and healthy. This is fresh flour, and from this we make our own bread, cakes, pies, pancakes, and much more. All very good," he grinned. The boys smiled as they patted their own stomachs agreeing.

"That pulley also runs our electric generator," added Smitty.

Austin asked, "You make your own electricity?"

"I guess it's too far to get it from a neighboring island," stated Ryan.

"Yeah, but Arthur didn't want the guests to know that. I mean we have music in the lodge, but most assume everything runs on batteries and in a way, they're right. But the office and the ovens in the kitchen take much electricity, so we make and store it for when needed."

"Wait a minute, how do you store electricity?" asked Ryan almost yelling above the noise.

Smitty motioned to follow him outside so they could hear him. "Do you remember the ditch and the pipe I told you about? Well, the wires from the generator run through those pipes. The pipes protect the wires from animal hoofs and nature. It also keeps the generators a secret. We never bring guests where I have taken you. The farm and the laundry are also a secret. It's all part of the magical mystery, as Arthur calls it. You're getting what he calls the behind closed door tour. Anyhow, the wires lead towards Arthur's house and end in a shed next to the house. In there is a large bank of batteries. All of his equipment runs off the batteries. That way, he never has to worry about surges or lighting storms. When the batteries become charged, the electricity stops flowing because of an automatic overload switch. There are control wires in the pipe turning the generator on and off. It manages something call a solenoid which changes the gears and pulleys. The waterwheel turns all the time, but the pulleys control the revolutions of the generator or the grinding stone. There is also a big wire coming from the shed to the kitchen but it, too, is in a buried pipe. This pipe carries two pairs of 220-volt wires operating the ovens and other appliances in the kitchen. Arthur did not want any telephone or power poles on this island. He felt such things would muck up the beautiful scenery, and tempt a guest to want to make contact with the rest of the world. Come on, it's time to hike back. We're going by the ocean shore this time."

He led them downward for more than an hour. He showed them where the freshwater from the mountain ran into the ocean. From the last hill, they overlooked a flat part of the ocean. The water was shallow for nearly fifty yards out and almost a hundred yards long. They pointed to a rock wall just inches above the water surface all the way around except for a wooden gate in the deepest section of the wall.

Smitty grinned. He liked this part of the tour. "This is our fish farm." He waited for the right responses. They didn't disappoint him.

Austin asked, "Fish farm? You grow fish here?"

"They gotta grow somewhere, why not right here? You see ancient Indian tribes were the first aqua farmers. We're using the same techniques. When the tide comes in, we open the gates and allow fresh fish to swim into our fish corral. Before the tide goes back out, we close the gate, keeping the fish inside our huge pool of seawater. We feed them so they grow larger. So when Tomas needs a bunch of fish for tonight's dinner, Johnny gets out his net and tah-dah, he scoops out plenty of fresh fish!" He laughed at himself.

252

FORTY-SEVEN

Ryan and Austin scratched their heads at the numerous unbelievable features created by Arthur and his team. This island was far more organized than Shark Island had ever been. They felt astonished at Arthur's astounding achievements. They followed Smitty down the shore to the village. It was lunchtime by the time they arrived. Arthur met them on the veranda holding drinks. He had somehow timed their journey right to the minute.

"I'm assuming you're thirsty after what I call Smitty's discovery hike. So what do you think of my little island?" he asked as he held fruit punches out to them.

"Thanks for the drinks. You were right," replied Austin. "I am flabbergasted. Is that a word? I just don't know what else to say. Arthur, you are a walking genius!" elated Austin.

"My sentiments exactly and my hat is off to you. This is the most amazing, self-sufficient place I know of," added Ryan.

"We try very hard to keep it natural. We don't allow the guests to discover how we cook or clean, and where we obtained their food. They assume we ship all the food in. We do ship some supplies in, but very little. We get a supply ship about once a month. We always need seasoning, rice, and other stuff. We also get our alcohol from the supply ship, which is an important part of their vacation experience. I had planned to build a liquor still, but just never got around to it. I hear North Carolina boys know a lot about moonshining, eh?" he teased. "Come, let's go in, and eat."

Tomas prepared large chef salads topped with either grilled chicken or shrimp. It was scrumptious, thought Ryan. Amazing had become Austin's favorite word on the island, and he said it over and over again as he discovered more and more of Elysian's magic. The entire village took a much-needed one-hour siesta after lunch. Austin and Ryan needed it after the long hike and their nighttime lovemaking. However, by three o'clock they were on the boat heading out to sea. They told Jim, who was also the captain of the boat, they had scuba dived a little in Key West, but were not yet certified.

"That's no problem. I'm a certified NAUI Diving Instructor. Give me a week of working with you and I'll have your dive card for you. Of course, you have some reading and lectures to do, but it's a piece of cake. Today, you'll dive near me. The other guests have their dive cards so they'll buddy up. They call this reef beneath our location Hunter's Cove."

Austin curiosity piqued. "Hunter's cove? Why?"

"Because big sharks come in and hunt the smaller fish lingering there," replied Jim with a grin. "They also love little white boys."

"I think I'll get a quick darker tan," laughed Ryan.

"Hang in there, guys. The sharks don't bother us because we don't bother them. You'll love it. Now let's check out your safety gear and the

253

plan." He lifted a harness with a tank attached for Ryan and another for Austin.

While organizing their dive gear, they also learned the electricity made by the waterwheel ran the air compressor that filled the air tanks. The guests had no clue, but just assumed the island had many tanks, because they never ran out. Jim took care of everything for the guests. He put the other divers in the water first, watched each diver carefully as they made descents, and then put the boys in the ocean. Once below the surface they immediately saw a huge difference from diving near Key West and the plentiful dive boats that scared away the fish. The ocean around Elysian Island was crystal clear, isolated, and the marine life plentiful. They spotted twenty or thirty fish they had never seen before and a huge grouper searching for lunch nearly mowed them over.

They had been diving about fifteen minutes when Jim spotted a six-foot reef shark. He led the boys into a coral cavern where they could watch the shark search for food and attack. The cunning and fierce looking animal, with its array of sharp jagged teeth, soon found its prey. It moved carefully, closer and closer, and in a flash it suddenly kicked its big tail fin and then swoosh it gulped down its lunch. Then the satisfied shark swam off into the deep blue while several small fish gulped the remains.

The boys soon enjoyed a short ride on a giant sea turtle, and just as they were about to surface, a dolphin swam alongside tempting the boys to chase him, but they were no match for his fins. Once aboard, they were delirious with excitement. Everyone on board had to listen to all the things they saw and did down below. Their joyous tales were infectious. They cheered the telling of their adventures.

To their surprise, Jim returned from below deck and opened a plastic Tupperware container filled with juicy slices of various chunks of fresh fruit. The boys devoured the pineapples and the oranges, but still passed on the bananas. They hadn't eaten many bananas since returning from Shark Island. Jim then opened a container of their chef's fresh apple fritters, which were like big cinnamon buns with bits of apple baked inside. The guests thought they were absolutely scrumptious. The hungry divers devoured their treats about as fast as the shark swallowed its prey. Ryan and Austin knew that Arthur and his staff had thought of everything, including the smallest details like fresh fruit and treats to restore their energy for another dive. Elysian was indeed a paradise.

Ten days had passed since their arrival. The time and the days managed to accelerate rapidly because each day became filled with adventure. This gave them time to learn more about the Elysian and time for the boys to love each other. They also learned to sail again, and thanks to Jim's eager coaching, they could steer and tack better than ever. Jim could do anything on the water, and yet he was the kind of person that was like a teacher or professor that took more pleasure out of watching someone accomplish something new than doing it himself. Ryan had long decided Jim would have made a great camp counselor.

He made a breath-stopping pause after that thought crossed his mind. He smiled as another idea took hold of him. He had realized Elysian was in fact, a grown up camp, a kid's paradise but adult style. They ate meals together like camp. They took part in various group sports from tennis and volleyball, to checkers and cards, to telling tall tales around the campfire, to roasting marshmallows, to going skinny-dipping, and horseback riding and hiking. It was the ultimate camp. He laughed as he told Austin his thoughts. Austin hoped Ryan's revelation was now a point for staying for he had already fallen in love with the place and very much hoped they could stay. However, if Ryan was not going to stay in his life, then if Arthur would let him this is where he decided he must stay to help others find the happiness and freedom he so desperately wanted and could not have.

The next morning, Arthur asked the fellows to walk with him after breakfast. They knew from time to time he had trouble eating, but he managed to get a few bites of eggs and toast down this morning, and so he felt more chipper than usual.

He pointed out to the beach. "I've looked at this beach a thousand times and more, and you know, each morning, it seems as if God has worked hard overnight just to make it a little better each and every day. Do you see the fish jumping over there?" He was pointing into the sun, but beneath the view of the sun were entire schools of small fish leaping into the air and then crashing once more in the water. It was as if they were doing their morning calisthenics as they frolicked and played.

"Yes, I see them," replied Austin enthusiastically.

"Me, too," added Ryan. "Arthur, I've got to hand it to you. You have imagined a special place, and worked hard to make your dream come true. I hope your guests realize how much of yourself and your life you have put into it. When Smitty gave us the behind the scenes tour, I was astounded at how creative you are."

"Thank you, my boy. Hard work does pay off, doesn't it? Come on in the office, I want to show you something." He walked between them holding on to their arms to steady himself as they went inside and cut across the great room to a big closed door. "Gentlemen, this is my office. I show it only to a few. I think it is time you saw it." He pushed the door open and led them in. The room was about twenty feet square with a high ceiling. A fan was hanging down on a pole and running slowly to keep the room cool. There was a row of four-drawer file cabinets, and a big huge oak desk with a high back leather chair like you might see in a banker's office. The desk featured a state-of-the-art computer. On a table to his right were a fax machine, copier, and even a postage meter. Behind the desk was a wall of shelves filled with books. Most successful professionals didn't have the quantity of books Arthur possessed. To their left was a wall on which they found a large painting of a very handsome man. They knew instantly who it was.

Arthur said, "As you may have guessed, there is the man that loved this place as much as I do. Without that love, neither one of us would have been able to make it a success. In the beginning life on the island was hard. We somehow built four cottages and just managed to open for business. At first, we were buying excessively too much food and having it sent in, but we pretended to live in style while our bank account nearly depleted. Then a white squall hit us one afternoon and in minutes, it blew the four cottages away. Our guests had to sleep on the floor in the living room of my house. The guests helped us with the clean up and rebuilding. Ironically, at the end of their vacation stay, the guests said they had the most wonderful time of their lives. They let me know they didn't need fancy things, but rather they found peace and serenity in the simple, natural setting of Elysian Island. It was a good lesson for us. We've tried to keep it simple since then and let the island work the magic.

"Paul did most of the cooking when we started until we found Tomas. I wish you could have met Paul. He would have liked you. He was smart. It was his idea to build the waterwheel and the generator. He and I cleared the land for our gardens so we could grow our own food. It took us a year to clear those few acres. You've never seen so much jungle vegetation, roots, and vines. We hauled numerous wagonloads of volcanic rock out of those new gardens. Every day at quitting time, we would sit down and look over the fields at the work we had accomplished for that day, and it gave us a great feeling of pride as well as a strong determination to finish. This place has our blood, our sweat, and even our tears on it. We love it dearly. To give it up, well, it is going to be hard."

He motioned to the big chairs in front of his desk while he went around to his big leather chair to sit down. "Please, rest your legs." He smiled and added, "Okay, so I can rest my legs." He moved slowly as if each leg weighed a ton. "After our chat, I'll have Smitty take you to where Paul is buried. I want you to bury me right beside him. I know I'm getting ahead of things a bit, but boys, forgive me for calling these grown men sitting in front of me boys, but it keeps me from feeling so blooming old, and besides, you fellows are so damned good-looking, the name boys just fits." They both blushed a bit and smiled. "Anyhow, where was I, oh yeah, Jerry and Terry explained things to me, so our deal is not about money, that's all taken care of. I plan to cut the money they gave me for the place in half. Half to the AIDS Foundation because they have to find a cure, and the other half will remain in the bank in Barbados drawing interest, so there will always be funds to keep Elysian going.

256

"Ryan, I'm told you're the one that is going to make the final decision. As I understand it, Austin was prepared to swim back to old Shark Island to seek happiness, but you feel drawn to live in the States. Do I have that right?"

Ryan replied, "Yes and no. There are some personal reasons in the way of my decision path. I love what you have here. I never dreamed such a place existed. I have always loved my stay at our summer camp where we met, and later I enjoyed working there. I love my adopted mother and almost love the senator, Austin's father, but that would be stretching things a bit."

Austin chuckled. "I feel the same way, and he's my blood father."

Ryan cleared his throat. "Austin and I have a special relationship that probably can't even come close to the many happy years you and Paul enjoyed. I can see why you loved him, because when I saw his picture, I could see a magical sparkle in his eyes." Ryan glanced back at the picture. He had touched Arthur.

Arthur's eyes glistened. "Yes, you're wise to have picked up on that. He could look at me with those eyes and I'd melt every time. I'd come marching in the house, covered in mud and bug bites, and I'd be furious because he had done something that infuriated me. He'd just smile while I spouted off and roll those big eyes at me, and in seconds I'd forget what I was even mad about. Now that he's gone and I finally have the upper hand, I can't think of darn thing to be mad at him about!!" He laughed at himself and the boys grinned, too.

"But Ryan, "he continued, "I sense something different about you fellows. It's not about sex because let me tell you, in the last twenty years I have been on this island I've had almost none. After being diagnosed with AIDS we became scared, but before that, we kissed, hugged, and cuddled, but we were two old farts who worked their asses off to build a dream. We shared a bond that goes way beyond sex and you get there only because of love.

"I'll not ask you how your sex life is because it ain't none of my business. However, I can tell from where I sit, Austin loves you more than anything in the world and I'm right, aren't I?" Austin nodded yes, as words just would not come to his tongue. He felt as if he had a huge lump in his throat. Arthur smiled and winked at him.

Arthur then turned back to Ryan. "And Ryan, somehow you're different and that's none of my business either, but you love Austin more than anything in the world. I would bet the whole farm on that. I'm right, aren't I?"

Ryan nodded. "Yes, but I..."

Arthur cut him off. "I want you boys to know that I think you can handle this place. I've turned down a few friends offering to take over for me, but I've seen your hearts, your genuine sincere smiles, and I believe you understand the mission of Elysian. I believe you will continue what we've started because you will have a chance to change hundreds of lives. You'll be able to do one special thing that Paul and I did that is more important than visiting a paradise, scuba diving, riding a horse, or going sailing. You'll be able to show them how to love each other. Not just tell them about real love, as they may not believe you, but show them. In addition, you cannot preach to them because they won't listen. You'll set such an amazing example they will almost die trying to emulate your love, and then settle for nothing less.

"We don't conquer mountains by trying to leap over them. We climb them one step at a time. You can change the way gays think and feel about themselves, and demonstrate how wonderful it is to be in love with someone. If the world can see how committed gays in love are then in time they will accept us.

"This would be your greatest mission if you take over. I propose you stay here more than the two weeks you planned. I think you should give me ninety days to train you, to introduce you to all my contacts around the world by fax, e-mail, postage mail, and by them coming to see us. We'll go to Barbados, and I'll show you where I shop to get the best bargains in equipment, how to handle the local island natives, and I'll even demonstrate my charm with the various local governments. I'll show you everything. You'll both learn at the same time so what one forgets, the other will remember.

"If you'll give me those ninety days you'll never want to go home. Now please think a little. Don't say 'no' and certainly don't say 'yes.' Your first deadline is fast approaching, if you want the job, it's yours. You'll train for three months and then you'll be on your own. This could well be the most important decision of your life. And don't you dare say yes because you feel sorry for me. Sorry wears off all too soon. You have to want to make this your life, your goal, and yes, your dream, too. Now run along. Smitty is waiting on you. He's on the porch. He's going to show you yet another special part of the island."

"Thanks for everything," said Ryan as he stood up and shook Arthur's hand firmly. Arthur winked at him.

"That goes for me, too," added Austin as he shook his hand, too.

"Have a good ride. I wish could come with you but I'll be going there soon enough, I'm afraid."

FORTY-EIGHT

Smitty led them out the south end of the village to the stable. They discovered a well-cleaned barn with piles of fresh hay and all the equipment hung neatly overhead. All the stall doors were open, allowing the horses to roam in and out as they pleased. Smitty explained Arthur's horses were a happy lot. Austin discovered how friendly they were when one horse came up behind him and rubbed the front of his head on the back of Austin's shirt that ended in a playful push. Ryan noted every horse was in excellent shape and well groomed. They eyed the oiled and cleaned tact hanging around the room. The Elysian horses were not too fat or too thin, and their hooves were shod. Arthur hadn't missed any details as the horses were well brushed. Once Smitty was confident the boys could indeed ride as they said they could, he gave his horse a slight kick to the side. They began galloping for a while for no other reason than just the pure fun of it. Smitty glanced back to see Ryan and Austin smiling from ear to ear. They loved it. It made old Smitty grin, and then he yelled as he charged on.

They had learned to ride many years ago at camp, but like learning to swim, they had not forgotten how to manage a horse. Smitty slowed down before crossing over a rambling stream, and then turned inland and upward. They climbed and crossed the cascading river several times until suddenly the trail leveled out into a small but beautiful valley. On the upper side of the valley the mountain continued climbing another fifteen hundred feet to a rocky peak.

Smitty did not say a word as they casually allowed the horses to walk across the field. The boys assumed they were somehow going to climb the mountain on the backside, but Smitty got off his horse and began to walk slowly while leading the horse by his reins. Ryan and Austin followed suit. Soon Smitty pulled up his horse and pointed to the ground, "That's the gravestone of Paul. Alongside Paul, we will bury Arthur. He's asked me to make sure that happens so that none of his relatives try to take his body back to the States. Only the workers and you will know this location. His legal will dictates that he is to be cremated. He did this to throw the relatives off. He does not want them to take his body. They also don't know that he has sold the island and they are not getting a dime of Arthur's money!" he chuckled at the thought.

Ryan turned around in a circle and instantly realized this was perhaps the most beautiful spot on the entire island. Below him was the lush green foliage of the jungle. Off to his right was the rich, deep blue ocean leading right up to white sandy beach. Off to his left the sun climbed rapidly into the sky. Paul had insisted on his burial on the steep upward slope of the mountain at the back of the valley. Most graves are on flat ground, but this was a steep spot. The grass grew over the grave, but there were fresh flowers at the headstone.

259

Austin asked, "Who puts the flowers there? It's too hard of a climb for Arthur, isn't it?"

"Yes, but he did it once a week for years. I do it now for him. I don't mind. The horses get a good workout, and I owe Paul and Arthur my life. It's the least I could do because they've been so good to me."

Ryan tied off his horse to a branch and then walked up closer to the grave. He turned around to face Austin and Smitty as they stood there holding the reins and that's when he got it. He smiled. Smitty winked at him and smiled back because he knew Ryan had just caught on. Austin felt left in the dark.

"What are you smiling at?" asked Austin inquisitively.

"Come here," urged Ryan. Austin gave his reins to Smitty and walked over to Ryan.

Austin made a puzzled face by wrinkling his brow. "What?"

Ryan took him by the shoulders and turned him around. Austin's face broke into a huge grin. Ryan asked, "Don't you see? Paul had himself buried on a downward slope, his head to the top so he could see the most beautiful view in the world even after his death. Below us is the village, his home, and farther out, the spectacular ocean."

"I see, clever, and pretty funny. Wait, I bet the sun dips into the water almost straight in front of us. Am I right?"

Smitty laughed. "Yes, you are. Paul left nothing to chance. He found this place in their early years on the island. At first we considered using this river to turn the waterwheel, but at the bottom it turns away from the village. The other waterfalls are much closer to the village. He never forgot this spot. He told everyone, 'I want my body buried here, but not for a long, long time, so don't go getting any ideas.' Ryan and Austin grinned at Paul's plans and comments. He must have been a special person, they thought silently.

"It's a beautiful, almost sacred place," said Ryan quietly.

"So peaceful," murmured Austin.

"I think Arthur wanted you to see this place because it's like Elysian's heritage. People come here to live a special life, but yes, time does march on, and one day we must pass the torch on to some younger white knights to take up the battle of life. From what I gather, you are the new white lords and it'll be my pleasure to serve you as well." He let his words sink in a bit before adding, "Okay, enough sentimental talk. Come on, let's ride!"

He led them up a steep narrow trail, but the long upward climb was worth it. The horses were sweating hard as they made their way to the top. Soon they were on the highest peak of the entire island. Smitty galloped to a grassy spot and then abruptly pulled his horse to a quick stop. "Turn your horse around in a slow circle. From this spot you can see YOUR entire island."

It took a second before the 'your' stuck in their brains because the view was so gorgeous and magnificent. They saw lush green valleys, cascading waterfalls, white sandy beaches, and finally they looked out across the blue ocean as far as they could see. It was then that they noted there was not another island in sight. No boats or planes, and no one to cause them harm or call them names.

Smitty climbed off his horse so without prompting Ryan and Austin slid off as well. He reached down and took some dirt in his hand. "This is Elysian dirt. It takes a lot of dirt to make a beautiful island. However, if you're not afraid to get your hands dirty, and your back sore, you can make something beautiful, too. Hold out your hands." He placed some dirt in each of their hands. "Ah, yes. Elysian likes you," he smiled and then laughed heartily. "Don't ever take her for granted, and don't let anyone take her away from you. Not man, his governments and taxes, not bad weather or even hurricanes, and certainly not the attitudes and prejudices of the world. Elysian is now your paradise." He pointed to the dirt in their hands, took a deep breath, and sighed with a new smile and added, "Her future now rests in your hands!"

FORTY-NINE

You would have thought they would have spent their last two days of the two-week period discussing whether they were going to stay or not. Austin had already made up his mind he was going to stay, but he had no idea if Arthur would let him run the place by himself. He sensed Arthur hoped for a couple to do it. Austin felt it unfair to put pressure on Ryan to stay simply because Austin wanted to, plus he was also afraid Ryan would say no, and that was something he didn't want to hear or feel.

Ryan had been thinking a lot, but didn't want to share his feelings with Austin until he had made up his mind. The past few days had been special for him, too. He knew if he used the world's standards and man's rules about what is right and wrong then he was a heterosexual. He also knew if he went back to the States he would live the life of a straight person and maybe even try to marry again. However, he also knew if he stayed on Elysian, it would be much like Shark Island, only better. Here he had a purpose in his life. He would be helping others find the peace they so desperately sought, and maybe he and Austin could teach them how to really love their chosen partner. It was like a camp for adults and he couldn't help but like that. However, he would not have to travel alone six months out of the year like he currently did for the camp. In addition, he would not have to face the political world of the senator. His only ambition in this world would be to help others learn how to make their life better. Their mission was a noble one, full of purpose, passion, and promise.

However, if he stayed, he felt like he would become gay, but then his brains told him that was not possible. Part of him believed the more popular belief that you're born straight or gay, but if that is true, are you also born to love or hate? For the first time he allowed himself to wonder if perhaps he was gay, a latent gay, and a real johnny-come-lately. He and Austin had met other gay men at Big Ruby's and in Raleigh who did not know they were gay until they were in their thirties. They met men who had married and had children, long before realizing their true nature. He also felt perhaps his mind was playing tricks on him, one minute he was straight and the next perhaps he was gay, but how could he be gay if he was attracted to women? Then he laughed at himself because most of the gays he met in Raleigh seemed excessively attracted to Madonna or Marilyn Monroe, Judy Garland or Barbra Streisand. How could they be gay and yet love so many female stars? How complex was all this? These thoughts ran thru his head endlessly.

He had taken a long walk by himself to sort things out. He ended up walking to the stable. On their first visit, he hadn't noticed the riding ring, but inside there was a baby horse playfully galloping behind its mother. He knew Smitty and the mother horse would teach the little horse exactly what he should do and what he shouldn't do. The horse would learn by both example from the mother and direct attention by Smitty. How easy it was for the little horse, thought Ryan. All the little horse had to do was follow the plan they designed just for him, and he would have a happy life. How simple, he thought.

On Shark Island, there had been no one to teach Austin and Ryan. They were without human examples to go by. They taught themselves. They learned how to cook, make traps, successfully fish with a spear, and how to prepare for storms and even enemy soldiers. They also learned how to love, a special love, and a very different love. It was a love that gave them the confidence to endure and the courage to take on new things. It provided an inner joy and a lasting peace. They genuinely felt loved by the other. He knew the straight world could not possibly understand how two men or two women can feel that awesome love between each other. They think gay love is all about sex. They've missed the point. Ryan knew in his heart that two people of any orientation can love as well as any heterosexuals, and perhaps because of the adversity of being different, they make the love they share even more special.

He assumed most straight men never felt the type of tender touches only a man can give another man, and that loss made Ryan a bit sad for rest of world. Nor would they enjoy the pure ecstasy of sex with the man that knew exactly what turned a man on, and how it could make their lovemaking so incredibly arousing. Straight men often call gay sex nasty and disgusting, much like a child might call broccoli or spinach nasty. However, if they followed the recipe to the letter, preparing everything perfectly, while adding the spice of love as the ultimate seasoning, then gay love is far from nasty, and certainly never disgusting, but rather exhilarating. A man's orgasm is always on at least two planes. The outward visible plane of pure satisfaction while making their bodies explode. However, beneath the surface, there is an inward plane of electricity that flows from head to toe in the moment of expulsion. This makes one feel like their entire body might just burst, and yet it is in the very moment of churning triumph that their toes simply flinch in victory. Like the child, they didn't know how good broccoli tasted because they simply didn't want to taste it, and worst yet, they didn't know how good it could be for them. Moreover, he thought, perhaps the reason a gay man's lovemaking aroused his partner so completely was because the man doing the giving always knows what he wanted in return.

Men and women have different bodies and yes, the sex between them is also special, but is it not the only satisfying sex. While most women might perform oral sex on their partner they may not do as well as gay men do, nor continue to ejaculation. Some may allow anal sex, but perhaps not on the same level that gay men enjoy. Neither could they both be tops and bottoms in turn both orally and anally. Ryan stopped and laughed at the deep thinking that seemed to suddenly roll out of his head. He kept walking.

Ryan had already discovered the beautiful, enchanting, natural splendor of Elysian that provided him an opportunity to become a philosopher, or more simply put, the time and solitude to hear the words of his own inner voice. The lack of human noise made such an impact on him. There were no cars rushing by, phones ringing, doors slamming, or people yelling. His thoughts magically bounced off empty shores like an Australian boomerang. He smiled as they gently flowed back to his ears.

With Jennifer, he had become aroused during deep kissing. He undressed her, kissed, and fondled her breasts, and then she would push his mouth to her crotch. Nevertheless, as much as he wanted what she wanted done, he could never do what she wanted convincingly. Only once did she perform oral sex on him. More commonly their sex was simple. He would excite her with his kisses to her breasts, then she would command for him to enter her, and five minutes later, it was over. Many times, he never had a chance to ejaculate, leaving himself pent up and frustrated. She would immediately leave him alone in the bed while she cleaned up, and then they went to sleep. Rarely did they cuddle afterwards. He thought their lovemaking had become almost as ritualistic as the goats on Shark Island.

However, with Austin, the kisses lasted longer and deeper. Austin knew how to twirl his tongue around the inside of Ryan's ear making his manhood swell even larger than the last time. Without even the advantage of a stopwatch to check them, they both equally took long periods of time in kissing ears and necks, or blowing gentle angel-wing kisses to the eyelids and giving a light nuzzle to their partner's nose. Austin would willingly kiss Ryan's bare chest while softly biting and tugging the nipples that always excited him even more.

On Shark Island, they had discovered the popular six to nine sexual position and often, for far more than an hour, they performed oral sex simultaneously. Temptingly, they rolled wet tongues over the head of the penis, while adding thousands of pleasurable kisses, over and again. They followed no similar pattern, but always brought about loud moans and sighs, and it was like nothing he felt when doing it with a woman. Austin knew exactly what buttons to push and yes, Ryan knew Austin's triggers as well. On most nights, he exploded not once, but three or even four times. However, what surprised him was that the quantity of his load far exceeded any and all efforts with Jennifer.

He felt like he had tasted the wine from both sides of the fence, so to speak. Who knows, he thought, had it been a different woman that treated him well, or perhaps a different man that would have treated him far less than Austin, would he now feel like he does, or would he even know what it feels like to be loved by a man?

He pondered the questions for a long time before remembering what Arthur told them. In the end, as you get older, it is not the sex one shares that makes a life worth living, it is the love between two people that matters, that gets you through the tough times, that makes your life more exciting and jubilant. It gives you purpose, pride, and the promise the other will always be there.

Ryan didn't know a woman who loved him as much as Austin did. He didn't know a woman that cared as much for every facet of his well-being as Austin. He didn't even know anyone that would fight for him without regard for one's personal safety, even if that meant giving his life. Ryan never had to ask Austin if he would die for him. If required he knew he would, and yet he never asked Jennifer if she would do the same for her honesty would have seared him like a hot knife to butter.

He hadn't realized it, but perhaps Jennifer never measured up to both the lovemaking he and Austin did so freely and so often on the island, nor had she measured up to the devoted love Austin gave him.

He continued walking until he reached the beach. He kicked playfully at the white sugar-like sand as he strolled along, stopping now and then to pick up a rock, and sending it spinning and dancing across the water until it ran out of steam and sunk quickly beneath the surface perhaps forever. For a moment, he forced himself to imagine that Jennifer still loved him. Therefore, he now had to make a choice just as he had done when they were in college. Should he choose the straight world and Jennifer, or the gay world and Austin? By doing so would he choose the love the world expected, or the more powerful, unending love Austin that gave generously and most unselfishly?

He wished he could make that decision all over again, but back in college, he took the path he thought was right, the one the world assured him was right, and he couldn't help but smirk at the results. His wife left him for a realty salesman and yet, there was Austin still loving him anyhow. In fact, he realized that no matter what he did, nothing ever changed Austin's love for him. If he had found a woman that loved him as much as Austin did, perhaps things would be different, but aloud he said, "Man can't live on what-ifs."

He stopped walking for a moment as if trying to listen to his heart. After a while, he began walking again. He tossed another rock and immediately memories flashed through his brain of a time when he and Austin used to skip rocks on Shark Island, always trying to outdo each other. He noted a flock of white birds flying overhead. They made their journey with what appeared to be effortless flaps of their beautiful wings. In a way, he pondered, the loyalty Austin displayed to him made him feel guilty for having wasted those years with Jennifer, when he could have just kept on soaring like the birds with Austin.

There were many times he wished they hadn't been found on the island, but left alone to grow. However, now that he had met Arthur, he could see that living alone in paradise with just your lover was a selfish act. Arthur and Paul didn't build Elysian so they could get rich because there was little sign of their own extravagance. They wore no fancy rings or thousand dollar watches. Their clothes were simple and except for the office, their house was void of all opulence. They put everything they earned right back into building the village up and making themselves self-sufficient. They were emphatically dependent on no one and certainly never chained to a bottom line or a failing economy.

Arthur had explained the island's bank accounts, including the trust accounts they started many years ago. They were growing and multiplying so Elysian would always have money should it be needed. Financially, the island paradise could survive even if another guest never came, but their goals had been far higher than just continuing their existence. Curiously, Arthur said there was an even greater miracle on the island that would forever guarantee a promising future for Elysian. When each visitor returns home they share what they learned on the island with others, and thus, the waiting list for a vacation in paradise was forever long, insuring occupancy forever.

So, he rephrased the question, should he stay with the heterosexual love he thought he had with Jennifer, or go back to the man he knew loved him above all others, and would die for him at the drop of the hat? Forgetting manly ego issues, he seriously doubted even in her best days, Jennifer would never have died for him. He nodded to himself while thinking, there was no question about it, she wouldn't have, but in his heart, he never once doubted that Austin would die a thousand deaths for him. Ryan would have died for Jennifer had the deed become necessary, however not solely for love, but undoubtedly for honor. For Austin, he would have done so for love and honor. This revelation became a turning point for him, for indeed he had crossed a point in his thinking. He continued walking.

Here on the island, he began to rationalize, it was not a choice of being straight or gay, but rather a choice of a life that brought far more opportunities to love, to be loved, to give love, to cherish love, and to grow in love. In addition, if they were fortunate, their bond of simple but loving lives would inspire others to seek love above all else. Above casual sex with strangers, above risky adventures, and away from one-night stands, rotating partners, mindless affairs, and soap opera-like breakups, and on to seeking a lifetime partner that loves them no matter what.

A scripture verse he had heard when he was a boy during a Sunday chapel service at camp just leaped out of his memory. He hadn't thought about the verse in more than fifteen years. He would have to think hard to remember what Bible book and chapter the scripture came from, but somehow he still knew the words clearly. "Greater love hath no man that this, that a man lay down his life for his friend." He repeated the words aloud to no one but himself and the ocean before him. He paused while deep in thought. It was the most complicated thinking he had done in his entire life. He chewed his lip.

He stopped walking. He didn't move a single muscle. He let his entire energy surge to his brain while willing his body to lie still and dormant for just a minute or two.

He made the difficult decision to not become gay because he felt you had to be born homosexual. However, he also decided not to even think he was straight as he felt he didn't have to prove his sexual persuasion to anyone. He knew in his heart his decision was not about being born gay or straight, or what kind of sex he liked, but rather he chose a partner, a life-long partner, a loving partner, a caring partner, and a very special devoted partner. A person he could trust with his heart, his soul, his body, and even his life.

Compared to every other living being on the entire planet, he knew Austin, and Austin alone was his mate. It was their love for each other that complemented their life, and made their togetherness work despite all obstacles. He now knew their love inspired others to love and be loved. He thought about Jerry, Terry, Jim, and Larry at Big Ruby's and all their guests, and he remembered how Terry told him the love Austin and he shared taught and challenged all others. These were words he marveled and took pride in.

Suddenly, Ryan began to walk once more, slowly at first, then confidently, and then a bit a faster almost skipping along on the wet sand of the shoreline. He laughed aloud. He smiled. He threw rocks way out into the water like an exuberant child. When Austin spotted him coming towards the pier where he somberly sat, he thought surely Ryan had either lost his mind or been drinking heavily. Ryan danced around in circles to the silent symphony playing in his head. He kicked his heels in the air that brought a big chuckle from Austin, and then to top it off, Ryan abruptly did a cartwheel in the sand. Austin laughed aloud at him.

On spotting Austin waiting for him, Ryan sheepishly walked to him, and said nothing as he sat down beside him and tenderly took his hand and held it. He didn't tell him he had made an important decision, or offer a hint he had been able to make the decision. Austin could feel Ryan's quickening pulse in his hand. Ryan's unusual behavior puzzled Austin, but he was afraid to ask what he was thinking. Not knowing was still better than hearing the expected negative response.

"Isn't this place just beautiful?" stated Ryan as he broke their silence.

"I have been nowhere better. We're lucky to be here."

"I'll say. We must invite Jerry, Terry, Jim, and Larry for a visit as soon as we can. We owe them a lot."

Austin squeezed Ryan's hand. "You're right."

"Come on, let's go for a swim. I feel as free as a dolphin!" Astonishingly, Ryan leaped to his feet, stripped off his pants, and took off on a run down the pier before leaping way out into the water. Austin was slower, stunned by Ryan's burst of enthusiasm, but almost as quickly, his pants came down, too. He would still follow Ryan anywhere. He ran off the edge of the pier while performing a flawless swan dive into the water. He swam up under Ryan, grabbed his foot, and unexpectedly pulled him under.

Ryan half expected the maneuver, a pattern they had done since they were little boys at camp. What surprised Austin was that Ryan came down easily, and then kissed him squarely on the lips under water. They surfaced, took a breath, and swam along the spectacular coral reefs hand in hand, kissing and caressing as they sank downward, and then racing to the surface for yet another breath.

They failed to note Arthur watching their natural play. His eyes saw Austin and Ryan, but his mind replayed a similar time when he and Paul had also swam lovingly among the fishes. His eyes moistened, he knew in his heart he had found two special people to run his island, and he was joyous this important goal had been accomplished. A badly timed sharp pain spread deep inside him that almost caused him outwardly to curse the disease robbing him of more years on his beloved island. He waited for the pain to subside and instantly prayed that God would give him the ninety days he felt he needed to train them. "Just ninety days", he begged, and then as he looked up to the heavens he almost silently whispered, "After that, I'll go peacefully, I promise."

FIFTY

On the morning of the last day of their arranged two-week stay, Ryan slipped out of bed early, trying not to wake Austin. He didn't know Austin hadn't slept all night, fearing Ryan would leave forever. Austin expected to find Ryan packing the next morning and when Ryan slipped out of bed, he felt certain of it. He kept his face in this pillow as silent tears rolled slowly off his cheeks onto the beautiful white linen. When Ryan left the room and quietly closed the door, Austin sat up and quickly looked for Ryan's luggage in the closet. It was still there. His heart nearly stopped. He rubbed his eyes, feeling afraid he might be dreaming. It puzzled him. He wondered why hadn't Ryan packed his clothes? He was afraid to allow his mind to think positive. He was afraid to hope and even acknowledge the possibility in his mind. He fell back and pulled Ryan's pillow to his face. His nostrils inhaled Ryan's scent. He sighed heavily before pulling it close to his chest, fearing it would be a smell that all too soon would be gone.

Ryan had made the complicated, life changing decision, but he wanted one last walk alone to check and double check his thoughts, knowing there would be no turning back once he committed to Austin and Arthur. He walked out on the pier and watched the sunrise, and found it as beautiful as the daily sunsets the guests enjoyed. Most of the village missed sunrises, but no one missed a sunset. He sat down on the end of the pier and watched the multicolored tropical fish swim in circles beneath him. They were so free and careless, and yet he knew they had to be happy. He wanted the same thing, for him and for Austin, but was it possible? He pondered these thoughts once again like hitting rewind on a tape player. Could a biologically straight guy and gay man live together as partners, enjoying all the love they could muster and be happy? Would Ryan miss the real world? Would he miss the touch of a woman? Would he miss civilization?

He grinned at his analytical thoughts and knew God knew the answers to any of the questions he produced. He'd decided it was just something they were going to have to try to make work just like any other married couple. His first marriage had failed, mainly because they had not worked at it as a couple. Jennifer was never committed and often he wondered if he had been, too. Had Austin's love become an unknown measuring stick, and though he thought he had been satisfied with Jennifer, perhaps he had not been and felt too inhibited to even consider the possibility?

Here on Elysian he was learning to forget everything he knew about life and many things taught when it came to love and sexuality. His self-esteem suffered greatly when Jennifer took up with a salesman. It damaged his pride, but more importantly, the loss of feeling loved, cared for, and cherished, did the most harm. And while it is true a good woman might have restored those feelings, Austin possessed them, generously bestowed them to him, and he could not help but feel more confident, more powerful, more excited, and more in love with life itself. They say behind every good man is a good woman, said Ryan to himself, but then he laughed when he realized in his case, behind this man, was an excellent man. He reached the same decision each time he went through it. It was the right thing to do, he said to himself, and then aloud to no one but himself and ocean, "It's the right thing to do!"

He stood up, pulled his shoulders back, turned around with a big smile on his face, and then looked up as Tomas began clanging the big breakfast bell. He grinned as he began walking back to wake Austin up. He smiled and waved at the other guests as they stretched and yawned, and made their way up the slight hill to the lodge. No one missed breakfast no matter how sleepy they were. From time to time, he saw a man kiss another man hello. Hugs were given freely to partners and neighbors. He was already used to seeing one man hug another man and it didn't bother him, but rather it made him happy for the lovers. It was indeed a loving place to be, a special wonderful place, and he felt like he was the luckiest man alive to be here and to have such a magnificent opportunity.

He pushed in the door to their room, and saw Austin pulling his shirt over his shorts as he entered the room. "About time you got your butt up," he barked teasingly. Austin almost said something in reply, but fearing he would break down he sat down and slowly pulled on his Teva sandals. Ryan continued, "You can't sleep in like this. From now on, you're going to have to get your butt up on time. No partner of mine is going to sleep in like some lazy old dog. We've only got ninety days to learn how to manage this place. So come on, get your cute little ass in gear. Let's go to breakfast! I'm starved!"

Austin looked up quickly. He stared intently into Ryan's eyes. His ears transmitted the last few sentences to his head, but his heart and brain were spinning out of control, and it took perhaps another second or two before the meaning behind the words took hold. "You're staying?" he finally muttered timidly. It was the question he had been so afraid to ask but the time had finally come. The moment was here. He had to hear it. He had to take it, he thought.

Ryan laughed as he tossed a pillow at Austin's face. "No," he paused for theatrical effect, and then not able to wait another second he grinned slyly and yelled, "WE'RE STAYING!!"

As the pillow bounced off Austin's face, the realization took solid hold of him. He began to shake nervously. Ryan came to him and pulled him to his feet. He hugged him tight. "We're staying, partner. We're staying. Now give me a kiss and let's go eat breakfast. I've been using my brain all morning, and I'm all tapped out. I need some brain food!"

Austin looked up into Ryan's face as the tears flowed like tiny clear rivers down Austin's face to his chin. They kissed quickly three times and then a long kiss.

"Thank you," said Austin as he wiped his face.

"Thanks for the bath. Thanks to you I'm now drenched and there's not a cloud in the sky. Would you quit crying and come on?" Ryan teased as he turned to walk to the door.

"Ryan?" Austin said quickly. Ryan turned. Austin threw the pillow. It caught Ryan squarely in the face.

"I'll get you!" yelled Ryan as he leaped across the bed, tackled Austin and knocked him onto the mattress. They rolled over and over trying to pin each other and when that didn't work, they resorted to tickling until finally they fell into each other's arms laughing, giggling, chuckling, and then finally deeply kissing.

Arthur began his task of teaching and training immediately after breakfast. He never doubted that Ryan and or Austin would stay. He felt it was their destiny. He had felt nothing like that with the other prospects. He also knew they were not choosing to do this out of sympathy for him or his cause. They were perhaps the only couple on earth that could prove they could live on an island entirely alone and prosper in health and in love. These boys belonged together, and he knew they would be able to take Elysian to another level.

"We'll spend part of this morning on learning how to read the weather information. I must teach you all I've learned about weather because a warning of a storm is crucial to both the safety of our guests and our staff, and of course the survival of the village itself. You must not let divers or sailors go for long journeys when storms are brewing. Being caught at sea can be disastrous," he stopped in mid sentence and then smiled at himself. "Listen, at me, you of all people knows that, now don't you." They laughed and smiled. He continued, "Okay, as you know from Smitty's tour, if a bad squall or God forbid a hurricane is coming our way, we move the valuable stuff and the perishable food to the cave." He set a red three-ring binder notebook on the desk in front of him. "This is our emergency procedures manual. I realize that outside these walls, everything seems footloose and fancy-free, but it is only that way because we make it all possible through hard work and good planning. Once a quarter, I go over the details with the staff so nothing is forgotten in the fleeting moments before a storm hits shore.

He pointed to the book. "In there, you'll find I've written what I feel is the proper solution for just about any accident or emergency. For instance, suppose one of our patrons had an appendicitis attack. What do you do? We list the topics alphabetically so turn and see. Austin, read the instructions to us." Arthur had immediately taken on the role of a teacher who knew the end of the semester was coming all too quickly.

Austin flipped the page and read, "We get on the satellite phone and call Barbados. I see you have five doctors on call there. Then arrange for a seaplane to come immediately, transport the victim to Barbados, and on to the hospital."

Arthur added, "Right and we have established accounts with the physicians, the hospitals, the ambulance service, and the airline service. Should a need arise there's even a list of private pilots. I want you to read this book cover to cover and then we'll talk about it tomorrow. Now let's talk about other possible emergencies..."

The class went on for hours. They looked through medical books, and then compact computer disks with even more information. Arthur explained the operating systems for the phones, the satellite hook-up, and more. Arthur knew they were mentally drained by midday so he changed the training. After lunch, they boarded a waiting seaplane and flew to Barbados. Jim went along as well. There they met the doctors, pilots, lawyers, mechanics, and all the other services they had at their disposal. The medical staff gave the boys unexpected physicals. Jim saw to this detail because Arthur wanted to be sure they were in the best of health and disease free. Then they met with the bankers and suppliers, and they brought back some supplies Arthur had ordered weeks ago.

The next day, Arthur had the faxed results of the tests on his desk when they met in the office once more. "I'm sorry to put you through the hospital tests, but I wanted the personal peace of mind of knowing you are not only disease free, but that you wouldn't fall victim to AIDS, too. I am pleased that in fact you'll be fortunate enough to be around Elysian longer than I was. Thank you for allowing us to do that and by the way, the doctors say you're in the best possible health. They also said that neither of you look your age. Your bodies, according to the doctors, are in excellent shape. Congratulations, now let's get to work!"

272

FIFTY-ONE

The weeks ticked by. The guests came and went while the training of the boys exposed them to everything on the island. They cooked with Tomas and prepared special food orders for a diabetic guest. They cleaned the stable, fed the horses, and ordered medicine from the veterinarian in Barbados. They learned how to repair the turbines in the generator, and perform maintenance on the batteries and electrical systems. They helped with the laundry. They filled scuba tanks. They cleaned the boat, worked on the boat's engine, drove the boat and then took refresher courses on rigging the sailboats. They checked and double-checked all the backup supplies and parts for everything that had a function on the island. It was like preparing a ship for an around the world journey. Each day they gained more confidence in their knowledge and skills. Austin impressed Arthur and Ryan with his newly designed, better functioning spreadsheets for running the business. They were just like the reports and software programs he did for his former bank job.

Arthur quizzed them constantly on the emergency manual. He reminded them repeatedly that problems always come quickly and like a lifeguard, they must know what to do and then take action and do it. There would be little time or opportunity to consult the manual. They must know the answers by heart. Ryan and Austin accepted the challenge and thus, pushed and quizzed each other relentlessly. Arthur's expectations were high, but they were determined to measure up. Often Arthur had to lie down on the couch to rest, but he never stopped teaching. The boys' determination and jubilant attitudes won over the staff. The boys were not afraid to help anyone, ask for advice, and then offer new ideas and suggestions. Their enthusiasm was catching, and just as Arthur had predicted, the guests and staff loved them.

They had also melted his heart by the affection they gave each other. They were prone to giving Arthur hugs and kisses as well. They treated him like a beloved grandfather, a role he never expected, but deeply treasured.

At the end of the seventh week, on a Saturday night preceded by a glorious golden sunset, the guests were deeply in awe of nature's magic and were grinning from ear to ear, as they filed into the dining lodge. Tomas had prepared his often-requested stir-fry specialties including chopsticks and chest napkins or bibs for the expected accidental droppings.

Austin was trying to teach the guests how to use the chopsticks. He had picked up a piece of pineapple and had it close to his mouth when it broke free and bounced off his chin to his lap. Everyone busted out laughing at him.

Like a mother hen, Ryan silently scanned the crowd to make sure all the guests had arrived for dinner and noted Arthur missing from the table. He leaned over Austin's shoulder, retrieved the dropped pineapple from his lap, tossed it in the air, successfully caught it with his teeth and gobbled it down.

"When all else fells, just throw it in there! We don't want you to go away hungry," he said with a laugh to the guests.

The guests clapped for him. He smiled and did a slight bow and leaned into Austin. "Where's Arthur?"

"I don't know. He's probably just running behind. I saw him enter the house about an hour ago."

"I'll go check on him," said Ryan as he kissed Austin's hair. "You look after the guests."

Austin smiled and nodded, but Ryan noted the worry lines on his brow as well. Ryan spoke casually to the guests as he left the room, trying hard not to spoil their vacation. Once out of sight, he walked quickly to the house. He pushed open the big door and called, "Arthur? Arthur?"

He heard no reply. His nervous habit of chewing his lip immediately returned. He spotted the office door open and made his way there. He found Arthur on the floor beside his desk, gasping for air. Ryan ran to him and turned him over on his back.

Ryan asked quickly, "Arthur? Are you all right?"

Arthur's eyes were open. He struggled to focus on Ryan's face. Ryan took his hand and squeezed it. Arthur's skin had a strange, white powdery look to it, but Arthur's face began turning blue. Arthur's fingers flinched in Ryan's hand. Arthur took several shallow breaths before gaining enough strength to speak. "Ryan? I'm sorry. I have run out of time," he labored. "My body can't wage the war against the AIDS virus any longer."

"Not to worry, Arthur. Hang on. You'll be okay," urged Ryan while knowing he was looking at a friend who was about to die. He had never been so close to death. His parents had slipped out of his grasp without him seeing their death. He didn't know what to do. He tried to be comforting. The manual hadn't explained how to accept the death of his teacher.

Ryan looked up as he heard footsteps. Relieved, he spotted Austin. It took but a second for Austin to realize they were about to say goodbye to their new friend as well as their mentor and tutor.

Austin asked as he took Arthur's other hand, "How is he?"

"Austin?" whispered Arthur as he tried to smile.

"I'm here. We both love you very much."

Arthur smiled once more. The boys' eyes watered as their pupils floated on pools of clear water. Arthur desperately tried to continue speaking, but his voice was failing him. "I must quickly tell you a few things. There is a tropical depression forming to the south. Check the computer. I had some printouts done. Be prepared," he warned. "Now, the good news, I canceled the deal with Jerry, Terry, Larry, and Jim. As you know, they had offered to buy my place for you, and you were to return their money with interest from the profits."

His words puzzled them and for a moment. They assumed they had somehow failed to measure up, but their minds wouldn't allow them to even think of this possibility at this moment. Death lay before them. Arthur's eyes were already fading. His organs were shutting down. He had little time left. They could barely feel his pulse. His hands were cold.

"Last week, my attorney prepared new papers and I signed them a few days ago and faxed the copies back to the attorney. Instead of selling Elysian, I am giving it to you both, equally. I didn't want you to have to worry about paying a mortgage, even to our good friends. Now you are free to demonstrate love in its simplest form. Try to send some profit money to AIDS research, okay?"

Tears began dripping from the eyes of the boys. "Yes, of course. Thank you, Arthur," began Ryan. "I owe you my life."

"And I thank you, too. You saved us as well," added Austin.

"I know I'll soon be with Paul and I can't wait to tell him about my two princes I left in charge. Be good keepers of the gate. May everyone hear of your work here by the examples you send back to the real world. I will pray for you. I will miss you both and I love ...."

He gasped once as his heart stopped, and then he was gone. They held his hands for a few minutes longer. Ryan then reached over and closed Arthur's eyes. Gently, they stretched his arms out on the floor, and then reached for each other and sobbed.

It took fifteen minutes before they could talk.

"We must tell the staff," stated Austin.

"Yes, but let's wait until after the guests have left the lodge. We'll call a staff meeting so as not to alarm the guests."

"When will we bury him?"

"I don't know, but I think tomorrow. He didn't want a funeral and certainly no embalming. Without such, we should probably bury him quickly. He didn't want us to invite anyone. He just simply wanted to be laid to rest beside Paul. He talked about cremation, but I don't think he has to worry about anyone taking his body home. He is home."

"I know," said Austin as he took Ryan's hand. "This is by far the hardest thing I've ever done."

"Me, too, now dry your face. We must be strong for the others. Remember, our promise to Arthur."

"I know, but it will be hard."

"He said we should check the computer. There is a tropical storm coming." Ryan walked around the desk and for the first time, he sat in Arthur's chair. Austin came alongside, noted the printouts and tore the pages off the printer.

"Jeez, Ryan! Look at this. The barometer has dropped and winds are picking up quickly just a hundred miles from here."

"Yeah, look at the satellite shot. You'd never know it. Tonight was the best sunset ever."

"I think maybe God ordered it up the sunset for Arthur."

275

He smiled. "You're probably right. He deserved it." He began walking to the door. "Come, let's go. We've got things to do."

They told the staff of Arthur's passing after dinner. It was more than an hour before the sobbing stopped and the healing began. They decided to bury him at sunrise, and then return to the village and continue with the day as best they could. They didn't feel it was fair to penalize the long-awaited vacations of their guests, and they knew Arthur would want it that way. Smitty left immediately and went to work on building a simple casket. Jim and Bob took shovels and went to dig the grave. They had to use lanterns to see as clouds began to swirl inland. The clouds blocked the moonlight from reaching the island.

Ryan and Austin set up a table in the living room and placed a tablecloth over it. When Smitty arrived with the box, Austin placed a blanket in the bottom, then a small pillow, and together, the three of them gently and reverently lifted Arthur's body from the floor and placed it in the box. Then they lifted casket to the table.

Ryan then went to the door and met the staff that had lined up to pay their last respects to Arthur. It was a somber time. No laughter, no smiles, but there were many hugs. When everyone had left, Smitty placed the lid on top of the box and nailed it down. Tears rolled down Smitty's face as he finished the last nail. Ryan put an arm around him as he walked him to the door.

"Ryan," called Austin from the office. "Come here. You'd better look at this!"

Ryan hustled through the living room and into the office. "Is it coming our way?"

"It is a tropical storm for sure. Looks like Barbados and surrounding islands are going to be pounded either late tonight or early tomorrow."

Ryan asked, "It's not a hurricane is it? They haven't occurred this far south in long time, right?"

"I contacted the National Climatic Center in Asheville, North Carolina. It took them a while to find us on the map, but their research shows only one hurricane that skirted the eastern part of Barbados and that was over fifty years ago. Communications weren't so good then and it might not have been an actual hurricane, but just a big tropical storm. Back then there was nothing on Barbados to record wind speed, but there were reports it did blow houses down and caused much flooding and tidal damage."

"Do they predict it will come this way?" asked Ryan as he moved around Arthur's desk and knelt down beside the computer. He slipped his arm over Austin's shoulder.

"No, so I called the Hurricane Center in Miami. It is good that Arthur had all these phone numbers in the red procedures book, but there were no predictions available from them either. We're not on their forecast map."

"Let's call Barbados and talk to some of our friends there and see what is going on?"

They made call after call but they couldn't get through. Either the circuits were down for some technical reason, or the storm had already hit them. It was midnight when they went to bed. Their nerves felt frayed and spent. Every muscle ached from the strain and tension of the day. They couldn't sleep so they leaned into each other and did their best to just rest. Together they worried how they would handle the storm. Their first day on the job could be the most harrowing day they had ever experienced. They knew they had survived a hurricane before, but hoped they would never have to do so again. If they didn't lead their staff accordingly, they could lose the village to a big storm. Throughout the night, the emergency manual information kept replaying in their minds.

FIFTY-TWO

The sun broke the horizon when the line of mourners made it to the top of the mountain. Smitty, Joe, Johnny, and Alley had carried the box the whole way. Everyone had picked flowers so they could carry a bouquet. Ryan and Austin led the marchers to the gravesite. When they reached the top of the mountain the wind was blowing hard. Leaves were flying through the air. They looked back across the ocean at Barbados and could see dark clouds coming towards them.

"We'd better speed this up," muttered Austin.

"I agree. Go ahead and lay his casket in the grave. A big storm is coming, so we'll have to hurry," began Ryan to the rest of the staff. "Austin and I were not as fortunate as most of you. We only knew Arthur a short time. To us he was like a special grandfather. He was a man you could respect, love, and look up to. He had given us so much. We feel privileged. We all will miss him. Everything we do on Elysian will be a tribute to his life, his work and his love. He loved us all."

Austin squeezed Ryan's hand as he saw the tears slide down Ryan's cheeks. "I have been trying to think of words to say, but there are no words to describe what Arthur did. Recently I found two reasons to remind myself of one of my favorite Scriptures that goes like this, 'No greater love hath a man that this, that he lay down his life for his friends.' Arthur might have lived another year or two had he gone back to the States to take care of his disease, but he wouldn't go. He stayed here to make sure Elysian was ready for the new leaders. He gave everything he had to this magnificent place and to his friends. I know we will never be able to thank him enough."

Ryan smiled at the staff. "Let's all bow our heads and pray for Arthur and Paul."

With tears flowing down their tanned cheeks the staff prayed. Once finished, Ryan and Austin began hugging the staff one by one. The wind picked up as Smitty and Alley began covering the casket with the fresh soil. Once completed, the staff formed a line and placed their flowers on Arthur's grave as their final goodbye.

Austin said, "As you can see, a massive storm is coming. The satellite report tells us this is going to be a bad one. We must prepare for the worst. Cancel all ocean trips and secure the boats. We have tons of things to move to the cave. Let's hurry back down the mountain, feed the guests, and get to work."

It did not take a satellite printout to convince the staff of the pending storm. You could see the white caps of waves breaking up all across the ocean for as far as they could see. Dead limbs began falling out of the trees. Coconuts hit the ground as the workers moved rapidly down the mountain. When they reached the village, waves were crashing strongly on the beach.

278

Many of the guests had already awakened and were watching the storm coming towards them.

Once assembled, they ate breakfast quickly. Ryan and Austin explained the storm to the guests and their plans for their safety. The guests and their luggage were moved to the cave after their breakfast. Austin and Ryan began moving much of the electronic gear while the staff took care of securing the food and the animals. They brought the boats around the point and into the safety of the fish farm, hoping the waves would not be as strong in the cove. They left the radio and telephone online for a while longer. Though they shut down the generator, the satellite dish was still in operation as it continued running off the battery system.

At noon, the staff fed the guests sandwiches and soup from their makeshift kitchen in the cave. Austin and Ryan were still in the office watching the satellite. Realizing what they were seeing was finally taking shape. Their fears had become a reality. The tropical storm had developed into a hurricane and it was rapidly tearing up Barbados. They were watching the Weather Channel's reports on the storm. Weather planes out of Miami had already flown over the storm and reported the wind speed over hundred and fifty miles an hour. As they listened to the forecasters, Austin nervously began biting his nails.

"We're in trouble," muttered Austin.

"Big trouble, but have we done everything we can do?" asked Ryan as he chewed lightly on his lower lip.

"Everything, I even went through the manual again. The staff helped Johnny harvest as many of the crops as they could. They knew if that storm hits us, there wouldn't be any fresh food for a while."

"Let's finish securing the house. Put all the lamps on the floors. Bolt the windows and let's pray this hurricane falls apart before it gets ..."

Before he could finish the sentence, they both jumped as a huge bolt of lightning hit the ground near the corner of the house and their bedroom. The whole house shook. The violent burst of wind blew Ryan and Austin to the floor. The thunder echoed through the valley.

"Ryan?" yelled Austin.

"I'm fine, you?"

"That scared the piss out of me! Come on, I smell smoke."

Austin and Ryan ran down the hall and found the corner of the house seared black and smoking. They quickly grabbed buckets and put out the hot timbers.

"More water," yelled Ryan over the howling wind.

"Roger!" replied Austin as he took two buckets and headed to the bathtub.

A roar abruptly went over the house. They both assumed it was lightning and dropped to the floor, but suddenly they saw red and green light

279

beams shown briefly through the windows and onto the floor. It scared the daylights out of them. It was as if some alien spaceship was landing on their roof.

"Come on!" yelled Ryan over the noise as they ran out the front door, and then struggled to close the door with the wind howling around them.

As they made it to the steps, the rain and hailstones began pelting them in the face. They tried to shield their faces as they quickly looked up to see a small two-engine airplane flying over the village. The plane was barely a hundred feet over them and tossing around by the wind like a floating bottle in the surf. One of the propellers was barely turning. Smoke was pouring out of the other engine's housing. The colored lights were from the wings of the plane. Ryan spotted the pilot as he desperately fought to keep the plane in the air. Austin stood there flabbergasted. There was no place for the plane to land as there was no airstrip on the island. As the wind continued to gain velocity, they grabbed the porch poles to hang on to. Huge waves were crashing high up the beach. Helplessly they watched the plane skim the tops of several palm trees, and then it hit the water just a hundred feet from shore, bounced and then slammed head on into the next large cresting wave. A wing ripped off the fuselage, then the other, before the plane flipped over and stopped upside down a hundred yards from shore.

The hurricane showed no mercy for the downed plane. Waves and wind blew over the twisted metal. The body of the plane spun around and tumbled over, moving it closer to the island shore. Ryan and Austin watched in horror as a body flew out from the plane and into the sea. Caught in the open door, another body jerked helplessly back and forth like a rag doll in the jaws of a dog. The hurricane did not offer any sympathy, but kept on pounding the poor accident victims with growing waves.

"Oh jeez!" yelled Ryan.

"We must help them!" screamed Austin.

"We can't. The storm is too strong," replied Ryan as he yelled over the noise of the thunder and lighting, the wind, and the hail as it bounced off the roofs of the village.

"I'll take the aqua launch!" yelled Austin as he started to run down the deck.

Ryan bear hugged him to stop him. "You can't. You could be killed. The hurricane is coming at us. We must take care of the village."

"You can do that. I can't let those people drown."

"You can't save them!" pleaded Ryan.

"Elysian is all about saving people. You take care of our guests and our staff. I'll help these people and I'll be right back. Now go!" Austin hugged him quickly, and then turned and ran across the sand to the first guesthouse nearest the beach. Underneath the house, he found the rubber launch tied up. He quickly undid the knots and began pulling it to the beach. The winds caught it and flipped it over. He struggled to right it once more. He fell as the rain, hail, and the wind attacked him. He forced himself up and pulled the boat to the surf. He pushed the boat into the water, leaped in, and fired up the engine. Thankfully, it cranked up. He steered hard to the right and raced over the first wave, which sent him airborne. He nearly fell overboard as the boat crashed hard into the surf, and then he raced over the next wave.

Ryan ran the path to the cave to make sure everyone was inside.

"Where's Austin?" yelled Smitty in the doorway.

"A plane crashed in front of the pier. He's taken the rubber launch to get the survivors!" yelled Ryan.

"He'll never make it in this storm," replied Smitty. Instantly, he realized he had just hurt Ryan. He could see it in Ryan's face. "Damn!" he cursed. "Come on. Let's help him!"

Ryan helped Smitty close the big doors to the cave and then they ran back down the path. A sudden blast of wind blew Smitty off the path and he landed in the nearby bushes. Ryan helped him to his feet. They made it to the house. Just as they started to cross the yard, they had to fall flat on to the sand as the guesthouse closest to the water came apart and began tumbling end over end through the air. Chunks of plywood sailed over their heads like sheets of paper. A single chunk at that speed would have severed their heads.

"Run!" yelled Smitty as he leaped to his feet and ran to the pier.

Ryan looked down at the pier as the waves almost engulfed it. Wave after wave crashed over the boards and shot high into the air like geysers at Yellowstone.

"I see him!" yelled Ryan.

Smitty turned to see the launch in the water just forty yards away. The sea was blowing them to the beach. Austin was standing up and struggling to pull a man from the water into the boat. Two passengers were already inside.

"Hurry, Austin!!" yelled Ryan. "Hurry!!"

Austin couldn't hear him over the storm. The wind howled loudly. The surf had turned into a solid roar. Large chunks of hail bounced off the roofs of the village, knocking holes through the wood structures as if they had been made of paper. The ice tore away the leaves of the trees and punched holes in the ground vegetation as if they had been sprayed with a machine gun. Off to their right a palm tree suddenly uprooted and spun end over end through the air, and then inexplicably up and over the house. Smitty was blown off the pier. Ryan leaped down to the sand and helped him back up just as a big wave crashed into them and rolled them up the beach like a beach ball.

Ryan struggled to his feet in time to see Austin sit down in the boat and begin steering the launch towards the beach. Ryan and Smitty ran back to the pier. Austin's boat crashed over wave after wave. Ryan was waving his arms frantically. Austin caught sight of him and grinned. He had the throttle

281

wide open. Twenty-five impossible yards to go, he thought. Suddenly, a huge wave lifted the boat high out of the water and sent it hurling through the air. While in the air the boat pivoted into a spiral. The rescued passengers were unceremoniously dumped into the swirling sea once more.

"Oh no!" yelled Smitty.

"Come on!" replied Ryan as he ran down the pier towards shore as the waves began taking it apart. Boards exploded upwards one after another as the big waves crashed into the shore. Ryan leaped off the end of the pier onto the beach and began running as fast as he could into the wind. Smitty ran after him. When he was near the overturned boat, he ran into the water and began swimming towards the spilled passengers. Ryan rescued a woman with a broken arm. The woman was in shock so he quickly turned around, grabbed a fist full of hair, and began swimming for shore. Smitty grabbed a man bleeding about his head and followed Ryan to shore.

As soon as Ryan could stand up, he began pulling her across the sand to a bush and told her to hang on. He then turned ran back into the surf. He glanced around looking for Austin. He didn't see him. Smitty made it to shore and dropped off the man. He saw the woman crawling farther up the beach. He couldn't believe it but the wind was getting even faster. Smitty struggled to his feet and leaned into the wind as he looked out to the sea once more. His face turned pale as he took in the horror before him. He stared disbelievingly at a gargantuan waterspout that stood two hundred feet high and was heading right for Elysian. Terrified, he ran back into the surf to show Ryan.

Ryan had found a small boy floating in the water face down. He quickly turned him over and blew some breaths in the boy's mouth. The boy coughed. Ryan sighed with relief. He screamed out for Austin but could not find him. He saw the boat roll over another wave, but then the wind caught the lightweight craft and flung it up and over their heads, and across the beach and into the bushes.

Smitty reached him. "Where's Austin?" he yelled.

"I can't find him. I don't see any other survivors. Here, pull the boy in. I'll check a little more." He handed the boy to him. The boy was in shock. His face was pale and expressionless.

"You'd better hurry. There's a waterspout heading for us!"

Smitty pointed out to sea.

Ryan glanced at the spout and urgently swam further out. Constantly he felt his body turned over and over in the water. He swam back and forth. He yelled over and over again. There was no sign of Austin. Reluctantly, he swam to shore. He stood on the beach but he could not find him.

"Come on!" yelled Smitty as he led the survivors across the yard, heading for the cave. "There's nothing more you can do!"

Ryan looked at him with great confusion and despair. He again turned back to the sea. "Austin!! Austin!!" he yelled. He cupped his hands and yelled again. "Austin!! Austin!!" The sound of the storm overwhelmed his ability to signal by yelling.

Smitty began pulling the survivors towards the cave after putting the woman over his shoulder.

Ryan looked again at the rapidly approaching waterspout. It was just a hundred yards away. The waves crashed into him. Terrified, he moved further up the beach. A gust of high wind lifted him off his feet and rolled him over and over in the yard. He struggled to his feet once more.

"Austin!!!" he yelled frantically.

There was no reply. Ryan ran to the edge of the house and tried to stand on the deck, but the wind blew him off and into the already trampled flowerbeds. He struggled to stay afoot as he ran up the path to the cave. Johnny was holding the door after helping the survivors and Smitty inside. Ryan stopped just six feet from the cave and turned around to yell for Austin once more but he was too late. The waterspout came straight into the village as if it had been aiming for it all along. He saw the remaining planks of the pier swirling high into the air. He saw pieces of the plane slam into a cabin. He saw some of the guesthouses implode and disappear in an instant. Exhausted he turned and ran into the cave and collapsed onto the floor. Johnny struggled but managed to close the door and bolt it tight. Debris began slamming against the door causing it to vibrate as if they were inside a big drum. The shaking of the door terrified everyone so they moved deeper in the cave to get away from it.

The staff suspected Ryan had injuries but that was not the case. He was on the floor sobbing. His chest heaved and his breathing labored, but they could hear nothing over the roar of the wind and the surf. Ryan felt his life coming apart. In the last twenty-four hours he had lost Arthur and now Austin. After losing Austin for weeks and searching everywhere for him, Ryan had finally found him in Key West. Ryan had eventually come to peace with their relationship, made an abrupt change in his way of thinking, living, and loving, and now felt compelled and ready to show as many as he could what true love was all about. However, on Elysian and in just a matter of minutes, he had lost the person that loved him more than anyone in the world. The person in whom he trusted completely and to whom he freely gave of himself.

He cried until the tears would flow no more. His spent body curled up into the fetal position as a glazed, hypnotic, terrifying look took over his face. The staff felt it best to leave him alone for a while. They all sat against the strong walls of the cave and prayed the storm would soon be over. Silently they all looked at one another as if searching for some comfort from a nearby friend. Guests looked the staff, and they in turn looked at the guests, and then they all looked at the battered and beaten survivors of the plane crash. They owed their lives to Austin. He had saved them. Sure Smitty and Ryan had assisted but without Austin, they never would have been close enough for Smitty and Ryan to help. Austin was the hero. Austin had saved them.

FIFTY-THREE

Waiting out the storm in the cave for three frustrating hours seemed like an endless eternity of torturous hell. They placed their palms to their ears to keep the whine of the turbulent, high-speed wind from entering their brains any longer. Though the cave walls were thick and strong, they felt the ground shake as the waterspout hit the beach. The spout broke apart on land, but left the island to contend with the raft of hurricane. The big doors to the cave mysteriously shook slightly in and out as the air pressure constantly changed. Logs and boards bombarded the door with heavy thuds as they were tossed easily through the air. Single boards were flung through the air like blazing arrows from a giant bow. Suddenly, a six-foot long two-by-four inch board pierced the huge thick wood door. It was a strong reminder they were completely at the mercy of the storm, and anyone that attempted to exit sooner than the hurricane allowed, would face certain death.

Hours later, the wind finally died down, and the gut-wrenching wail stopped. Smitty cautiously opened the door to the cave. To their surprise, his face immediately lit up with brilliant rays of sunlight. They had never seen the sun so intensely bright, which was partially because of their eyes adjusting from the dimly lit cave, but also because the storm had blown away all the dust in the air. The cave dwellers felt they were seeing a miracle, while marveling at their survival of the killer storm.

Smitty ventured out a few steps, pushing piles of boards, logs, sticks, and limbs out of his way. The rest of the staff followed him, each one pulling, and pushing debris to the side of the path. They stood with the other guests and looked down at the remains of the once beautiful village.

The pier was gone, as were three guesthouses. The roofs had vanished on several others. The dining lodge remained intact though covered in tree limbs, but to their surprise and bewilderment, Arthur's house was still standing. Debris covered the roof, but it held fast to its frame. Oddly, the storm broke only a few of the windows. A few pieces of the siding were missing. Sand and jungle rubbish engulfed the porch. They noted the bent radio antenna, but marveled that the rest of the house survived so well. It was as if God protected the house. Ryan was sure that Arthur and his angel buddies helped spare the house as well as the rest of the village.

Smitty immediately took charge of organizing the cleanup. He was following the plan that Arthur taught them. Ryan stood at the top of the hill looking over the village, and everyone continued to pass him by as they exited the cave. His heart felt heavy and his spirit was broken. He sighed with great despair as he followed the last of the guests down the path to begin cleaning up the mess. Tomas took the plane survivors to his kitchen to get their wounds cleaned and to feed them. Ryan walked around the staff and the guests, and slowly made his way to the beach. He stared at it intensely as the waves continued to pound the shore. He could see the remains of the fuselage as it remained stuck in the sand. He let his eyes scan where they pulled the other survivors from the water. He turned from left to right, but saw no sign of Austin.

His eyes filled with tears. He struggled to walk down the beach a bit, but it was of no use. There was nothing alive anywhere. Dead fish scattered the sandy beach. He could not find a shoe or a torn piece of clothing. He turned to walk back to the village, but he was so overcome with emotion and sorrow, he collapsed to his knees. He pounded his fists in the sand until his arms loss all their strength. Feeling hopeless, he glanced up from the sand into the heavens. "Please God," he whispered. "I need him. I can't do this alone."

He hadn't expected the ocean to split apart, as it did for Moses, nor had he given any hope a whale might just swim over and spit Austin out. He didn't know what he expected, he just prayed for a small miracle that would allow Austin to be alive. He waited. Nothing happen. He dropped his head into his hands and sobbed some more. His tears fell from his cheeks to the white sand and quickly disappeared.

After a few minutes, he struggled to his feet, but feeling so spent and drained of life that he could hardly walk. After several attempts, he managed to take a wayward step or two towards the village. He came across a short stick stuck vertically in the sand by the wind. He picked it up and held it in his hands for a minute or two before angrily bringing his arm back and flinging the stick towards the brush near the beach. He watched it sail through the air and expected it to crash in to a tree. His eyes followed it until it hit the brush beside something black and gray. He didn't recognize the object. His brow wrinkled as he stared at it. His brain tried to register where he had seen the object before. It puzzled him for a long moment.

Suddenly, he realized he was looking at a bottom piece of the rubber boat. He ran down to the beach, over a dune, and into the brush. There he found several sections of the boat, and under some twisted palm limbs, he dragged the bent motor out into the clearing. He stepped through the debris of broken limbs, branches, and several fallen trees. He kept pulling limbs out of his way. He found a bigger section of the boat that was a few yards of gray rubber. It was all that remained of the craft.

He reached down and pulled a section of the rubber panel towards him. Instantly, his eyes spotted a bare foot. His heart leaped to his throat. He gasped and froze with fright. Though afraid of the touch, he gently knelt down and put his hand to the bare foot. His eyes blinked quickly, as he realized the foot was warm.

He sprung into action like a tiger suddenly after its prey. He yanked the remaining rubber raft away, urgently pulled back some limbs, and joyfully found Austin lying face down in the dirt. Ryan yelped at the sight of him like a beagle pup spotting a rabbit. Smitty heard him and came running. Ryan quickly crawled on his hands and knees under the trunk of a fallen tree until he managed to get to Austin's face. Gently, he rolled Austin onto his back. He put his face to Austin's mouth and felt a warm breath on his cheek.

"He's alive!!" he yelled. "He's alive!"

Smitty ran up to him. "Is he okay?"

"I don't know, but he's alive. Look, I think his arm is broken. It looks bad."

"I'll splint it and then we'll carry him to the house. Check for broken ribs," urged Smitty as he tore pieces of his shirt to form the splint.

"Right," Ryan replied as he carefully and tenderly roamed his hands all over Austin's body. He found no other obvious broken bones. He found a cut in Austin's scalp. Blood had oozed out and dried in his hair. Thankfully it had stopped the flow of his blood.

Smitty quickly found two sticks, tore more pieces from his shirt, and tied the splints onto Austin's arm. He then knelt down to pick Austin up.

Ryan gently stopped his arms as he looked up earnestly into his Smitty's eyes. "No, I'll do it. He is my responsibility. I'll carry him," said Ryan as he lifted Austin into his arms, and began walking gingerly through the debris towards their house. Smitty led the way, making a path as best he could. They finally reached the steps. Ryan struggled across the porch as Smitty opened the big doors to the house.

Ryan stepped through and made his way to their bedroom, which was thankfully intact. Just as he laid Austin's head down to the pillow, Austin's eyes suddenly opened. He tried to talk, but no words would come. For a moment, the two boys communicated through silent eyes, their windows to their hearts, in a place where words were not needed, but yet understood. Ryan smiled. Austin tried to.

"Hang on," urged Ryan aloud. "I love you."

Austin swallowed hard, wanting desperately to speak. "I...knew... you ...would...come."

He closed his eyes and for a brief moment, Ryan thought Austin might have died. Nevertheless, he held on to his good hand, and he could feel his pulse in his palm. He smiled, then leaned down and kissed Austin's bruised lips. "I love you. Now sleep while I clean you up."

FIFTY-FOUR

Austin slept until nearly noon. The sound of power saws and hammers awoke him, as well as the empty growling sound coming from his stomach. He stretched his sore muscles, and instantly felt some pain from his broken arm. He forced his eyes to open, and stared up at the clear blue skies overhead. If it hadn't been for his damaged arm, he would have sworn the hurricane had been nothing more than an extremely realistic nightmare. He drew into his lungs the wonderful flowery smell of Elysian and instantly felt better.

"You're awake!" announced Tomas as he brought in a breakfast tray. Austin struggled to sit up while Tomas straddled the tray across his lap. Before him on the tray was a large glass of fresh orange juice, his favorite ham and cheese omelet with extra cheese, a fresh biscuit, and a cinnamon bun. He also noted a little bowl of strawberry jam, three strips of bacon, a cloth napkin, and a gorgeous orange flower in a crystal vase.

"How in the hell did you manage all this the day after a hurricane hit us? This is fabulous and I'm starved to the gills," blurted Austin as he began by taking a bite of the omelet.

Tomas, a big man that looked like a cross between a Hawaiian Native and a Japanese sumo wrestler, broke into a huge, satisfied grin. His hard work on the breakfast already acknowledged, he teasingly replied, "Ryan said I was to take good care of you, and get you up and around as soon as possible. He's outside directing all the reconstruction. And besides, it never hurts to butter up your new boss!"

Austin laughed and took a bite of the ham. "Hmm, this is good. How is everyone? Was anyone hurt?"

Tomas began picking up the wet clothes and towels all around the room. "Everyone is fine. Let's see, I'll explain it this way. The guests are all fine with not a single scratch. Most of them suspect we planned the hurricane as part of their adventure' vacation!"

Austin laughed again. "I think not. I mean, where in the world do you buy a waterspout."

Tomas chuckled. "The staff is fine, too. Smitty got a bump on his head when a board from the pier slid off the roof and nicked him a bit. If you ask me, it was a small bump, but he has been playing it up, trying to get all the sympathy he can from the staff, and most unhappy they are too smart to oblige him. The man, woman and child from the plane crash are doing great. I have them in your guest room. The man is resting in bed, as he is weak from all the blood he lost, but another day of my cooking and he'll be fine. Though bruised and sore, the woman is otherwise happy to be alive. The little boy has no visible injuries at all. He's outside running up and down the beach exploring. He's so excited. He thinks landing here was the best vacation ever.

I think he has a permanent grin on his face. It's been a long time since we had a child on this island, so I think we have sufficiently spoiled him."

Austin smiled and continued eating until he could eat no more. Tomas helped him out of bed, and got him into the shower with his bad arm sticking out. He cleaned up a few scratches about his head and shoulders, and then dressed him.

"I suppose Ryan and I managed to disappoint Arthur on our first day on the job. We let a hurricane come right through the village. Are all the guests packed and ready to leave?"

Tomas led him down the hall. As he approached the door he said, "I think you'll be pleased at how well you did on your first day, even though you slept through most of it." Austin stepped out the door and onto the porch just recently cleaned of the sand and debris. Tomas then continued, "If you ask me, you and Ryan did very well. All fifty-two guests are safe and sound, the fourteen staff members are doing great, and you saved three people from the plane, so we didn't lose any of our team and in fact, gained three new people. Arthur would be happy about that."

Austin winked at Tomas. "Yeah, but look at the mess. We couldn't protect the pier, the guesthouses, and the crops in the fields."

Turning to him and pointing a finger, Tomas responded quickly. "Now you just hold on a minute. Don't you go putting yourself down around me? You did more in one day to save lives and this place than any five men I know. Besides, Arthur never did like the way he built the pier. He wanted steps down to the beach and he wanted it farther out so bigger boats could tie up. In addition, we'll rebuild the guesthouses a little farther in so they'll be in the shade all day. The guesthouses that blew away were the first ones built. We'll make new stronger ones. Storms are nature's way of pruning dead limbs, and in our case, it forces us to improve our island."

"I think you may be right. Have the guests already left?"

"On the contrary, they wouldn't leave. Just look at all the people working. Do they look familiar?"

Austin shaded his eyes and scanned the village. There were groups of six or more working on each guesthouse, pulling down limbs and debris, and fixing walls and doors. He spotted Ryan working with a group of twelve. They were building a new guesthouse wall by wall, and to his amazement, this was the third one they had built already. He squinted as he focused his eyes, and realized most of the workers were the guests themselves. "Our guests are working? Arthur would never approve of that."

"Sure he would, because he believed the island belongs to everyone. The guest didn't want to leave. They wanted to help rebuild Elysian just as the island rebuilt many of their lives. You couldn't run them off with a stick. They are doing a great job. Why don't you walk on down there and see for yourself?" urged big old Tomas.

Austin turned and hugged Tomas. "Thank you for a spectacular breakfast, and for everything you do for all of us. Ryan and I appreciate you so much."

"You're welcome. Not get a move on," he playfully popped Austin's butt with his big hand. "Get on now. I have to go work on my kitchen. It is a mess."

Austin grinned and strolled easily across the sand as the soreness in his limbs began to loosen up. He waved to guests and staff as they called out his name and waved at him in return. He made his way to the new guesthouse Ryan and his crews were building. Ryan spotted him so undid his tool belt while letting it slide to the ground. He quickly came running across the sand to meet him.

"How you doing?" he asked as he approached.

"I feel like you jumped up and down on me all night and tossed me out the window," grinned Austin.

"How did you know?" asked a chuckling Ryan. "I admit I thought of doing just that, but not last night." He gave Austin a good hug and then a long kiss.

"I can't believe how much work this group has already done. Isn't it just wonderful how everyone has pitched in," stated Austin.

"At daylight, the damage depressed me, but an hour after breakfast, the generosity of our staff and guests alike overwhelmed me. Their enthusiasm is contagious. Yesterday, I would have said it was impossible to improve Elysian, but today, so many ideas are flying back and forth among our gang of workers, I think we'll make it better and stronger."

"I guess the pier will be the hardest to rebuild."

"Well, maybe harder, but we can do it because all the pilings are still in place, so we just need some good beams to bolt in place, and then replace the flooring. I think we'll add some steps down to the beach, and a covered area to provide some shade from the sun. Some of our guests can't take as much sun as we can."

"I hear that Arthur wanted to make the pier longer so big boats could tie up. Let's walk a bit," suggested Austin. "Maybe we can do that after the rest of the repairs are made."

Ryan took his hand and walked him towards the beach. They didn't say a word for a while. In Austin's mind, he was replaying the events of yesterday. He walked across the sand just opposite where the plane had gone down. He recalled finding three people in the water, and felt horrified as he caught a memory of the pilot who had already drowned due to being trapped in the wreckage. Later, he recalled the man's body tossed through the air and into the water. He then turned his head inland, and he remembered flying wildly through the air, and suddenly dropping hard to the sand, knocking the breath from him.

Ryan sensed Austin needed a moment of quiet time, and so he just held his hand, giving it a gentle squeeze. After a while, Austin turned to him. "Three tropical storms in our lifetime, and we have lost people we love, but three times you and I have survived together."

Ryan replied, "Yes, I know. You and I are survivors. It's a special part of us. We're also lucky. We could have died at sea like my parents, or blown away when the hurricane hit Shark Island, or we could have died in America the victim of disease, hatred, or even depression. We could have split up and just endured our time on earth, and that would have been that."

They had stopped talking for a moment. Slowly, Austin raised his chin revealing a sly, mysterious smile highlighted with twinkle in his eyes. "Yeah, but we have become bookends."

"Bookends?" quizzed Ryan.

"Yes, neither one is good without the other, but together we hold everything together."

Ryan slid an arm around Austin's waist and hugged him. "Clever, aren't you? I was hoping that bump on your head had knocked some sense in you."

"It did. I know I have found my perfect bookend, my perfect occupation, and the perfect place to live," smiled Austin.

"Me, too, but more importantly, together, we have found our purpose. We can help change humanity, one person, one couple, and one group at a time."

"Did I ever tell you I loved you?" asked Austin as he turned to face Ryan.

"Yes, and I believed it every time. I love you as well."

They kissed deeply. All the staff and guests stopped their work, gazed at them, and then spontaneously began applauding. The boys broke off the kiss, turned and faced their audience, and blushed.

"Whoops! I guess we're teaching by example again," laughed Austin.

"Well, don't stop! The lesson's not over!" exclaimed Ryan.

They kissed again, this time deeper and longer, and they didn't hear the 'ooo's' and 'aahs', or the catcalls, only the sound of their hearts beating in unison. Their passionate loving example made everyone on the island instantly feel better about the boys, themselves, and even the world. Momentarily, the monstrous hurricane was forgotten, as did their daily struggles with life's problems. Elysian's magical paradise had not faltered to the storm, and neither did their love for each other.

Five Years Later

They could still remember celebrating their first year on the island, and today they began the fifth one. Tomas spent the entire day in his kitchen preparing a feast to celebrate the event. They had accomplished numerous improvements, but their biggest triumph was the steady success of Elysian's spirit. Word of this magical island spread around the world, and the waiting list grew longer, but they resisted expanding the quantity of guests. This had a been another lesson of Arthur's to forever keep the personal touch of humans relating to humans, and if allowed to grow too large, soon no one would know everyone's name, nor their problems.

Ryan and Austin had spoken to Bonnie from Key West before the surprise journey to Elysian. Since then, they convinced their mother to visit them at least twice a year. The senator lost his bid to become Vice-President and showed no interest in visiting their new island home. They never let his absence bother them, but they delighted in spoiling Bonnie as much as possible. She loved their home, and the staff treated her with great kindness. She loved them all, and almost as much as she loved her boys, Austin and Ryan.

Jim, Larry, Jerry, and Terry visited twice a year as well with standing reservations for life. Their visits made their decision to help the boys a proud accomplishment, but they also continued learning from the boys, recharging their relationships with their partners.

Ryan spotted Austin standing on the pier waiting for him. He had been diving with a new group. Behind Austin, he could see their island village, the lofty mountains, the vegetable grove, and even the fish farm. He allowed his eyes to scan the guest cabins and dining lodge. He noted how beautiful their house looked on the white sand. He felt so lucky to have it all: a great job, a great home, a great family, and a great partner.

Ryan turned his eyes back to the pier. Austin's blond hair was blowing in the sea breeze. He thought Austin was as handsome as humanly possible. To his left was little Johnny, just three years old, and to his right was Eddie, now eighteen months, and thankfully, out of diapers. He waved at their sons. Austin pointed to their dad's boat, and they gleefully waved back at him. Austin lifted Eddie and sat him on his shoulders. Eddie clung to Austin's hair with one hand and waved wildly with the other. Ryan beamed with pride at his little family.

He never thought they would have kids and he had no clue Austin wanted kids as well, but one day they just blurted out the possibility and instantly fell in love with the idea. A lesbian nurse from Holland agreed to their pleas after meeting her in Barbados where she worked. It took six months to work out the details, but in the end, she became a surrogate mother with Ryan's sperm donation that produced Johnny. Ryan no longer felt guilty or at fault about failing to produce a baby with Jennifer. A few years later, Austin's sperm produced Eddie. They became the proudest parents on the face of the earth. Even a stranger could see Ryan's features in Johnny, and

Austin's features in Eddie. Bonnie also loved her grandchildren and did her best to spoil them with love and kisses.

They had not planned the educational value of having sons, but the results came along anyhow. The guests played with the kids, and laughed at their childish games and adventures. Their guests loved their children, and some left with the possibility of having children, too.

"Ahoy!" yelled Ryan as the boat neared the dock.

"Ahoy!" replied Johnny.

"Ah-choo!" yelled little Eddie as they all laughed. He had not yet mastered the proper pronunciation of the nautical term, so they all responded the same. "Ah-choo!"

Tom Flack
December 24, 2008
Revision April 24, 2010

EPILOGUE

There are many examples in history where it took entire armies to change a part of the world. However, there are other exciting changes that took just one person, or perhaps only a few, like Ben Franklin and his kite flowing with electricity, Thomas Edison and the light bulb, Louis Pasteur and his pasteurization process, and Jonas Salk and his polio vaccine. These individuals created huge changes achieved only through their total dedication and determination.

Changing our world's attitude and level of respect towards gays will take no less. It begins with one or two people, then ten or a hundred, and then thousands until an army of people worldwide join the struggle but stay on course.

Nevertheless, finding true love amongst a world of opportunities is a magic that only some of the luckiest of couples ever truly experience. However, hope keeps the journey for that joyful goal alive!

I hope it is you and your love that find the happiness and joy like the guests of Elysian, and if so, encourage others to follow by your example. Make your love contagious, and watch it magically spread around the world.

The island of Elysian only exists in the minds and hearts of those who seek true love. Therefore, the island of love exists in your state, your town, and even in your house. Seek it, as if searching for a great treasure!

TJ Johnson
December, 2008

Acknowledgements

I finished this story over four years ago, designed the cover, and then began the editing process. Creating a tale of adventure is a bit like Tom Sawyer avoiding a fence in need of a coat of paint, but I love the fun in fiction!

I am most grateful to those who help me every day along the journey of my life.

Author TJ Johnson

TJ began writing his stories in the eighties, mostly for fun and for friends. He was still working full-time for someone else and the career took up more time than he wished. In 2005, he began working for himself with hopes of spending more time on his writing. On the computer were several novels not yet produced, so while writing new material, he began searching for outlets for the books he had finished. His favorite part of writing is the crafting of the rough draft, a period in the process when the words fly from the storage center deep in his brain like a movie stuck on fast-forward. The agonizing part begins with the painstaking restructuring as the editing begins, but it is a joy when the tale is finally finished. TJ often works on three stories at once, each in different stages of production. He does this to keep his creative skills at peak performance, and because he believes fiction is just too much fun!

His most recent releases: **Gay Grifters** about a gang of thieves robbing rich gay men. The **Raceboys** about a national champion forced to come out as a gay driver, and **A Writer's Fantasy** about his favorite college basketball team and their handsome star player. Also available is **The Will** and **Stranded.**

Currently, TJ is editing **Crosshairs,** a continuing story with the cast of Gay Grifters – an Eric and Tyler Story.

Fans of the War Series (**The War Apart - Part 1**, **The War Ahead - Part 2 Revised 2010**) will be pleased to know that the research is finished, and the editing has begun on **The War Beyond - Part 3**.

Requests for additional information and Inquiries can be obtained from **Hard Title Publishing,** at **Info@ItsFiction.com**

You may also signup for free publication notices, read a chapter from other books, and check out TJ's blog at:

WWW.ItsFiction.Com

Contact TJ Johnson at:

Info@ItsFiction.com

1. I try to answer all my email myself; however please read "Bio & Info" at www.ItsFiction.com before writing as your question – saving time for all! Many readers ask the same questions repeatedly.

2. Please do not add my email address to any group for jokes, thoughts, prayers, or riddles, etc. I always delete these without reading.

3. I do not open any emails with attachments as these may contain viruses or other nonsense!

4. Please do NOT write suggesting plot lines as I delete these quickly, too. I like to write my own stories. If your plot is good, write it yourself! Do not send your manuscript to me – I am a writer, not a publisher, and I do not have the time.

5. All characters and names are part of my imagination and indicate no one particular. If I like a person's name, I may use the first or the last name but never both at the same time. It is true some of the events in my books are historical in nature but many are not. Choosing which to believe is your job, but this is why fiction is fun.

6. If you do not receive a reply, perhaps "Bio & Info" contains the answer already, or your email address is not functioning correctly.

7. If you have read all the above, I cannot wait to hear from you!

8. If you think a sequel should be added to your favorite story, please send an email to the above address!